The Chronicles of Wizard World: Book I

Charlie Watson and the Golundrus Cube

R.J. Scott

PublishAmerica
Baltimore

First printing

ISBN: 1-4241-6903-8
PUBLISHED BY PUBLISHAMERICA, LLLP
www.publishamerica.com
Baltimore

Printed in the United States of America

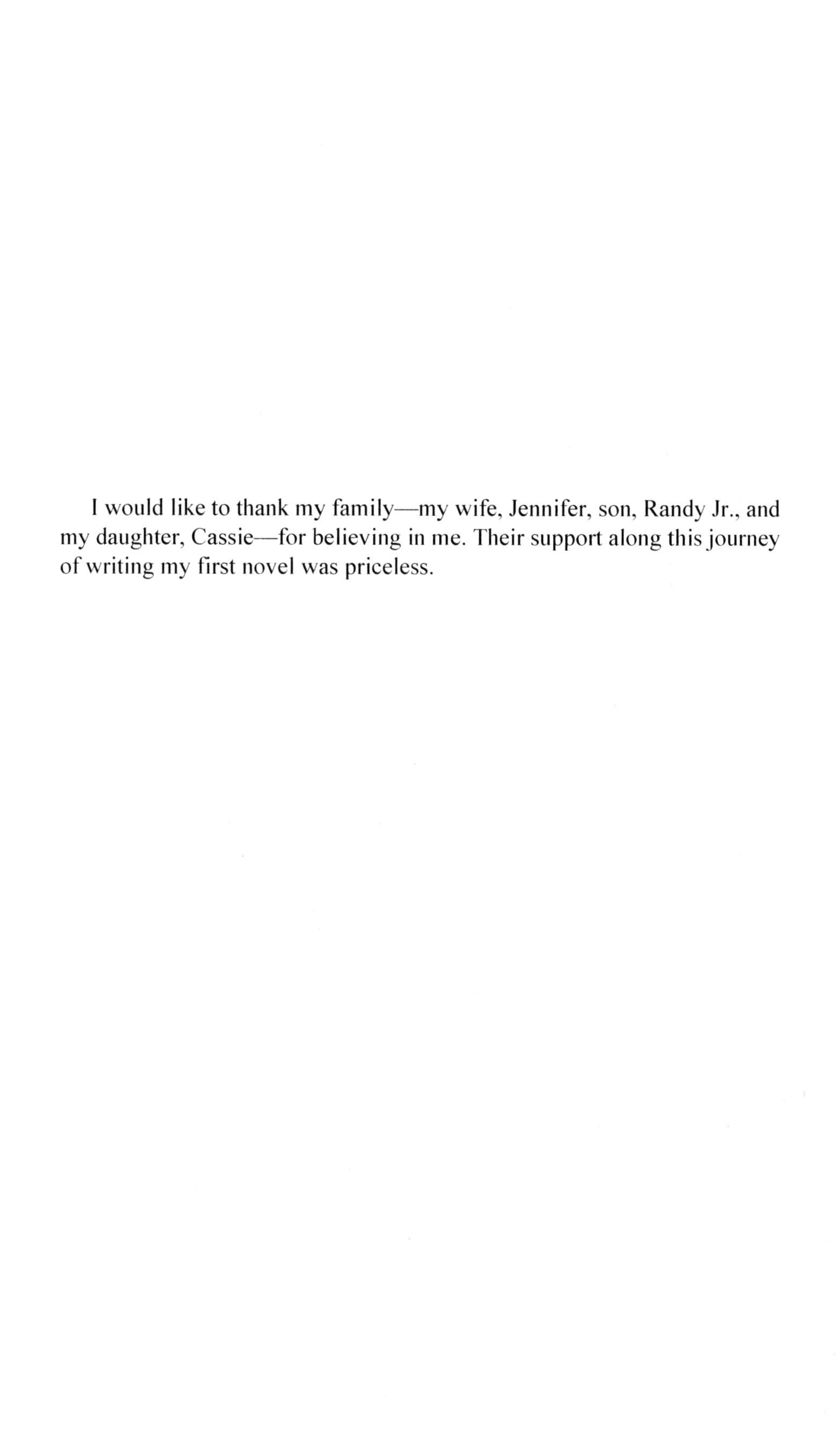

I would like to thank my family—my wife, Jennifer, son, Randy Jr., and my daughter, Cassie—for believing in me. Their support along this journey of writing my first novel was priceless.

Chapter 1

Meeting a New Friend

Yet another summer was about to come to an end and another school year was about to begin. Charlie and Tim had a wonderful vacation. They spent their time playing video games, watching movies and of course, getting into a bit of trouble here and there, which seemed to be one of their favorite things to do.

When Charlie and Tim could sneak away for a few hours they would spend their time exploring Boston and some of its more shady and mysterious locations. They would go down dark alleys, explore empty buildings and make detailed maps of the locations. The boys would often bring their digital camera and GPS along just in case reference material was needed. More than once while on one of their adventures exploring empty buildings they had run-ins with the local police. Although they were never actually caught, they had established themselves quite the reputations nonetheless. Charlie was the one with the ideas and Tim was the brain behind all the detailed maps and creative use of the Internet along with a vast array of electronic gadgets.

The last day of summer vacation painfully had arrived. Charlie and Tim depressingly said goodbye to their summer fun but wanted to complete one last quest before it all came to a crashing halt. They planned to sneak off to an alley behind Charlie's house to continue doing research on a strange cobblestone they had discovered a week earlier.

Grandma Watson looked through every room of the house and couldn't find Charlie anywhere. She laughed to herself knowing all too well where he must have gone. She headed out the back door and stood on the back porch of Scott and Sarah's house smiling. "Charlie, Charlie Watson, are you in that alley again?"

"Yes, Grandma."

"And I bet your friend Tim is there with you too, isn't he?"

"Yes, Grandma."

"Hi, Grandma Watson."

"Hello, Timothy."

"Well, you need to get out of there right now. You know how your parents hate it when you play in there."

"Just give us another minute, Grandma; we think we might have found something important."

Grandma just smiled, knowing all too well there was no way either Charlie or Tim was leaving that alley until they finished their investigation. "And what did you find this time?"

"It's some kind of symbol embedded into a cobblestone. Why don't you come back here and take a look at it?" asked Charlie.

"No thank you, Charlie, it's bad enough that you two are back there, let alone me encouraging you. After all, you know how your parents feel about your so-called adventures," said Grandma Watson.

"But it's the last day of summer, Grandma, and we really, really need to finish our investigation of this alley before tomorrow," said Charlie.

"All right, boys, five more minutes and that's it. Not a single minute more, understand?" said Grandma Watson.

"Yeah, and thanks, Grandma," said Charlie. "Hurry up, Tim."

"I am. Just two more photos, that's it. We're done. These will make excellent additions to our collection."

"Great, let's get out of here before my parents get home and I end up grounded again. There would be nothing worse than starting school tomorrow and already being grounded," said Charlie.

"I see your point," Tim said. "Speaking of that, I need to head home myself before the nanny lets me have it."

"Okay, Tim, I'll catch up with you tomorrow on our walk to the torture chamber."

"Yeah, thanks for reminding me how much fun school is really is."

After a restless sleep the first day of school finally came and Charlie depressingly walked out his front door and met up with Tim just like he did on most every school day. Tim was a short, blond-haired, blue-eyed, almost round boy who has been attending Golvert's School for the Advanced and Gifted since he turned four years old. He was not the bravest soul but was a dedicated friend nonetheless. He has never set foot in a public school and has enjoyed the easy life. His parents, John and Laura Smittens, own Smittens's Crafts for All Occasions. They have stores worldwide and are very well off. Tim spends most of his time with a nanny or hanging around Charlie's house as if he were a second son due to his mother and father's frequent business trips. Charlie can't remember a time of not knowing the Smittens or when he and Tim were not best friends.

After fifteen minutes of lazy walking the boys finally reached their destination, Golvert's, a private school for the upper-class children in the surrounding suburbs.

Golvert's is a traditional Boston building. Built in the early 1800s, it has the classic style of large pillars at each side of the entranceway. Built into the trim surrounding the uppermost level of the building could be seen ancient gargoyles perched at every corner of the building. The school had been remodeled many times in the past to keep up with modern requirements but it still had that feel of a building that was built long ago. The stairways were wide and had the original railings that were worn from the many years of use. These railings were carved from marble embedded with small gargoyles and other odd-looking symbols. The hall floors were made from either marble or hardwoods that also showed the signs of the many students' treks through the years wearing shoes that were not meant for these types of surfaces. Long black streaks could be seen along with the occasional chip or two in the wood placed there by a student with too much time on his or her hands. The lounge was sporting velvet curtains covering the nearly twenty-foot-high windows yet they still nearly reached the floor. There were round cherry tables and long stretching oak tables that stretched for nearly twenty feet. These tables showed the marks of the years of abuse by overzealous students with too much time on their hands. Here, students could spend free periods studying and quietly chatting amongst themselves about the newest and most important school gossip of the day. The separation of students in this area was obvious, as the higher-ranking kids took up seats in the large depressed velvet seating areas separate from the nerds and the occasional punks while the rest of the not-so-lucky kids pulled up old chairs and worn-out benches.

Everything seemed normal for this first day of school. It was Monday, rainy, cold, and Ron Colstrun and his group of miscreants were torturing anyone smaller and younger than they were just for the fun it. The four, Ron Colstrun, Beth McGrigger, Sean Tolvert and Ron's brother, Clive, seemed to be in particularly foul moods today. Charlie and Tim were glad it was not their usual morning to be the victims of their daily ritual.

The boys made their way through the crowds of gathering students and headed for their morning classroom. After all the initial hustling and bustling of the first day of school finally settled down and most of the students were seated in homeroom there was an announcement over the intercom stating that a new student would be starting today and her name was Crystal Kildroy of the famous Kildroy family. Like usual, most students couldn't resist chatting and whisperings and it was especially heavy because of the fame of the new student. Crystal's father, James Kildroy, was a world-famous soccer player and her mother, Lourdes, was a renowned publisher and author.

Crystal Kildroy was the embodiment of today's modern teen. She carried the most expensive backpack, all leather with silk straps, an MP3 player and a rather expensive-looking cell phone. Her hair was long and blond with just a small hint of waviness to it. She wore her hair down and it framed her slightly tanned face. Her eyes were a sparkling blue and her lips were full and a beautiful red. Standing about five feet five and very athletically built, Crystal was the centerpiece of all the morning chatter.

After the morning announcements were over the children were dismissed to leave and head to their first class of the morning. While heading out and getting pushed aside like usual by Ron Colstrun and his cronies, Charlie and Tim heard a very unfamiliar voice speaking to them.

"Hi, boys, my name is Crystal Kildroy. I'm new here and I need a bit of help getting around. Hello? Are you two listening or what? Today is my first day of school here." Taken back for a moment, neither Charlie nor Tim knew what to say. They usually were not the type of boys girls sought out. As the initial shock wore off Charlie introduced them. Speaking in any kind of a congruent sentence was almost impossible.

"So Charlie, I noticed you have a slight accent, are you from England?" Crystal asked.

Charlie was almost speechless. "Uh, yeah, my family and I moved here from England when I was three. My parents still speak with that accent and it seems to have stuck a bit."

Tim still had nothing to say at the moment and was staring with a vacant look on his face. He simply couldn't believe that Charlie—yes, his friend Charlie Watson—was talking to Crystal Kildroy and she was actually speaking with him and not saying anything insulting. She genuinely seemed interested in the conversation. Immediately, the not-so-friendly Ron picked up on this along with his friends, who were now circling like vultures getting ready for their next meal. They proceeded to rudely step right in front of Charlie and Tim, acting as though they were not even there.

"Hey there, Crystal, Ron Colstrun is my name and this is Beth McGrigger, Sean Tolvert, and my younger brother, Clive. We are all members of, dare I say, the 'in crowd' if you know what I mean. If you want to have any type of success here at Golvert's School you definitely want to be a part of the right crowd, meaning stay away from the common kids and the ones who cannot pay their own way."

"Well, hello to you all and it's very nice to meet you," said Crystal as she looked awkwardly at the newest group of students who had just been rudely introduced by Ron Colstrun. Ron acted like he owned the place and it was obvious that the rest of his friends thought the same way too. Crystal was astonished at how this turn of events caused Charlie and Tim to look terribly uncomfortable and awkward. Crystal was so taken aback that she was no longer paying much attention to what was being said to her by the members of the so-called in crowd.

Crystal noticed Tim and Charlie walking away with their heads hanging low. Both were walking as though a dark cloud of misery had just appeared overhead and gloom and doom was raining down upon them. They had that walk that you often see by a team that has been defeated too many times in the past. Ron and Beth just laughed and started to throw insults at Charlie and Tim that were reserved for bars and alleys and definitely not a place of learning. Crystal turned and started to walk away with a look of disgust on her face. She stormed away from the group without paying them a bit more of attention. She walked with such grace and elegance that most of the students in the hall stopped to watch the situation unfold. Ron and his group were simply aghast at being snubbed like this, even if it was the famous Crystal Kildroy. After all Ron, Beth, Sean and Clive were the most popular kids in the school and nothing happened at Golvert's without their approval.

"You are making a huge mistake, Crystal," yelled Ron. "Worrying about those kinds of kids will only get you into unwanted trouble while you are here at Golvert's." Ron casually glanced at Beth and she was off without a word. Beth pulled a pack of gum out of her pocket and proceeded to place five pieces into her mouth. She began chewing frantically as she started down the hall after Crystal. A rather evil grin proceeded to take the place of Ron's mouth as he and the others waited for the show to begin.

Crystal kept walking and was unaware that Beth had started after her. Beth had an unfriendly look on her face as she headed out. In no time she was right behind Crystal. She then reached into her mouth and pulled out the largest wad of gum that Charlie or Tim had ever seen! She was now a foot or two behind Crystal with gum in her hand when it happened. Without thinking, and totally out of character, Charlie proceeded to drop his backpack right in front of Beth, tripping her and sending her sprawling right onto her face. Beth had fallen so hard that her nose was already swelling to twice its size in just a matter of seconds. The gum that she was carrying and obviously meant for Crystal's beautiful hair was now stuck to the front of Beth's school uniform and on the side of her face.

Charlie, still in shock at the look of Beth's face, promptly realized what he had just done and decided a hasty retreat was in order. With Tim grabbing his left arm they ran down the hall as fast as they could and into their next class—Business Class for Young Adults—with Ron, Sean and Clive hot on their heels.

Crystal had no inkling of what had just taken place on her first day of school as she headed to her very first class, but she was aware that something strange had happened. Many of the group's frequent victims had watched with utter enjoyment and now were bursting out with laughter at the sight of Beth.

Crystal looked on, wondering what all the commotion was about; looking behind her she noticed Charlie's backpack lying on the floor a few feet behind her and Beth along with it and not looking all too well. She then noticed an enraged Ron, Sean and Clive in hot pursuit of Tim and Charlie and slowly started to put it all together, quickly realizing that something very wrong had just happened.

After running into their class nearly knocking over desks, both boys assumed their seats. As the rest of the class filed in, Charlie and Tim tried to remain inconspicuous but they both knew this was not over. Ron leaned in the classroom doorway and was calling Mrs. Roust into the hallway. She hastily exited the classroom to see what was going on. Ron, Sean and Clive were still fuming; they could be heard out in the hall explaining everything to Mrs. Roust. The story was totally exaggerated of course and Charlie and Tim had no doubt what the outcome would be.

Crystal had now entered the classroom and was standing by Mrs. Roust's desk waiting for her new textbook and to be instructed where to be seated. She was thinking to herself that this had to be the strangest first day of school ever.

The entire class were whispering and pointing in Charlie and Tim's direction. Every student knew this was just the beginning but most thought that this was the best thing that had happened to the school in quite a while. Someone had actually gotten the best of the school bullies for once. That person was sure to pay dearly but for one moment there was a bit of relief in Business Class for Young Adults.

Most students, especially Charlie and Tim, generally despised the class, Business for the Young Adults. Mrs. Roust was a very old woman who had an angry look on her face even when she was smiling. She particularly disliked Charlie and Tim and made her class as uncomfortable as she possibly could for them. After all, she was Ron Colstrun's aunt and they were both sure that he told fabricated stories to her all the time to make sure she would continue to make their class time as miserable as possible. Ron loved it when she would bully and insult Charlie and Tim on an almost daily basis. No matter what kind of project Tim and Charlie did they always received the lowest grades in the class.

"Charlie Watson and Tim Smittens, both of you get out here right this instant," exclaimed Mrs. Roust from the classroom entrance. Charlie and Time timidly proceeded out the door and met Mrs. Roust along with Ron, Sean and Clive. The three started to smile and waited for the punishments to be handed out.

"Okay, you three, I have your sides of the story so please go and take your seats," said Mrs. Roust with an evil smile. All three proceeded into the class without another word but were smiling happily, knowing all too well how the next few minutes would turn out.

"You two are in some serious trouble. I have heard a great deal of how you assaulted Miss McGrigger and she is now off to the nurses' office with a bleeding nose and gum stuck all over her beautiful uniform and even in her hair! I cannot believe on the first day of school that you two are already causing trouble like this. How could you two assault one of our most popular and excellent young adults here at Golvert's? I will be taking the both of you straight to the principal's office and with any luck you will be suspended or expelled!" said Mrs. Roust.

"But, Mrs. Roust, Beth was going to put that gum in Crystal Kildroy's hair! She was walking right up behind her before I stopped her," said Charlie loudly.

"Yeah, Mrs. Roust, I saw her too. It's exactly what Charlie said."

"Well now... So you both admit that you did trip up Miss McGrigger and that she was doing nothing but chewing gum and walking down the hall and minding her own business on her way to class?" said Mrs. Roust triumphantly. Right then and there both Charlie and Tim knew they were not going to get out of this one.

After their trip to the principal's office and a call to both their parents, Charlie and Tim were assigned in-school suspensions for three days and given a stern warning that if anything like this happened again they would be expelled. Charlie and Tim were resigned to the fact that they would be spending the next three days seated in a small room with long tables, shades drawn and no talking allowed, leaving nothing to do but schoolwork or the occasionally helpful reprieve of rearranging books in the library with Mrs. Flutterfen. They also realized that when they left school today trouble would be waiting for them on their journey home.

One-forty-five p.m. came and school was being dismissed. The time Charlie and Tim had been regretting had come at last. It was like an old western with Tim and Charlie just staring at the clock and waiting for the final bell of the day and the beatings that would soon take place when they attempted to go home. When the bell finally did toll Charlie and Tim were surprised to see students lingering about and they were even more surprised to receive the occasional pat on their backs from strangers who had never acknowledged them in the past. Apparently their earlier exploits had spread through the school and most if not all the kids were pleased with their accomplishments. Things were changing for the both of them and hopefully they would not be beaten too badly to enjoy their newfound fame.

"Well, Tim, this is it. There's no use in putting it off. We have to go home eventually. We can try to hide or take a different route but they will find us sooner or later. It might not be today or tomorrow but they will catch us without a doubt," said Charlie.

"Yeah, Charlie, I know. Let's just go for it, it's time to face the music," said Tim.

With a determined look on both their faces and the chanting of their names coming from the hallway behind them, Charlie and Tim headed out the school's front door to face whatever kind of challenge awaited them.

"Tim, let's just take our regular route and let the events play out as they may."

"Yeah, Charlie, let's just go already."

As Charlie and Tim were walking they noticed what they thought was a head following them, carelessly hidden behind a row of hedges on the left side of the street. They were not sure but it did look like the top of Clive Colstrun's head. He was rather tall, making it almost impossible for him to crouch down behind the low set of hedges.

"Tim, I think this is it. I'm sure that's Clive. His head is so fat there is no mistaking it. Any second now the chase will begin. Let's stick together no matter what happens, okay?"

"Yeah, Charlie, you can count on me. Even though I'm pretty sure I will curl up in the fetal position, I will be right there with you till the end."

"Thanks, Tim, that's all I can expect from you. It's good to know you are getting a bit braver in your teen years. "

"Thanks, Charlie, that makes me feel much, much better."

Charlie and Tim rounded a corner and took a quick left onto Seventh Street when the chase began.

"Get ready for the beatings, you two morons!" yelled Ron as he ran right at Charlie and Tim. After all, Ron knew all too well that he had Sean, Clive and Beth to back him up. Charlie was sure he wouldn't be so arrogant if the shoe was on the other foot. Unfortunately it was not and all Charlie had was his not-so-gallant but best friend, Tim. He was a very smart kid but not the bravest—that's for sure. However, he has always stood right by Charlie's side no matter what the odds.

"It's over for the both of you this time; you two need to be put back into your places once and for all. Evidently the time off we have given you from the usual embarrassments at school has not served either of you too well. You two should have just kept your noses out of our business and stayed under the usual rocks you hide under."

"What you did to Beth today just guaranteed the worst beatings we have ever given to either one of you," said Clive as he and Sean grinned and cracked their knuckles dramatically. They looked like a pack of stray dogs that had just treed a cat and were looking to tear it to pieces.

"This is it, Charlie. I will assume my position and get ready to be pummeled like usual," said Tim as a look of total fear spread across his face.

"Don't sweat it, Tim. I will protect you for as long as I can," said Charlie with a concerned look on his face.

Right when it looked like there was no hope to stop the beating that was about to commence, a stretch limo pulled up right between the two groups and a door swung open.

"Get in, you two, and be quick about it," said Crystal. "Well, close your mouths and stop staring. Just get in already! I don't think your friends over there are going to wait on the other side of this limo forever, you know."

Charlie and Tim rapidly jumped into the car, falling over each other, and Crystal closed the door as the limo pulled away. You could see Ron, Clive, Sean and Beth screaming some rather nasty words and waving their hands in disgust at the opportunity that had just been so rudely taken away from them.

Charlie couldn't believe their luck. "Crystal, we are so very happy to see you! Surprised, but very happy nonetheless; another second or two and it would have been a rather sticky situation for the both of us, that's for sure."

"Yeah, Crystal, that was awesome! You are the best. We have been embarrassed, kicked, punched and had countless other miserable moments at the hands of those four. It was like a ritual to get beaten by them at least once a week. Ron, Clive, Beth and Sean just seemed to always get away with everything and no one ever stands up to them. If anyone ever did they would usually end up wishing they were going to the dentist or worse the doctor's instead of having to spend another day at Golvert's," said Tim.

Charlie was grinning from ear to ear. "Did you see their faces as we sped away? It was priceless."

"You do realize this will only make it worse when they finally do catch up with us?" Tim questioned.

"Of course but it was worth it," said Charlie. "So, Crystal, do you make rescues every day or was this just a one-time thing? Because if you do, I'm sure this is not the last time we will need it. This is a frequent happening here at Golvert's, especially for Tim and me. How did you know where we were anyway?"

"Yeah, I was wondering that myself," said Tim.

"Well, after what you two did for me at school it was the least I could do. A few other students said they watched you two leave out the side door and gave my driver directions so I figured I would take a drive by and check up on you two. After all, I never did get to thank either one of you for rescuing me from Beth McGrigger, a wad of gum and probably short spiked hair. The rest is history and I'm pretty sure will be all over the school by tomorrow," laughed Crystal.

Crystal reached into the limo's bar and grabbed three glasses and a bottle of punch and the new friends toasted their new friendship and recent victory.

"This has to be one of our best adventures yet!" said Tim.

"I totally agree and the best part is there were no police involved and neither one of us has a black eye either," laughed Charlie.

Tim looked on grinning from ear to ear. "I know! Isn't it great?"

"Adventures, what do you mean adventures?" Crystal questioned.

"We thought you would never ask," said Charlie smiling.

"We'll fill you in while we are heading home," said Tim.

"We sure will," said Charlie with an even bigger smile than usual.

Chapter 2

Mysteries, Plans and Discoveries

The second week of school was starting. Charlie, Tim and Crystal had spent the first week barely avoiding the seemingly never-ending attempts of revenge by Ron, Clive, Beth, and Sean. Almost as if by magic, anytime Charlie, Tim or Crystal were alone even for a moment, seemingly out of nowhere Ron, Clive, Beth, or Sean would appear and attempt to exact their revenge for the week earlier.

"Charlie, we can't keep this up; eventually they are going to get us and the constant pressure is starting to get to me," said Tim.

"I agree," Charlie replied.

"They seem to be everywhere," said Crystal.

Charlie looked deep in thought trying to figure this all out. "How do they know where we are going and when we are alone? It's like they are tracking us somehow."

"Well, it's possible but highly unlikely. They are not the sharpest bunch around but they do have money and access to electronics. And don't forget Mrs. Roust," said Tim.

"That's right, I forgot about her. She is a ball full of laughs, that's for sure, and one of my favorite people. I would put her right up there with you, Tim and Crystal too," said Charlie with a laugh.

"You never know what lengths they will go to for revenge," said Tim. "Once they waited a whole year to get even with the Tritter kid, remember? He had mistakenly caused Ron to lose at his favorite video game while at the arcade. It was plain to see it was an accident but they never stopped for a second. Poor Dave Tritter! They would put dead animals in his locker or dog poop in his gym shoes. They even loaded his backpack up with all kinds of nasty bugs once. Dave was to the point where he was afraid of his own shadow. He would not go to the bathroom all day. He was in total fear of all four of them and what they were going to do next. They never stopped until they finally laid a good beating on him, when no one was around to witness it of course."

"They really did that just over a stupid video game?" asked Crystal.

"Yeah, Crystal, they did, and still to this day Dave Tritter has not forgotten. He gets the shakes and runs the other way when he sees any of the four punks. I suspect he will never recover from this and probably has nightmares about it," said Tim.

"It's almost time for first period and I have to get to class. I'll see you two later, I don't want to be late to my first class of the day," said Crystal. She turned and left and Charlie and Tim shook their heads in amazement.

"It's a strange year already," said Tim.

Charlie nodded in agreement.

Both Charlie and Tim hated Golvert's and most of their classes except ancient history. Both boys hurried to arrive on time for this class and to their surprise Crystal strolled in right behind them and took the seat right across from Charlie. The instructor of ancient history was Mr. Nilrem. He had been a teacher at Golvert's school for twenty-five years. Mr. Nilrem was a short, rather portly man with long hair and a rather scraggly-looking beard. He tended to wear strange outfits that resembled dress robes more than the usual suits that most the other male teaches wore.

"Well, hello, boys! I had my schedule changed because of a scheduling conflict and ancient history had an opening so it looks like we will be together in class. Any info on this Mr. Nilrem, is he a good teacher or what? What will we be going over in class anyway? I like old Egypt and early European history and stuff like that. And one other question—can I expect to run into Ron, Clive, Beth or Sean?" asked Crystal.

"Well, this is our one sanctuary here at Golvert's. Fortunately for us it seems that none of them are smart enough to pass this class so they all dropped out after the first week, with the help of Mrs. Roust of course. And our curriculum in this class is kind of strange. When I say ancient history I mean ancient history. Some students will tell you what Mr. Nilrem teaches is a bunch of fairy tales and fabricated stories but Charlie and I love his lectures and field trips so much we spend our free periods here too," said Tim.

"Mr. Nilrem spends a lot of time, well, discussing fairies, goblins, trolls, wizards and stuff like that. You know like Merlin and the Knights of the Round Table, the ancient Norse gods, and the Greek gods and goddesses. He is just awesome," said Charlie. "It seems like he has so much knowledge of the past, it's almost like he was really there. It's very strange sometimes. He seems to know every little detail, and not like he is making it up either; he just knows. I don't know how old he is but I suspect he is older than anyone here at Golvert's and probably anyone alive for that matter."

"It seems like he has always looked out for us in some way," said Tim. "He always is there to help us out of sticky situations here at school and gives us great advice when we are on one of our adventures. He never seems surprised by what we ask him or what we're doing. He just smiles and gets right into the meat and potatoes of it all and wants to know everything that we did and what we had seen. He is just a great teacher."

"All right, everyone it's time for class to start," said Mr. Nilrem. "Everyone turn to page seventy-nine please. This is our second week back from summer vacation and it's probably as good a time as any to go over something really interesting. There have been many books, movies, and poems written about wizards, and especially, Merlin. Some people will tell you he is a fictitious character that never really existed, others will tell you that he did exist but had no real magic and was a sort of parlor magician. What I am here to do today is tell you the facts as they have been told to me plain and simple. Please get your notebooks at the ready, people, there will be lots of little tidbits that will not be found in any textbook discussed here today and believe me, you don't want to miss any of them.

"Now, back in the 1200s, give or take, there was a man called Merlin. He was born to an ordinary mother and father that was said to have been one of the gods himself. He came down to Merlin's mother one fateful night and rescued her from a group of road bandits. She was very thankful and invited the young hero back to her humble shack for a quick meal and some honey mead. He gratefully accepted and their relationship began.

"After many years a son was born and his name was Merlin. Now, Merlin's father would leave from time to time to deal with other business. At first it would be for a day or so and then his time away seemed to become more frequent and extended. He was gone for weeks at a time and sometimes longer and never really explained where he was or what he was doing. He just had a way of sidestepping any questions and never really answering a single one.

"Now this boy Merlin was no ordinary child, mind you, he seemed to be very special. The forest creatures took an immediate liking to him and almost watched over him no matter where he went. His mother was so shocked by his special abilities that she had trouble with him from the beginning. Merlin would wander off for days at the tender age of five and his mother would be grief stricken until his return. Merlin would return as if by magic out of the thin air and be at the front door when she missed him and was worrying about him the most. Eventually, Merlin's father stopped coming by as much and seemed to fade into history as if he was never really there in the first place. No one seemed to remember his face or really what is name was or where he came from. He was just gone and drifted out of everyone's memories like a storm comes and goes and is eventually forgotten altogether. "

"Mr. Nilrem, you believe that Merlin was alive and that he could do magic?" asked Crystal.

Mr. Nilrem grinned and then smiled broadly from ear to ear. "Let's not jump ahead, Miss Kildroy. Please give me time to finish the story before we get into open discussion.

"So, as the story goes on, Merlin's magical powers continued to grow. He was able to see the future using a seeing stone, talk to the animals and manipulate any person's appearance, including his own, actually changing down to every minute detail his appearance to look like anyone that he had ever seen. In time Merlin's many magical gifts were viewed by powerful lords and kings as a way to expand their empires and fortunes. Kings and queens alike wanted to control Merlin and his magical power, often wars were fought, but Merlin always remained his own master and answered to no one but himself.

"Obviously Merlin did assist King Arthur—yes, I did say King Arthur—in gaining access to the throne of England by pulling Excalibur from the stone. But that's another story altogether. Today we are just discussing some of Merlin's special powers and if he really existed at all.

"Now, class…any comments at this time?" questioned Mr. Nilrem. The entire class raised their hands and the open discussion began. Many questions were asked and they were very strange indeed.

"Mr. Nilrem, is there any evidence that Merlin could change his shape, like morph into someone else and sound like them and everything or that he could talk to animals and see the future too?" asked Crystal incredulously.

"That's what the legends tell us and there is some history to back this up. There are many entries in a few ancient texts that managed to survive the test of time that refer to the shape shifter, fairy or something along those lines and these references are really pertaining to Merlin himself," said Mr. Nilrem.

"Where is all the hard evidence? Is there anything at all like drawings, sketches or things like that? Maybe a statue of Merlin or his wand or his cauldron?" asked Tim. The class began to laugh loudly.

"Children, there are many things that are there for us all to see; we just have to believe and know where to look. Look at your textbook right now for instance. There is no actual reference to there being anything of Merlin's ever discovered and this book was written as if he was a mere legend, correct? Now take a look at this book that I'm now holding up in front of all of you. What do you see? This book was recovered from an ancient burial site in England in the 1400s. The grave was not marked except for a tall tree that seemed to flower year round, no matter what the weather was. Some people say this is the burial site of Merlin himself. The book was recovered within fifty feet of the burial site and there seemed to be some remnants of what might be called a cauldron. Of course the metal object in question was badly rusted and flattened and it's left to the imagination as to what it really was, but nonetheless it could have been a cauldron. There was no author listed for the book but there are many references to herbs, animals and some rather peculiar potions that no one has deciphered to this very day. Now, is this Merlin's book? I don't know for sure but there is always a chance. So, what I am trying to say is that there is always a chance that some stories are not really tales but that without actual hard evidence and through the many centuries they are eventually put into the category of a fantastic story or tale as time marches on. But remember, legend is almost always based on fact," said Mr. Nilrem.

"Mr. Nilrem, I kind of see what you are saying, just because there is little or no hard evidence that sometimes you have to believe anyway because there is always a chance?" clarified Tim.

"Exactly, you have to decide for yourselves what's real and what's not. Don't let a textbook or some fact-finding teacher tell you what to believe as real and what simply cannot be," said Mr. Nilrem.

"Mr. Nilrem, can we take a closer look at that book?" asked Charlie.

"You sure can, but you need to come during your free period and I will explain anything you would like to know, within limits of course," smiled Mr. Nilrem.

"Thanks, Mr. Nilrem," said Charlie.

"Yeah, thanks," said Tim and Crystal too.

"Mr. Nilrem, where did you get the book?" asked Charlie.

"I can tell you that maybe another day. At this point in time it really doesn't matter. Let's just say someone I know let me borrow it for a while," said Mr. Nilrem mysteriously.

"Now please gather your belongings now and get ready for the bell. I believe physical education is next for most of the school," continued Mr. Nilrem.

"What do you think of his story, Crystal?" asked Charlie.

"Well, it seems a little far-fetched, doesn't it? There is really no hard evidence whatsoever except for a book and a tree that flowers too frequently. Is that enough to believe in magic or Merlin? I need more if I am going to believe either one," said Crystal.

"At least wait until we get to check that book out more closely and see what it really says. Charlie and I get along great with Mr. Nilrem and he always lets us look at the most interesting stuff he has, of course within reason," said Tim.

"Yeah, Crystal, some of his stuff is awesome, you'll see. He has really cool armor and swords that date back to Arthur's time and even earlier," Charlie said.

"He has like a storehouse full of old things like books, maps and all kinds of old jewelry, rings and stuff," said Tim.

"Did you say jewelry?" asked Crystal.

"I knew we would hit the jackpot eventually and that was it," laughed Charlie.

"Every person has his or her vice and apparently Crystal's is the shiny stuff," Tim chimed.

"We better get going. We don't want to be late for physical education. You know that means extra laps for sure," groaned Tim.

"What's wrong with extra laps? I thought that was the reason why you were always late," said Charlie. We'll see you after phys ed, Crystal. Try not to get too beat up while you're playing that crazy game of tennis."

Crystal laughed. "Oh, I'll be careful; I know how tough that game really is."

An hour later Tim, Crystal and Charlie met at Mr. Nilrem's classroom door and discussed the fun they had while playing tennis and lacrosse.

"Well, kids, how was physical education? Did you enjoy your game of tennis and lacrosse?" asked Mr. Nilrem.

"Yeah, Mr. Nilrem, it was great. So can we look at that book now?" asked Charlie.

"You sure can," said Mr. Nilrem. "I'll be back in thirty minutes to check up on you three so please stay out of trouble while I am gone. Just remember to be careful. The book is very, very old and very powerful."

"Powerful?" asked Charlie.

"Yes, powerful in its own way. Remember there are many things that are not black and white or on and off. Some things are outside the realm of the norm. So just be careful," said Mr. Nilrem.

"No problem, Mr. Nilrem. I will keep an eye on these two," said Crystal.

"Oh, finally someone who can hopefully keep these two out of trouble for longer than five minutes," said a grinning Mr. Nilrem.

"Well, you two, let's get down to business and this Merlin guy," said Crystal.

Charlie, Tim or Crystal had never touched a book quite like this one. The book itself seemed to be made out of something resembling leather although they could not be sure. The binding was worn from the many years of handling. At some time in the book's past there was something imprinted on the cover but it was illegible at the present time. There was just an imprinted, faded image left. The pages were made out of paper that was also unfamiliar to any of the three. They seemed to be very thick and had tinted yellow through the ages. The book was handwritten and most likely a one-of-a-kind. There was no glossary or anything like that and it was more like a personal journal or just random thoughts that had been jotted down.

"The first thing we need to do is copy as much of this book as possible for later translation and reference. So let me get my handy handheld scanner and digital camera and get the ball rolling." Tim proceeded to open his backpack and in it were some of the most impressive electronics you could find in any electronics store. He had a digital camera, handheld scanner, laptop, PDA and an incredibly small cell phone.

Charlie just shook his head and told Crystal not to ask at the moment. This was Tim's deal. He loved using his technology to get to the bottom of almost everything.

"This book makes no sense at all. How are we going to decipher any of it? I have never seen anything like it. Have either of you?" asked Crystal.

"And what's up with these maps? They make no sense at all. It's like they were drawn upside down or something. What was this guy thinking when he wrote this, that we would be hanging upside down to read it?" said Charlie.

"Crystal, Crystal, Crystal, Charlie, Charlie, Charlie…you both need to have a little faith. Remember, I am the biggest Internet geek in this school and possibly the entire city of Boston. Do you think for a second I don't have my ways of obtaining information? Well, do you, because I do and I will. We just need to make sure we get all the data and I'll do most the rest. Let's get going because we only have thirty minutes, remember," said a determined-looking Tim.

Charlie, Crystal and Tim each took turns documenting as much as possible and scanning and copying every single page in the book. Although they had no idea what any of it said at the moment they were sure it was important and that they had to figure it out. They had just finished scanning the book when Mr. Nilrem returned.

"Well, how goes the deciphering? Any luck?" asked Mr. Nilrem

"We're just at the beginning of our investigation, Mr. Nilrem, so this could take a while. We'll let you know if we have any questions," said Tim.

"If you do think of anything don't hesitate to ask, of course if it's within reason, I will gladly answer," said Mr. Nilrem.

"Thanks again, Mr. Nilrem," said Tim.

"Oh, and one last thing, kids, there is another source of information that you could use and I'm relatively sure he would love to assist you in any way that he can. That person would be a certain grandfather, Mr. Watson. He has an extensive amount of knowledge ranging from ancient writing to ancient sites and is a very reputable source. He has personally helped me on many occasions in the past," said Mr. Nilrem.

Charlie looked shocked at this turn of events. "What, you know my grandfather?"

"Yes, Charlie, I have known him for many years. He asked me not to tell you so you would not expect any favoritism from me while you are my student. He and I decided it was definitely for the best and I have stuck to that promise until thirty seconds ago. I hope he understands. I am sure he will. I thought it was about time that little secret was let out," Mr. Nilrem said.

After leaving the class and getting safely from earshot, Crystal, Tim and Charlie stopped to discuss the news of Charlie's grandfather and Mr. Nilrem.

Charlie, still sporting a look of total disbelief, was almost speechless for once. "I just can't believe that he knows my grandpa. Why would they keep something like that from me? It makes no sense at all."

"I'm sure there is a good explanation—just ask your grandfather," Crystal replied.

"I think so too, Charlie. Just ask your grandfather and I'm sure he will explain it. It's probably just like Mr. Nilrem said, that he didn't want any favoritism for you so he asked it to be kept private. It's really not a big deal, is it? Mr. Nilrem genuinely likes you it seems, so just let it go until you see you grandfather."

"Hey, it's almost lunch and then just art class and home for the day. Then we can meet later and discuss this in more detail and prepare to go over the photos and notes we took from that really old book. You know? The Merlin book," laughed Tim. "I suspect there will be reference material all over the Internet with something that old, but then again you never know."

"Let's make plans to walk home together," said Tim. "We can meet at the west exit and take the usual route home. Besides it being the quickest way, the best part is that we usually don't run into our long-lost friends, Ron, Clive, Sean and Beth all that often since they go in the opposite direction."

"That was a good one, Tim," said Charlie.

"It sure was a good one," said Crystal. "So we can meet at 1:45 at the west exit and chat along the way. See you both then."

Charlie walked away deep in thought, wondering why his grandfather had never let on to knowing Mr. Nilrem in the first place. This whole thing made no sense at all. Was it something to do with the Merlin book or could it be just like Crystal and Tim said, that there was a logical explanation. Charlie was not paying a bit of attention to a certain group of kids that were taking a particular interest in him and the conversation that just went on between himself, Crystal and Tim.

"Well, well, well, it looks like we know where we are going to be at 1:45 today," said Ron.

"Where's that?" asked Clive.

"Where do you think, you dummy? We are going to be waiting for Charlie, Tim and his little girlfriend Crystal," said Ron angrily.

Ron grinned maliciously. "Clive, go and get the spray paint, gum, scissors and the digital camera and let Sean and Beth know that today is our lucky day and we will finally get our revenge."

"This is going to be great, but do you think we should get the spray paint too?" Clive asked.

"Of course I do, Clive. This time there will be no doubt as to who is the head of this school. They will never mess with any of us again. We will embarrass them so bad by putting their pictures on the school website. And the auditorium, too! Hurry up and get going, Clive! We don't want to mess this up and I'm sure Beth won't want to miss this after what happened to her. She will probably make a trophy out of Charlie's hair or something," laughed Ron.

Clive laughed, "Now that would be a sight to see hanging off her backpack!"

"Hey, Charlie, where's Tim? It's just about time to get heading home. I'm totally excited to check out all the pictures we took and start trying to make sense of all that stuff that was in Mr. Nilrem's book," said Crystal.

"Me too, I can't wait to see what we can find out. I am really anxious to get home and talk to Grandpa too and see what he has to say about Mr. Nilrem.

I just don't understand and I think it could be another mystery for us to look into. It doesn't add up to me and I certainly plan on getting to the bottom of it. And of course you and Tim will be helping me."

"We sure will," agreed Crystal.

"Hey, guys, I am almost all set to get going. Just give me a minute to put all my planned work away in my backpack and we can get out of here. I'm totally excited about trying to translate all this data. I am curious if my newsgroup will be able to assist me with this. You can find anything on the Internet if you know the right people and know how to ask," said Tim.

Charlie, Tim and Crystal headed out without any idea that Beth Ron, Clive, and Sean were closely following them. Ron had gotten released fifteen minutes earlier and was waiting ahead of them to set the plan into action.

As Charlie, Tim and Crystal walked about two blocks from the school they noticed Ron standing in the street sporting a spray can in each hand and smiling so broadly it looked like his face would get stuck. A quick glance behind them and they noticed Sean and Clive closing in fast with scissors, a paint can and Beth carrying a digital camera happily strolling towards them. Realizing a calamity was about to unfold, Charlie yelled, "Run!" and pulled Crystal by the arm down the nearest alley with Tim hot on their heels. They were all well aware that this could turn into a socially crippling and quite embarrassing event. Charlie, Tim and Crystal ran as hard as they could down alley after alley. They took a quick left and ended up at what looked like a dead end. Thankfully there were some rather stinky dumpsters and barrels lining the alley walls. Charlie, Tim and Crystal swiftly ducked behind four rather repulsive barrels. These disgusting barrels were overflowing with fish parts that were primarily indescribable. The stench was beyond disgusting.

In the background you could hear Ron yelling at the top of his lungs. He was furious and did not want to let his prey escape so easily.

"All of you keep looking! They have to be down here somewhere. I don't care about the stench, just keep looking. There is no way we are losing them today," said Ron.

"I don't see them anywhere, Ron, and I have no idea where we are. This place totally doesn't look familiar to me," said Beth. "I'm getting creeped out! Can we get out of here?"

"Oh, stop being a wimp and keep looking! They have to be here somewhere," said Ron. "Clive, do you see anything over there?"

"I got nothing," called Clive.

"How about you, Sean?" asked Ron.

"I got nothing over here or behind the dumpsters either," said Sean.

"Beth, anything over by the fish barrels?" Ron asked.

"Nothing over here," Beth replied while trying not to gag. Luckily Beth was so disgusted by the smell of fish and the filth that was littering the entire alley she never actually made an attempt to look behind the barrels. After all, she was Beth and this was far below her to even think about touching anything that smelled that bad anyway. How dare Ron even consider for one moment that she was actually going to go behind the barrels and look around or even touch one? These things were smelly and gross beyond description and far below someone of her stature.

Ron was infuriated at the failure to get even with Charlie and Tim. "Okay, you three, I know you can hear me and don't think for a second that this is over. It may not have been today but there is always tomorrow. Have fun hiding like the pathetic cowards that you are."

After a few more moments of poking around without any luck the stench finally got the best of them. Ron Clive, Sean and Beth unanimously decided it was time to go.

"Let's get the heck our of here. This place is starting to give me the creeps too," said Ron.

"Yeah, it's definitely creepy and the stench is incredibly disgusting. It's making my eyes water and my stomach turn. And you know I have a strong stomach," said Clive.

"With the way you eat you would have to," said Ron.

"Speaking of eating…" Clive wondered.

"All right, I get the point. There is nothing more to do at this point but go get cleaned up and head for a pizza and soda. I will call Mother and have her order it like usual," said Ron.

"Excellent," said Clive.

"Thanks, buddy, you're the best," said Sean.

"Oh, shut up already and stop kissing up!" Ron grumbled.

"See you later, losers," yelled Clive.

A few moments passed and Crystal finally built up the courage to whisper a few words. "Do you think they're gone?"

Charlie took a peek over the barrel he was hiding behind and all was clear but he decided it's better to be safe than sorry. "We should wait a bit more before we get out of here, just to make sure."

"That was way too close," said Tim.

"This stinks," said Crystal.

"Look on the bright side. At least we still have all our hair," said Charlie smirking.

"I mean the fish, Charlie. It really, really stinks. Let's wait a few more minutes to make sure they're gone then we can get out here. This place is creepy. Has either one of you ever been down here before?" asked Crystal.

"Nope," Charlie and Tim replied.

"I think we waited long enough, I can't stand the smell anymore. It just might be worth getting a smiley face spray painted on my backside and a Mohawk to match to get away from this smell," said Tim. "This stench has to be the worst thing I have ever smelled and that's counting that Wenstral kid after gym class too."

"Well, I don't know this Wenstral person but I totally agree, this smell is horrendous and I can't take it anymore," said Crystal. "Hey, guys, wait a minute. Do either one of you have any idea what that means?"

"What are you talking about?" asked Tim.

"Turn around and look!" Crystal exclaimed. Tim was already looking and Crystal proceeded to manually turn Charlie's head to the left so he could see what she was talking about. Charlie and Tim just stood in awe of what they were looking at. Neither said anything and they both kept staring at the wall of the alley. What they were looking at seemed so out of place that they simply could not think of a thing to say. There mounted on the alley wall behind the barrels of rotten fish was something that just did not belong. Seemingly appearing out of nowhere at eye level was a beautiful plaque made from either solid gold or maybe brass. The screws were also made from the same material and screwed tightly into the brick. The plaque seemed spotless even though it was right behind barrel after barrel of rotten fish.

The plaque read:

Come to where the wizards are, it could be near it could be far.

To open the lock to magic and mystery insert the key for your chance at history.

The key could be round,

It could be a square,

It could be here or it could be there

So find the right symbol and open the lock, fit it just once and turn it like a clock.

Most people live in one either large or small,

Kings or Queens tend to rule them all.
People come and people stay.
There are places to meet and to go and play
Some families keep them as treasures and such.
One finger can hold them or a neck just as much
Some look the same and some do not
There could be more than one but then again not
But in the end they are the same lot.
This key can be held close to the heart or far away when we point or do not.
A fist would not hide it but a shirt sometimes can.
It could be a woman's or a man's.
Look to a volume where some will be found
Next to a tree that flowers year round.
Plans need to be read wrong and from the ground
Use a stick for ambling around.
The symbol is created in the ground.

Tim looked on, amazed at what he was seeing. "That plaque is absolutely amazing! I have never seen anything like it, that symbol or that poem. Whatever it is this thing is totally out of place. Is that thing made of gold or what? Charlie, I think we might have stumbled into another adventure moment, and the biggest one ever. Congratulations, Crystal, you are right here to get caught up in the middle of it, so welcome to the club. I hope you're ready because this sure looks like a winner to me."

Crystal looked on almost speechless. "That has got to be the oddest and most wonderful thing I have ever seen. That symbol is astonishing. It looks almost like a key or something should fit in, almost like it's a lock. What is it doing in an alley in Boston behind a load of rotten fish?"

"I have no idea what any of this means but I plan on finding out," said Charlie.

"I figured that would be the case, so give me a minute to get out my camera and a quick GPS reading so we can get back here after doing research. Of course, I need to get a quick sketch and a rubbing too," Tim remarked as he dug out his equipment.

"Oh, of course," Crystal said with amusement. "You always need to get a rubbing. Did you say GPS? You are carrying a GPS with you? Are you kidding?"

"Oh no, he never leaves home without it—to him it's like a cell phone or your purse," laughed Charlie.

"Very funny," said Tim.

"What would a plaque with a rhyming poem be doing out in the middle of nowhere on a beautiful golden plaque with a symbol like that? It's way too bizarre. That does look sort of like a keyhole, but not for a regular key. More like something you would fit into it and press or turn. Maybe it's a that was left here a very long time ago by pirates or something like that," said Tim excitedly. "The only question I would have is why hasn't it been discovered before? I just don't see how it has not been noticed by one of the workers dumping fish guts out here. Someone is spending a lot of time filling all these barrels and all they would need to do is look up to see this thing. I just don't get it."

"I really have no idea why we see it and no one else has that we know of. This just might be the biggest mystery we have ever come across to date," said Tim, smiling broadly from ear to ear.

"I totally agree. Thanks to Ron and his gang for chasing us in here or we would never have found this in the first place. So I guess they're good for something then," said Charlie.

"Okay, let's get out here and get going already. I'm all set with my digital camera; rubbings and I got that GPS reading. I will do some research tonight and I suspect it's going to take a while. Hopefully I will have something for you two by tomorrow," said Tim.

"I definitely think it's time to get going too," said Crystal. "It's getting late and we do not want to end up grounded! Then we will never get to the bottom of this."

Charlie, Crystal and Tim exited the alley and Tim marked the entrance to the alley with his GPS so they could get back easily for later reference. All the way home the three couldn't stop talking about the plaque in the alley and the strange saying or poem. None of the three had any idea what it meant or where it came from but they all intended to find out. This was a mystery that they just could not let pass by.

Charlie had almost forgotten about Mr. Nilrem and what he had said about his grandfather. He was so caught up in the alley and what has just transpired that he completely pushed it out of his mind. He finally remembered after Tim and Crystal were gone and he was alone walking to his front door wondering what it all meant and how it fit together. It sure seemed like a lot to take in for one day, but then again Charlie was used to excitement from his many misadventures with Tim and just loved a good mystery.

Chapter 3

Grandpa Watson and the Facts About Fairies and Such

Grandpa Watson loved telling stories to anyone who would listen. He had spent most of his life exploring the world's mysterious places. Many years of his life were spent searching for items and artifacts thought to be pure legend and nothing more. He enjoyed proving the experts and skeptics wrong. Although he had reached the ripe old age of seventy-four, you would never know it. He still acted like he was forty and looked like it too. He had a sparkle in his eye that said he was a very confident man with a clear and bright mind.

Grandpa had a slight limp from one of his adventures, although he never really discussed how it happened or where he was when it did. Charlie was sure some of his family members knew the truth of the injury but it seemed that Grandpa was very leery to discuss it. The details are sketchy but the family grapevine states that he was in Burma in an unidentifiable temple unknown to the entire archaeological world. Grandpa was looking for an artifact that was supposedly left behind by a magical group of what he called "Wizards." Just mentioning Wizards or the supposed temple was considered archaeological suicide by most mainstream archaeologists and of course this was one of the main reasons why he went looking for it in the first place.

It has long been rumored that the temple is protected by ancient magic. Many magical traps guarded the entrance to this sacred location. Hieroglyphs supposedly depicted ancient wizards and sorceresses doing all types of spells and creating potions.

These rumors were spread by a small group of villagers who had supposedly been to the site many times. This was enough to convince Grandpa that there must be something there worth studying after all, so off he went to Burma along with Grandma Watson. After that journey to Burma Grandpa always carried the one thing that he values most, his trusty cane. It has been widely speculated that it was recovered from Burma. This cane had an odd symbol embedded in the head of the cane that looked somewhat like four lollipops in a beautiful large clear crystal. The crystal itself seemed to be alert and looking at you as if it were waiting. Grandpa never let the cane out of his possession for a moment. This was his most special and favorite discovery.

"Hey, Grandpa," said Charlie.

"Well hello, Charlie," said Grandpa. Tim said hello and Charlie proceeded to introduce Crystal Kildroy but was cut off by a smiling Grandpa Watson.

"Crystal," said Grandpa, "of the famous Kildroys, I suspect? You look just like your mother. She is a most beautiful woman with the wittiest sense of humor." Looking puzzled, Crystal was getting ready to ask Grandpa how he knew her mom, but by the look on Charlie's face she just let it go for the moment.

"Can you tell me all about your trip to Burma?" Charlie asked. "I know you don't like to talk about it, but we'd love to hear it."

"Yes, Charlie, I think I will, but first you must listen to what I have to say before you hear any of the story whatsoever. I have not discussed this in many years and there are reasons why," said Grandpa Watson

Crystal and Tim looked on anxiously waiting to hear all about this mysterious trip to Burma that Grandpa Watson had taken many years earlier. They hoped to pick up a few details that might be helpful to their quest, trying to crack the riddle they had found on the mysterious plaque in the alley on Wolworts Street.

"As far as the facts go, kids, here they are. The first thing all of you should know about my trip is that some individuals in the field of archaeology will state that what I am about to tell you is utter rubbish and there are no facts to back up my story. Scholars and professors would say that there couldn't possibly be anything that cannot be explained with either a textbook or simple science. I would like to tell them to stuff their textbooks, facts and the notion that if it cannot be found in a book, the Internet or a shopping mall it simply cannot be true. These past statements are some of the many reasons why I hardly go into detail about my journey to Burma, or adventure, as you would call it, Charlie.

"The first challenging thing about this journey that made it difficult to complete was the tumultuous time in Burma. The government was in constant flux with warlords popping up across the countryside. Most of the warlords and gangs were very unscrupulous and would think nothing of removing your head from its comfortable normal location atop your shoulders and placing it somewhere else, if you know what I mean.

"Burma was under the control of a general who dominated the country for many years. He appointed himself president along the way and then became a sort of kingpin in Burma and its underworld. Getting passage into his land can be a bit costly and definitely not the sanest thing to do. Illegal activities are one of their biggest money producers and they are not too keen on outsiders who might interfere with their cash cow.

"I left for Burma with Grandma Watson with many hopes and thoughts that I would finally be able to put to rest this notion that I was a crackpot searching for dreams and fairy tales. We left for Taiwan on August 13, 1960, and landed four days later. We slipped over the Taiwanese border and followed the Irrawaddy River into Burma. There we met our guide, Utritcka, in his home village of Yutrgang. Our gear was packed into what you might call a canoe that was about twenty feet long. We set off at first light and headed down the river towards our destinies. We followed the river for two straight days. Finally we reached the landing that was marked by two very old carved lions. These two lions were weather worn to the point that they were hardly recognizable. Utritcka stated that these lions were left as guards to scare off would-be treasure hunters and adventures. We pulled up between these great lions' heads and left our boats behind on the sandy shore and headed into the deep and rather forbidden-looking rainforest. Utritcka, our guide, stated that the path we were now on had been cleared many times in the past and it always is overgrown again by the very next morning. I began to realize that this would not be an easy journey. It was a four-day walk with many perils and miseries such as snakes, mosquitoes, thorns, pumas and the occasional warlord or two popping up. We spent many hours dodging groups of militia, hiding in the jungle and not making a sound, fearing for our lives. After walking for miles we realized that if the rebels did not kill us then surely the malaria-carrying mosquitoes would. We cut our way through dense brush and jungle for a day straight. It was as if the jungle itself was trying to deny us access to the location we were seeking. Finally, after days of hacking and stumbling through the thick forest, we ended up at a clearing with a strange large depression that must have been caused by a rather large explosion of some type. I still don't know what caused this and there seems to be no known records that the public would have access to that we were able to track down. This depression was deep and wide. Figuring that there might be some artifacts around the hole, we spent hours searching and came up with absolutely nothing. This surprised Grandma and myself. We figured there would surely be something, anything, a small artifact, carved stone or something, but there was nothing."

"Mr. Watson, how is it you were able to find this location and convince a guide to take you to this hole?" asked Crystal.

"That's an excellent question, Crystal, and I will give you a quick overview of how I was able to gain their trust," said Grandpa.

"I had spent many years with the inhabitants of Yutrgang and learned a few of their secrets from their elders. It took quite a while to earn their trust. The Yutrgang are a very skittish people and do not trust outsiders whatsoever. I was spending many days with Grandma Watson trying to decipher their hieroglyphics and translate it to a language that we could understand. While doing research on a small site, Grandma and I heard loud screaming and many Yutrgang were seen running past us into the jungle with weapons raised at the ready. After spending quite some time trying to find out what happened, finally one of the elders was able to explain using a crude form of sign language that a child was missing and the Demon was seen in the vicinity of the child's last known whereabouts. I proceeded to follow some of the villagers into the jungle when I heard a faint sound coming from my left and slightly overhead. I immediately noticed the puma, or Demon has they called it, trying to pull the child into a tree and to certain death. I proceeded without thinking to pull my hunting knife and slowly edge towards the beast. He was rather large for a puma and I was terrified. I knew that if I did not act promptly it would be over for the child. I noticed a tree to the right of the mighty beast and started to slowly move towards it. Slowly and steadily I climbed till I was just above the beast and I leapt with all my might and thrust my hunting knife deep into his neck right below his skull. The beast screamed in great pain and immediately dropped the child back to the jungle floor. I fell with the beast and landed awkwardly on my left leg and now you know the reason for the limp. I have had it ever since.

"Anyway, after our long and arduous journey we finally arrived at our destination. Grandma and I were most anxious to get this archaeological fact- and relic-finding part of our journey underway. I proceeded to the edge of the great pit and examined it as closely as possible. Neither Grandma nor I could see the bottom of the pit even when dropping a flashlight or two. The pit was as dark during the day as the darkest night. Through the long years the entrance had been overgrown with heavy vines and local vegetation. The vines and brush seemed to have woven themselves together to form an almost impenetrable wall. It was hard to tell the difference between the brush and the actual edge of the crater itself.

"We set up camp on the rim of the cavern and prepared to journey into it at first light tomorrow. Three tents were set up. One tent we prepared was set up for supplies and the other two for sleeping. We had set up a fire pit in the middle of the site for cooking and lighting purposes only. No matter how hard we tried that first night we were unable to light a fire. We tried matches, a lighter and even the fire-starter kit we had brought along. Even with our best efforts alas nothing would come of it. We decided to have a cold ration meal that night and would try and figure this out in the morning.

"When waking the next morning I was well aware that our surroundings had changed. Most of the landscape seemed to have completely morphed overnight. Trees were moved, plants were present that were not there previously, and the overhead of trees seemed to be creeping over the camp, giving it an eerie feeling and making early morning seem like dusk. I was first in shock at the sight of this but I later learned the truth of what had transpired. I noticed while making my morning walk around camp that at least half of our climbing gear was missing and a third of our supplies had disappeared. I promptly alerted Grandma to this and she and Utritcka went off into the surrounding jungle to see if any of the equipment would turn up. After about an hour search it became very obvious that whoever or whatever removed our supplies during the night had made sure they would not be found," said Grandpa Watson.

"I have some small details to add in that may sound a bit strange but here they are nonetheless. While walking through the dense forest for the past two days I had begun to notice some rather strange things. First, let me explain that I have seen these in the past at various locations while doing archaeological work. I have noticed what I call orb fairies. They are small glowing creatures with wings and they have the most beautiful little laughs. The fairies seem to giggle when they are about to do something mischievous. The orb fairies come around every time I am close to a magical site.

"Now don't roll your eyes and think I am crazy, because I am not," Grandpa said with a stern loud voice. "I have seen these orb fairies many times in the past and Grandma has too. So let's get back to the story. Where was I now? Oh yes—magical sites are places where I think at one point in time great wizards, sorceresses or magic folk lived and left a sort of trace behind. Sometimes it's just a feeling or it could even be an artifact of some sort."

Now Tim decided to chime in at this point, being a highly scientific person and a computer buff for most of his young life, "Grandpa Watson, do you mean like magic? Actual magic? Like spells and wands and magical chants and people flying on broomsticks?"

"No, Tim. Wizards and sorceresses do not ride broomsticks. They either morph or they dissipate and go wherever they need to," said Grandpa Watson very sternly and looking a bit red in the face.

"Daylight was breaking on our first day while we were attempting to try and explore the pit. With the dense overgrowth, large trees and vines growing from the walls of the inner rim for hundreds of feet on every side it made it very difficult to decide how to go about getting to the bottom of this. Grandma and I noticed even with the naked eye that it looked like the brush itself was alive, as if it were moving even though there was little or no wind. The more I focused the more obvious it became that the movement was not the brush but snakes, and I mean not a few or a hundred but thousands of them hanging on every branch, it seemed. I have no doubt that this place is in some way guarded by the wood spirits. The wood nymphs or tricksters, which they have sometimes been called in the past, changed this large entrance into what me, Grandma and Utritcka are now seeing."

Immediately Tim and Crystal had that usual look of skepticism you see when someone was just asked to buy a bridge or swamp land from Florida. Before they could even get a word out Grandpa shook his head with a look of disgust on his face and said, "Give me a minute to explain the wood nymphs, as Grandma so expertly had named them. Wood nymphs are beyond beautiful. There is no word in our language to describe them to do them justice. Grandma and I have tried many times either talking to one, catching one or getting a picture of one of these wonderful woodland creatures. We have failed at every attempt. I will do my best to describe what I have seen. The woodland nymphs range in height from three to five feet. They have hair that is colored so beautifully it cannot be described fully. It is always flowing like the wind is blowing even on the calmest days. They seem to float on the winds like the smoke billowing from a chimney on a cold winter day or glide like a feather so graceful it's almost as if they are made of nothing but pure beauty. Their eyes glisten like the water on a pond, so serene and peaceful with so much life and happiness.

"The wood nymphs are as tricky as they are beautiful. They are able to manipulate the forest, jungle or any type of plant or vegetation. They are able to change the appearance of a path you just walked down minutes earlier to look completely different. They have caused many explorers and adventures to be confused, end up lost and sometimes not turn up at all. Now do not think for a second that these beautiful creatures are evil, because they are not. They are protecting something of great importance when they are being mischievous. The also seem to behave differently depending on the travelers they come across. They have been known to save children and weary travelers by projecting paths and lights to guide them to safety. But beware if the wood nymphs sense you are evil in any way; they will work as hard as they can to make sure you do not ever leave the forest of jungle ever again." Everyone was silent for a moment and trying to decide whether to laugh or if he was serious.

After a long pause, Grandpa continued on with his story and we were left hanging on every word. "Now here we all are—Grandma, Utritcka and myself—standing near the edge of this great hole. We cannot see the bottom, we have no idea what is down there but I know in my heart that I have to try and rappel down nonetheless. Utritcka is very nervous about this place and says it is cursed by the wood spirits. He is very edgy and does not want any part of trying to attempt to rappel down into this hole created by the gods, as he put it. His people have avoided this place for centuries. Utritcka stated that many of his relatives and friends had tried to gain access to this sacred place and have never been seen again. It is said that a great demon god lives down there and will eat the flesh of anyone trying to gain access to the great treasure that lies in the tunnels below.

"Nonetheless I had decided I was going down there. Nothing is going to stop me at this point. I decided that I was much too close to proving that the ancient guilds did exist and that I am not a crazed lunatic. So I loaded up my backpack with extra rations, a flashlight, strapped on my sidearm on my right side, my hunting knife on my left side and my trusty white cowboy hat that I always wore on many of my adventures.

"Utritcka and myself proceeded to the edge of the pit and started setting up the ropes for the dangerous climb ahead of us. The mysterious unknown was calling to me and I just didn't want to be denied. We proceeded to put on our climbing harnesses and started to edge towards what we thought was the edge of the hole. We prepared to traverse the hole by first proceeding to the task of arduously chopping away as much of the vegetation as possible to try and start rappelling. It seemed like a tedious task and almost like the very jungle itself was trying to stop us. Once we had made a clearing big enough for me to squeeze into Utritcka started slowly lowering me into the hole while I continued to chop the vegetation. I had to be very alert and attentive to all the rather poisonous snakes and spiders that seemed to pop up out of nowhere mere feet away from me during the entire rappel. They seemed to be present more as a deterrent; it was as if they were waiting for something before they would make any kind of an aggressive move. I tried to stay focused on the chopping, lowering and the occasional tree branch that would seem to have a mind of its own and avoid my machete. My leg was a bit of a hindrance but I would not let that stop me."

Tim had a perplexed look on his face. "Grandpa Watson, how come the spiders and snakes were not attacking you? That sounds really strange. And what do you mean the jungle itself was trying to stop you? It's not like the jungle can think for itself or anything like that, right?"

"Timmy, some things cannot be explained, they have to be experienced. There are things out there that words cannot describe. Mysterious things happen all the time and people write them off to either an overactive imagination, exaggeration, or that you are simply nuts," said Grandpa.

"Well, Mr. Watson, there is a sensible explanation for all of this, I'm sure. I bet the jungle has really good soil and that you, Grandma Watson and Utritcka just got confused and the landscape really did not change. Some animal could have dragged off your extra gear in the night and the snakes and spiders probably did not bother you because you were not threatening them," said Crystal

"Crystal, you can believe what you want after I finish this story, if that's okay," said Grandpa with a smile. "If you still believe the way you do now then that is your choice and remember, all I am telling you is a story plain and simple."

Grandpa continued, "While I was about a third of the way down to what I thought might be the bottom I realized that this main line was not going to be long enough to get me to where I wanted to go. I signaled up to Utritcka and Grandma Watson that the rope was just not long enough and I was going to tie off and use my backup line to make the rest of the descent. Both Grandma and Utritcka were totally against this, realizing that I would have to pull myself out if something went wrong. Both of them signaled frantically for me to stop right there and come back up this instant. I am not one to quit or be deterred by something as little as a piece of rope, so I went with my plan anyway and started to descend even deeper until I could not longer see Grandma Watson or Utritcka.

"The vegetation started to subside along with the snakes and spiders and I began to notice what looked like very old and weather-worn statues and large blocks of what looked like marble or possibly granite. I was trying to get a better look when I realized that I was very close to the bottom. That's when the adventure really began.

"Immediately to my left I noticed a torch that had not been lit for many long years. I pulled out a wood match and lit it, glancing about. To my total amazement it looked like this cavern was the size of a small city. All along the walls were beautiful broken statues along with broken pillars that were lying about strewn from some sort of cataclysmic disaster from long ago. There seemed to be an apparent circle-type layout to the whole place like the middle was the focal point of this entire location. Realizing that this was the find of a lifetime, I pulled out my camera and started snapping pictures as swiftly as possible. The place was overwhelming with all the artifacts and hieroglyphs all about the walls and on odd-looking plaques. The plaques seemed to be almost like street signs or directions, I wasn't sure. I started to take notes in my scratch pad and jotted down a general layout of the place. After about five minutes I realized that this place was immense and that I would never be able to document it all in one visit. I went back to the hole and yelled up to Grandma Watson to throw me down some supplies and that I would be staying the night. She was not too keen on this but I could not leave this place. It was just too impressive to not try and view every little detail."

"After gathering up the supplies, I headed back to what was apparently the entrance. It looked like the remnants of an ancient arch that had long ago fallen. I stepped through the arch and to my amazement I noticed that everything around me seemed to brighten, as if a spotlight was just turned on. I proceeded to put out the torch and continue with my sketching and picture taking. I wandered for what seemed to be hours until I found myself standing in front of an ancient staircase. The steps were so large an ordinary person would have trouble climbing them. They seemed to be built for a giant. Now, I am not saying giants, before you interrupt, but the steps were about two feet high so it was kind of awkward to get up them with my injured leg but I persevered anyway. After reaching the top I realized to my total joy and excitement that this temple-type structure was complete! I was in shock. I had discovered a temple underground in the middle of Burma. This would put me over the top finally. I would not be ridiculed for my ideas and research. I proceeded to enter the temple. It seemed to be guarded by two of the strangest creatures I had ever seen. Two statues on either side of the great entranceway both seemed to be almost waiting for something as if they were alive but just waiting. I sketched one of them and proceeded cautiously by them and into the main entranceway of the temple."

"Grandpa, what did they look like? You know—the two creatures?" asked Charlie.

"I'll get to that later, Charlie. Please let me get to the end of this, okay?" asked Grandpa.

"So I have just entered the temple. I will call this the great hall, as it was immense. The hall was possibly 600 feet in length and about 400 in diameter, give or take. All along the edges were statues of what looked like people from long ago. Most of them were wearing long robes and carrying strange items like orbs or long staffs. Most had long hair and very long beards. They looked incredibly lifelike. I would not have been surprised to see one of them move or say hello. It was a very eerie feeling walking through there to the end of the great hall. Once I finally reached the end of the hall there was another staircase leading to another floor. I proceeded up the stairs and into another long hall. At the end of this hall the room seemed to be lit by the sun itself. At the greatest point of light there was a pedestal with what looked like a walking stick or cane resting in a stand that closely resembled two lion's paws. A very nice abstract statue if I do say so. Just two lion's paws manipulated into a beautifully handcrafted pedestal holding this walking cane. The detail was exquisite. I moved ever closer, expecting something crazy to happen. I walked right up to the pedestal and slowly reached out for the cane. As my hand got closer I noticed that the light was getting brighter. The closer my hand got the brighter the light was, until I could barely see my hand or the cane. I reached farther into the light and felt the solid object and grabbed it. The light instantly dimmed and the paws seemed to release the cane to me. Now I am not exaggerating, the paws seemed to actually let go of the cane.

"I was amazed at what had just happened. I was holding a cane that could be thousands of years old in a place that had not yet been discovered and was not in a textbook from here to China. I was going to become the most famous explorer of all time!

"I started my walk back through the first great hall and down the stairs. When getting downstairs, to my amazement it surely seemed that some of the statues were either missing or moved. I checked my reference sketches and it definitely seemed that way or I misinterpreted it in the first place. I was certainly feeling a bit shaken after this strange turn of events and decided I would exit this place promptly and explore more in the morning. As I exited the temple I had no doubt that both the statues turned to watch me leave. I was petrified at this point in time and proceeded to run to the arch, not daring to even glance back for a second, fearing of what was coming behind me. At this point in time I was too tired to try and attempt to climb out of so I decided to find a safe location and curl up for the night.

"When waking the next morning after having the strangest dreams of wizards and sorceresses, magic and spells, I decided to take one last look at those two statues and get a bit more detail for my notes. To my utter and total amazement they were no longer there and it looked like there were tracks in the dust heading off towards the darkness of the cave that I dared not explore. I went right back to my rope and climbed with all my might at a sprinter like pace. This time I noticed there were no spiders or snakes. The jungle almost seemed to have quit and even the vines and brush seemed to be much lighter than it was just a few hours earlier. When reaching the point of where I had originally tied off my line, Grandma Watson was shouting down to me that our guide was missing and she had no idea what had happened to him. She could not find a trace of him anywhere.

"I picked up my pace, climbing even faster to help with the search for our guide, Utritcka. Grandma and I spent a few moments to run through all the details of where and when she had last seen Utritcka. After a considerable search of the entire area of our camp and surrounding jungle we didn't find so much as a trace of Utritcka. Not even a bent branch of a tree or a shred of his clothing. Nothing could be found, no blood, no animal tracks, just nothing. It was as if the jungle had taken him away. We decided to take turns guarding the camp through the night and journey to Utritcka's village in the morning to give the bad news to his village elders and family.

"That night I couldn't sleep, so I filled Grandma Watson in on every amazing detail about the temple. She was in total disbelief and shock. I told her everything and showed her the cane to prove it. After cleaning the cane we examined it more closely and realized that there was a beautiful crystal at the head of it. This crystal was oddly shaped and seemed to have something embedded in it. This amazing discovery would have to wait for further analysis once we got back to England and had the proper equipment on hand.

"We spent the next two days working our way back to where we thought was the location of the Yutrang village and were unable to locate it or a trace of any of its inhabitants. It was like it was never there. We spent a solid day rechecking our steps and searching for anything, to no avail. We could not find it again. It seemed like the jungle had just swallowed it. We proceeded over the next two days quietly back into Thailand and caught a flight back to England the next day.

"Well, kids, it's getting late so we will need to finish this some other time," said Grandpa.

"What do you think happened to the villagers and what about the strange creatures and the signs that you saw in the temple and the missing statues?" Tim asked.

"Yeah," said Crystal. "We need to know what happened. Did you get the film developed and if so where are the pictures? What happened to your notebook too?"

"Well, Crystal and Tim, that's a good group of questions. First let me tell you about the film. After getting back to England and having it developed, every single picture was blank. It was as if I we had never taken even one single picture. Now that was absolutely horrible but I thought, at least I have the notebook. But to my total astonishment the notebook was completely blank too. It was as if by magic. The only thing that was still present was the cane and that I still carry to this day, right here. This cane is the only thing that survived my adventure.

"Three years later Grandma Watson and I went back to try and find the lost city and there were no guides who had heard of the Yutrang or the lost temple. We spent weeks searching through Burma on our own and were unable to find a trace of what we had found only years earlier. Determined, we went back four more times and came up empty. Utritcka was gone, along with the Yutrang and the lost temple. It was as if the jungle itself had again decided to keep its secrets hiding the temple along with the Yutrgang and Utritcka. They seemed to have been removed from the very fabric of the world. Like I said, the only thing surviving to prove my story is this cane and I never let it out of my sight for a moment," said Grandpa Watson.

"Grandpa, we have one more question for you," said Charlie. "How come you didn't tell me that you know Mr. Nilrem?"

Laughing loudly Grandpa Watson said, "Charlie, I was just looking out for your best interests. I didn't want people assuming that you were getting ahead based on the people you know. I just wanted Mr. Nilrem to let you find your own way, so to speak. We agreed that it was best not to tell you. There is really nothing more to it than that. And besides, I didn't want him assisting you in any way on one of your so-called adventures."

Charlie, Tim and Crystal smiled and decided that some of the facts of this amazing story were best left for another time. Although they all wanted to see the cane up close and Tim was practically drooling to study it, we could all tell that Grandpa was not going to let that happen at the moment.

"Grandpa, we need to get going. Thanks for the story," said Charlie. "We have some other things to take care of."

"Charlie, please tell me it's not another one of your so-called adventures? You know how your father and mother feel about that stuff. They are not all too happy when they get calls from the principal or even worse—the police."

"No, Grandpa. It's just some schoolwork that we need to get done and we are going to help each other out."

"Okay then, but please try to stay out of trouble!" instructed Grandpa Watson.

"Charlie and Crystal, I will catch you both tomorrow. I am going home to do some research tonight and I'm sure it's going to take a while since as usual I will be doing this alone," stated Tim.

"Like always, buddy," said a smiling Charlie as he patted Tim on the back a bit too hard.

"The more things change, the more they stay the same," said Tim.

"Okay, Tim, I will talk to you first thing tomorrow. We can make plans to meet at my house and go over what we have learned so far," said Charlie.

"See ya, guys," said Crystal. "It's getting late and who knows how much longer my limo driver will wait before he gets all upset."

"I have the same problem with my limo guy too," said Charlie.

"Doesn't everyone?" asked Tim.

"Funny, guys," said Crystal. "Good luck with the research, Tim. I hope you find something really interesting for us to go over tomorrow morning."

Chapter 4

MTM and Backwards Thinking

Friday night Tim spent searching the Internet for anything and everything pertaining to Merlin. He entered countless chat rooms and used every other resource he had available. However, much to his annoyance he couldn't find a single thing connected to either the maps or symbols they had copied from Mr. Nilrem's ancient book. Hour after hour went by and still nothing. Eventually he decided to give Merlin a rest for a while and focus his efforts on the poem or the even more mysterious key-like symbol.

Desperation was now setting in so Tim finally decided to do something drastic. He spent an hour or so chatting with some of his least favorite members in the ancient history chat room who go by the group name, "The Ancient Mediators." They were a group of longstanding members of the ancient history chat room who were so-called know-it-alls. They are extremely frustrating to just about anyone who might try to have an educational conversation that was not going to be entirely one-sided. Nonetheless, Tim dug in, not wanting to leave any stone unturned, and begrudgingly sent them an IM to go and meet him in a private chat room. After a rather lengthy and utterly useless chat session with four members of the group it was quite apparent that they had nothing to offer whatsoever. Tim was reaching a point of total frustration. He had no answers and seemingly nowhere to find any. The aggravation built and he was about ready to call it a night when a new name appeared in the chat room. This was a name he didn't recognize. Initially he didn't pay MTM much notice. He then viewed a few of his recent posts from earlier in the evening and decided it was worth a shot to see what if anything at all this person had to offer.

Tim and MTM spent a good part of the evening going over ancient history and information of historical nature. Hour after hour passed and Tim started to realize MTM just might be able to offer something to this mystery.

"Hey MTM, I have this problem that I have been working on and every lead ends up at a dead end. All this researching and nothing to show for it is really starting to give me a serious headache. I searched what seems like the entire Internet along with every group I can think of and came up with nothing," typed Tim.

"What is this all important data," replied MTM, "and when can I see it?"

"That's just it. I have to make sure I can trust you before I send this stuff to you. This data is sensitive," stated Tim, "and as far as I know, only known to myself and two other people. So you have to understand why I'm so hesitant to share it with you."

"I definitely understand, but I am wondering what I can do to convince you I am on the up-and-up so to speak," typed MTM.

"I can't think of anything that will help solve this problem," typed Tim.

"How about this, you can encrypt the data so it can only be read and I can't copy it in any way," typed MTM.

"That sounds like a plan, just give me a minute or two and I will have this data locked up so tight a locksmith couldn't open it," typed Tim.

"Here goes nothing; I'm posting the data right now."

"I assure you I will not disappoint you," typed MTM.

I hope not, thought a now doubting Tim.

After sending the data, Tim was second-guessing himself and wondering even with his security steps if he had made a monumental blunder. He had just met this guy only hours earlier, knew hardly a thing about him and now he had access to the biggest discovery he and Charlie had ever made. However, moments later doubt turned to happiness. It became very apparent that MTM was quite the student of ancient symbols and maps.

Making small talk, Tim asked more than once what MTM stood for and was disappointed when there was no valid explanation given. MTM simply explained that the name does not matter, it's the facts that do, so he should just let it be for the time being. Tim was surprised that he had not seen MTM in this chat room before. The expertise that he was displaying seemed rather extensive. It seemed as if he had a vast library to reference and would be a great future source in the ancient history and odd historical facts chat room. His knowledge reminded Tim of someone but he couldn't quite think of whom. He seemed more like a professor or maybe an archaeologist.

Tim spent some time researching MTM during his free minutes while waiting to hear back from him and couldn't find a single bit of information related to him on any message board or newsgroup. The only posts Tim could find were the ones he made this very night. Tim thought this was strange but decided that it was something that could wait until another time to figure out.

Right now the only thing he wanted was answers and he was sure they would soon be coming.

Finally all this waiting was over and MTM had some answers.

The two spent hours discussing the data and the possible answers to it all. Even though it was quite apparent to Tim that MTM had knowledge that could possibly crack this, he seemed to be holding back, especially when it came to the poem and the key. Tim was not going to let it rest and he kept prodding MTM to assist in any way possible. After all, Tim was really interested in the book and the map but he was obsessed with that symbol and poem from the alley. He just couldn't get it out of his mind and he was not going to stop searching and pestering whoever he had to until he had the answer.

"MTM, have you ever seen that poem anywhere that you can think of? Take your time and think on this. How about while you were reading or doing reference work for a report or a fact-finding mission for yourself? Anything would be helpful at this point. As far as I can tell this poem seems to exist only in that alley and the same with the symbol. I am still coming up totally empty with this one and it's killing me!" typed Tim.

"Tim, I might be able to point you in a different direction. Have you truly looked at the poem? The question I would ask you is what does it actually say? Is it a poem or something else maybe? Let's take a step back for a moment and look at it again from a different perspective and try to break it down, starting from the symbol first instead of from the poem. Now you said you think the symbol is a key, right?

"Yeah, I believe so."

"Well then, if it's a key what kind of key is it? Where is the key and where do we find it? Now that's the way I would look at it if I were you."

"Ah ha," laughed Tim. "It's not a poem at all is it? I get what you're saying now! It was right in front of my face the whole time. I feel so stupid to tell you the truth. Excellent! I knew I would figure it out eventually, with your help of course."

"Well thanks, Tim. I appreciate the vote of confidence but you actually did it yourself, I just pushed you in the right direction. However, I am a bit surprised it took you this long since you do seem to be very bright indeed."

"Thanks a lot, MTM. When will you be back in this chat room so we can get together again and discuss this and the maps from the alleged book of Merlin?"

MTM replied, "I'll be back here at midnight tonight if you can make it."

"I sure can. I'll be bringing a few friends along to chat if you don't mind."

"That's great, the more the merrier. I look forward to going over your discoveries that you may make during the coming days," typed MTM.

"Thanks for everything, and I'll talk to you later," typed Tim.

"Good luck with your research and remember sometimes you have to believe," typed MTM.

"What? That sounds like something I have heard said in the past and I don't quite remember where," Tim said distractedly.

Morning came mercilessly quick for Tim after staying up past 3:00 a.m. researching symbols and maps from the old textbook. He realized he had made a monumental breakthrough with the help of MTM and was anxious to talk to Charlie and Crystal. Tim decided that it was not the appropriate time with it being 3:00 in the morning and fell asleep, satisfied with his night's work. He dreamed of opening the plaque and was awakened just when he was about to get a look inside by a very distinct ringing noise next to his left ear. He had deliberately left his cell phone next to his head knowing that Charlie would call first thing when he got up and wake him for information. Of course Charlie did not disappoint, but this time Tim would not have minded a bit more sleep.

"Hey, Tim, it's Charlie. How did you make out last night? I've been anxiously waiting to call you until a decent hour but I couldn't wait any longer. The waiting was killing me. You know how impatient I get."

"Well, Charlie, it's 7:00 a.m. and I have been asleep for exactly four hours if that answers your question somewhat."

"Oops, sorry!"

"That's all right. It was worth staying up that late for what I learned last night. Call Crystal and wake her up and we can meet at your house and get together in the basement to go over some of the new information I gathered. I think you will both be as excited as I was, that's for sure."

"Well, I can't wait to hear what you have to say. I'll call Crystal and wake her up and get her over here ASAP."

"Okay, Charlie, I'll see you at 9:00-ish give or take. Make sure there are some donuts handy and maybe some caffeine-loaded beverages too. I am totally exhausted!"

"Will do!" Charlie replied.

Two hours later Tim and Crystal met at Charlie's house to discuss the night's discoveries thanks to Tim's diligent research. Both Crystal and

Charlie were hanging on Tim's every word and trying not to miss a single tidbit of information. Of course he was so excited that he was rambling on and on so rapidly that Crystal and Charlie both knew this was impossible.

"Tim! Please slow down a moment and take it from the top, "said Charlie.

"Sorry, guys. I guess I got all caught up in a caffeine moment. Okay, here goes," said Tim. "First I would like to tell you all about MTM. I met him in a chat room that I have frequented in the past. The chat room is called Ancient History and Odd Information. Charlie, you know this one, we have used it in the past." Charlie nodded. "Well anyway, I spent hours finding absolutely nothing related to that poem or symbol until I met up with this MTM. He would not tell me what the initials stood for but I will continue to try and get that information. He was very knowledgeable about things but he would not directly give me any real information. He was leading me but not really giving anything away. After a long chat he asked me to look at the poem and the symbol together. I knew the symbol was some sort of key assembly and we all agreed on that. So he then asked me to think simply about this and to analyze it from that perspective instead of the poem. So after taking about a minute or so I realized it was not a poem at all but a riddle describing the key and where to find one. It was totally right in front of my face the whole time and I never realized it. The riddle is what we need to figure out, not the symbol. The riddle will point us to the key!"

"Excellent," exclaimed Charlie. "That's amazing. I would never have thought of that for a second."

"Yeah, I agree. I thought it was some stupid poem and had nothing to do with the key at all. I was stuck on the key and didn't even think about the poem and the connection," said Crystal.

"Now all we need to do is figure out that riddle and we can find ourselves a key and get into whatever is behind that plaque thing. However, I still have not figured out any part of the riddle, but I will. Just give me time," said Tim smiling broadly, "and of course you two are going to help me."

"We sure will," said Charlie. Crystal nodded her agreement also.

After spending hours writing down the riddle line after line, backwards and forwards, the three were no closer to the answer than the day they first read the riddle in that alley almost a week ago. Charlie and Crystal tried to cross-reference any of the lines in the riddle to any reference they could find on the Internet and this was not helpful at all. Tim kept on using his message board contacts and had the same result. They were stuck.

"Well, 'It could be round, it could be square' means that it could be either. That's no help. Is it round is it not? Should we be looking for a square that fits in a round peg or a round peg that fits in a square?" asked Charlie. "Is it possible the key can be found in more than one shape then? Does that mean it could be either? And what does this 'A fist cannot hide it but a shirt could'? That makes no sense at all. Crystal, any ideas?"

"Let's try and look at it from 'A fist cannot hide it.' Make a fist, Charlie, and let me see what it could hide. And what about 'a shirt,' how does that figure into this?" asked Crystal. "I think you were right, Charlie. It must be two different objects. One could be in a shirt and the other on a hand like maybe a ring?"

"Excellent! You just might be onto something there," Charlie exclaimed.

"What do you think, Tim? Maybe a ring?" asked Crystal.

"It sure sounds like you two are onto something. I think it is definitely referring to different objects and one just might be a ring, but what could the other one be?"

"A shirt could hide it, which could be anything," said Tim.

Crystal thought about what she would wear and then it came to her. She had no idea why it took her this long to figure it out. "How about a necklace? It can be held close to your heart and a shirt could hide it. That's it, guys, it's jewelry, a necklace and a ring. Think about it for a second, women and men can wear either one. We did it! Now here comes the twenty-dollar questions, what ring and what necklace and where are they and what do they look like?"

The group was quiet for quite some time. Neither Charlie, Tim nor Crystal had any idea where to look for either a ring or a necklace or what either looked like for that matter. It seemed like an impossible task. There are millions or rings and necklaces; the magic question is which one they should be looking for.

"Well, it looks like it is going to be a long day, so we better get three more bottles of soda and a dozen more donuts for sure," said Charlie, rubbing his suddenly tired eyes.

"I totally agree, but let's make it pizza since it will be lunch soon, agreed?" asked Crystal.

"Pepperoni and cheese and do not spare the pepperoni," said Tim.

After quite a few hours, two pizzas and two bottles of soda later, they didn't seem any closer then they were at 9:00 a.m. They knew about the keys but had no idea what one looked like or where on this planet to find one. At this point they decided to break for dinner and would meet back at Charlie's around 7:00 p.m. for more research and hopefully a breakthrough. Although they were still feeling rather excited, the grim reality was setting in that this could be a riddle that cannot be solved by them alone and that they would need help. Charlie thought this through and decided he just might have to ask Grandma Watson or even Grandpa Watson if this MTM guy could not assist them further.

7 p.m. came and Crystal was dropped off by limo, of course, and Tim wandered over from his house right down the street. Tim had spent a few more hours searching the Internet but had come up with nothing really helpful except that it was going to be a nice day tomorrow according to the local weather channel. This little bit of information caused a bit of a chuckle from Charlie and Crystal.

"Breakthroughs, anyone?" asked Crystal.

"Nope," Tim said with a sigh.

"Nothing," said Charlie.

"I think that right now we should consider any and all resources, no matter who they may be, and luckily I happen to know two who live just right across the street," said an already up and moving Charlie.

Tim smiled, already knowing it was going to be either Grandma or Grandpa Watson who Charlie would try and convince to come over and help.

"Wish me luck, you know how Grandma and Grandpa Watson hate getting involved in our adventures," said a grinning Charlie.

"Yeah, Charlie, but this time its different. We might actually have something," said Tim.

Charlie knew all too well that Grandma Watson was an expert in ancient symbols so he decided to go to her first. Surely she could be helpful with the plaque they discovered in the alley. Charlie had decided he would ask for Grandpa's assistance after Grandma Watson had shed some light on this. Charlie didn't want to cause any grief between his father and Grandpa Watson if he was helping them with one of their so-called adventures again. Grandpa Watson had encouraged Charlie on more than one occasion and his parents just didn't agree with this. Charlie's parents wouldn't understand how important this was and would probably ground him just for being in that alley in the first place.

Charlie reached his grandparents' front door and barged in like he always did, catching Grandma Watson by surprise.

"Charlie, you scared me half to death!"

"Sorry, Grandma Watson, it's just that I have something really, really important to ask you."

"And what's that?" asked a skeptical-looking Grandma Watson.

"It's just that we found something amazing and we really need you to come and take a look at it—oh please, Grandma Watson," said Charlie with his best puppy-dog eyes.

"Charlie, you know how your parents hate it when I encourage you with any of your adventures," said Grandma Watson.

"I know, Grandma, but this time I think we really have something," said Charlie.

"Okay, Charlie, but this is the last time I am doing this so it better be good," said Grandma Watson.

"Thanks, Grandma," said Charlie as he grabbed his grandmother in a large hug.

After a few anxious moments Charlie came running down the basement stairs smiling from ear to ear. With this smile Tim and Crystal knew that help was on the way in the form of Grandma Watson.

"How did you get her to come over?" asked Tim.

"It was really simple. I just told Grandma that we found something really important and that we needed her help. She said that she would come over and check out what we found and if she thought it was legit she would go and get Grandpa Watson," said Charlie. " I was just hoping to get Grandma but if this turns out to be really important, like we think it is, then she will go and get Grandpa too, so that will be even better."

Grandma arrived carrying her usual backpack and large purse slung over her shoulder filled with all kinds of reference material. "Hello, children," she said. She then immediately turned to Crystal with a large smile on her face. "Well, hello there! You must be Crystal Kildroy. You do resemble your mother. Grandpa Watson already told me that he had met you yesterday and he was right, you look just like her. Before you ask I will fill you in some other time, dear." Crystal just smiled and would wait till another time to get that information.

"Tim and Charlie and of course, Crystal, I am really anxious to see what you have for me this time. It's not an old can again or something you found by the river, is it?"

"No, Grandma. We have something I think even you will be interested in this time," smiled Charlie.

"Yeah, Grandma Watson, we sure do," said Tim as he started to unpack all his electronic gadgets and multiple folders, all organized to his specific standards, of course. First he laid out all the folders with pictures of the plaque in all different angles. He then laid out all the paperwork on the riddle and what they had figured out so far. Smiling from ear to ear he anxiously waited for Grandma's reaction. He looked like a kid on Christmas morning impatiently waiting to open his first gift.

Grandma Watson proceeded to open the first folder with the images in it. Her expression stayed serious and didn't change after she flipped though picture after picture without saying a word. Charlie couldn't remember seeing his grandmother this serious before when reviewing anything he or Tim had found in the past. Charlie was thinking to himself that this was finally something important and Grandma knew it too. She stopped staring at the photos and proceeded right to the riddle or poem. She read it over and over and still said nothing to anyone and went right back to the photos. Charlie, Tim and Crystal were silent and waiting patiently to see what Grandma Watson had to say. Grandma Watson smiled broadly without saying a word, but Charlie and Tim knew this time whatever they had found was the real thing.

"Well, well, well, children. I must say this is quite impressive. Where did you happen to see this plaque anyway?"

"We found it in an alley while we were hiding from Ron and his gang again," said Charlie.

Grandma Watson looked at Charlie rather skeptically, "Oh really, so you were not out on an adventure and just accidentally stumbled across this?"

"Yeah, that's exactly what happened," said Charlie.

"So maybe your parents won't be so upset at you this time if they happen to find out," chuckled Grandma Watson. "Okay, kids, let's get right down to it then, I suppose."

Charlie, Tim and Crystal were on the edge of their seats waiting to hear what this all meant. Grandma Watson prepared to speak and then she looked down once more at the photos and just shook her head.

"Here is what I think this is, I'm still not sure so please bear with me. I also should let you know that we need to get Grandpa Watson over here right promptly to let him take a look at this. I think he can contribute more to this than I can, but I will do what I can nonetheless. I just want you to understand that this is all speculation on my part and I have little or no actual facts to back up what I am about to say. One other person that I am aware of has seen that plaque of yours, to my knowledge. There is no documentation of it, I am afraid, of any kind. It all kind of disappeared, and rather oddly too, I might add. The one person who saw the plaque did document it and take photos of it but none of the film would develop and the notebook seemed to be magically blank when it was checked for reference material. Obviously not too many people believed the story in the first place, but with this new evidence everyone from the most serious doubter and skeptic will have to. Charlie, I would suspect you and Tim would have figured that the person I am referring to is your grandfather. There are some differences to the plaques but he did mention seeing something that resembled the plaque I see before me now. Charlie, I am going to go and get Grandpa right now. I don't want to discuss this over the phone and would prefer to tell him in person. Please don't share any of this information with anyone at the moment because I'm relatively sure there will be many people and some of them not so nice who will be most interested in using that plaque for their own personal gain. Children, give me a few minutes to gather up Grandpa and we will both tell you all that we know."

After a few seemingly useless moments of complete silence Tim looked at Charlie and Crystal and knew what was going to be said next.

"Do you think we should tell her about MTM?" asked Crystal.

"Yeah, Tim, I think we should tell Grandma and Grandpa when they get back," replied Charlie.

"Unfortunately I have to agree with the both of you. Maybe I should not have said a thing to anyone and I should have waited. I'm sorry, guys, I jumped the gun," said Tim with his head slumped down in despair.

"Don't worry, Tim. I'm sure this MTM is okay. We will just have to check him out a bit more closely and find out," said Crystal.

"Yeah, Tim, don't sweat it," said Charlie. "Let's just wait and see what Grandma and Grandpa have to say and I'm sure it will be all right."

A few moments later a very excited Grandpa Watson came barging down the stairs with Grandma Watson hot on his heels. He was so excited he seemed to have forgotten about his injured leg and almost fell trying to get down the stairs two at a time. Grandma had to grab him from behind to stop him from falling. Grandpa finally reached the bottom of the stairs in one piece and was carrying a handful of maps and charts. On his back he was sporting a backpack, bulging at the seams, with what, was anyone's guess. He had his cane in the other hand but was not using it to support his weight at the moment. He was totally moving on adrenalin and didn't seem to even notice the usual pain he suffered in his long-ago-injured leg. Grandpa Watson seemed so excited he did not know where to start. He was at a complete loss for words. His eyes were ablaze and his cheeks were red. His shirt was not tucked in and one of his pant legs was stuck in his left sock. He had left so suddenly he didn't seem to notice he was wearing a slipper on his left foot and a sneaker on his right. The kids took in the scene and laughed aloud for a few moments.

"Kids, kids, please give me a moment to gather my composure," said Grandpa breathlessly.

"You better make it a few minutes it looks like," Grandma quipped.

"Tim, my boy, can you please hand me the photos that Grandma has told me about?" requested Grandpa.

"Sure, Grandpa—here you go. I hope you enjoy them. I have placed them in sequence of when they were taken and also grouped them by angle and exposure quality of course," said Tim smiling.

"Thanks so much, Tim, I expected nothing less," said Grandma Watson with a lopsided grin.

Grandpa spent the next ten minutes just gazing at the photos, looking from one to another and back to some of the first images he had initially viewed. Primarily he just kept shaking his head and mumbling. After a few moments he broke out a notebook and started to take down notes swiftly as if he was afraid he was imaging this and would not be able to finish them before they disappeared. He was smiling from ear to ear now. He then proceeded to grab his cane that was leaning on the wall beside him and started to hold it tightly and look at it with total happiness. He seemed like he had just removed a great weight from his shoulders and could stand up straight again. There were a few tears now forming in both his eyes and he hastily wiped them away and just continued to smile and shake his head. Grandma just stared at Grandpa with a caring and smiling expression that made the children realize they had discovered something that was very important to Grandpa.

"Children, the first thing I would like to say is thanks to all of you. For the past thirty or so years I myself was wondering if I was going insane. Quite often I thought to myself if what I had seen in Burma was just a dream or a made-up memory of some old man. The only thing I had to hang onto was this cane and my fleeting memories," said Grandpa. Tears were now streaming down his face and Grandma dabbed them away with her handkerchief.

"Thanks for what?" asked Charlie.

"Yeah, Grandpa Watson…thanks for what?" Tim asked.

Crystal said nothing, leaned back in her chair and just took it all in. She was putting two and two together. A grin developed that caught Grandpa's attention. The way Grandpa Watson gripped his cane immediately made her think of the Burma story she had heard a day earlier. She had a good idea what they had discovered in the alley was directly related to the missing information from his journey all those years earlier. She was now relatively sure that they had discovered something absolutely spectacular and beyond anything they could have ever imagined.

"I can tell by the look on your face that you have figured this out. Good for you, Crystal," said Grandpa with a broad smile. "This plaque is almost an exact replica of the one I saw in Burma the night I was down in the cave and first found the great hall. I had taken a photo of it, and sketched it too, but alas, none of that proof survived after we left the jungle. Now this proves without a shadow of a doubt that there was something there and I am not crazy after all."

"Grandpa, I'm sure the kids would like to know what they found. So let's not keep them waiting any longer and get down to business," said Grandma.

"Oh, sorry, dear, I do get carried away! Kids, buckle your seatbelts—this could get a little bumpy," said Grandpa.

Grandpa spent the next two hours going over the riddle and the key. However, he didn't mention anything related to the data that Charlie, Tim and Crystal had collected from the supposed book of Merlin. He seemed transfixed on the riddle and seemed to care nothing for the maps and ancient symbols. Grandpa spent an hour going over every single line of the riddle. He seemed to be able to break it down very easily with a little help from Grandma, of course. Crystal seemed to be very sharp also and had a good sense of riddle solving. Tim was strictly a facts guy and had some trouble with simple things like this. Charlie tried to be helpful but seemed to offer little useful information.

"Grandpa, we are all wondering the same thing," said Charlie. "I remember you telling us that your data seemed to have disappeared; you know, the photos and your notebook. We're wondering… well, why our stuff didn't?"

"Charlie, I believe we can get into that another time. I have a few theories on what actually happened but they are not important now. What's important now is going over the data that we have here right now and in front of us. I can explain my theory after we finish going over these wonderful photos and this riddle. I think at this juncture focusing on the present is more important than focusing on the past," said Grandpa Watson.

"Hey, Grandpa, how come we have not gone over any of the data from the book that we collected?" asked Charlie.

"We can get to that in a few minutes. I have seen that stuff a hundred times and it really never meant a thing until I saw this riddle," said Grandpa.

Charlie questioned, "So they are tied together?"

"Oh yes, Charlie. Wasn't that obvious?" asked Grandpa.

"Well no, but I guess it is now," said Charlie.

"Kids, the riddle is broken down into segments. The first segment is describing what the key could be and where it might be. For instance the key could be round or square, so we know it's not an actual key, now is it?" stated Grandpa Watson. "The riddle is describing where it could be or what it might look like still. Think, where do most people live?" asked Grandpa.

"Maybe in a house?" Tim said tentatively.

"Well, yes. That could be it, but where else do they live?" asked Grandpa Watson.

"How about a country?" Tim asked again.

"Yes again," said Grandpa.

"How about a city or town?" Grandma offered.

"Exactly!" Grandpa exclaimed.

"So now if you put together the verse 'One finger can hold them or a neck just a much' with 'this can be held close the heart or far away when we point or not' and what do you get?" asked Grandpa anxiously.

"How about a ring or maybe a necklace?" asked Crystal.

"You are so bright, dear!" Grandma said. "That is correct!!! Now we need to put it all together. We know it could be a key or a necklace. It has something to do with a city or possibly a town. Now we need to know who has one and where to look for it? Any ideas?"

"How about the last clue?" Tim suggested. "There seems to be something there."

"Well done. I think we are headed in the right direction, now we need to put it all together," said Grandpa. "The last clue states, 'look to a volume where some will be found,' anyone?"

"A volume could be a hard drive," said Tim smiling.

"What about a book?" asked Charlie.

"Excellent ideas, both of you, however, if I were a betting man I would suspect the latter," said Grandpa. "So we know that it is a ring or a necklace or possibly both. We also know it's in a city or a town. Now we know that the probable location of a key can be found in a book. The next question is obvious, which book and were do we find it?"

"I remember Mr. Nilrem telling us that this book we studied was supposedly Merlin's and it was found next to a tree that always flowered year round no matter what the weather." informed Crystal.

Smiles were everywhere along with hugs and pats on the back. This riddle that seemed to be unsolvable just a few days earlier was just about figured out. Charlie was amazed at how smart the people were in this room. He felt very proud to be associated with every one of them.

The celebration was short-lived, as Grandpa and Grandma got right back to work examining the maps and symbols very closely. Charlie, Tim and Crystal were really no help at this point but they all paid close attention. Tim continued to do the only thing he could think of, take the most detailed notes that either Grandma or Grandpa had ever seen. Charlie was wondering why Grandpa had never mentioned this book in the past or why this had come together like this. It all just seemed so strange to him that this book would magically appear right when they discovered the plaque in the alley. It was almost like the book was waiting for the plaque to be discovered or the plaque was waiting for the book. Charlie couldn't decide, but either way he thought it was really weird and kind of creepy.

Charlie asked the group, "Does anyone else think it is extremely strange that the day we found this plaque we were also given access to the very book that would help us figure this all out?"

"Yeah, I was wondering the same thing. I know there is coincidence and all, but that was way too perfect if you ask me," Tim stated.

"Well, I have to agree with the both of you on this one. It just seems too coincidental, first viewing the book and then ending up in that alley. An alley that neither one of you has ever seen before. Considering the extensive so-called adventuring you two do every free moment that you can get away with and to not have found that alley before, it's—well, almost like magic," chimed Grandpa.

Everyone smiled and Tim shook his head. He was strictly about the facts after all and this was not adding up for him just yet.

"I think we'll have to wait to solve that mystery for another day. Right now all I can tell you is that sometimes when things are meant to be, nothing can stop them from happening. Destiny is what some people call it, and that I believe is all we have at the moment," said Grandpa. "However, I'm sure there is a logical explanation for Mr. Nilrem showing you that book on that very day but unfortunately it is not coming to me at the moment. We will have to ask him what the reason was for that, but I suspect he was simply following his lesson plan. After all, he is a rather excitable man. He was probably caught up in the moment of one of his Merlin lessons and could not resist. He knows Charlie, and you too, Tim, obviously love this stuff and I am sure that Mr. Nilrem picked up on the obvious that Miss Kildroy is also a fan. I know it's not the explanation you were hoping for but it seems to fit for the moment."

"Let's all focus on figuring out these maps so we can get on with this. There is a light at the end of the tunnel but it is still far, far away. We have figured out some of the riddle but the most important part still is not resolved," said Grandma determinedly.

Grandpa yawned. "I agree, so let's get back to work, everyone. We have a mystery to solve and it is way past my bedtime."

Grandma couldn't help but smile and laugh like she was fourteen again. She saw that gleam in Grandpa Watson's eyes that was brighter than ever. She realized that he would not let this mystery go until he had completely solved it. After lengthy discussions, they were no closer to figuring out the last clue than they were when they started. Tim was dozing off and Crystal had curled up an hour ago and was fast asleep. Charlie was fighting to stay awake but was losing the battle. Grandpa's eyes were bloodshot and he was rubbing his face with frustration. Grandma was resting her head on her right hand and tapping her pencil in rather annoying rhythm. Her disappointment was quite obvious. She decided it was time to call it a night. It was decided they would meet again at Grandma and Grandpa's house at 10:00 a.m. for breakfast. They would take up the discussion and continue searching for the answer to the final clue.

Tim had completely forgotten about his midnight meeting with MTM and fell asleep at 11:30 p.m. with his cell phone right by his head. MTM signed on and left a message for Tim that he would talk to him soon and not to worry about missing their meeting.

The next day came and they all met at Grandma and Grandpa Watson's house. Everyone was spent and seemed totally out of new ideas. Tim discussed the details about MTM and how he had forgotten to meet with him last night. Grandma and Grandpa did not say a word and just listened. Tim was sure he had done something disastrous and felt horrible about not waiting to talk to the both of them first. Both Grandma and Grandpa assured Tim that everything would be okay and that they would straighten it all out soon enough. They were all sitting around the dinner table drinking hot cocoa when a knock was heard at the door. Grandpa smiled at Grandma and he proceeded straight to the front door without a word. After a few moments, a familiar voice was heard.

"Well, hello, children," said Mr. Nilrem. "I am so glad to see you all. How are my three favorite students doing this fine Sunday morning?"

"A bit tired but well, thank you," said Charlie.

"Well, enough pleasantries. Let's get right down to it," Mr. Nilrem said. "I have a good idea of why I was called here. Mr. Watson, I presume that you have something to show me and I am guessing it is related to your precious cane?"

"Mr. Nilrem, as you already know from our previous conversation, Charlie and his two friends have made quite the discovery in this past week. I did not give you all the details as I thought this was a conversation best kept private, if you know what I mean," said Grandpa. "First I would like to show you the photos I told you about. Then we can go over the riddle and the last two clues that we haven't managed to figure out just out yet."

"So what you were telling me over the phone is true then?" asked Mr. Nilrem.

Grandpa Watson replied, "Yes. A portal has been discovered."

"I figured it was only a matter of time. After all, with the discovery you made over thirty years ago…" said Mr. Nilrem.

"Okay, you two, it would be nice if you let the rest of them in on what you are talking about," Grandma Watson suggested. "After all, it was Charlie, Tim and Crystal who made the discovery."

Charlie, Tim and Crystal were sitting on the edge of their seats with almost uncontrollable anticipation. All three were intently listening to the conversation between Mr. Nilrem and Grandpa Watson and waiting for any bit of information to come forward.

"Kids, as you obviously figured out this is not the first time something like that plaque has been found. Mr. Watson found something very similar to this many years ago in Burma. Unfortunately all of his data was lost and there is still no known reason for this. We tried many times in the past to retrace Mr. and Mrs. Watson's steps but were unable to rediscover what they had found those many years earlier. We were sure that someday something similar would be found but we had no idea it would be right in our own backyards," laughed Mr. Nilrem.

"That was sure a surprise to Grandma and I, that's for sure," Grandpa chuckled.

"What we have been able to figure out with our years of research is that these plaques are portals. Now where they go is another story altogether. That we will not know until we finally open it," said Mr. Nilrem.

"So you are saying this is not a safe but some sort of door to another room or something in the alley?" asked Tim.

"Tim, it is a door of sorts, just not a door to a room," said Mr. Nilrem cryptically.

"So what does that mean then?" asked Charlie.

Mr. Nilrem replied, "It means that we think it's like a door to another place, time or location. We are not sure which one at this point but we are sure it's something along those lines. Thanks to your grandmother for many years of research she has been able to translate many runes and symbols and we have at least figured this much out."

"I just don't believe it," Tim said shaking his head.

"I have to agree with Tim, said Crystal. "This all seems a bit too far-fetched for me. How can that be possible? You are telling me if we can open this portal we can travel to another place or possibly time travel?"

"Yes, Crystal, that's exactly what we are saying," said Mr. Nilrem.

"Now I know, children, this is very hard to swallow but please try to have an open mind. Grandpa Watson spent many years researching this and Mr. Nilrem has been kind enough to always help us out as much as he could along the way," said Grandma Watson.

"Thanks, Mrs. Watson, but all I have done is point you in the right direction. You have done most of the work," said Mr. Nilrem.

"Of course we could not be this far along without you three, now could we? No, I guess we would not, so all three of them need to be let in on all the details," said Mr. Watson.

"This story starts in Burma and continues on with the recently-made-public book that everyone here has already reviewed. This book was found quite a few years ago but it has been kept out of the public eye. I had spent many hours with Mr. and Mrs. Watson reviewing the book but it did not seem to pertain to anything in particular. I had not taken that book out in years until this very week. There was just no information obtainable to Mr. Watson's past discovery so we just kept looking and kept it on the back burner. We hoped beyond hope that someday another discovery would be made and we could continue our research and make the final breakthrough and crack this mystery wide open. Now that this plaque has been found we need to figure out what the key is and where to find it. From what I have heard already we know what it might be but we have no idea where to find one," Mr. Nilrem stated.

"Well, that seems to be the million-dollar question at the moment," said Tim.

"We need to take a closer look at the last clue right now. So please get everything together and I will show you what I think it means and where we might find the answer to it," said Mr. Nilrem. "The last clue says something about it could be found in a volume so we figured it was a book, correct? So we know we need to find one. Now the rest of the clue reads, 'Next to a tree that flowers year round' so we can assume it might just be a reference to the book that we have in our possession. The rest of the clue reads, 'Others need plans to be read wrong and from the ground.' Does anyone have an idea about this last part of the clue? Any ideas would be helpful," said Mr. Nilrem hopefully. Everyone looked thoughtful but offered no information. "Okay then, here is what I think it could mean. I think it's a map; one of the maps located in this very book.

"Now we know we have the map and we know what the key might be but we need something to read this map. Don't we?" asked Mr. Nilrem.

"Well, this is where I will step in," said Grandpa. Smiling like a child holding his favorite toy, Grandpa presented his cane to the group. "The last two clues are tied together. The first part of the clue says use a stick that's not lying around and the symbol is created in the ground. Now what could be created in the ground?"

"How about a crystal?" Charlie offered.

"Well done!" said Grandpa Watson proudly. "So now what about this part of the riddle, use a stick for ambling around? This one should be easy with my presentation a moment earlier," smiled Grandpa.

"It's the cane!" said Tim.

"It sure is. Now we need to figure out how to read this supposed map and try and find a key," said Grandpa Watson.

The group gathered together smiling with their recent breakthrough. All six of them knew this was a special moment and none of the group wanted it to end. These types of discoveries come once in a lifetime for some and never at all for others. They spent the next few hours going over the map and trying to read it correctly. They still had not found anything related to a key or where one might be. Hour after hour passed without a single breakthrough and the group was becoming frustrated and beginning to lose that fire inside that had been set with their earlier successes. Finally, almost by accident, Charlie was lying on the floor in the living room on his back with his hands behind his head when it came to him. Excitedly he jumped up and grabbed the cane and the map and proceeded to dive back down onto the living room floor. Everyone watched with curiosity as Charlie held the map in one hand and placed the cane below it. In an instant as if by magic small dots could be seen scurrying about the map this way and that. Charlie could not believe his eyes! Grandpa Watson, Grandma Watson and Mr. Nilrem were hugging each other as tears streamed down their faces. Tim was speechless. Crystal was crying with happiness. The adults' faces shone with great respect and admiration for these three kids, who had just achieved what seemed to be an impossible chore a few days earlier.

"This is the most amazing thing I have ever seen!" said Tim. His legs were shaking wildly and Crystal helped him to remain upright.

"Children, what we need to do is find one of these keys and open that lock," said Mr. Nilrem. "The easy part is done, now we need to figure out what these small dots are and where do we actually find one." It was decided that a break for dinner was in order. They would meet again around 7:00 p.m. At this point they would make plans for their next meeting. The search for the key would soon begin.

Chapter 5

Portals and Sneaks

The rush of finally cracking the secrets of the mysterious map was finally wearing off and weariness had promptly set in. The lucky discovery accidentally made by Charlie while he was lying on the floor was a monumental breakthrough but there was still one more bridge to cross, finding the all-important key. The oddest thing about this map was the way the keys seemed to be moving about as if they had minds of their own. No one seemed more surprised by this than Tim. He hated it when he couldn't explain something with logic or by the use of one of his electronic gadgets. He spent hours staring at the map and shaking his head and making notes. He was not talking to anyone, just staring and taking notes. Charlie and Crystal were laughing a bit when they looked at him and quite a bit more when they were out of earshot.

Grandma and Grandpa Watson were still carrying on, acting more like school kids than senior citizens. Mr. Nilrem continued to smile and be the most relaxed of the bunch. He seemed excited but more in the way of relief than of the actual discovery.

The weekend was spent doing endless research. Tim could not have been more excited by the never-ending studying. He loved the proposition of spending hour after hour trying to crack the riddle of the keys. Not everyone was so dedicated as he was but not one of them wanted to stop until they had this mystery solved. Unfortunately weariness was finally taking over and it was then decided to put everything on hold until Wednesday night. Charlie, Tim, and especially Crystal were completely against this and wanted to continue the quest for the elusive key but were outranked by the three elder members of their group. Grandpa explained to them that they had to attend school tomorrow and that it was very important that they get their rest. Mr. Nilrem also chimed in that everyone was mentally spent and nothing more productive would come tonight. The key could wait another day or two; after all, they were not really going anywhere so to speak. Although Crystal pointed out candidly that they did seem to be moving about.

Goodbyes were said and they all went their separate ways with each knowing that it would be hard to get any rest with what they had learned over the past week.

Monday morning came and a very groggy Charlie and Tim prepared to start their usual walk to school. When they starting walking they were met with a nice surprise; a limousine pulled up beside them. Crystal shoved her head out the window and the boys lazily climbed in, thankful they wouldn't have to walk the rest of the way to Golvert's.

One glance at Crystal and Charlie noticed she looked a bit ragged and tired. She was lounging rather lazily in the back seat and looked beat. Her hair was in a ponytail and her makeup just wasn't as perfect as it usually was. Judging by her looks it was obvious that she had not slept much either.

"Guys, here we go back to school for another day of joy and learning," sighed Crystal. "It seems so lame compared to what we've been doing over the past weekend, that's for sure."

"It sure does," said Tim.

Charlie just nodded his head and continued to drink a soda he had pulled from the bar in the back of the limo. He was daydreaming at the moment and not paying any real attention to either Tim or Crystal. He was just too tired to focus on anything at the at the moment and was just looking forward to getting through the day without anything tremendously exciting happening. They were moments away from another school day and Charlie was hopeful they would get a few minutes to talk to Mr. Nilrem when they were in his class.

"I still don't believe what I have seen over this past weekend," Tim said. "It all seems totally unreal. I keep expecting to wake up every morning and come to the ugly realization that it was all just a dream. Of course I wake up and there it is all over again and to my surprise it is real; I see the laptop, maps, papers and pictures, all these facts looking me straight in the face mocking what I have based my entire life on, the facts and science."

"Tim, it's not all bad now, is it?" asked Charlie. "I know a lot of this stuff is really weird and almost unexplainable, but you did use the Internet to help us out. Don't forget about your GPS; without that we would never have been able to keep track of the location of the alley and without your digital camera where would we be now? So see, we needed technology after all. So there you go, buddy, the world's not completely upside down, it's just a little tilted.

Now you can sleep easy knowing that the world is not coming to a technological end."

"Tim, I agree with Charlie, where would we be now without all the stuff—well?" asked Crystal. "Think about it for a second, we wouldn't have been able to return to the alley, reference the maps or pictures that we had taken, and Mr. and Mrs. Watson would never have helped us and we would have nothing. We would be right where we started, just a plaque and nothing else. So your belief in technology is still safe and sound."

"Even with all that electronic equipment at our disposal we still haven't figured this out yet. We needed the help of a teacher and Grandpa and Grandma Watson more than that stuff," said a dejected Tim.

"Give it time, Tim. After all, as they say, Rome wasn't built in a day," said Charlie. "And there is no way we would be this far without you and your technological know-how."

"Maybe so, but all these weird things have definitely given me a new perspective on things, that's for sure," said Tim.

Crystal noticed the clock and knew it getting dangerously close to detention time. "Guys, I don't mean to interrupt but it's time to get to home room. You two better hurry since neither one of you can afford to be late again, so I'll see both of you on our way to first period."

"See ya," said Charlie.

"See you in a bit, Crystal," said Tim.

After homeroom and announcements were made, Charlie, Tim and Crystal exited their home rooms and were on their way to Mr. Nilrem's class. Tension was high and the air was filled with excitement as they reached their destination. However, when they arrived at the class they were in for a surprise; Mr. Nilrem was nowhere to be found. He apparently had taken a sick day and there were whispers that he was not coming back anytime soon. As if this wasn't bad enough, adding to their misery was Mrs. Roust standing at the head of the class and looking as mean and grumpy as usual. Charlie, Tim and Crystal were in total shock. Mrs. Roust noticed this and glared at Charlie and Tim with that look of disgust she often had when she spotted them. She hastily made a note in her trusty notebook. Both Charlie and Tim were not all that happy at the moment. This was of course their favorite class after all and they were looking forward to spending a free period here later in the day. Crystal just looked at both of them and knew they must be feeling absolutely awful and wanted to talk to them but knew better than that.

Mrs. Roust proceeded through a very dry and dreadful lesson. She despised this class and Mr. Nilrem. Both Charlie and Tim realized that she must be ecstatic at the thought of Mr. Nilrem not being here for a while. She disliked his strange teachings and more than once tried to have his class removed from the curriculum. Judging by the even more unusually miserable look on her face she was enjoying wrecking the best part of Charlie and Tim's day. She hated both the boys and could hardly control her excitement when she noticed the look of dread on their faces.

Class mercifully finally came to an end and Charlie, Tim and Crystal were the first to exit the class. They met in the hall and discussed the strange turn of events.

"Mr. Nilrem didn't seem to be sick at all over the weekend," said Charlie. "Did either of you notice anything weird about him?"

"Nope," said Tim.

"He seemed perfectly well to me, although he looked pretty tired," said Crystal.

"He was probably just worn out from all the researching and no breaks," said Charlie. "He must be pretty old, so it kind of makes sense."

Unknown to them their conversation was not a private one. Hiding just around the corner was someone listening intently to every word. Clive had been hanging next to them the entire time they were talking and when he was spotted by Charlie he hastily scurried away and out of sight, no doubt to go and see Ron and the rest of his gang of friends.

"I think we need to be a bit more careful what we talk about in the future," Charlie said.

"I totally agree," said Tim.

"Yeah, we do need to be more cautious when we have these kinds of conversations. It's obvious that we haven't heard the last of Ron, Clive Beth and Sean," said Crystal.

Clive continued down the hall and met up with Ron, Sean and Beth. They were anxious to hear what Clive had learned while he was skulking about and eavesdropping on Charlie, Tim and Crystal's private conversation. After he gave all the details to Ron and the gang it was decided that they needed to pay much closer attention to Crystal, Charlie and Tim in the future.

It had reached that dreaded time of the day when Charlie, Tim and Crystal would attend their least favorite class, but this day was even worse—they now had to spend two classes with Mrs. Roust. There she was like usual waiting at the door to greet most of her students. She had a look of total disgust when Charlie and Tim walked by.

She completely turned away from Crystal and outright ignored her. Ron, Clive, Sean and Beth showed up late as usual and Miss Roust waited for the three to get seated before she started class without saying a word to any of them.

Ron took his seat and looked towards Charlie, looking like he wanted to burst with whatever he was holding in. "Hey, Watson, I heard that your favorite teacher is missing in action. Maybe he's in jail or he went back to the alley he came from," laughed Ron.

"Just shut your mouth," Charlie said angrily.

Crystal jumped in as promptly as she could but the damage was already done. Miss Roust was on her way over with that look of total pleasure on her face. She enjoyed giving Charlie detention or extra assignments just to get under his skin.

"Mr. Watson, I will not have those kinds of disruptions in a class that I am teaching. Please step out of my class right now," said an evil-looking Miss Roust. "Oh, and Miss Kildroy, would you please join him." After exiting the class and waiting for a moment in the hallway Mrs. Roust arrived with that usual smile on her face.

"Both of you will be serving detention tonight. No ifs, ands or buts—that's it. I will not tolerate students acting out in my class. I cannot believe that you would be so rude, especially to one of our best students nonetheless. I will see you both right after last bell here in my classroom," said Mrs. Roust.

"But—s," said Charlie.

"But nothing, Mr. Watson, I will not tolerate any more outbursts, is that clear? Yes or no, Mr. Watson, nothing else is needed," said a grinning Mrs. Roust.

"Yes," said Charlie.

"Miss Kildroy?" Mrs. Roust asked.

"Yes," said Crystal.

"Now both of you back into class and please take your seats," said Mrs. Roust.

After returning to his seat Charlie noticed Ron was struggling to hold it together. His face was red from laughing while both he and Crystal were in the hall. He looked like he might cry from laughing too hard. Charlie tried to ignore him but it was almost impossible when Beth, Clive and Sean joined in. Of course Mrs. Roust did nothing to stop any of it and just sat back and smiled.

The rest of the class went by without any other interruptions. Charlie was furious but he held it together knowing that he would only end up in more trouble. When the bell rang he stormed out of class and didn't wait for either

Tim or Crystal. He needed a few moments by himself to get it together and let his rage die down. He was infuriated with Mrs. Roust and this was being escalated by the upsetting absence of Mr. Nilrem, his favorite teacher. Now he would have to wait even longer to try and find out what had happened to him.

The day rapidly sped by; Charlie managed to avoid any run-ins with Ron, Sean, Beth and Clive, which probably was a good thing since he was still irate. He met up with Crystal and Tim by the west exit; they said their goodbyes and headed off to detention and Miss Roust while Tim headed home alone.

Tim exited school and headed home using his usual route, unaware that two hooded figures were following him very closely. Up ahead in the distance two other people were seen leaning against an old fence next to a run-down building. Tim didn't pay too much attention to either of them and kept walking, caught up in his own thoughts about the map and the missing Mr. Nilrem.

Tim was now walking right in front of a run-down, long-ago-vacated building when the two hooded figures ran right up behind him and pushed him violently into a break in the building's surrounding fence. Tim stumbled through the fence, almost falling when two other hooded assailants were rapidly upon him; one punched him in the stomach while the other one grabbed both his arms from behind. He was hit with such force that he thought his insides were going to pop out. Tim doubled over and was then kicked rather hard in the butt and he fell hard, banging his face on the concrete walk. His left eye started swelling instantly shut and he felt really strange. Tim knew he was being kicked but was too out of it to really focus on the pain. His head was swimming and whatever he tried to focus on seemed to be all wavy like he was underwater. The light seemed to be hurting his eyes and his ears were ringing. An assailant came from behind him and cut his backpack straps off and that was the last thing he remembered. Tim could do nothing at this point in time. His stomach was killing him, dizziness had set in and he felt like he was going to throw up any second. As suddenly as it had began the assault was over and the attackers were gone and all Tim could think about at this point was falling asleep.

Tim was left lying on the walkway bleeding form his nose, mouth and left eye. Unable to think too clearly, he tried to stand but his head started swimming and he fell to his butt and decided to sit a bit more. He would have used his cell phone but when he reached back for his pack it was gone along with his GPS, pictures and maps. Luckily he didn't have his laptop with him today. Fortunately for him he had left it at home to run diagnostics.

After running a few blocks the four hooded assailants decided it was safe enough to remove their hoods. They were laughing hysterically. They couldn't believe their luck. This was a great day for all of them. They had beaten Tim to a pulp, stolen his backpack and totally gotten away with the whole thing. No witnesses and no way to trace this back to any of them.

"Beth, Clive and Sean, that was awesome! Did you see the look on his face when I punched him in the stomach? It was priceless I tell you, priceless," said Ron.

"That was awesome, I have to put it right up there with the Twitter kid," said Beth.

"Without a doubt an excellent day. Now we need to see what we have here in this so important backpack. I bet there's nothing but toys, candy and smelly socks, knowing this guy," said Ron.

"Hey, everyone, look at this," said Ron. "We have gotten our hands on a GPS, a digital camera, his phone and pictures and maps. I have no idea what some of this crap is though. Sean, take a look at these maps and tell me what you think."

"I have no idea what any of this stuff means so I'll to take a closer look at this stuff when I'm home and can access the Internet of course," said Sean. "Wait a second; these pictures look like they are from that alley we chased them into a week or so ago. It's definitely the alley; just look at all the gross fish-filled barrels and dumpsters around. I don't remember seeing this plaque though. I didn't notice it while we were. Did any of you see it?"

"Nope," said Beth.

"Me either," said Clive.

Ron just shook his head no.

"It sure seems like we might be onto something here. This was a great get for us," said Ron. "Now all we need to do is figure out all this stuff and what those two clowns are up to."

"I wonder how long it will take poor Timmy to get home," laughed Beth.

"Maybe he won't make it at all tonight," said Clive.

"That would be sweet," said Sean.

"It sure would. Okay, guys, let's get out of here and stash this backpack so we can properly place it tomorrow to make sure Charlie finds it," laughed Ron. "Sean, take all the rest of this stuff back to your house and keep us updated with what you find over the next day or two. We can meet at your place and plan for our next...what is it that Charlie and Tim call it? Oh yeah, so-called adventure," laughed Ron even harder this time.

"Okay, guys, catch you all later," said Sean.

Tim was still staggering down the street when Mr. Watson drove by and noticed him looking rather ragged. Mr. Watson hurriedly stopped his car and jumped out and caught Tim just before he collapsed. Mr. Watson proceeded to place Tim in the back seat of his car and head straight to his parents' house. Tim was coming in and out of consciousness while in the back seat and Mr. Watson knew this might be serious. Try as he might Mr. Watson was unable to get any useful information from Tim and decided that it could wait till later.

Tim was taken to the hospital and was diagnosed with a concussion and a broken rib. He needed about five stitches to close the gash over his left eye.

Charlie was just arriving home from detention when he got the news. His parents drove him over to the hospital where he was at least happy to hear that none of Tim's injuries were too serious. Tim would have to stay in the hospital overnight and take a few days of school off and would be fine in a couple of days or so.

Charlie was furious for not being there to help his friend. He recognized a setup when he saw one. He felt it was his fault that this had happened for letting Ron get under his skin. He planned to get to the bottom of this no matter what the cost. He already had a good idea who the culprits were and just needed some proof. Charlie called Crystal and let her know what had happened. She was shocked and upset upon hearing the news and headed off to the hospital to check up on Tim herself. When she arrived she couldn't believe her eyes when she saw how awful Tim looked. His face was swollen and all bruised. His left eye was completely closed and his face just looked awful. He was sleeping and never even acknowledged that Crystal was even there.

After leaving the hospital Crystal headed off to Charlie's house to try and calm him down. He wanted to go and storm off and lay a beating on Ron, Clive, Sean and even Beth for that matter. He was in a rage at this point and was barely listening to reason. Tim was his best friend and he felt he had let him down by not being there.

"Charlie, you need to calm down! There is nothing we can do right now. We should just be thankful that he is going to be okay. This could have been a lot worse, you know," said Crystal.

"Yeah, I understand that, but I just know it was Ron and his group of loser friends and so do you. They have wanted to get even with Tim and myself since that day we met you. I just knew they would not let it go but this is worse than anything I have seen them do in the past. They are mean and nasty kids but they usually have their limits and this time they crossed that line. I am not going to let any of them get away with this. I don't care how long it takes but this is not over with," said Charlie.

"Charlie, will you please calm down, okay? We can talk about getting even another time. There is a more important question I think needs to be asked. Did you see Tim's backpack anywhere? I know I didn't. Hopefully it is at his house or this mess has just gotten way bigger," said Crystal.

"I am sure it's at his house. I will ask him tomorrow first thing when I see him. He was in no condition to answer any of my questions when I just left him," said Charlie.

"Okay, then it will have to wait till tomorrow," said Crystal.

Tuesday morning came and just as Charlie expected there were Ron, Clive, Beth and Sean giggling and pointing at him while he walked by without his best friend. Charlie wanted to turn around and punch all of them right in the face but decided that it could wait till another day. He knew that if he did anything at school he would get detention, suspension or even expelled. He just held his head high and kept walking and did his best to pretend he couldn't hear a single one of them. Even when Clive asked where little Timmy was Charlie just kept walking and didn't mutter a single word. Miss Roust was leaning out her classroom door watching the whole thing unfold and just smiled when Charlie passed her by. He could hear her laughing but didn't care at the moment. He knew that he would get his revenge eventually.

Charlie headed to his locker to grab a few things when he noticed something hanging from the handle. There was Tim's backpack, spray painted pink and all torn up. Charlie just pulled it off and threw it to the ground without turning around. He knew that Ron and his gang were just waiting to see his expression. Charlie decided he would not give them any pleasure whatsoever and just pretended it was not there and continued on to his next class. He passed Crystal in the hall and they exchanged a quick hello while heading off to their next classes.

The day came to an end without anything spectacular happening and Charlie headed home anxious for any news on Tim. When he arrived he received some good news; to his surprise Tim had already been released from the hospital and was resting comfortably at home.

Charlie was excited about the good news and headed over to see his best friend but was turned away by Miss Tundrill. Charlie argued with her for a few minutes but realized it was useless. Miss Tundrill was a stubborn woman and would not give in one inch. Reluctantly Charlie decided to head on home and try again tomorrow. Miss Tundrill is Tim's so-called nanny. She is a six-foot-tall woman with a rather odd accent that Charlie did not recognize. Miss Tundrill is quite a bit overweight and enjoys being as mean as she can to Charlie whenever she gets the chance. She is sure that Charlie is a bad influence on Tim and tries to keep the two boys apart as much as she possibly can. Miss Tundrill blames all of the trouble that Tim gets into on Charlie. She takes care of the Smittins's house and Tim while his family is, like so often, away on business.

As Charlie headed home and walked into his bedroom his phone started to ring. And to Charlie's great relief he heard his best friend's voice on the other end of the telephone. Tim didn't sound that entirely well but was trying to explain what had happened. Although the details were a bit sketchy Charlie realized that Tim had been attacked by what sounded like four assailants. It didn't take Tim and Charlie too long to figure out who they were. Tim then broke the news to Charlie about everything that had been taken and told Charlie to go directly to his grandfather and let him know. Charlie promptly headed over to his grandparents' house and spilled the entire story to Grandma and Grandpa Watson.

"Charlie, it sounds like Ron, Clive, Beth and Sean knew how to set Tim up to get him alone."

"I'm relatively sure that Mrs. Roust had something to do with this. That was just way too coincidental that you and Crystal received detention that very same day that Tim was attacked," said Grandpa Watson.

"At the moment we have no proof that she had anything to do with this or that it was Ron and his gang of hoodlums for that matter," said Grandma. "But I can surely add two plus two and get the correct answer every time. The question now is will they figure out how to get a key and open the doorway before us? Charlie, I think we need to speed up our plans a bit and get together tonight. See if you can call Crystal and your grandfather and I will go and persuade Miss Tundrill to let Tim come over here for some tea. Grandpa, you go and call Mr. Nilrem and see if we can get him over here ASAP."

"Uh, Grandma, I have some news for you about Mr. Nilrem," stated Charlie.

"Well, what is it?"

"He was not in school on Monday and Mrs. Roust was subbing in for him. She didn't give us any other information either."

"Now that's a bit of a surprise. Grandpa, I think you and Charlie should go right over and check up on him. I will go and talk to Miss Tundrill by myself," said Grandma Watson.

"Grandma, I am on my way already. Charlie, let's get going. I am fairly certain that there is more to this than we are currently aware of. I think we should hurry up to check on Mr. Nilrem. I fear there may be something rather sinister afoot," said Grandpa Watson.

"I agree," said Grandma.

"First Mr. Nilrem does not show up for school and that very same day some of our most important data is stolen. I am sure this is not a coincidence," said Grandpa Watson.

"Hurry up, Grandpa, and Charlie, please call Crystal and let her in on everything that has transpired," said Grandma Watson.

Charlie called Crystal from the car while he and his grandfather were heading over to Mr. Nilrem's house. She would meet up with them in an hour or so at Charlie's grandparents' residence.

Grandma Watson headed over to have a nice chat with Miss Tundrill and get Tim released for a few hours.

Charlie and Grandpa Watson arrived at Mr. Nilrem's house after a thirty-minute drive to the outskirts of the city. His house was on a very secluded road and set far from the street. The house was immense for one person. The entire place resembled more of a castle than any other house in the surrounding area. There were no lights on and the garage door was wide open. Grandpa and Charlie exited their car and started to check the house. Once they headed around the back they noticed that the door had been kicked in. Grandpa and Charlie entered through the kicked-in back door and found it ransacked. The entire house was turned upside down. All drawers were dumped out and the kitchen cabinets were opened with their contents spilled throughout the room.

They headed upstairs to check out the bedrooms. In the master bedroom it was the same. The bed was turned over and the contents of both closets were strewed about the room. There were random holes in the walls also. There was no sign of Mr. Nilrem in any of the bedrooms upstairs or the kitchen. The living room was checked and was also the same, furniture turned upside down along with the couch cushions and a few paintings were ripped off their normal spots on the wall and were lying about the floor.

Grandpa Watson and Charlie checked the basement and this was also ransacked. Tools lying about and many statues shattered along with torn-open boxes and such.

Grandpa and Charlie decided to check the library and this had been completely emptied of every single book. Charlie had not been here in the past but Grandpa was a frequent visitor and he simply could not believe that the thousands upon thousands of books were all missing.

"Charlie, I cannot begin to tell you how many books Mr. Nilrem kept here. Try to think of the library downtown and then multiply that by two. How could someone do this and where have all the books gone?" asked Grandpa.

"Do you think they were looking for the book of Merlin?" asked Charlie.

"I am guessing you are probably right and unfortunately we have no idea if they got what they were looking for. I think we need to finish looking through the rest of the house for Mr. Nilrem and then get out of here and let Grandma know what has happened. She will be very worried about Mr. Nilrem. He has been a friend for many years."

"I am sure he will be okay, Grandpa. He is a pretty smart guy."

"I hope so, Charlie, but we just don't know at this point in time. Let's you and I go check out the guesthouse down front and see what we can turn up. If there is nothing there we'll head back home and see what your grandmother thinks we should do next."

They carefully exited out the broken back door and while heading down to the guesthouse Charlie had that ever-so-eerie feeling of being watched. He was not sure who or what was doing the watching but he just knew. Grandpa was gripping his cane very tightly and had a focused and serious expression on his face. It was as though the trees that lined the driveway themselves were moving although there was no wind. This made the atmosphere of the whole place resemble a creepy Halloween scene, adding to the uneasiness that Charlie was already feeling. One look at Grandpa however, eased his tension a bit, as he began to relax his unusually tight grip on his cane. The two proceeded to the guesthouse without incident.

The door here was also kicked in here but this place had not been torn apart just yet. Either the perpetrators found what they were looking for or something scared them off. There were strange scratches near the doorway and there were broken branches and leaves lying about. The leaves and branches were also in the front doorway and the foyer but Charlie paid no attention to this. He figured that maybe a gust of wind had blown the stuff in.

"Charlie, I believe we will find the book here. Don't ask me why, I just do. We need to be diligent and make sure that we leave no stone unturned so to speak."

"Grandpa, why do you think they didn't finish what they had started? I mean they could have ripped this place apart too, right?"

"Charlie, I'm sure you noticed the trees moving although there presently is no wind whatsoever, correct?"

"Yeah, but I just figured it was my imagination or something."

"Hardly, there is definitely something going on here that scared away the intruders and I suspect by the broken branches and leaves it was probably the trees themselves."

"That's not possible is it?"

"Remember, Charlie, everything is possible if you believe. I don't have time to get into the details about the trees right now but I suspect Nilrem left a little surprise behind before he left. Let's not worry about that right now; we need to focus on the task at hand and find that book. It's very important that it does not fall into the wrong hands."

"Okay, Grandpa, I'll look in this side room and you take the living room."

Charlie entered the room and headed right to a beautiful cabinet. It was like he was drawn to it. This cabinet was about eight feet tall and about six feet wide. It was carved with a tree on each door and what looked like fairies all along the edge. At the very top and in the middle was what looked like a ball-shaped thing on a pedestal. The two door handles were made out of what Charlie suspected was bone, brass and some very beautifully carved wood that resembled skeletal hands. The carving was intricate. If the hands had a skin tone they would have looked real. Charlie was hesitant to grab the handles because of the look of them. He finally worked up the courage and just reached out and pulled. To his surprise when the doors swung open there was the book. It was sitting on a beautiful stand that resembled the door handles. He grabbed the book and yelled for Grandpa, who came running into the room much quicker than Charlie would have guessed him capable of. He was looking around with his cane at the ready when he noticed the book and smiled.

"Excellent job, Charlie, let's get going. I think we have stayed here long enough and who knows if the people who were here earlier are planning on returning."

"Okay, Grandpa, let's get out of here. This place gives me the creeps anyway."

Charlie and his grandfather arrived home without incident. Grandma met them at the back door and they filled her in on the entire story. Charlie grabbed a snack from the kitchen and headed off with Grandma and Grandpa to the living room. Charlie entered first and to his surprise there was Tim lying on the couch and Crystal helping him to a drink.

Charlie and Tim just smiled at each other. Charlie was quite relieved to see his best friend up and about. Tim was not looking his best but he did have his trusty laptop with him and that grin that told Charlie he had something cooking in that wonderful mind of his.

"It's great to see you all here, together again. I'm sure that there are lots of things that need to be cleared up. First, Tim, I just wanted you to know how happy I am to see you up and about. It is obvious that you are a real trooper. Considering how you looked earlier I am most impressed to see you here," said Grandpa Watson.

"Thanks, Grandpa Watson. I'm not one hundred percent but I will do what I can to help out," said Tim.

"The second thing I would like to do is let everyone in on what we know about Mr. Nilrem. He was not at school and his house was completely ransacked. We have no reason to believe that he is in current danger, although this would not surprise me. With him missing school and not contacting anyone I am definitely concerned. However, I believe the item that they were trying to obtain thankfully eluded them and is now safely on our possession, the supposed book of Merlin. Thanks to Charlie's diligent searching it is now safe and sound.

"I'm sure without a doubt that these three recent events are related together. I don't know who or what they are trying to accomplish, but I am quite sure it has something to do with the plaque in the alley. I am inclined to think that this is quite a big issue and we all need to take it very seriously. At this point in time the more you know the less safe you are. So now would be the time to get out of this if you wish. There will be no hard feelings and no one here will think any less of you. I will wait a moment for your decisions." After a few moments no one moved or said a word. Grandpa proceeded to smile and decided it was time to put this all together.

"So this is it. Now, Tim, I am pretty sure by the continued smile on your face that you have something to add. I am going to guess that it has something to do with the map and the strange moving objects that we suspect are keys. Now don't keep us waiting any longer and let us all hear it."

"Okay, Grandpa, here goes. I would like to point out that we haven't been able to figure out where these keys are or why they are moving about. It is very odd behavior for a key and we can all agree with that. I could not understand how they were moving or where they were. I needed to put it all together somehow. I stayed up writing a program to track the movements and put them into a sequence. However, this led to nothing. I then tried putting the movements to one of the older maps that we had and this then led me to the breakthrough. I realized that this was like a GPS system tracking every single key in the entire area and possibly the world. First I used large maps and kept shrinking it down till I got to a regional level, then state and so on. This is when I realized that the keys were right here in the city!! Now take a look at this map with the moving keys and now look what happens when I put a transparent map of downtown Boston right over it, BINGO," said Tim. "There is a key right in this very room."

"Right here?" said Charlie.

"Yep," said Tim.

"Are you sure?" asked Grandpa Watson.

"Of course I'm sure, just look—wait—right over there!!" Tim turned and pointed right at Grandma Watson.

"Me?" Grandma Watson asked. "I think you need to check your—"

"No, not you, Grandma Watson, but I believe it's—right—there," pointed Tim.

Tim was pointing at a rather large odd-looking broach that Grandma Watson had pinned to her shirt.

Everyone turned to look at Grandma Watson. There pinned to her shirt was a large broach. She had no idea why everyone was looking at her. Grandpa moved over and pointed at the broach. Grandma then carefully removed it and they all stared at it. "Could it be that easy, right here in this very house in plain sight for all to see!" Yes, this was it—they had found a key at last!! It was right in front of them the entire time. Celebratory high fives and hugs were given. Tim avoided all of this, as he was not feeling that entirely well still.

"Grandma, where did you get that—well, well, Grandma?" impatiently asked Charlie.

"Yeah, Grandma Watson, where?" asked Tim

"Hold on a second now and let me explain. This broach has been passed through our family for many generations. It holds no particular monetary value that I know of and is more a family heirloom. This broach was said to have first entered our family in 1634, give or take. It was supposedly discovered while one of our ancestors was doing some remodeling on their farmhouse and discovered this strange box sealed into the stone foundation. Inside this box was this broach, which was then given as a wedding gift to one of your great, great, great and so on relatives, Miss Martha Watson. She then passed it on to her son and so on until it finally reached your grandfather, who then gave it to me forty-plus years ago. Now what ever happened to that box I could not say, but I'm sure that it would be something worth studying if it could ever be recovered."

"I wonder who sealed it there in the first place?" asked Charlie.

"Charlie, unfortunately that's a mystery that will most likely never be solved," said Grandma Watson.

"You never know, Grandma," said Charlie.

"Judging from the map and all the little moving objects scattered about there are lots of keys waiting to be discovered here and possibly around the world," said Crystal.

"Yeah, Crystal, that seems to be the case. There are a few keys right around your house and others just randomly moving about the city and others still that are not moving and have not moved since we figured out how to read the map. I bet that not a single one of those people has any idea what they have in their possessions," said Tim.

"I bet you're right," said Crystal.

"I think we need to pick a time to go and open that door, safe or whatever it is. But before we do that there's one more thing too, and that's we have to wait until Tim is a bit better since he was a major factor in us being able to figure this out," said Grandpa Watson.

"I totally agree," said Charlie.

"Thanks, guys. I can't wait to see what happens when we finally go and try to open the lock. This will be our greatest so-called adventure ever," excitedly stated Tim.

"For me it has to be the best one; after all, it's my first and only one," laughed Crystal.

Chapter 6

Entering a Strange Land

The rest of the week passed with continued planning for the coming Saturday. Not one member of the group had heard from Mr. Nilrem and the worry and concern were certainly growing. Grandpa finally decided that he would call the police if they didn't hear from him within the week.

There was a heavy debate over who should go and make the first attempt to open the lock. Grandpa thought it should be an adult but surprisingly Grandma did not. She stated that the kids made the discovery and that they should be the ones to go and try to unlock whatever was there. Reluctantly Grandpa agreed. Grandpa Watson would drop off Charlie, Tim and Crystal a block away from the alley to try and make it as inconspicuous as possible. The kids would then proceed to the alley and discreetly enter one at a time as to not draw any attention to them.

After reaching the entrance to the alley anticipation and tension was high. Charlie, Tim and Crystal were very restless and had no idea whatsoever or for that matter if anything would happen. First Tim headed into the alley, Crystal followed a moment later then Charlie pulled up the rear. The three met right by the dumpsters. The smell of the rotten fish was worse than they remembered. The stench was almost unbearable but this would not deter any of them from their goal. The three proceeded to crawl behind the dumpsters and looked up at the plaque once more. Charlie, Tim and Crystal were shaking and smiling with uncontrollable excitement. Charlie pulled the key out of his pocket and ever so slowly his hand edged towards the lock. You could cut the tension with a knife.

It seemed like hours were going by as Charlie cautiously pressed the key into the lock and started to turn it clockwise. First there was a loud click then an incredibly bright flash. Following this flash Charlie, Tim and Crystal, still struggling to focus, rapidly realized they were no longer in the alley but somewhere unknown and wonderful. It seemed they had been transported to another place and possibly time. Charlie turned and stared in wonder at the magnificent archway and its entire splendor. Charlie reached back and grabbed Tim and Crystal by the heads and turned them around to face the arch. Tim's jaw dropped and Crystal was left speechless. The arch was a wonderful achievement of architecture but that was not the main issue. They could no longer see the alley they were just standing in. Instead they were looking right though the arch and the alley was gone; what was now in its place were flowing hills and mountains, beautiful rivers and fields that seemed to go on forever. Charlie was still clutching the key in his hand when he noticed something familiar; there was another keyhole present on this side of the portal to reinsert it. This keyhole was a bit different than the other one. On this side of the portal the keyhole was located in the mouth of a carved person that resembled some sort of a wizard or possibly a priest. The entire archway, from top to bottom, had more of these strange figures running up and down both sides, each different, with longer beards, or shorter robes. The overhead had another wizard carved into it holding what resembled a cracked cube that had been broken into four pieces. It seemed to Tim that this was a story like ancient Egyptian carvings and if you followed the arch from left to right you could read it like a book. The cube seemed to be either broken by the wizard standing below it or he was possibly assembling it again. This wizard was holding a stick and was pointing it at the cube and lightning seemed to be coming from the end striking the cube.

Charlie was now grinning from ear to ear and Tim was shaking his head. "I guess it's time to do a bit of adventuring."

"Do you really think we should? You know this could be dangerous," said Tim.

Before Tim could get in another word Charlie started strolling down the walkway with Crystal right behind him.

Tim, still shaking his head reluctantly, followed along. "I guess we go."

"Off to see the wizard!" laughed Charlie.

After stepping off what they thought was a marble walkway the grass they were now standing on seemed to be the greenest and softest that Charlie, Tim or Crystal could ever remember feeling. The grass seemed like it would bend almost like it was made out of velvet, every blade soft as a feather, but it was still firm enough to stop their feet from reaching the dirt below. There were strange trees to their right and to the left was the largest city any one of them had ever seen. All around all the colors of the flowers, the sky and even the trees seemed to be of a brilliant tone. There were strange birds chirping and other odd-looking animals could be seen far off in the fields.

Their attention promptly turned to this wondrous city. Although they were still quite a distance away it was obvious that this city was massive. The towers seemed to grow out of the very ground and almost reach the clouds themselves. The buildings and archways all seemed to be created from marble. All of the structures seemed unnaturally tall for the type of buildings they were but it was still too hard to judge from the distance they were currently at. It was hard to actually take in the whole thing because it was so incredibly large.

"That city is larger then New York and Boston put together," stated Tim.

"Only you would know such a thing," said Charlie. "Get out your GPS and see what it says."

Tim gazed at this for a moment and realized it was reading as if they were still in the same location they were in only moments ago. He couldn't make any sense of it and checked his readings over and over again and came to the same conclusion. "These buildings must be somehow or another right in downtown Boston." How this was being pulled off without someone seeing them was anyone's guess at this point in time.

Charlie, who at first was excited to explore the area, was now starting to think that maybe a little caution was not such a bad thing. Tim and Crystal were also getting a bit nervous and decided that maybe they should not wander too far and should instead work on getting the portal open again. They could always come back when they were more prepared. It was decided to use the key to go back and get some supplies just in case.

They turned around and headed back up the path towards the archway. All the while Tim was taking pictures with his digital camera for reference of course. They were within ten feet of the arch when something really strange happened. Six beings appeared as if out of the thin air pointing staffs at Charlie, Tim and Crystal. They proceeded to stop dead in their tracks and just looked on in total amazement. Suddenly a seventh being appeared, again out of thin air, but at least he looked human. He also was carrying a large staff or walking stick and had it pointed at Charlie, Tim and Crystal.

The person who seemed to arrive out of thin air was a well-dressed individual in long and beautiful flowing black robes. The robes were trimmed with what looked like gold. This trim ran along the entire robe from top to bottom. He was a rather short, balding man that resembled a politician who had been to one too many fund raisers and had quite a few too many glasses of brandy. He wore rings on every finger but the thumb on each hand. Hanging from his neck were gold chains of all lengths and thickness. His cheeks were red and chubby, causing his eyes to look like small slits, and his stomach was as round as a beach ball. Charlie couldn't make out his feet to see if he was wearing shoes or not. He almost looked like a bad Santa Claus for a moment.

The six original beings that had appeared were hooded and stood anywhere from three to five feet tall. It was hard to make out what they really were. All six of them were wearing long black robes and hoods that completely covered their heads and faces. They seemed to have streaming hair growing right out of the backs of their robes. The hair resembled a horse's mane. These beings had very broad shoulders and chests deep like a barrel with arms that hung much too long and low to be human. They were hunched over as if their spines were bent from years of slouching. The hands of these creatures seemed to also be abnormally long and bony, which was strange, considering the bulk of the rest of their bodies. On all the beings' right hands were strange-looking gloves. These gloves were made of leather, with chain mail all along the palm. Along the cuff of the glove there were loops and chains that extended up the sleeve of their cloaks. Where the chain went could not be discerned. Charlie thought he could make out what looked like an elongated face with sagging skin that looked like it had been stretched too far. This gave him the creeps and reminded him of something you would see in a horror film. They did not speak in any language Charlie, Tim or Crystal was familiar with. However, all six of the creatures kept their walking sticks pointed right at Charlie, Tim and Crystal.

The man dressed in the long flowing black robes said nothing and walked slowly towards Charlie, Tim and Crystal. He remained silent at first and just kept staring at them with a surprised look on his face. To their amazement three more beings appeared out of thin air right next to the person now standing directly in front of them. Tim could not believe his eyes and figured it is some sort of trick of mirrors or lights. Charlie was speechless and just staring blankly at the six creatures that had surrounded them in rather orderly fashion. Crystal was shaking like a leaf and saying nothing. She was gripping Charlie's hand so tight that he was sure the circulation was being cut off.

Just then the person with the gold-trimmed robe turned and proceeded to smile at all three of them.

"I would like to introduce myself. My name is Gershrom Cadwalader. I am the Overseer and acting head of Wizard World security. I am responsible for all disputes, magic or otherwise. Now I have a few questions for the three of you and please take your time and answer them thoroughly. Otherwise you will find yourself spending some time locked away in our restraining cells."

Charlie, Tim and Crystal were still speechless. They were transfixed on the six mysterious beings that were surrounding them. They were not paying much attention to this Gershrom Cadwalader guy at the moment at all.

Although Gershrom Cadwalader seemed a bit agitated by being ignored, he stayed calm nonetheless. "Children, please focus for a moment and listen. The first thing I would like to know is what your names are? The second is where you came from. And the third, what guild are you from? And finally where are you mentors?"

"Mr. Cadwalader, my name is Charlie and this is Crystal and Tim. We are from Boston. Right now we have no idea where this Wizard World is or what a guild is or a mentor for that matter."

"So you are not going to admit to which guild you belong to? Is that because you have something to hide perhaps?" asked Mr. Cadwalader with a rather sly look on his face.

Tim snapped to his senses and stated that they had come through the archway right behind him. And he also stated that he had no idea who or what a guild was either. He explained they inserted a key and simultaneously turned it and there was a rather bright flash and the next thing they knew they seemed to be standing on the other side of the arch. He was sure they were still in Boston and had never heard of this Wizard World either.

Crystal still had nothing to say and was now gripping Charlie with both her hands.

"That is absolute nonsense," stated a now-angry-sounding Cadwalader. "No one has come through that gate or any other gate for many thousands of years. Obviously you three are up to something and trying to hide your true intentions."

"So where are you staffs then?"

"We don't have any staffs," said Charlie.

"Do not lie to me, boy."

"I am telling you the truth—we don't have any staffs and we don't know this guild or a mentor either," said Charlie.

"It seems that our options are limited by your short and obviously untrue answers so you leave me no choice; it will be off to the Council of Elders or even the detention chambers for all of you. Of course that could be all avoided if you decide to start giving me some straight answers," said Cadwalader.

Two beings flanked each one of the kids while Gershrom Cadwalader led the way to the ancient city. Crystal did not want to let go of Charlie but decided it was better than having one of these things touch her even for a second. She was almost paralyzed with fear. Charlie kept telling her it would be all right and the group started walking towards the most amazing and wonderful buildings that any of them had ever seen.

Immediately Tim went for his digital camera and the two beings flanking him pointed their staffs at him very ominously. Tim retracted his hand from his backpack and put them both up as to surrender. He felt this was a golden opportunity to document this location and was a bit disappointed that he would not be able to at the moment. However, he had left his GPS running so he would have some excellent readings for future reference. The group continued to head towards the magnificent city. All around them there seemed to be things moving in the wooded areas that were lining the stone pathway. Crystal was sure she had just seen a rather small person with wings. She thought it looked like a fairy or something. She shook her head in disbelief and just kept walking without saying a word. Charlie was also staring into the woods and also thought he saw a rather small person too! However, he didn't hesitate to ask why there are one-foot-tall people floating about in the woods just over there. Tim would not even acknowledge any of this. He kept turning his head the other way to try and ignore the flying whatever they are. But no matter where he looked he continued to see these flying fairies.

Mr. Cadwalader laughed and wondered why the three of them were acting so strangely. After all it's just some wood nymphs working the forest into tiptop shape like they do every day.

"What do you mean they are wood nymphs?" asked Charlie. "There is no such thing. My grandpa mentioned them before but he was only telling a story."

"Charlie, why are you acting so peculiar? Of course there are wood nymphs and there has always been," said Mr. Cadwalader.

"Mr. Cadwalader, I can tell you without a doubt that I have never ever seen such a thing and I will continue to believe that they don't exist even though I see them right now," said Tim.

"What is going on?" asked Crystal. "None of this makes any sense at all; this can't be real. First these little hooded guys appear out of nowhere and now there are fairies all over the place. This is just not normal."

"Why are you three acting so strange? Stop playing games, all of you; everyone here in Wizard World, including you three, have seen the nymphs thousands of times in your lifetime," said an obviously frustrated Mr. Cadwalader.

"Maybe, Gershrom, it's just as they stated, they simply have not been here before," said another voice out of thin air.

A moment later another person seemed to appear as if from the air itself. He was rather tall with flowing gold hair. His beard almost reached the ground and his hair was not much shorter. His robes were of the most brilliant gold all laced with red highlights. He also wore some sort of a pointed hat of the same color. He was carrying a walking stick familiar to the one being held by Mr. Cadwalader.

"Ah, Phinneus, it's so nice to see you," said Mr. Cadwalader. It was obvious he was not too happy to see this Phinneus person.

"Gershrom, how are you on this lovely day?" Without waiting for a response Phinneus went right to the next question. "I see that you have brought some of the Shifters here to assist you with something? Judging by this I must assume that you are in great peril or this is a most serious situation."

Mr. Cadwalader was steaming. He looked furious and was almost speechless. He was holding his walking stick so tightly it looked like it might snap in half. The newest arrival, Phinneus, kept smiling as the events were unfolding. He seemed in quite the pleasant mood.

"Children, let me introduce you to the head of the Council of Elders, Mr. Phinneus Grabblemore. Mr. Grabblemore regulates everything here in Wizard World. He has the final say in all decisions, magic and otherwise," mumbled Mr. Cadwalader.

"So, Gershrom, can you tell me anything helpful about these most dangerous prisoners?" asked Phinneus.

"Phinneus, these intruders will not state which guild they belong to or for that matter who their mentors are. And to top it all off they claimed to have come through the archway, which is obviously some ploy to start major trouble. After all, who would believe such a thing?" said a snickering Cadwalader.

Phinneus just continued to look rather happy. He was smiling at all three of the kids and was motioning for the Shifters to step away. Initially none of the six moved and then Mr. Cadwalader made a rather casual hand signal and they all disappeared right then and there.

"Phinneus, you have no idea whatsoever what these children could be up to, or where they are really from for that matter. I say we throw them in a detention cell for a bit and we will certainly get the truth out of them after that," said a now excited Mr. Cadwalader.

"And what are they up to that merits such a thing, Gershrom? You yourself stated they have not a staff between them and that they came through the portal. Is this not what you said or did I hear you incorrectly?" asked Phinneus.

"That is just preposterous! I am going to bring this up to the council. They will want to hear about this. I tell you the lot of them should be detained and watched by the Shifters until they are thoroughly checked out. You are overstepping your boundaries like usual, Grabblemore," said Gershrom.

"That may be true, Gershrom, and you are surely entitled to your opinion and please do go to the Council and state your case. I am sure they would like to hear of your valiant capture of three unarmed juniors doing nothing wrong except walking towards our city," said Phinneus.

"One of these days you are going to make a decision that will cost us all," said Gershrom.

"That might be true but I feel fairly certain it is not today," said Phinneus, now grinning from ear to ear.

Mr. Cadwalader turned without a word and disappeared into thin air as if by magic. There was a quick puff and he was gone. Tim was taken aback and simply did not believe his eyes. He looked like he might become ill with the strain of it all.

"Children, I can see that you have had a most interesting entrance to Wizard World and I simply must hear all about it," said Mr. Grabblemore.

Mr. Grabblemore offered to give them all a lift to the city. However, there was no car or transport that could be seen. Mr. Grabblemore smiled and asked them to grab on to his robe and to hang on tightly. Charlie, Tim and Crystal reluctantly grabbed on and were instantly leaving the ground. Tim looked like he was about to hurl and Crystal was frozen with fear. She closed her eyes and would not open them, even with constant prodding from Charlie. Charlie was laughing and enjoying this experience. He looked up at Mr. Grabblemore and received a small grin.

They landed right outside the main gates of the city. Tim fell to the ground, followed by Crystal. Charlie, on the other hand, was laughing still and was having the time of his life. He was staring right at Mr. Grabblemore and was simply in awe of him. Before he could say a word four more Shifters appeared out of nowhere again and were pointing staffs at the group. Now this time Mr. Grabblemore was obviously none too pleased with this and had a definite angry look about him. He seemed to make a simple hand gesture and all four of the beasts turned to vapor. He smiled down at the children and motioned for them to follow him.

The gates of the city were enormous. Each was the size of a rather large house. Tim estimated them to be approximately forty feet by forty feet, give or take. He stated this was an educated guess and he could be off by an inch or two.

"Naturally," said Charlie smiling.

Crystal still did not say a word and just smiled. She seemed to be far too blown away by all of this to make a logical statement. Tim was trying to pull a notebook out of his backpack to take notes and quick sketches.

There were hundreds of men and women all dressed in long, often bright-colored, flowing robes or capes. Charlie thought they looked like throwbacks from a time long gone by. It seemed that everything had come to a standstill while Mr. Grabblemore was leading Charlie, Tim and Crystal through the streets. Everyone seemed to know him and stop to smile or wave hello. There were cots being pulled by animals that none of them could ever remember seeing or identify. Strange things seemed to be floating in shop windows. Streets seemed to be swept by brooms moving by themselves. Everything was beyond normal, so odd that it could not possibly be real, but there it was right in front of their eyes.

Tim continued to document everything he possibly could, although he was relatively positive that the majority of what he was seeing was just not possible. *After all, how could a broom sweep without someone to push it?* thought Tim. *And how can that robe over there in that window possibly keep turning around without someone wearing it? Maybe it was on wires? Yeah, that has to be it.*

"Charlie, are you catching all of this?" asked Tim.

"What? Do you mean the brooms sweeping the streets or the robe that is displaying itself?" asked Charlie.

"Yeah, that and what kind of animal is that? I have never seen anything that resembles it whatsoever," said Tim.

"Children, that wonderful creature is a kattergraff. I would have expected that to be plain to see," said a smiling Mr. Grabblemore.

"A kattergraff?" asked Crystal. "There is no such thing. What is this place, a theme park or something?"

"Crystal, it is what it is after all, Wizard World, the most magical place on the planet," said Mr. Grabblemore. "And a kattergraff is just what it sounds like, a cross between a cat and a giraffe. They have always been that way. Of course we still do have giraffes and cats, but there are also some other interesting species that you will see around here from time to time. We can get into that some other time; right now we need to get to the Great Hall and meet with the Council of Elders. I am sure they will be most delighted at the sight of you three and very interested in hearing your stories."

Charlie, Tim and Crystal continued their walk towards the Great Hall. All the while Mr. Grabblemore talked about this and that but nothing in particular. The general layout of the city seemed to be in a circle that was constantly rising to a central point. All of the structures were made from marble that looked to be thousands of years old. There were elegant statues of fairies, robed men and strange animals that were even stranger than most of the ones they had already seen. Along their walk they noticed that there was a waterfall that fell in the back of the city and filled small channels with beautiful crystal clear water. Floating through this water were strange fish and what looked like mermaids or fish people. Tim just continued to take it all in and jot down note after note. Crystal and Charlie were transfixed on this one building that seemed to be constantly changing its storefront from food and beverages to clothing and trinkets. Mr. Grabblemore explained that this was the newest wave in the city and that everyone was doing it to draw in more business.

He pointed to another building that had rotating windows displaying floating cauldrons and staffs that were rotating and flipping about.

Finally they reached what seemed to be the central point in the city and were staring up a rather large staircase. The staircase was lined with beautiful columns that had been entangled in vines. These vines wrapped themselves around all the columns and also the overhead structures. When reaching the top step there were cauldrons full of fires on each side heading towards doors that were even bigger than the set at the city gate. These doors had to be at least sixty feet high and wide. The key that would fit the door's lock would have to be at least six feet long and weigh hundreds or maybe even thousands of pounds.

"Excuse me, Mr. Grabblemore, I don't want to seem impolite but there is no way that you are lifting that key," said Tim. "It has to weigh at least five hundred pounds."

"Good guess, Tim, but it actually weighs a bit more than one thousand pounds, give or take, and yes, I will be inserting the key. Only a member of the Council can lift it or someone who has been told how," said Mr. Grabblemore.

"What do you mean 'told how'?" asked Charlie.

"I could explain that but then everyone in earshot would be able to use the key and that would surely defeat the purpose of making it difficult to gain entrance to the Great Hall," said Grabblemore. "What's important right now is getting you three in to see the members of the Council and discuss exactly what to do with you three."

"Maybe we can meet them another time; we have been gone a while and letting us just go home would be fine by me," said Crystal.

"If I am doing the math correctly I believe that the three of you have been here for approximately six hours by your time, correct?" said Mr. Grabblemore.

"Yeah, that sounds about right," said Charlie.

"There is no need to worry then, now is there. Time does not work the same here so to speak. I will not get into the details just yet, but let's just say to the Regular World you have been gone for mere seconds," said Grabblemore.

"How can that be?" asked Tim. "We have been gone for hours and someone is sure to notice."

"No, Tim, they will not. Like I said, time works differently here in Wizard World. A simple explanation would be that for every year that passes in here only a day passes on the Regular Side. So you see, there is nothing to worry about," said Grabblemore.

"That's just not possible at all, now is it?" asked Tim.

"Trust me, Tim, it is the truth and I assure you that no one is missing you at the moment. As far as they are concerned to them you just left. On that note I suggest we do what we originally came here to do and that's meet with the Council. So just give me a moment and I will open the doors and we can be off to meet with them," said Grabblemore.

Both Charlie and Tim smiled and were prepared to laugh when Mr. Grabblemore was preparing to lift the key.

"I bet ten men, never mind this old guy in a dress couldn't lift that key," laughed Tim.

"Tim, I am sure you are in for a bit of a surprise then," said Mr. Grabblemore with his usual smile.

Mr. Grabblemore pointed his staff at the key and it started to lift slowly off the ground. It headed straight for the lock and inserted itself without any great issues. Mr. Grabblemore was grinning the entire time. He was enjoying the distressed look on both Tim and Charlie's faces. Crystal did her usual and proceeded to squeeze Charlie's arm again until he felt it might fall off. With a mighty clunk the key turned and the great doors started to swing open. All the while Mr. Grabblemore simply smiled and kept his staff pointed at the doors and lock.

The great doors swung wide open revealing a long and rather wide room. This room had sparse furnishings and a large circular enclosure in the middle of it with round benches matching the curves of the rails. Along the edge of the great room were round-shaped chairs with round tables in front of each one. The walls were lined with beautiful bookshelves. Each shelf was filled to the maximum with book after book. These shelves reached to the ceilings, which were at least fifty feet in height. There was a crystal ball on a pedestal in front of each bookshelf. It seemed that they coincided with the seats. A bookshelf for every seat and a crystal ball and pedestal too. Currently all the seats were empty and the place was eerily quiet.

"Mr. Grabblemore, now that we have a few minutes can we please go over the time differential that you mentioned on the walk over here?" asked Tim.

"Tim, now is not the time and the council will be arriving any moment. They are all most anxious to meet the three of you and discuss how you came to be here," said. Mr. Grabblemore.

Mr. Grabblemore instructed the three children to go and be seated in the middle chamber. Here they found round bench-like seats that were surrounded by two desks that matched the curvature of the entire room. The desks were completely void of anything.

The children heard that strange sound, almost like a balloon popping, and suddenly there were four more people in the council chamber. There were three men dressed like Mr. Grabblemore and one woman wearing a flowing gown that was too beautiful to describe. The gown was so beautiful and flowing making it seem as if it was made from the very essence of the air itself. At the same moment Charlie, Tim and Crystal noticed that their desk now had three cups, a carafe filled with some sweet-smelling juice and a fruit bowl that appeared out of thin air. Also appearing were silver plates, knives and forks along with a quill, ink and parchment. Charlie stated that if he sees a pig fly he would now have officially seen everything. This brought a quick chuckle from Crystal and Tim.

The four new arrivals exchanged pleasantries and headed to their seats. All was quiet in the room as all eyes fixed on Charlie, Tim and Crystal. Mr. Grabblemore stood up from his seat and the rest of the group followed. "I would officially like to start this emergency session with a quick update of all the facts that we presently have. Firstly, we know that these three children have stated that they have come through the Great Arch. Secondly, we are led to believe that they do not possess any magical powers or have any knowledge of such things. And finally, we are under the assumption that they somehow have in their possession at least one key.

"We do not know where they received this key or if they possess more than one. We do not know if they are magical or not and we do not know if they actually came through the Great Arch. However, we do know that they are here right now before us," laughed Mr. Grabblemore. "With that this meeting can commence and the floor is open."

The beautiful woman in the flowing robes stood up gracefully and with elegance. She had flowing auburn hair that seemed to be blowing in the wind although they were inside. Her eyes resembled the color of purple and her lips were full and a dark red, glistening like a ruby. She was carrying a different style of a walking stick that looked as if it were made from diamonds and silver. The crystal or diamond on the head of the staff seemed to be perfectly clear and reflecting light in many directions.

"Greetings, everyone. For all of you who do not know me, my name is Efa Vanora. I am the head of the Great (Wilifrem) Guild from the North. We make our guildfaire in the outermost forest by the mighty Wilifrem trees that were created by Mistress Wilifrem herself many thousands of years ago. Our guild is a natural guild, meaning we are of the forest. We are able to communicate with forest animals, plants and even manipulate them to work in our favor. I was called here today by the Head of Council, Mr. Phinneus Grabblemore, for this most urgent matter and I am glad I decided to attend. I look forward to getting to know all three of you in the very near future. I am sure there is much we can learn from one another."

After a moment Efa Vanora graciously took her seat as if floating there and another gentleman prepared to stand up. He bowed graciously to Mr. Grabblemore then the rest of the council and also to Charlie, Tim and Crystal, who after a moment returned the bow.

With a booming voice this rather tall and thin man stood up. His robes were black and trimmed with blood red. He was wearing a matching hat and a matching patch over his left eye. He had very long dark hair and a beard to match. He was sporting a tattoo that ran from his forehead down the left side of his face and under his chin. It was hard to make out the details with his long goatee. His staff was in his left hand and it was dark wood and sporting blood red rubies throughout it. Adorning the head of the staff was a red ruby carved into the head of what looked like a menacing dragon.

"Good day. My name is Eblis Morfran and I am the head of the Blagdon Guild. This guild is located near the Great Mountains to the east. Our guildfaire is located in a valley with large caves surrounding it. Here the land is constantly dark, almost like night even at midday. We are of the dark. We associate with darkness, shadows and mist. We are like the morning fog that floats in and seems to make everything mystifying and invisible. We are like the wind and shadows that form at dusk."

Mr. Morfran proceeded to sit down again. The room seemed to have grown quiet and tense after Morfran presented himself. Tim noticed Efa Vanora gripping her staff rather tightly and her face looking rather tense. There was obviously something there that would need further investigation, thought Tim to himself.

The next person to stand was Mr. Vance Vortigern. He is the head of the Calder Guild. Mr. Vortigern stood about six and a half feet tall. He was wearing a solid silver cloak with the sleeves cut off at the shoulders. The cloak was cut v-neck style down to his navel and pulled tight with a bright red jewel-encrusted belt. He had flowing blond locks that were pulled into a perfect ponytail. His face was clean-shaven and he was sporting hoop earrings in each ear. His staff was very tall and was also silver with diamonds and pearls embedded throughout it. The head of the staff had a pearl the size of softball atop it. Crystal thought that this was the most handsome man she had ever seen. She was transfixed and could not take her eyes off of him. Charlie and Tim were not all that interested and just waited patiently for him to finish his introduction.

"Hello, my dear," said Vance Vortigern, smiling ever so politely. He proceeded to kiss the back of Crystal's right hand, which of course caused her face to turn a lovely shade of pink. Charlie and Tim giggled at this and promptly stopped when they received a rather harsh look from Crystal.

"Hello, young sirs," said Vortigern, who proceeded to bow accordingly to both Charlie and Tim, who both returned the bow.

"The guild that I represent is Calder Guild. Our Guildfaire is located near and upon the great river to the South. Let me enlighten you as to what we are about. We are of the water. We flow and bend like the water and also move like the mist that is sometimes created when water is flowing over the rapids. We are like the great rushing water being able to manipulate, move and adapt to almost any obstacle. We are able to move mountains or glide by them gracefully."

After finishing his speech Mr. Vortigern proceeded to do a rather graceful back flip and land right next to his chair without any effort whatsoever. Of course Crystal was again all flustered and started to clap and smile rather enthusiastically. She stopped when she realized she was the only one.

Without much fanfare Mr. Grabblemore graciously bowed to the three children and introduced himself as the head of the Golundrus Guild.

"Children, since we have already met let's just skip all the pleasantries, shall we? Our guild the Golundrus Guild is one of the original guilds here in Wizard World. It is many thousands of years old and has persisted through the most horrible and joyous of times. We are of everything and nothing in particular. Our guildfaire is neither here nor there. We can bend the wind and crush a boulder. We can talk to animals or become one with them. We can manipulate the ice and the cold or simply say hello with a smile."

The room grew steadily silent as everyone waited for Mr. Grabblemore to take his seat. It was obvious to Tim, Charlie and Crystal that this Grabblemore guy was very important and greatly respected. However, Tim did notice that Eblis Morfran was not paying any attention to Mr. Grabblemore and didn't seem impressed whatsoever.

"Children, you have now met the Council of the Elders. We have given you a very brief summary of what each guild is about and some basic history. This information, however, is not complete and is just a minuscule tidbit of what each guild and Council Member has to offer. There is not enough time in a day to go over every single detail, now is there?" said Mr. Grabblemore.

"Now I am sure the Council Members have questions and we will begin shortly. However, right now we need to eat and relax for a bit and get all our bearings straight," said the ever-smiling Mr. Grabblemore. "So please partake in the food that has been supplied to all of you and we will begin the session once you are all sufficiently filled."

Without warning all of the council members disappeared into thin air, leaving Charlie, Tim and Crystal speechless like usual.

"What do you guys think?" asked Charlie.

"I think we have been here long enough and need to start thinking about heading back," said Crystal.

"Wait a second, Crystal, I don't think we are in any trouble and it won't hurt to stay a bit longer. This place is very interesting and I want to check it out a bit more, that is of course if the Council lets us out of here," said Tim.

"Okay then, we will answer some of their questions and then ask them if we are being held here or if we can leave," said Charlie. "If they say we can't leave then we will bide our time and wait for our chance to get out of here and back to the archway."

"I guess that's okay for now but I would prefer if we left really soon," said Crystal.

"We need to remember to ask about the time-differential thing. That could be very important. We could be aging faster or slower or time could be going by faster or slower," said Tim.

"Yeah, that is kind of an important one. I am sure Grandpa is wondering what has happened and is probably getting a bit nervous, especially with Mr. Nilrem missing still," said Charlie.

"Charlie, can I keep the key for now, just for safekeeping? It will make me feel better and maybe I will want to stay a bit longer," said Crystal

"I guess if it makes you feel better, but it's already safe with me," said Charlie. Tim looked questioningly on, wondering why Crystal would want the key. He did not see any harm in this and nodded for Charlie to hand it to her, which he did.

"Thanks, guys, I will kccp it safe," said Crystal.

Charlie and Tim glanced at each other and said nothing.

The three then spent a good half hour eating some of the fruit and drinking the wonderful fruity-tasting punch that had been provided for them. This punch seemed to be as filling as eating a four-course meal, thought Tim. He was very happy about this of course. Charlie was amazed at the flavor of the punch also. Crystal, on the other hand, was just poking at the fruit and barely drinking. She looked very antsy and seemed in a rush to get going.

Moments later Charlie, Tim and Crystal heard that familiar pop and four figures appeared out of nowhere again. This startled all three of them like usual but they were starting to get used to people just appearing out of thin air.

"Children, I hope that the punch and fruit was to your liking? Members of the Dernen guild specially made that punch, so please thank Efa Vanora, head of Dernen, for this most delicious meal." Charlie, Tim and Crystal bowed and Efa returned it with a gracious smile on her face.

"Now I am sure you three must have some questions for the Council, so please do not hesitate to ask and we will gladly answer if we are able," said Mr. Grabblemore.

Tim got up from his seat and opened his notebook. His first question was to be about leaving or not, but obviously he had other ideas of what was important. "Council, first let me ask a most important question, how do you keep disappearing like that? And second, can we leave if we want to? And third, Mr. Grabblemore, you had mentioned that time passes differently in Wizard World and we really need to know exactly how that works."

"All three are very wise questions and of course I will answer the easy one first. Yes, you can leave whenever you want. You are not prisoners here, you are honored guests. However, we would like it if you three would stay a bit longer and when you do decide to go I will gladly escort all of you back to the archway," said Mr. Grabblemore.

"Second, how we keep disappearing is a most complicated thing. I am not sure we have the time to go over it right now. Let's just say there are a few different ways to do it and it takes many years of training.

"And thirdly, how time passes is something I can give you a quick lesson on. When you are here in Wizard World time seems to pass normally to all of us. We age the same and days and nights are the same. However, when you go back to the Regular World time over there is not quite the same. For instance, when a day passes by in the Regular World a year passes by in Wizard World. So to anyone waiting for you on the other side you have been gone for mere seconds. We are still basically in the same location but not in the same space. We are what you might call dimension shifting of sorts. Think back to when you thought that a shadow seemed to be there and then gone the next moment. Well, what causes that is when our two dimensions become so close that we are almost one and things seem to fade in and out of existence.

"I hope I have thoroughly answered all your questions satisfactorily," said Mr. Grabblemore, smiling and bowing ever so slightly. Tim returned the bow and sat down transfixed on his notes and not saying a word.

"Thanks for all the information, Mr. Grabblemore," said Charlie. "So we can go if we want right now?"

"Correct, but like I said I would prefer it if you decide to stay a bit longer so we can go over all that you have learned related to the other side of the portal," said Mr. Grabblemore.

"Can you give us a second to talk it over?" asked Charlie.

"Certainly," said Mr. Grabblemore.

After a brief discussion Charlie stood up. "Tim and myself would like to take you up on the offer and stay, but Crystal would like to go as soon as possible. We are not sure if we can do that because we only have one key."

"I must agree that certainly presents a problem. As far as I know if Crystal takes the key then you two will be trapped here until she comes back or someone else figures out how to use the portal. I would strongly recommend that she wait until you two are ready to leave, as I cannot guarantee if when or even ever for that matter the two of you will be able to get back," said Mr. Grabblemore.

"Crystal, can't you wait a bit longer? There is so much to learn here. We have hardly broken the surface at this point. This is the opportunity of a lifetime," said Tim.

"Tim, I know you and Charlie are really excited by all of this, but I don't feel comfortable right now. I think we need to head back and see what

Grandpa Watson and Grandma Watson have to say. After all, we can always come back, right?"

"Yes, you can use the portal to return as long as you have a key," said Mr. Grabblemore. "But I strongly suggest that you keep this information to yourselves. I am sure that there are some rather unscrupulous people who would love to get their hands on that key of yours to try and gain access to Wizard World and its many secrets. If you do feel that strongly about leaving then you probably should. Charlie, Tim and yourself can take her back through the portal and then talk to your grandfather and then come right back. After all, it's not like you have been gone for that long, remember?"

"Yeah, he's right, Charlie. Let's take Crystal back and let Grandpa Watson know what's going on and then come right back. We can always go back and get Crystal again if she decides she wants to return," said Tim.

"Okay then, it's settled. We will drop Crystal off, talk to Grandpa Watson and come right back," said Charlie.

The Council of Elders bowed to the group and the three returned it. Like usual all the members vaporized into thin air again. Tim just shook his head and started to gather his things. He placed his notes in his backpack and asked graciously if he could take this parchment and feather quill with him. "Of course," said Mr. Grabblemore with his usual gracious smile.

"I will lead our small group to the portal. I think it's best at the moment if you stay with a member of the Council. The Overseer has a different view on why you three are here and we do not want any problems occurring," said Grabblemore

"I am sure that Tim and Crystal would agree that we have no interest in meeting up with any Shifter any time soon, that's for sure. They were the creepiest little guys I have ever seen," said Charlie.

"Yeah, no doubt," said Tim.

"I most definitely agree, they sure were creepy," said Crystal.

As they headed out of the Great Room all eyes in the city were transfixed on them. It was blatantly obvious that there was an immediate leak of information to the entire city and the residents were certainly inquisitive. None of the residents attempted to speak to Charlie, Tim or Crystal; instead they would lower their heads with graceful bows. This made their journey out of the city gates last quite long with all the bowing that was going on. Tim's back was killing him by the time they had reached the gate. He stated he would be glad if he never has to bow again and that if this keeps up he would need to see a chiropractor when he gets back home for sure. Charlie and

Crystal just smiled and Mr. Grabblemore had no idea what Tim was referring to and just continued to lead the three of them to the city gate.

"Children, we can either walk or you can hold on to my robes again and we can take the rather exciting route of vaporation, it's entirely up to you three of course," said Mr. Grabblemore. Of course Charlie and Tim wanted to vaporate but Crystal wanted to walk and enjoy the sights so that was the choice of travel. Charlie and Tim were not too happy about this but decided to go along nonetheless. After all, they would soon be back in Wizard World and could do whatever they wanted after Crystal was safely through the portal.

"Alas, we have reached the arch of entrance or the portal; whichever you prefer to call it is fine with me," said Mr. Grabblemore. "Now I will bid you farewell and good travel. I hope to continue are friendship in the very near future. I am going to give you this orb in order to call me as soon as you enter Wizard World again. This will of course allow me to greet you here at the portal and hopefully stop any unnecessary meetings with the Shifters and the Overseer. It is very easy to use; once appearing on this side of the portal just look into the ball and say my name and it will call me no matter where I am. Of course I will immediately drop what I am doing and vaporate here and we can continue on with your introductions to Wizard World. There are many things for you to see and experience here and far too much for me to discuss in a mere day's time."

"Thanks for everything and we will see you real soon," said Charlie.

Tim, Charlie and Crystal all bowed and prepared for their trip home. Crystal pulled the key out of her pocket and inserted it into the lock and turned it without waiting a single moment. There was the usual bright flash and they were now again standing back in the alley with the stench of rotting fish and a not-so-enjoyable surprise waiting for them.

Before either Charlie or Tim could say a word to each other Clive and Sean immediately grabbed onto them while Beth and Ron started to punch and kick them without mercy. In seconds both Charlie and Tim were on the ground and still being pummeled by Ron and his gang. Charlie glanced up at Crystal and she looked away and didn't say a word. Charlie realized they had been betrayed. He was furious but there was nothing he could do at the moment. He could not believe this was happening. Tim was being hit rather hard again and there was nothing Charlie could do. Crystal just walked away and handed the key and orb to Beth. A moment later Grandpa came running down the alley and Ron, Clive, Beth, Sean and Crystal ran right by him without saying a word.

"Charlie, Tim, what just happened? I saw Crystal run by with Ron and his gang. What is going on?" asked Grandpa Watson.

"She took the key, Grandpa, and the orb too," said Charlie.

Tim was holding his stomach and moaning. He still was not fully recovered from the last beating he had suffered a week earlier. Grandpa helped them both to their feet.

"Unfortunately there is nothing we can do at this point in time. Let's get back home and we can try and figure out our next step," said Grandpa Watson.

"But, Grandpa, they have the key… It's over—what else can we do?" Charlie stated.

"Remember, Charlie, there are always options. Have a little faith; we are not out of the game yet. Now help me get Tim into the car and we can talk on the ride back to my house," said Grandpa Watson.

"Okay, Grandpa, but I just cannot believe it. How could Crystal do that to us after all we have been through together? "asked Charlie.

"Charlie, I am sure she has her reasons and I bet they will become quite clear eventually," said Grandpa Watson.

The ride to Grandpa's was very quiet. Tim was holding his left eye again that was swelling shut and Charlie was trying to get his nose to stop bleeding. They were both furious with Crystal. Charlie could not understand why neither of them had seen this coming. After all, they had helped her when she was about to get all gummed up by Beth McGrigger those weeks earlier.

"Charlie, I guess it's just you and I again like it always has been," said Tim.

"No, Tim, not this time, we have Grandpa, Grandma and hopefully Mr. Nilrem when we find him. Together we are still a great team and we will get to the bottom of this."

"Now that's the spirit," said Grandpa. "We will figure this all out without a doubt."

"All right, let's get going then. I am not going to let Ron or any of his cronies get the best of any of us for that matter," said Tim. "They might have our key but we still got one thing they don't, and that's brains."

Charlie and Tim filled Grandpa Watson in on the entire experience. Grandpa Watson could not stop smiling the entire drive home. He was not paying much attention to the road and twice just missed two mailboxes that were close to the rode. Had it not been for Charlie's warnings they surely would have hit at least one of them. Grandpa just couldn't control his excitement and was rather anxious to get home. After arriving at home and assisting with the injuries to both Charlie and Tim Grandma Watson was filled in on all the details and what Crystal had done to them. She assured them that there was probably a logical explanation and eventually they would hear all the facts and maybe it would all make sense. Nonetheless Charlie and Tim were still furious with her and could not wait to see her at school.

"Children, the first thing we need to do is figure out how to get another key. I believe that should be our number one goal at this point," said Grandpa Watson. "Everyone agreed?"

Everyone agreed and the map and the cane were brought out once more to try and find another key. Oddly enough it seemed that there was another key right in their very neighborhood. Judging by the mapping information that Tim had put together he estimated the key was within two blocks of their very location. He could not be one hundred percent positive of this as there was a bit of guesswork involved but he was fairly certain that there was a key waiting to be claimed and that they would be the ones to do it.

Chapter 7

Ron, Crystal and Mr. Buttons

Crystal met up with her new friends the very next morning. They were discussing how they had beaten Charlie and Tim and taken their precious key away with ease. Ron was so pleased with himself for setting this whole farce up in the first place with the help of his parents and tricking Charlie and Tim into thinking that Crystal was their friend when all along she was just playing a part. After all, if his parents had not known the Kildroys and arranged for their meeting before the beginning of the school year none of this would have been possible.

"Can any of you believe how gullible Charlie and Tim really are? I mean come on already, how could they think for even a second that you, Crystal Kildroy, would want to spend even a single minute of your time with the likes of either of them? They are losers and always will be. Just see how this has worked out for us; they spent weeks doing stupid research and studying and we stepped in and took it all away from them. The first day of school in the hall worked out perfect. Well, not so perfect for you, Beth, but it sure made this more believable. Just imagine if they had realized you really never had any intention whatsoever of actually putting that gum into Crystal's hair? They are so easy to fool and manipulate, like stupid children who have no idea when they are being played. When will they ever learn?" asked Ron.

"Ron, when are we going to go through the gate?" asked Crystal. "It was kind of creepy there. We should definitely make sure we are prepared. It's not like being here in Boston. There are strange people there, and even stranger things."

"Oh, Crystal, just calm down, I am sure we'll be fine. These strange creatures or whatever they are will recognize our high-ranking stature and soon enough we will be treated like the royalty that we are. So there is no need to worry; after all, you will be with me, Beth, Clive and Sean. It's not like you will be going back with the two losers."

"I know that, but it's still not normal there. Remember what I said about the Overseer and the Shifters and how absolutely creepy they were."

"Yes, yes, yes, I do but I'm sure this Overseer will recognize us for what we are and these Shifters will be thrilled to see us all," said Ron.

"I can tell you they were not too happy to see Tim, Charlie or me for that matter so I doubt that, but we do have the orb to call Mr. Grabblemore."

"This Grabblemore guy sounds like he will be able to assist us. I am sure he will be of some use, although if what you said is true about him liking both Charlie and Tim I am not so sure. The Overseer guy sounds more like our kind of people; he hates Charlie and Tim so he can't be all bad, now can he," said Ron.

"Beth and Sean, get your sorry butts moving and get everything on that list I wrote and make sure you don't forget anything. No cutting corners like you two normally do—just follow the list to the letter, got it? We need to be prepared when we arrive in Wizard World. Like I always say, better safe than sorry," said Ron.

"And when do you always say that?" asked Beth sarcastically.

"Oh, just shut up and go already before I get some gum or something and you know I will definitely stick it in your hair," said a sneering Ron.

"Okay already, no need to get nasty; I was just joking around," said Beth.

Beth and Sean headed out without another word. Crystal did not say a thing. She seemed a bit down in the dumps at the moment. Although none of her new friends were aware of it she was still feeling pretty bad about what she had done to Charlie and Tim. She had done what was asked of her and she was not sure she had done the right thing. It was too late to turn back now, she thought. She was fairly certain that Charlie, Tim and the Watsons must absolutely hate her for what she had done and she couldn't blame them one bit.

Charlie and Tim spent an entire day looking for a key and were no closer to getting back into Wizard World than they were the day theirs was taken. Tim was sure of his data but they were still unable to locate another key, although there seemed to be one right in this very neighborhood. An hour or so earlier the key seemed like it was going to walk right up to the front door. Tim peered out through the front door more than once and did not see a thing. In disgust he walked back to his seat and continued to study his data and the map. Grandpa and Grandma Watson were both assisting in the search and were also coming up dry. This mysterious key seemed to be moving and walking right next to them in the very streets they were walking upon.

"Charlie, this makes no sense at all. That key should be right in front of us, here right now, give or take," said Tim.

"I know and I just don't understand it either. Maybe your map is a little bit off or something," said Charlie.

"My data is never off," said a defiant Tim.

"If your data is right then where is they key? It should be right here and I don't see it, do you?" asked Charlie.

"I am telling you it has to be here. Just look at the map—it has to be correct, I just know it," said Tim. "That key should be right in front of us walking towards us as we speak and all I see is Mrs. Flutterfen's fat old cat Mr. Buttons. This whole thing makes no sense."

Suddenly Charlie got up without a word and slowly walked towards Mr. Buttons. He was calling the cat and wiggling his fingers to try and get the cat's attention. Tim kept studying the map and wondering what the fascination was with Mr. Buttons. Then it all became obviously clear and he hastily got up and joined Charlie calling the cat with great enthusiasm. Tim could see the key they were looking for hanging off Mr. Buttons's neck on a beautiful red leather collar. However, Mr. Buttons was not cooperating even though he was purring and rolling about. The silly cat would not come any closer than five feet to either Tim or Charlie. This was a frustrating moment to see the key mere feet away and to be at the mercy of a cat named Mr. Buttons.

"Tim, go and get some tuna fish from Grandma ASAP. Hurry up, we may not get another chance at this," said Charlie.

Tim ran as fast as he could right into Grandma Watson's house. He barged into the kitchen, throwing the door open without knocking, and explained they had found the key but that they needed tuna fish to get it. Grandma Watson had no idea how tuna fish played into this, but pulled a can out of the cupboard nonetheless and opened it and handed it to Tim. "Thanks, Grandma Watson. I will be back in a few minutes, hopefully with a new key and I will explain everything then."

"I don't see the significance of a can of tuna but here you go and good luck."

"Thanks, Grandma."

She shook her head, smiled and continued on with preparing the evening meal.

Tim slammed the kitchen door on his way out and hurried to the side gate and slowed to a cautious walk. He placed the tuna can about ten feet from Mr. Buttons and started to call him as nicely as possible. "Here, kitty, kitty, kitty, come and get the nice tuna fish." Mr. Buttons could not resist the smell of tuna and headed towards the can. The cat became oblivious to its surroundings, allowing Charlie to easily circle behind Mr. Buttons while Tim stayed in front only a few feet away. They could both see the ring hanging from Mr. Buttons's collar. Charlie was now within a foot of the cat when he heard a very familiar voice.

"Hello, boys, can I help you two with anything?" asked Miss Flutterfen.

"No, Miss Flutterfen, we are just playing with your cat. We fed him a can of tuna. I hope that's okay," said Charlie.

"It sure is. Mr. Buttons loves tuna fish. It's nice to see the both of you taking interest in a fine and beautiful animal like Mr. Buttons. He just loves being scratched behind the ears and having his belly rubbed. Well, boys, I will see you at school so have a great day," said Miss Flutterfen.

"We will," said Charlie.

The boys waited a minute or two until Miss Flutterfen had gone back into her backyard and closed her gate. The cat was still enjoying the feast of tuna and not paying either Charlie or Tim a bit of attention. Slowly Charlie reached down and started to pet Mr. Buttons behind the ears. Just as Miss Flutterfen had said earlier, Mr. Buttons started purring and rolled on to his back. Tim reached in and started to remove his collar and Charlie continued to pet Mr. Buttons. Within moments the ring was off the collar and they both headed into Charlie's grandparents' house hardly able to control their excitement. They were going to be heading back to Wizard World after all and nothing was going to stop them.

"Grandma, we found the key," shouted Charlie. "We found it! We found it! It was right here all along just like Tim had said."

"Like I said all along, my data was correct," said Tim.

"I never doubted you for a moment," said Grandma Watson. "Well done, both of you, well done."

Grandpa Watson arrived moments later to hear the rather funny tale about Mr. Buttons and the tuna fish. After enjoying the story for a few moments the group decided it was as good a time as any for planning their next excursion into Wizard World.

It was decided that Grandpa would join the boys. Grandma feared that if there was another run-in with the Shifters that they might not be so lucky this time and they might need all the help they could get. And after all, Grandpa Watson did provide the cane and discover the lost city many years ago and was quite looking forward to exploring this Wizard World. There was no stopping Grandpa, and Grandma Watson decided it was not a bad idea either. Charlie and Tim could surely use Grandpa's expertise in this strange world.

Within the hour Grandma dropped off Grandpa, Charlie and Tim a block or so from the alley. They were off for what was to be Grandpa's greatest adventure ever. He was like a small child shaking with excitement. Charlie and Tim both smiled and were glad Grandpa was going with them.

While walking down the alley both Tim and Charlie were sure they had seen a flash around the corner. When rounding the last corner in the alley there was nothing there however. They proceeded to lead Grandpa Watson behind the dumpsters and fish-filled barrels to the plaque on the wall. Grandpa smiled with amazement and touched the plaque ever so slightly. He had reached a point in his life where he was sure there was no way he would ever make a discovery like he had so many years earlier and now here he was on the verge of not only doing something even more spectacular, but having to thank his grandson and best friend for this great opportunity.

"Charlie and Tim, I would like to take this moment to thank you both. Through all these many years the both of you have listened to my stories and never once treated me like I was losing my mind. You have no idea what this means to me and I am forever in your debts," said a choked-up Grandpa Watson.

"No problem, Grandpa," said Charlie.

"Yeah, likewise," said Tim.

"Okay, now let's get that key into the hole and let the magic begin," said Grandpa Watson.

A moment later there was a flash and a pop and Charlie, Tim and Grandpa were standing on the other side of the arch. Grandpa looked around for a moment and was surprised to hear a strange popping noise that was all too familiar to both Charlie and Tim. Within moments they were surrounded by at least ten Shifters who were pointing staffs at each one of them. The group raised their hands but it did not matter to the Shifters; bolts shot out from three of the staffs and Charlie, Tim and Grandpa were promptly on the ground unable to move or even speak. Three more Shifters motioned with their staffs and Charlie, Tim and Grandpa started floating in the air. Still unable to move or even talk, all they could do was look straight up at the beautiful clear sky above them.

"Well, well, well, it looks like you two did not learn your lessons the last time you were here. I see you have brought another criminal with you and that's fine with me. One more for the detainment cells in the pit of Dulgeon.

I am sure the two of you are wondering where Grabblemore is, but do not hold your breath waiting for him since he has no idea that any of you have returned here to Wizard World. Thanks to our newest friends Ron, Clive, Sean, and Beth, and yes, Crystal, we were quite prepared for your illegal entrance. This time there will be no stopping me from my required duty. The three of you will do some hard time in the pit. I am sure you will find the living quarters quite to your likings. Oh, and just remember to watch out for the hanging Sloggers as they are known to leave a nasty scar after the poison works its way into your system over months and months of agonizing constant prickling pain. I have heard that the worst part is the constant leaking from the large pustules that form. Well, let's get a move on and get these three criminals out of sight before word gets back to Grabblemore," said Cadwalader.

Charlie, Tim and Grandpa Watson were magically floated along for what seemed like days, although in reality only an hour or two actually had passed by. It was hard to tell which direction they were heading in because all any of them could see was the beautiful clear sky. They were unable to pick up any useful information since the Shifters did not talk whatsoever. Occasionally the Overseer did give them a direction or two but that was about it. Finally they stopped moving and were dropped rather hard to the ground. Charlie noticed he was now able to speak and some of his movement was returning. Tim was making some sort of sound but Charlie couldn't make it out and Grandpa remained silent and unmoving, which made Charlie a bit nervous. Without warning Grandpa came to life and surprisingly pulled a staff from one of the Shifters but before he could swing it he was zapped again by a bright red bolt and unable to move lying on his back staring straight up again.

The three were moved down tunnel after tunnel until there was no longer any natural light. There were torches burning every ten feet or so on either side of the cave. Lower and lower they went and finally they stopped. Charlie could see lots of movement but could not really ascertain what was happening. He could hear moaning and lots of hammering and these constant slashing noises all about. Finally they were carried into what looked like a cell. Here they were dropped to the floor and left. Charlie heard the gate close and lock then he saw three quick bright red flashes and they were instantly able to move again. However, Charlie, Tim and Grandpa stayed still, fearing they would be hit again with this curse or spell. They still did not know entirely what had happened or where they were at the moment but at least they could look around and talk quietly amongst each other.

"Tim, Charlie, either of you have any idea whatsoever where we are or what just happened?" asked Grandpa.

"Grandpa Watson, I can give you my best guess, and that's Ron, Crystal and the rest of that group arrived here and tipped off the Overseer that we would probably be returning," said Charlie.

"That part was easy to figure out, but I can speak for Charlie and neither of us has a clue as to where we are at the moment. We did not see all that much outside of the main city where we were here earlier," said Tim.

"The first thing we need to do is figure out where we are and how to get out of here and get in contact with Mr. Grabblemore," said Grandpa Watson. "It seemed quite obvious that the Overseer did not want us to have any contact whatsoever with Mr. Grabblemore, so he is obviously who we want to get to as quick as possible. I have a bad feeling that we will not last all that long down here in this mine and I am sure that is part of the plan. They do not have to kill us, just assist us along that path, if you get what I mean?"

Tim thought all about this situation for a moment and it all hit him. "Wait a second, no one knowing of our return—"

"Exactly, Tim, we're on our own on this one," said Grandpa.

"I get what you mean," said Charlie.

"So we need to stick together and figure this all out. We do not have anyone else to depend on but ourselves," said Grandpa.

"Grandpa, I can say without a doubt that we are not going to dig ourselves out of this one. This cell was carved right out of the mountain itself and who knows how deep we are," said Charlie.

"I would measure a guess at about three thousand feet, give or take," said Tim. "I was counting in my head while we were being moved or floated down here."

Grandpa just laughed. "Well done, Tim, like usual I should expect nothing less. So now we know how far, the next thing is to figure out if we can get this cell door open somehow."

Suddenly a voice from seemingly out of nowhere spoke. "Don't bother, the cell doors are magically sealed and can only be opened from the outside by a Shifter or one of the Goblins. I have tried for the past ten years, give or take, and have had no luck. When you come down here there are only two ways out, either dead or by someone helping you from the outside."

"Well, stranger, thanks for the information, but we are not going to quit just yet. By the way, my name is Mr. Watson and this is Charlie and Tim. We come from what I believe you might call the Regular World."

"So it is true then, people have finally come through the portal. Did you meet with anyone before you were taken down here? Well, did you?"

"The first time we arrived we met with the Council of Elders and Mr. Grabblemore gave us an orb to call him but unfortunately one of our ex-friends and some of her new friends took it. So we do not even know if Grabblemore or any member of the Council even knows we are here," said Charlie.

"That is good news and you should keep a little faith. Mr. Grabblemore is a very able-bodied wizard. He knows most everything that goes on here in Wizard World. Luckily you have at least met with him so there is a chance that he will figure out your whereabouts. I, on the other hand, do not think I will be so lucky.

"Excuse my rudeness; I am so sorry I have not properly introduced myself. My friends call me Alston so please refer to me by that. My surname is not important. I have been down here for the past ten years, give or take. I was unfortunately on the wrong side of a dispute and was ceremoniously locked up down here. I worked for the Council of Elders doing, how you say, undercover work of sorts. Unfortunately I was betrayed and arrested on a rather fabricated story by the Overseer and here I am. There was no trial to speak of or hearing for that matter. Since I was reporting directly to Mr. Grabblemore there is no trace of me to be found. Only he knows what I was doing and he cannot know what has happened to me because there is just no evidence. I was there one day and then gone the next. The Shifters detained me and whisked me away in the dead of night here to this secret location and I fear here I will remain till the day I die. I hope your fortunes turn out better than mine have."

"So what is this place for anyway?" asked Mr. Watson.

"You have unfortunately found your way into a dungeon or as I like to call it, forced labor camp," said Alston. "This is where many of the crystals that you have probably seen either in staffs or worn about individuals' necks are mined. However, it's backbreaking work and not too many villagers want to spend their time down here working in this most horrible place. You will soon learn that there are many things down here much worse then the Goblins or Shifters. I hope the lot of you avoids these beasts, with a little luck of course, and lives to tell the tale of this wretched place."

While Charlie, Grandpa and Tim were locked up, hungry and cold, Ron, Sean, Beth and Crystal were enjoying themselves being treated like kings and queens. The overseer was most pleased with their assistance in detaining what he called a most dangerous lot who illegally entered Wizard World and were allowed to skirt the law with the assistance of Mr. Phinneus Grabblemore.

"Mr. Cadwalader, what happened to Charlie, Tim and his grandfather anyway? Where are they now?" asked Crystal.

"Dear child, that is really not important, now is it? The important thing is that you did the right thing and assisted in the detaining of three known criminals," said Mr. Cadwalader.

"But, Mr. Cadwalader, are we guilty too? We entered Wizard World without an invitation," stated Crystal.

"Ah, child, but you did not since you returned with an invitation from Mr. Phinneus Grabblemore, head of the Council of Elders himself. You are still carrying the orb he gave you, correct?" asked Mr. Cadwalader.

"Well, yes, but I took that from Charlie and Tim, so—"

"So nothing. You have it, dear, and they do not, plain and simple. The law is the law. They got what they deserved. I hope the lot of them don't enjoy the sun much because they will never see it again," laughed Mr. Cadwalader.

"They got what they deserved in the end," said Ron.

Sean, Clive and Beth laughed and kept enjoying the feast and servants they had at their disposal. Crystal was quiet and not having all that much fun. After all she felt quite responsible for what had happened to Charlie, Tim and now Grandpa Watson.

Charlie, Tim and Grandpa Watson spent their first night in this horrendous location. They could hear screams and moans off in the background and strange-sounding animals. They had no idea whether it was night or day when their cell door swung open, and what was waiting at the doorway was something out of a nightmare. There stood the most grotesque, beastly-looking thing any of them had ever seen! This thing stood at least two feet taller than Grandpa and must have weighed at least four hundred pounds. Its left eye was missing and patched with what looked like a piece of steel screwed right into the flesh and probably the bone surrounding his eye socket. He wore a leather collar with short spikes that had a large metal loop at the front. Two more leather straps extended to his waist from the main loop and held up what looked like some sort of armor-type pants that stopped at the knees. He wore no shoes but instead had spikes strapped to the top of each foot. On his waist hung a large rusty dagger with jagged edges. He was carrying a whip in his left hand. Also there were wristband and forearm guards that were spiked with rusty tips. He was the most menacing thing that any of them had ever seen. Immediately all three started to step back towards rear of the cell but stopped in their tracks when the beast cracked its whip right over their heads.

"Come now or be whipped," said the beast. "Now or whipping!!!"

Charlie, Tim and Grandpa slowly headed towards the beast. The beast then reached around its back and threw three sets of shackles at their feet and instructed them to put them on. Charlie, Tim and Grandpa reluctantly obliged and were led out of their cell by chain into the pitch-black darkness. After a good ten minutes of stumbling and being pulled along there were torches ahead and the outlines of what seemed to be other prisoners could be seen. Their chain was hooked high on the wall by the beast and they were handed pick axes. The beast then pointed to a place along the wall for them to start digging. His whip cracked once in the general location of their heads and they promptly started to pick away at the wall.

Tim was struggling in a moment and hardly able to swing his pick. The beast promptly came and pushed Tim to the ground, causing him to drop his pickaxe. Grandpa reacted with great speed, spinning around and swinging his pickaxe with great purpose, hitting the beast right below his armor on the back of his right leg. The beast fell to the ground screaming in agony, although the pickaxe barely broke the skin and shattered in the process. Grandpa then picked up Tim's pickaxe and started to strike the shackles about their ankles to break them free. In a moment both Charlie and Tim were loose but they were far from freedom still. Another great beast had seen the attack and escape attempt and was heading over with whip and dagger drawn. Grandpa smiled at Charlie and Tim and proceeded to run straight at the beast. Charlie yelled for his grandfather to stop but he did not turn around or even pay him a bit of attention. Tim grabbed Charlie by the arm and started pulling him away.

"We have to go now, Charlie, or this was all for nothing."

"But we can't leave him down here, we just can't. We have to help him, Tim."

"Your grandfather knew what he was doing and he can take care of himself. Right now if we don't get out of here then we will all be in for it, I am sure."

Off in the distance Charlie could make out another shadow swinging a pickaxe and he knew right away it was Alston assisting his grandfather. "Go swiftly! This will be your only chance to save yourselves and hopefully your grandfather and me. Do not look back and take the tunnel to your left. Hurry now, there is not much time. I will see to your grandfather so don't worry. Just get out of here and get in touch with Phinneus. He can help you and hopefully stage a rescue. He is the only one you can trust."

Charlie was being dragged away by Tim and he could see in the distance the shadow of his grandfather and Alston swinging their pickaxes in all directions.

Charlie and Tim both ran as fast as they could and occasionally had to duck into small crevasses to avoid detection. They had no idea how far they had traveled or if they were even close to escaping. They both decided to rest for a while in one of the offshoots they had stumbled into earlier.

Charlie could not get his grandfather out of his head. How could he just leave him behind like that? He was miserable with himself. Tim could do nothing to console him at the moment. They were not sure if it had been days or hours but they finally reached the entrance. It was heavily guarded by more of these beastly-looking things and there seemed to be no means to get past them.

The boys ducked into another crevasse and watched for hours as cart after cart came in and out with loads of supplies. The supplies came in and the empty barrels were filled with the crystals that were mined by the slave labor. It was decided that they would wait for a cart to approach and try to either get under the cart or into one of the barrels. After ten or so carts passed by there was a bit of a backup forming. Charlie and Tim took this opportunity to approach the last cart and cautiously check to see if the barrels were empty or not. Finally the next to last barrel was empty. What a stroke of luck. They quietly removed the lid and slid into the barrel, closing it as tightly as they possibly could. The barrel smelled of stale beer or mead but they both figured it was better than being stuck in a damp musty cell. A moment later the cart was searched and sent on its way. All the while Charlie could not stop thinking of his grandfather and that way he had sacrificed himself so the two boys could make their escape. They realized they were in debt to Alston and were both hoping that they would be able to repay it someday.

After long hours of a rather bumpy ride the cart finally came to a sudden stop. The barrels were unloaded rather unceremoniously and piled along with many other barrels. Charlie and Tim were quite relieved to realize their barrel had not been stacked too high and after a few quick peeks they were able to escape rather easily. However, even though they were free, neither of the boys had any idea where they were nor what they were going to do next.

Cautiously Charlie and Tim made their way to the back of the storage shed. They checked out their surroundings and concluded that they had arrived in a rather large village. They were cautious not to be seen, remembering what Alston said about not trusting anyone. However, this put Charlie and Tim at a sizeable disadvantage since they had no idea where they were or how to get in touch with Mr. Grabblemore.

"Charlie, we need to use a bit of stealth and gather some supplies. After that we can try and get our bearings and head back to the main city."

"But what about the Shifters and the Overseer? I bet our escape will be discovered in no time and they will be out looking for us in force," said Charlie.

"Charlie, that might be true, but like Alston said, Mr. Grabblemore is the only one we can trust and that means heading back to the main city to look for him."

"Okay then, let's wait until tonight and do some exploring of this new place and gather what we can. Maybe we can come across a map or something to make our trip a bit easier. There's nothing else to do but relax until nightfall. Moving around during the daylight is definitely going to get us spotted or worse caught by those beast things again. I can tell you right now I am in no hurry whatsoever to head back to Dulgeon. I think I would rather spend the day with Ron and his gang," said a laughing Charlie.

"I see your point and sadly I agree," said Tim.

Nightfall came and Charlie and Tim cautiously emerged from their hiding place under the barrel-storage building. Doing their exploring at night had its benefits of stealth but also the disadvantage of not being really able to take in the entire location. Charlie realized it had been at least a day since their last meal and was starving. Tim agreed that their first priority should be getting some food and drink. They decided to split up, hoping for better success. They each spent the first night sneaking along alleys and behind carts and around barrels hoping to come across an easy score. Finally their efforts paid off when Tim was able to procure a bag of what looked like fruit and two containers of some sweet-tasting water. Tim spotted someone unloading a cart and waited for just the right moment and grabbed the bag and drink then ducked under an empty cart for a moment or two before heading back to their original hiding place. Charlie also returned a moment or so later sporting two cloaks, a parchment and a quill. He also managed to get his hands on a rather impressive dagger from a sleeping beast. This took great courage and a steady hand, knowing all too well what these beasts were capable of. Fortunately this particular beast seemed to have either passed out or just slept so heavily that he did not notice or even stir at all while Charlie pilfered the dagger. After spending some time eating and enjoying a drink they decided to call it a night and get ready for tomorrow. After all, it would be daylight soon and they would be stuck under this porch again for the entire day with nothing to do.

Tim woke first to the sound of cart after cart being drawn by what looked like rather large oxen. What was being pulled behind the beasts of burden were what resembled war wagons. When the caravan stopped hundreds of the beasts exited and immediately were lined up in military-style formations. Tim knew right away this was not a good thing at all and nudged Charlie to wake. However, there was no need—he was already waking and looking on with a rather distraught look. Neither Charlie nor Tim needed to speak about this. They were both feeling reasonably sure that these beasts were in fact looking for the both of them.

"Charlie, we can't wait any longer; we need to get out of here. Tonight's the night we leave. We will have to ration our remaining supplies and head out towards where I suspect the city will be located."

"I agree, we need to get out of here as fast as possible. It looks like they are going to tear this place apart looking for us and I am sure it will not take them forever to figure out that we are in fact here and then we will end up right where we do not want to be. Let's bury everything that we are not going to take with us so we do not leave any traces that we were here. We can make it as hard as possible for them to find us."

Charlie and Tim remained silent throughout the day, watching the beasts rip the town apart piece by piece. More than once they heard the storage room right above their heads being ransacked. There was this certain beast directing the entire operation and he did not look all too friendly whatsoever. This beast was missing his left hand, had massive scars all over his face and his hair shaved down to one long ponytail right in the middle of its head.

"That's one scary-looking thing, that's for sure," said Tim.

"Hopefully we will not get all up close and personal with that thing and our exit goes undetected tonight. We have enough food and drink to last for three days so we should be all set. That should be enough to get us back to where we started, assuming of course that we head in the right direction," said Charlie.

That very night Charlie and Tim cautiously crawled out from their hiding place under the storage building. Less than one hundred yards away they could both see thick underbrush and trees. This would make excellent cover for their escape. The streets were silent and the war wagons seemed to be packed up for the night. There were very few guards within sight so Charlie and Tim crawled towards the nearest brushy area. Just then not one hundred feet from them the big ugly walked out of the woods with two of his cronies right behind him. They did not look either way and just headed straight for the closest battlewagon. They mumbled a few incoherent words and two uglies went towards the center of the town and the big ugly continued his walk to what must be his sleeping quarters. Charlie and Tim lay motionless and completely quiet for a few more moments and within moments had reached the safety of the forest.

"That was just way, way too close for comfort," said Charlie.

"Yeah, no kidding, all they needed to do was just glance our way and our luck would have run out," said Tim. "I cannot believe they did not see us. I wonder if there is more to this than we are aware of. It is quite possible they have either night-vision issues or their peripheral vision is very sub par."

"Again, Tim, nothing you say amazes me. You never miss a trick, no matter how small."

"Details, Charlie, always the details," said Tim.

They spent the rest of the night moving slowly and ever so quietly through the brush until they reached what they figured was a good enough spot to stop and rest till first light.

Charlie and Tim both experienced rather restless sleeps. There were far too many strange sounds heard often far too close for either of their likings. More than once Charlie pulled the dagger from its sheath and prepared for battle only to have whatever was stalking about wander off. When first light finally did come they were able to get a good look at their new surroundings and were not so pleased to at all after this.

They were in the middle of a very dense forest. This canopy was so overgrown they thought it still might be night. However after Tim did a quick calculation he was sure it was morning, although he was not sure of the exact hour. These trees that were surrounding them seemed to be ancient. The trunks were at least forty feet in diameter and they seemed to have grown to such heights that they would rival skyscrapers in downtown Boston. Tim took some quick notes while Charlie explored the general area of their makeshift camp.

"Tim, I have no idea which way to go. This place is so overgrown it's hard to get a bearing. And besides that, these trees are giving me the creepy crawlies. They seem to be watching us. Not with eyes or anything like that, but like they are watching us somehow."

"I will keep a sharp eye out and possibly an ear too and maybe one of these trees will let me know which way to go," said a laughing Tim. "Of course I will ask it politely."

"Funny, Tim, really funny. Now why don't you put that brain of yours to good use and get us the heck out of here."

"Well, give me a minute and I am sure I will figure this all out."

"It's obvious that we cannot use the sky for any sort of navigation but we do know in general which way we came from if we simply retrace our steps. So let's take a quick look for our tracks and then keep heading north. Charlie, take a look over by that tree and point in the general direction from which we came and I will plot our new course."

Charlie searched and searched but was unable to find a single track. It was as if the forest had swept all trace of them away overnight. Tim, looking a bit agitated, joined in the search but even he realized that this was a fruitless action at this point.

"Charlie, I think you just might be on to something."

"What's that?"

"That this forest is really watching us somehow or someway, and the magic question is why? At first I thought you were crazy but I think you are right. This new twist leaves me one option and the best I can do is make an educated guess and hope for the best."

"See, I told you it wasn't my imagination after all, and did you just say guess? It's nice to see that you are still human."

"And what does that mean?"

"Well, I was not sure you even knew what the word 'guess' meant, never mind that you would actually make one," said Charlie.

Hour after hour they wandered and seemed to make no headway whatsoever. They checked their bearings and Tim figured that they were back exactly where they had started from within twenty feet, give or take. "Well, Charlie, this is quite the little predicament we are in, that's for sure. Maybe it's time we ask one of these trees to help us out. After all, you were pretty sure they are watching us, right?" asked Tim.

"Yeah, but I don't know tree language and I don't believe you do either. Right but we need to try something."

Hours passed and they were still stuck in the same clearing they had started in earlier in the morning. Tim was staring off into the wilderness and Charlie was poking around with a stick he had found. Out of the corner of his eye he was sure he had seen something move. He gestured to Tim to be quiet and still while he looked again. A moment or so passed and there it was again. A small person was moving about the underbrush poking and prodding and not paying any attention to Charlie or Tim. Charlie again gestured for Tim to get up and circle slowly to the left and Charlie headed to the right. They used the classic squeeze play but when they got to the point where the little person should be there was nothing there. Again Charlie and Tim tried this and still the same thing happened. Over and over this game played out with the same results.

"Tim, obviously we are going about this the wrong way. Let's head back to the clearing and just be patient and wait."

"Wait for what, our supplies to run out?" asked Tim.

"No, we are doing something wrong and I don't know what it is. Obviously chasing that person is not the right way so let's wait and see. We can afford a few more hours; after all, we are not getting anywhere anyway."

"Okay, two more hours then we try and walk out again."

Time slowly ticked by and the little person could be seen wandering about and seemingly not paying a bit of attention to either Tim or Charlie. Tim was growing frustrated but Charlie was just leaning against a tree and pretending to ignore the little person. Tim finally followed suit and this seemed to interest the little fellow. Slowly he started to wander closer and closer to the makeshift camp. Cautiously the little person finally made his way to the edge of the clearing. Still not saying a word he moved slowly within five feet or so of Charlie. Charlie continued to ignore the little fellow and just kept staring in the other direction. Finally the little person was within mere inches of Charlie when he decided it was time for action.

"Well, hello there," said Charlie. "This is a wonderful forest you have here."

"Why thank you," said the little person.

"Do you mind sitting for a bit and chatting with Tim and myself?"

"Of course not, now that you two stopped trampling my forest and chasing me," said the little person.

"Sorry to have offended you and the forest, but we are not from these parts. We are lost and trying to make our way back to the city where we journeyed to a few days earlier. You know the one, all white marble, Council of Elders and Mr. Grabblemore?" asked Charlie.

"Well, of course I do. Phinneus is a wonderful person and he has wandered these woods in the past. Is he a friend of yours?"

"He sure is and I am sure he would be most delighted to meet with us again. I am sorry for being so rude but I have not asked your name yet. I am Charlie and this is Tim."

"Well, Mr. Charlie and Mr. Tim, my name is Ambrose of the Wood. I watch and protect this forest and have since its creation. Long before man and beast there was this forest and long after they are gone it will still survive with me watching over it."

"Ambrose, we are very happy to meet you and this great and wondrous forest. It is indeed very impressive. I have never seen its equal here or in what you would call the Regular World," said Charlie.

"The Regular World, surely you are mistaken. There has not been a traveler from those parts for many a century," said Ambrose.

"Ambrose of the Wood, I am not mistaken and that is one of the reasons we need to get back to the city and in touch with Mr. Grabblemore ASAP," said Charlie.

"What?"

"Sorry, as soon as possible," said Charlie.

"Charlie and Tim of the Regular World, I will be of as much assistance as possible. I can see you to the edge of the wood and point you in the right direction from there. However, before you set off on your journey I suspect some supplies will be helpful, so we can take care of that back at my homestead."

"Excellent, and thanks, Ambrose," said Tim.

An hour or so passed and the end was finally in sight. Just through the brush ahead a stream could be heard and smoke was billowing from an unknown source. Ambrose, Charlie and Tim quickened their pace and arrived at the clearing in just a few moments' time. Here Charlie and Tim were exposed to a most wonderful sight. Built out of what seemed the wood itself stood a cabin, but not just an ordinary cabin. This cabin seemed to grow out of the very floor of the forest. The trees and brush shaped themselves into what looked like a rather large half balloon. There were what looked like windows and doors. The windows seemed to be made out of the water itself and the vines and brush had intertwined to shape both entrance and door. The chimney was made out of wood and this seemed amazing to both Charlie and Tim. The stream flowed right through the heart of the dwelling but yet there was no feeling of wetness upon entering. All the furniture and accessories were made from wood. Charlie and Tim sat down at a round table and Ambrose prepared a quick meal.

"Ambrose, we cannot thank you enough. After we escaped from a town not too far from here and wandered into your forest we never expected to get out or have a chance for that matter to reach Mr. Grabblemore," said Charlie.

"So you are the escapees that the overseer is searching for then. That explains a lot and is most interesting indeed. The overseer has made every attempt to keep this secret of course," said Alston.

"He does not want Mr. Grabblemore to know we are here so he locked us away in this place called the pit of Dulgeon along with my grandfather," said Charlie. "Thanks to Ambrose, whom we just met at Dulgeon we were able to escape but my grandfather is still back there."

"Did you say Alston? Please be sure, as this is very important."

"Yeah, it was Alston. I am sure of it, right, Tim?"

"Yes, that's definitely what he said his name was. We did not get to thank him since we were in quite a rush to get out of there."

"I was sure he had been killed. This is most wondrous news. And you said Alston and your grandfather are still at Dulgeon?"

"Yeah, they couldn't get away so they started a diversion so we could get out and get help," said Charlie.

"Well, my boys, help you have found and help will be on the way."

"How do you know Alston?" asked Tim.

"He is my bother after all," said Ambrose, "and this is most happy news, yes, yes, happy indeed." The trees seemed to sway right and left and the grass seemed more springy than usual. "As you may have guessed he is also of the forest as am I. We are what you might call Wood Spirits or something of that sort. We are of the wood. What happens here affects us as if it actually happens to us. When the forest is sick so are we and vice versa. All the forest speaks to me from the largest great wood to the smallest hultra.

"Now that we have heard the joyous new of my dearest brother Alston, I think it is time we get both of you on your way. Your journey will be at least a three-day walk from here but there are other ways to travel," said Ambrose.

"Other ways?" asked Charlie.

"Yes, my friend, and I will show you," said Ambrose.

Ambrose seemed to suddenly be taller than just a moment ago. He tilted his head back and made a loud noise that made both Tim and Charlie cover their ears. He kept this up for a minute or two until there was some noticeable rustling from the forest. Something rather large was moving through the forest with great agility. Neither Charlie nor Tim could make out what it was but they were sure that Ambrose had called it for some purpose. Closer and closer the sound grew until suddenly breaking though the brush came the strangest-looking creature either of them had ever seen.

"This, friend, is a grizzantalor. Now do not be afraid of this mighty animal. They are very intelligent and noble beasts. They are able to carry great weights for long distances at a rather quick pace. They have been friends of the Wood Spirits for many generations. They will carry us to the edge of Donlorg Forest and save you a day of walking," said Ambrose

The grizzantalor reminded Charlie of a grizzly bear that had the muscular legs of a gazelle. It had fur like a bear; the head of a large bear and the stripes resembled the hind area of the gazelle. Although the legs resembled a gazelle they were thick and muscular like a bear's but much longer. This creature seemed strong yet graceful, able to jump over downed trees and gracefully trot at a steady pace.

In a matter of moments Charlie, Tim and Ambrose were all packed up and sitting on the back of the Ggrizzantalor. The seat was strapped to the animal's back so the rider could see just over its head.

Swiftly they were off covering large chunks of ground effortlessly. Tim estimated that they were going approximately twenty-five miles an hour on average. Of course Charlie did his usual headshake and just enjoyed the ride. Soon they had reached the edge of the forest and the great beast came to a halt. Charlie, Tim and Ambrose dismounted and unloaded the supplies.

"My friends, this is where we say our goodbyes. You will head north for the next day and you will reach the outskirts of the Great City. I would like to thank you both for the wondrous news of my brother Alston," said Ambrose.

"Thanks for all your help, Ambrose, we could never have gotten this far without you," said Charlie.

"There is no need for thanks, my friends, as anyone who is friends with Phinneus is surely a friend of mine and always welcome in the Donlorg Forest. Good luck with your continued journey, but beware; there are still many perils that you will likely have to face along the way. Let us all hope that you avoid them all," said Ambrose. "Oh, one more thing, when you do arrive at the outskirts of the city look for the red-roofed house and ask for Groulder. Tell him I sent you and he just may be able to help you out a bit. Hand him this and he will know it's from me."

"If we can ever help you out someday do not hesitate to ask," said Tim.

"Thank you, my friends. Maybe someday I will take you up on that," said Ambrose. "Oh, boys, I almost forgot, this parchment might just come in handy when you enter the tunnels below the city. If you get to the right location you will know what to do." Ambrose smiled, turned towards the forest was gone before either Tim or Charlie had a moment to open the parchment.

After spending a moment or two reviewing the parchment, neither Charlie nor Tim had any idea what this parchment was meant for but decided it must be important, so Tim safely put it into his backpack for later reference, wondering what new mysteries and challenges awaited them in the next part of their journey here in Wizard World.

Chapter 8

The Red Roof and Stench-Ridden Places

Charlie and Tim bade farewell to their new friend Ambrose and headed north towards the Great City. The next day was rather boring, walking and more walking with the occasional Grizzantalor spotting but nothing else.

They followed Ambrose's instructions and reached a well-worn path that closely resembled the description that he had given them. If his directions were correct this path should then lead them to the village and hopefully a meeting with Groulder.

"From what Ambrose said yesterday we are to follow this road for the next mile or so and look for the tree that reaches the sky and forks like a snake's tongue and follow its shadow until we reach the edge of the Truggla River. We are supposed to follow the river's edge for two thousand steps and then veer back towards the main road, at which time we should be able to see a house with a red roof just on the other side of the road. Then we are to try and make contact with Groulder and see if he can help us get back to the Great City," said Tim.

"Sounds easy enough so let's get to it," said Charlie. "I'm sure this Groulder guy will be just pleased to see us and will just drop everything and gladly help us in any way possible on our most urgent journey to the Great City. I bet Groulder is just sitting at home wondering when he will be able to turn his life upside down and help two kids he doesn't know. It's probably a common and everyday occurrence in these parts."

"Charlie, Ambrose has gotten us this far and we really don't have any other options at the moment so I say we go for it and play it by ear."

"Tim, I have to tell you something and it's that you are definitely changing—if it's for the better I'm not sure, but changing without a doubt. I thought I would never hear the day when you would just go for it."

Tim thought about Charlie's statement for a moment, and then grinned. "Yeah, well, crazy times call for crazy measures."

"Again something I would never expect to hear from you, but you are right, these sure are crazy times."

"Hey, Charlie, have you given any thought to what caused Crystal to go Benedict Arnold on us like that?"

"Yeah, I have—she is obviously shallow and an inconsiderate jerk just like her new friends."

"Charlie, she didn't seem like that to me but I guess you could be right."

"Actions speak louder than words and her actions were definitely loud and clear, that's for sure."

"I see your point, Charlie."

"Enough about Crystal already, let's get this over with."

After leaving the river's edge and heading to the edge of the road remaining concealed in the brush, Charlie and Tim spotted the first Shifter they had seen since they escaped the Pit of Dulgeon a few days earlier.

"Look at that—just two of them walking down the lane, cloaks all covering their heads to avoid the sun as casual as you or I while at Golvert's," said Tim.

"As casual as can be with Ron and his pack around anyway," said Charlie.

"It looks like we need to wait till at least dusk before we decide to head over to the red-roof house down the lane and try to contact Groulder," said Tim.

"Okay then, let's hang by the river for a bit and dig into some of our supplies. I'm starving. This Wizard World will definitely get you into shape in no time," said a ravenous Charlie.

"Yeah, I agree," said Tim. "I feel like I lost ten pounds since we arrived here. Not that it's a bad thing but ten nonetheless."

"Agreed," said Charlie.

Hours passed and dust was soon turning into darkness. The beautiful landscape had now taken on its usual eerie feeling it does around this time of night. The trees started to resemble their typical creepiness and every noise sounded like that spine-chilling something that goes bump in the night. Charlie and Tim grew weary of the shadows and hastily packed up their remaining supplies and quietly headed back towards the main road. Carefully they again surveyed the landscape looking for anything out of the norm. Everything seemed well enough for an attempt at the red-roof house just down the lane.

"Timmy, let's not disappoint and head out for Grouldy's house."

"Yeah, let's get a move on. You know how dark it gets around here. Right after dusk this place will turn pitch black and if we are not hidden away safely somewhere we will definitely regret it."

Initially Charlie and Tim stayed close to the edge of the road but after a moment or two they both realized that this town was strangely quiet and unnaturally dark for what looked like a bustling village. They were now walking by what looked like two small houses. Each house had a corral attached to it. In the darkest recesses of the pens they could just make out what might have been a few kattergraff wandering about. Besides this and the occasional what looked like large chickens with the biggest legs and future drumsticks wandering about, all was quiet. Tim thought this strange that all the shutters were shut on all the houses and no activity could be picked up anywhere.

"Charlie, I think we need to pick up the pace a little. There is definitely something not right here."

"It's kind of creepy if you ask me, dead quiet except for the occasional giant chicken or kattergraff," said Charlie

"Yeah, and why are all the lights out and the shutters closed?" asked a now concerned Tim.

Charlie and Tim headed towards the nearest dwelling and cautiously rounded the corner towards the barn. Walking by the corral Tim noticed a fairly large herd of corralled kattergraff huddled together as if scared by some unseen evil. Off in the background Charlie and Tim thought they could hear thunder, but listening more intently led them to a different conclusion. It was definitely off in the distance but the sound was growing clearer by the moment. The sound was almost rhythmic, as if a drummer was playing a constant beat. There was no doubt that it was growing rather obvious why the town was all but closed. Something was approaching and the people didn't want any part of it. They both focused and intently listened to the ever-approaching rumble. It became more and more obvious that the approaching sound was not a storm but an army. An army of obvious large proportion judging by the stomping feet and the loud clanking carts that moved in harmony. This was an army of whom or what Tim and Charlie had no idea, nor did they want to be out and about in the open when it arrived.

The marching grew louder and louder and became almost deafening. Charlie and Tim covered their ears and had to yell to communicate. They both realized that standing in the street or by this corral was not a good idea at all. Unfortunately they were now in an uncomfortable spot: try to make it back to the woods for cover and risk being seen by who or what was coming, or try and make it to the red-roofed house a few blocks away.

"Charlie, now or never, what do we do? If we wait any longer we are going to be trampled by whatever is coming this way."

"Let's head for the house. I don't think we can make it back to the woods at this point. We'll definitely be spotted and I'm not so sure we'll be all that pleased by what is doing the spotting," said Charlie.

"I can't argue with that," said Tim.

Moving swiftly and stealthily Charlie and Tim moved towards their destination, not knowing whether they would find salvation or rejection.

"There is no more time," said Tim.

"Tim, follow me," yelled Charlie as he ran for the back of the nearest house with Tim hot on his heels. They headed for the corral, jumped over the fence and tried their best to mix in with the kattergraff herd.

Tim more fell over the fence rail than climbed it, almost falling face first into the muddy-looking corral. "I guess it's better than just standing here and waiting to get trampled by what is definitely a really big army, possibly a goblin army!"

"Yeah, I thought you would pick up on that but I didn't want to freak you out. This is definitely not the best of plans but then again it's better than nothing," Charlie said.

"Hopefully we get out of this one and meet up with this Groulder," said Tim.

"I hope we do too, but this is definitely not one of my best ideas. Maybe we'll get a bit lucky and not end up snacks on a stick or back in Dulgeon," said Charlie.

"Look on the bright side, at least we could check up on Grandpa and Alston," said Tim.

"Being stuck in a cell wouldn't be too productive in assisting them in their escape," said Charlie.

The stomping grew so loud it sounded like the freeway during rush hour in downtown Boston. Charlie and Tim could not tell exactly what was going on but they were sure there were war wagons and the army looked like it was going on for blocks. There seemed to be no end to them. The goblins were being led by a lead goblin riding some strange creature. Neither Charlie nor Tim could make out enough details to decide what it really was. Behind them heading out of the barn could be seen the silhouette of a man that must have stood at least eight feet tall. Charlie and Tim were now not only facing a goblin army marching thirty or so feet in front of them but a giant walking mere feet behind them. Charlie and Tim froze in the hiding place beneath the kattergraff herd. They were standing knee deep in some rather unpleasant substances mixed with some heavy mud. The smell was unbearable but the alternative was much worse. Neither expected this hiding place to keep them undetected for long. Charlie almost out of habit reached for his newfound dagger; this would not be much of a deterrent to an army or the large man coming straight at them but it was all they had. Finally the large man who closed the twenty or so feet between them in a mere three or so steps was close enough to make out and Charlie and Tim were amazed at what was now standing right in front of them

"Whoa! Charlie, that has to be there biggest person I have ever seen," said Tim. "I bet he is the biggest person alive!"

"Great, now we can get killed by a giant or by the goblins," said Charlie.

"There will be no need for such worries at the moment, little ones," said the bellowing giant. "I assure you that you are quite safe right where you are. The goblins will not come back here and they will keep on marching right up that street. Give it a few more minutes and they will have gone. Then you can tell me what the both of you are doing in my homestead and harassing my herd of kattergraff. I am hopeful you will come up with a good reason for this uninvited intrusion into my yard or I will surely drag you both right out into that street to meet with the friendly fellows merrily marching by. I would wager a guess that they would spare a moment or two from their current malicious errand to have some fun with the both of you. The goblin army has moved on down the street and it's now safe to come out, so please do. One more thing—be very careful not to spook the herd any more than you two already have."

Charlie and Tim were now in a most precarious position caught hiding under the bellies of the kattergraff to avoid the goblin army and being discovered by a giant of a man. This giant was simply massive to say the least. It was obvious there was not an ounce of fat on him whatsoever. He looked like he had been carved from a rock. His shoulders were broader then the grizzantalor and his neck was just as thick. His legs were the size of both Charlie and Tim put together and the girth of his chest must have been the roundness of at least four large men. His hands looked like they could hold both Charlie and Tim's heads at once. He had bright red hair and a beard to match. His bright blue eyes sparkled like the river water rushing over the rocks. He was most impressive and intimidating to say the very least. When he spoke his voice bellowed like it was coming through a megaphone.

Charlie put on his most pathetic puppy-dog face he could muster. "We are very sorry, sir. We didn't mean to cause you any trouble. We were just trying to hide from the goblins when we accidentally stumbled into your corral looking for a good hiding place."

"Yeah, we sure are sorry. We were just looking for someone named Groulder who lives in the house with the red roof," said Charlie.

"Thank you for the most gracious apology, but there is something else that is more pressing at the moment and that is why are you looking for Groulder?" asked the giant.

"Ambrose told us to come here to the red-roofed house and look for Groulder, so here we are," said Tim.

"Oh, did he now? And what proof do you have that either of you even know Ambrose for that matter?" asked the giant.

"He gave us this." Charlie pulled a small wrapped object about the size of a baseball from his pocket.

"Ah, I see. Well then, I can assist you from this point on. I am the one you seek, Groulder. Some call me the man of the mountain because of my great size but I just prefer Groulder. What should I call you two little gentlemen?"

"I am Charlie and this is Tim. Ambrose said you might be able to help us gain access to the ancient tunnels that run under the Great City."

"That is a dangerous journey that you wish me to take the both of you on and I might consider it, but first I need a good reason to do so. There must be a dire cause for you two to want to enter the Great City undetected and I would love to hear why.

"However, first now we shall go and enjoy a bite to eat and go over the reasons my assistance is needed. Ambrose has provided you with a very impressive token to present to me so it must be a very serious circumstance or he would not have taken the chance to send the both of you here with it, but nonetheless I need to hear the reason just the same," said Groulder.

After exiting the corral Charlie and Tim spent the next half hour cleaning off as much of the muck as possible. The stuff was now caked into their hair, ears, eyes and other personal unmentionable places. Charlie pointed out to Tim that they actually smelled worse than the alley with the rotten fish back in Boston.

Finally they were heading into the small home of Groulder. The front door was made from one solid piece of wood with a very plain handle. It must have weighed a ton, Charlie was guessing. The wrought-iron black hinges were at least four feet long and hammered in with nails that had heads the size of a dinner plate. Once walking in there were two rooms—the main room, which consisted of the living area, kitchen and sleeping area; and another room that was used as a lavatory and storage. The place had high open-beamed ceilings and the roof was made out of what looked like red clay tiles. The floor was wood or stone that had been worn smooth after years of heavy walking. There were no cabinets, just shelves with many handmade containers filled with strange-looking food jars and additives. There was a large fireplace in the corner that was blazing with an old cast-iron cauldron gently smoking and occasionally bubbling since it had reached a boiling point. Whatever was cooking smelled wonderful to both Charlie and Tim; their last hot meal seemed like weeks ago although it was more like two days. Groulder led them into what was the kitchen area and they took seats surrounding a table made the same as the front door, one solid piece of wood. Charlie and Tim were unable to reach the floor with their feet since the chairs were built for a giant. Groulder placed bowls in front of both Charlie and Tim and he then headed over to the fireplace to fetch the cauldron. Groulder placed the cauldron right in the center of the table and grabbed a rather large ladle hanging from the rafters and proceeded to fill both Charlie and Tim's bowls right to the top.

"Eat, my young friends; this will energize and warm you both. This is my secret recipe made from the herb of Frotrolon found only deep in the forest to the west. This herb when mixed with the proper amount of Gratfeltin and hot water produces a porridge substance that not only tastes great but also is simply wonderful for the weak and weary. Dig in, boys, and then we can get down to business," said Groulder.

The tasty meal left both Charlie and Tim feeling re-energized and fresh. This was a wonderful meal and Tim was wondering if they could take some with them on their journey. Groulder gladly offered to fix them up with two containers that should last them till they reach the Great City. Tim asked for the specific recipe but was denied with a smile by Groulder.

"This, young man, is an ancient Patagonian recipe that only we are able to recreate. Even if you were to get the exact recipe it would never work for you. So that is the reason, my friend, that I will not bother wasting either of our precious time going into these details and specifics."

Tim reluctantly let it go and decided this was not a battle he could win.

Charlie and Tim spent the next hour or so reliving their entire adventure in every detail, leaving Groulder speechless. He was hanging on every word and rather anxious when there were stops in the story.

Groulder looked on wondering how these two boys were still alive, but here they were asking for his help. "My little friends, I'm most intrigued by this tale, yes indeed. It's most unfortunate that your grandfather and Alston are missing. Hopefully I'll be able to assist the both of you in getting back to the Great City and in contact with Phinneus Grabblemore. You are both welcome to sleep here tonight in the safety of these walls and I will give you my answer first thing tomorrow. There is no need to worry for your safety; I can assure you that no harm will come to either of you while you are in the walls of this dwelling."

"Okay, Groulder, we accept your offer to stay the night and look forward to your answer in the morning. We are definitely beat and haven't had a good night's sleep since we arrived back in Wizard World. I for one am personally looking forward to waking after not having slept on the rocky ground for a night so I can hopefully get this kink out of my back," said Charlie.

"Very well then, I will roll out these two fur beds and I'm sure you'll have a most wonderful sleep. Now I must go and prepare the kattergraff herd for their evening slumber and make sure the homestead is secure for the night," said Groulder.

Charlie and Tim were sleeping within minutes. Fatigue had finally caught up with them. Neither stood guard and both slept with reckless abandon, not worrying about their safety for a moment. After all, they were in the house of Groulder the Patagonian giant. Morning came and Charlie was awakened by the front door opening and closing rather loudly. There stood Groulder smiling and covered in sweat. Charlie guessed this was from his morning work with the herd of kattergraff he had in the corral. Tim was just stirring and still half asleep and by the expression on his face savoring the most relaxing and comfortable bed he could remember.

Groulder walked in and took a seat at the dining table. "Children, it's obvious that your sleep was most pleasing. I would like to point out before we get down to business that it is probably a good idea to keep the shutters closed. After all, you never know who might just wander by and spot the both of you and report it to some unscrupulous individual. So please gather round the table for another round of porridge and we can discuss why I should help the both of you or not."

"Groulder, you have heard our story and how desperate we are to get help for Grandpa Watson and Alston," said Tim. "We also need to stress to you that we really don't have many friends or options. Ambrose helped us out because of the information we were able to give him about his missing brother and now we are here in front of you with whatever Ambrose asked us to present to you."

"Yeah, Groulder, we need some help. I know it could be dangerous but if you don't help us we will just have to go it alone. My grandpa and Alston risked their lives so Tim and I could escape and we are not going to leave them trapped in that god-awful place the Pit of Dulgeon," said Charlie with a rather heated and passionate tone to his voice.

Tim was sure that Charlie's speech would have convinced him to go on this crazy journey and he is not an easy sell for too many things.

"Little Charlie, it is quite evident that you feel very strongly about helping your grandfather and Alston. What impresses me most is the fact that you only met Alston just once and you are concerned for him and his well-being. That shows great character to say the least. And, Tim, it is quite obvious that you are very dependable and trustworthy or I'm sure Charlie would not have brought you along in the first place," said Groulder

"To be honest he's a lot more than that to me," said Charlie.

"So after thinking on this last night and talking in more detail with the both of you today I have decided to assist you with this most urgent journey back to the Great City. We shall pack during the day today and start our journey later tonight," said Groulder.

Charlie and Tim smiled and thanked Groulder rather enthusiastically patting him on his back and trying to teach him the high five, which is a bit difficult for a Patagonian giant over seven feet tall.

After spending the early part of the day packing there was nothing much left to do for either Charlie or Tim but some idle small talk and the occasional catnap.

"Resting is not such a bad idea, my little friends, since our journey will be both difficult and taxing," said Groulder.

"How far away is the Great City?" asked Charlie.

"Little friend, it is two days by the way of the grizzantalor or maybe five walking with your little legs," said Groulder.

"So three days, give or take; that's not too bad," said Charlie.

"It does not sound too bad but I assure you that most of your previous journey was the easy part," said Groulder.

"Why do you say that?" asked Tim.

"We need to cross a most dangerous land called the Swamp of Tomorrow," said Groulder.

"Swamp of Tomorrow, that doesn't sound all that bad," Tim said.

"If you understood what we were going to face while we are there you would not have such an opinion," said Groulder. "The Swamp of Tomorrow is a place filled with magic and mystery. Here you will be tantalized with the very things that you either want most or dread most. Many men and beasts alike are never seen again after they enter the Swamp of Tomorrow. I recommend great caution and strong will while we are in that ancient evil magical place. Now rest and be merry because tonight our journey begins."

Groulder noticed that the light was fading and dusk would soon be turning to darkness, so he instructed Charlie and Tim to gather their gear and to mentally prepare for the next step in their journey.

"We will walk through most of the night continuing north. By morning we should reach the edge of the Swamp of Tomorrow where the test of our mental strength will begin," said Groulder.

"Hey, Groulder, what is that thing you are carrying?" asked Tim.

"Tim, this a lightner. Many villagers from this area use these devices when moving about at night to light the way," said Groulder.

"What's in it?" asked Charlie.

"These little creatures are called lighteners and have been around for as long as I can remember. The little beings do not mind being caught as long as they are treated well and let go in a day or so. They always return as long as you follow those simple instructions. So when and if we exit the swamp I will thank them for their assistance and release them so I can again call on them when needed," said Groulder.

After four or so hours of walking Charlie was sure that someone or something was following them off to the left. He nonchalantly tugged at Tim's shirt and casually pointed this out. He nodded for Tim to keep it quiet for the moment. Without notice Groulder stated he was aware they were being followed and was trying to judge the numbers of the uninvited guests. He figured there were about six goblins judging by the noise and movement he has been hearing for the past hour or so. Both boys were taken aback by this and wondered how many other hidden skills Groulder possessed.

"My young friends, as you already know we are no longer alone and unfortunately must prepare for battle. I am relatively sure we will be attacked within the next few moments. Please stay close to me and try to avoid obstructing my movements as much as possible. I should without much difficulty be able to defeat these goblins. When we reach the coming clearing just a bit in front of us I will stop and casually set down my gear and the both of you should do the same. Charlie, keep your dagger close at hand, and Tim, please hold on to this staff," said Groulder.

The attack came from above, left and right. Two goblins jumped almost on top of the group and just as swiftly one came from the front and one from the rear. Off in the distance the silhouette of at least two more could be seen lurking and waiting. The goblin running straight for the group swung a rather ugly-looking club sporting rusty six-inch-long spikes right at Groulder's head. Without much effort Groulder grabbed the club with one hand and the creature with the other and threw the thing out of sight. The goblin careened off at least three trees before coming to a stop in the branches of what looked like a pine tree. Surprisingly aware of the goblin coming up behind him and aware of the club about to split his head with a nasty stroke to the back of his skull, Groulder ducked, spun and grabbed the second creature right by the neck and rather unceremoniously threw this goblin out of sight in the same general direction as the first one. Branches could be heard breaking along with most likely bones when the creature made a sudden thudding stop in the brush. There was no time to enjoy their early success as Charlie was now squaring off with one goblin and Tim the other. Tim was visibly terrified but held his ground and his staff at the ready. The goblin made a few lunges and rather nasty hissing sounds at him but he managed to keep it at bay with occasional pokes and jabs with his staff. Charlie was tackled to the ground and the goblin was on top of him. He was much larger and stronger then Charlie and was gaining the upper hand. Tim, noticing this out of the corner of his eye, swung the staff with all his might, cracking the goblin right upside his head. The beast rolled a few times before coming to a stop. There was an obviously heavy flow of blood now running down the side of its face. Charlie noticed that the color was more black or brown and not normal looking to him. The goblin hissed and spat then rather gingerly lumbered off into the forest. The last goblin had drawn his dagger and was just about to plunge it into Tim's back when Groulder snatched it by the back of its neck and again proceeded to effortlessly throw the foul thing a good twenty or so feet from the group. The goblin could be heard crashing through trees and hitting the ground with a rather large thud. The two goblins that had not joined in the attack could be seen heading over to their fallen comrades and assisted them in making a hasty retreat deeper into the woods.

Charlie was still on the ground lying on his back and staring at Tim. Tim was shaking and still gripping his staff and ready for more action. He was sweating and still trembling from the battle just a few moments ago. Charlie had a newfound respect for his friend. Tim was definitely changing and in Charlie's eyes for the better. Groulder reached down and snatched Charlie from the ground and lightly placed him in a standing position. Charlie noticed there was not one mark on Groulder even though he was sure he had seen him grab one of the clubs with his right hand. He did not mention this but made a note of it for a later private discussion with Tim.

"Is everyone okay?" asked Groulder. Charlie nodded and Tim, still shaking, smiled rather meekly.

"Judging by what I just witnessed it's quite apparent that the both of you can take care of each other. We should gather up our supplies and continue on with the rest of our journey," said Groulder.

"But what about the goblins, will they return?" asked Tim.

"I don't know for sure, my little friend, but after the beating we laid on them I would suspect we would not be hearing from the likes of them any time soon. They will head back to wherever they came from and lick their wounds for the next few days and we will be long gone by then," said Groulder.

"Do you think they were following us?" asked Charlie.

"Goblins have many spies that lurk all about us. It's quite possible that we were simply spotted by one of them accidentally or we just ran into a patrol by simply being in the wrong place at the wrong time," said Groulder.

Charlie skeptically looked at Tim and neither said a word but both were wondering if there was more to this chance encounter then Groulder's explanation.

"My friends, the important thing is that we are all safe. We shall continue traveling until daybreak and then rest by the edge of the great swamp. We will not enter during nightfall because I fear we would surely fail on our quest. So at daybreak on the second day we will make our way into the Swamp of Tomorrow," said Groulder.

Groulder continued to lead Tim and Charlie deeper and deeper into the forest. While walking Charlie and Tim started to notice a rather foul smell blowing their way and getting stronger with every step. This nasty smell was beginning to get a bit overwhelming to the both of them. Groulder did not seem bothered by this and continued to walk as if not noticing the stench that was growing ever stronger by the moment.

Finally Charlie yelled, "What is that smell!"

"Whatever it is it sure stinks," said Tim.

"That, my little friends, is the smell of the Swamp of Tomorrow. After a bit you will adjust to the stench and not be bothered as much," said Groulder.

"I doubt that but if you say so," said Tim.

"I actually think the dead fish smell back in the alleyway smells like roses compared to this place," said Charlie.

"I didn't think anything could smell worse than that place but I guess I was wrong," said Tim.

They broke through the final thickets of the forest and arrived at their destination, the Swamp of Tomorrow. The smell was even stronger now that they had left the forest. Strange cries and gurgles could be heard coming from this eerie place. A rather heavy green-tinted mist seemed to entirely engulf the swamp, adding to its eeriness. It was as if the swamp itself was trying to hide its wonders and secrets. Groulder and the boys set up camp and set a nice fire to cook by. After finishing a nice meal of what the boys were now referring to as porridge, Charlie and Tim were lazily lying about while Groulder wandered about the edge of the swamp stopping at random moments and just listening and not saying a word. Slowly the boys nodded off and were relatively surprised to be awoken by Groulder. It seemed like only moments had passed since they last spoke to him but it was obviously the next morning already and very early at that.

"My little friends, our journey begins. Remember to stay strong and focused, as things are not what they always seem to be here," said Groulder.

Within moments of taking their first steps into the swamp it was obvious to both Charlie and Tim that this was not going to be easy or enjoyable. Although the ground was somewhat firm each step caused a sloshing sound and their shoes were waterlogged along with the bottoms of their pant legs. There were small insects buzzing about and occasionally biting, which made Tim dislike this place more and more by the bite of each little pest. Groulder stayed in the lead of course and continued to stop, motion for silence and then continue on without saying a word.

They reached what looked like a clearing but instead they had come to a rather large murky mud hole the size of a small lake. It was hard to tell that there was water below the thick layer of algae, leaves and what looked like dirt. The smell was atrocious to even Groulder. There were large lily pads seen floating about with the biggest frogs that Charlie or Tim had ever seen. Groulder explained that these frogs were called Gantoads and that they projected small darts that numb and can kill if not treated properly. He motioned for silence and pointed off in the distance. Without notice a large creature could just be seen through the mist rising from the murky water and flying away.

The water began to bubble violently and two more of these flying things popped out and took flight following the first one off to the west. Groulder leaned in closely to the boys and requested extreme silence and care. He explained that if these bog dragons discovered them that this could very well be the end of their journey right here and right now. He motioned for them to move quietly back into the small brush and after seeing those creatures this was done without hesitation.

While moving backwards Tim accidentally stepped on a swampspatter plant, releasing a large puff of red dust that engulfed Charlie, himself and Groulder. Groulder took a deep breath to avoid most of it but Charlie and Tim didn't and promptly were under its spell.

"Hurry now, the both of you must listen to me and try and stay focused. That mist that the both of you just inhaled will cause hallucinations. Some are not all that bad but others can be deadly. Focus now please or it will be too late," said Groulder. But it was already too late; Tim was looking at Groulder and all he could see was a goblin the size of a giant. He was backing away from Groulder and was absolutely petrified. Charlie was also doing the same but he was heading slowly into the swamp itself. Tim pulled his staff from his back and started to swing it in any and all directions, causing quite a ruckus. Charlie reached for his dagger, turned and then took off running in the opposite direction, yelling at an unseen enemy. Groulder, not knowing which one to help first, tackled Tim to the ground and hastily bound him to a nearby tree. Tim was terrified and yelling for Charlie but he was long gone. Groulder tried to instruct Tim to drink but he kept closing his mouth, fearing he was about to be poisoned by a giant goblin. After three attempts Groulder finally gave up the nice approach, reached over and pinched Tim's nose closed and waited for his mouth to open. After fighting it for a moment or so Tim finally opened up and Groulder poured a rather generous amount of antidote down his throat. Tim gagged and tried to spit it out but was unable to do so. His eyes, which were just moments ago glazed and hazy, were now finally clearing. Tim's first thought was that his head was pounding and he had no idea where he was. He kept closing his eyes and shaking his head and yelling for Charlie to untie him.

Groulder just smiled and tried to reassure Tim that all would be well in a matter of moments. "My little friend, please have some patience, in just a few more moments all will be clear again except for your headache. That is an unfortunate side effect to the antidote but a small inconvenience to what could happen if the mist was allowed to finish its work."

Minutes had passed by and Charlie was nowhere in sight. He continued to run and scream at his own demon. He thought he could just make out Cadawalader in the mist laughing and taking his grandfather. He was just always out of Charlie's reach no matter how hard he ran. Charlie was running out of control, oblivious to the environment, and accidentally stepped on at least two more swampspatter plants along the way, only amplifying the effects of this most dangerous drug.

"Tim, you must get it together, I fear we do not have much more time if we are to save Charlie. He has taken off chasing his own dream phantom and the longer he runs the worse our chances are of discovering him," said Groulder.

Charlie continued his pursuit of his demon and ran harder and harder, becoming frustrated by not being able to get his grandfather back. He was not paying attention to his surroundings and just continued his chase of Cadwalader farther and farther into the swamp. However, they continued to remain out of his reach and the taunting by Cadwalader sent Charlie into a rage. He ran faster and faster and without noticing he was now standing almost waist deep in a nasty and unfriendly-looking bog. The water's stench here was even worse than it was at the earlier bog. Charlie didn't care and was completely focused on catching the imaginary enemy of his who was now halfway across the bog and moving very fast. This unscheduled change of plans had put Charlie into the most precarious situation of his young life and the strangest part was that he was completely unaware of it. A foul creature burst from the bog. Its size was enormous and its stench-ridden hair and face almost snapped Charlie out of his trance. Right before Charlie's very eyes this creature promptly changed form. No longer was it this ugly thing seemingly growing from the very sludge of the water, but now taking its place was his grandfather, standing right before him and calling him forward. Charlie shook his head and could not believe his eyes. After all, he had just seen his grandfather run across the bog only moments earlier with Cadwalader. Now his grandfather was standing right before him smiling and calling for him. Charlie couldn't straighten this out in his head. He was just so relieved to see his grandfather that he really didn't care at this point in time and decided it was best to go to him. Slowly he waded into the ever-deepening water and heading right towards the Bogblagger and certain death. If Charlie were not stopped he would become one of these very beings trapped here forever, luring innocent creatures and people alike to their deaths. Closer and closer Charlie walked, reaching out to his grandfather, almost about to touch him and finally save him from his fate with the Shifters and Cadwalader. Something buzzed dangerously close by Charlie's right ear, hitting his grandfather square in the face. Groulder had thrown a Gantoad and when they hit anything they release their spiny thorns into the object that they strike. Grandpa stumbled backwards and Charlie reached for him but was yanked from behind with such force that for a moment he fell below the water's surface. When he finally did emerge he could not see his grandfather anymore and started to strain with all his strength to get loose and search the murky water for him. Charlie had no idea what just hit his grandfather but he was sure that he needed his help more now than ever. For all Charlie knew Grandpa could be hurt badly, or worse, drowning. However, Charlie could not break the steel grip that had him about the neck. He struggled with all his might but he realized he could do nothing to help his grandpa. The water surface settled for a moment and Charlie was completely downtrodden at the loss of his grandfather. Charlie stared at the water and it started to bubble and rising from the murky water appeared a grotesque creature instead of Grandpa Watson. The creature was moaning and squirming and making a noise that made Charlie cover his ears. The Bogbladder was now focused directly on Charlie. It was preparing to take him down to the depths to join its legions of the damned. Again, seemingly from nowhere another Gantoad buzzed by Charlie's head, hitting the creature squarely in the face, forcing it to once again disappear into the stench-ridden filthy water from whence it came.

Charlie was still in a hazy dream-like state but he was sure he could hear Tim in what he thought must be a dream. He sounded far away although he was actually standing right behind him and pulling him backwards with all his might. Even though Charlie was a better athlete and much stronger than Tim on this day he would not let that get in the way of him saving his friend. Tim pulled and pulled and would not be denied on this day. His friend's life could still be on the line and there was no way he was going to fail on this day. Charlie finally stopped struggling and was sobbing about the loss of his grandfather and his failure to save him when he realized it was Tim who was pulling him from the murky waters. Once they reached the edge of the bog and Tim released Charlie, he turned to face Tim and was filled with anger, rage and a feeling of total betrayal. Why would Tim stop him from saving his grandfather? This made no sense at all. Tim has always liked Grandpa and they treated him like he was one of their grandchildren. Charlie pulled his dagger from its sheath and headed straight for Tim. Tim backed away and kept talking to Charlie but he did not hear a word. Groulder grabbed Charlie from behind with one hand and with the other poured the antidote down his throat. Charlie gagged and struggled to no avail. Groulder placed him against a tree and tied his hands so he could not move a muscle. Just like earlier with Tim, Charlie's eyes started to clear and his head started to pound.

Tim stepped in front of Charlie and smiled at him. Charlie smiled back and Tim knew everything was going to be all right. Groulder took a moment to untie him and explain the whole ordeal to Charlie.

Charlie was so sure of what he had seen that he was having a hard time believing either of them. They wasted hours going over this and now would have to spend the night here in the swamp. Groulder did not want to be moving about in the darkness and did not like the idea of being here overnight, but decided it was the better of the two evils. Through the night there were strange noises but Groulder stayed on guard the entire time. He did not rest for a moment, fearing what might happen if he did. Charlie dozed off and had miserable dreams of his grandmother yelling at him for not saving Grandpa. Tim also didn't sleep that well, fearing he would without a doubt be attacked once his eyes closed. Morning came and the three weary travelers had a quick bite to eat and headed out into the swamp once more. Soon they would reach the end of this horrible place and hopefully their disturbing memories would end too.

"My little friends, we are very near the end of our journey. Soon we'll be able to see the outskirts of the Great City. However, once we reach the tunnels there my journey will end and yours will continue. I cannot help you any further for it has been many centuries since I have been inside the walls of the Great City," said Groulder.

"Why can't you go with us?" asked Charlie.

"I am unfortunately unable to enter the city because of very ancient magic that was put into place a very, very long time ago that till this very day stops any Patagonian giant from entering. Do not spend a moment preparing to ask me why because that, my little friends, is best left for another day and time. We need to just spend the next hour or so avoiding any more of the swamp's surprises and you will reach your goal, the tunnels of Etrallia," said Groulder.

"What does that mean?" asked Charlie.

"Yeah, what are the tunnels of Etrallia?" asked Tim.

"I am not the one to answer that. Just remember to follow the map that I have drawn for you and eventually all will be explained. I cannot tell you any more for it is not my right or place to do so. Please take these supplies and the evening lightner for use during the rest of your journey. But do not forget to release them after you are through or they will never again allow themselves to be captured by either of you," said Groulder.

"Wait a second, Groulder, is there anything we should be watchful for down in the tunnels? You know, like any creatures, pits of doom and that sort of stuff?" asked Tim.

"My little friend, just follow the map and watch for the occasional Cractors that lurk about," said Groulder.

"Cractors? What's a Cractor and why should we watch out for one?" asked Charlie.

"They are creatures about the size of a dog but to you they would be called a large rat," said Groulder.

"Excellent! A large rat, sewers, swamps of mist and bogdragons, what we need now is a twister and the crazy lady riding the bike to complete the picture," said Charlie.

"No kidding," said Tim.

With that last word Groulder headed back into the swamp. He didn't look back and was soon swallowed up by the haze and mist of the Swamp of Tomorrow and out of sight.

"Tim, it looks like we are on our own again, my friend."

"Yep, we sure are."

"Now the fun begins, exploring these pitch-black tunnels the lead into the bowels of the city with only a sketch on a piece of parchment drawn by a giant that we met two days ago," said Charlie.

"I feel really good now," Tim said.

"Yeah, me too! Well, at least we have the lightner and that piece of parchment Ambrose gave us to help us out," said Charlie.

"Excellent!" Said Tim

"And look on the bright side we can see where we are going in the darkness and get into an excellent game of x's and o's if we get bored," said Charlie.

"Yeah, that'll be really productive," said Tim.

An hour passed and Charlie and Tim were now deep into the bowels of the city. They were trying their best to follow the map that Groulder had drawn out for them but there seemed to be lots of discrepancies. Many of the tunnels were closed or had collapsed over time and possibly Groulder didn't remember correctly.

Charlie looked at Tim knowing that a decision had to be made, and with a little luck it would be the right one. "It looks like we need to make a decision. The map says go straight but obviously that is not an option since the tunnel is completely collapsed. So we can turn back, go left or go right."

"Charlie, let's not be too hasty now, we can spend a few minutes reviewing our options. Looking left we can see that the tunnel splits again, looking right it only goes to the right again and straight for as far as we can see. We can also go back to the beginning like you said by retracing our steps correctly and try to find another way into the city. I for one vote for us going left and then taking the split to the left again hoping we can meet back up with the collapsed tunnel. Now what do you think?"

"Tim, I agree—going back is really not an option and going right just does not seem right to me, so left it is. Let's make a mark on this tunnel wall just in case we don't like what we run into and need to make a hasty retreat. It's probably the safest thing to do other than tie a string and hope it reaches the end."

"Okay then, off we go," said Tim.

The boys headed left and left again only to find another split heading north and one south. They marked the corridor and headed north, figuring it would eventually take them in the right direction. Rounding another corner to the east they ran into a small group of Cractors eating something indescribable. The lightener fortunately caused the creatures to scatter in random directions. It became apparent that the Cractors didn't deal that entirely well with bright lights. Charlie and Tim were both relieved by this discovery since these creatures were foul and nasty looking amongst other things.

"Let's hope there are not any other surprises down here because I have just about reached my limit on surprises, that's for sure," said Tim.

"At least there aren't any bogs or swampspatters or bogblaggers around, said Charlie.

"Okay then, which way now?" asked Tim.

"I say we keep going straight for a while, it looks like it's getting cleaner that way," said Charlie.

"Okay then, let's get a move on," said Tim.

The tunnels seemed to go on forever. Tim was kicking a rock and Charlie kept dragging a stick along the tunnel wall for amusement. At last they finally reached something different, significant and most likely important, a four-way intersection of sorts that had an old broken and battered statue right in the middle. Along the walls there were ancient pictures that had been hastily thrown about obviously in a rush and many other broken trinkets, statues and much-worn books. Tim looked on excited at all the books that were lying about and hastily put down the lightner and started randomly picking through the books. Charlie spent the next few moments looking at the worn and broken statues, pictures and the intriguing statue. *This statue must be here for a reason,* thought Charlie. He was intrigued by it. *At one point in time this person was someone important,* thought Charlie. It was very large and intricately carved. It had worn over many years but the detail was extravagant nonetheless. This statue was of a beautiful woman wearing what looked like a crown. She had a beautiful half broken staff in her right hand and a book in her left. She wore a gown that would have dragged on the ground if she were real. Her features were of perfection. If she were alive Charlie was sure he would not have been able to look away from her for a moment. He analyzed the statue and enjoyed every detail.

"Tim, you have to look at this statue—it's amazing. The detail is without equal. It looks like she could move any moment. Tim?"

"Yeah, yeah, hold on a minute. This book is interesting—I think it's a diary or something like that."

"Take it with you and read it later, right now we need to get our bearings and get out of here. I believe the answer has to be here at this statue somewhere somehow."

Tim reluctantly put the diary back where he found it and took a GPS reading for prosperity. He noticed what Charlie was talking about. This statue was amazing. The beauty was beyond anything he could remember.

He spent a moment studying the face and every curve and worked his way down to the staff and the book. The book—"That's it!! Charlie, look at this book. Take a real close look. Right in the open page there is something written. Give me a second to clean it off so we can try and read it."

After a moment of cleaning the words were legible but did not make sense. Tim was stumped and without an answer. Charlie could think of nothing that made sense.

"It looks like until we figure this out we are going to spend a bit more time hanging with our new friends the Cractors." Tim turned and could see three of them lurking just at the edge of the tunnel's entrance. He picked up the lightner and pointed it in the direction of the Cractors, who hastily scattered.

"Tim, I would bet that eventually they will get used to the lightner and then we will have a problem, so we need to get on with figuring out what those words mean on that book and how to get out of here."

"Let's take an inventory of our situation. We are lost in a tunnel, have the lightner, and we have my brains and your never-quit attitude. Okay, now all we need is a rescue party and cable TV and all will be right with the world."

"Don't forget we also have that piece of parchment that makes no sense too," said Charlie.

"That's it," said Tim. "Give me a minute and I will put it all together."

"My friend, it looks like that's all we have—take a look."

Tim looked up and noticed that most of the tunnels leading to the chamber were rapidly filling with Cractors who were starting to look nastier by the minute.

"Hurry up, Tim I think we are out of time."

"Yeah, I agree, just hold them off a littler longer and I'll have this all worked out." Precious moments passed while Tim tried to figure out the puzzle. Charlie kept waving the lightner this way and that to hold the Cractors at bay. This was working but he was sure it would not work forever.

"Tim, hurry up!! I think we are going to need a new plan."

"Okay, I almost got it. Just give me one more minute."

"I can try but by the looks of it I would say we are out of time."

The Cractors were slowly starting to get into the tunnel now and scurry about hissing and snarling at Charlie, now apparently not being bothered by the lightner or Charlie.

"I got it!! FOLLOW ME NOW!" yelled Tim.

Tim and Charlie were now back to back, Tim waving his staff and Charlie the lightner. Slowly but steadily they worked towards the tunnel that Tim had figured was the correct one. Tense moments passed as they continued to push the Cractors back and away, all the while focusing on the light that could be seen getting brighter and brighter.

"Tim, we are there, finally. I never want to see another rat again for as long as I live. One question though, now that we are almost at the end of this maze of tunnels, what do we do now?"

"Charlie, that's the best part of this—he already knows we are coming."

"What?"

"When the text in that book is read it alerts the person of your choice to your coming. Think of it like an invitation, one part is the statue, the other is this writing. When you put it all together it sends a sort of a private call to the person of your choosing. That's why Ambrose gave this to us. He figured we would find the statue and be able to call Mr. Grabblemore," said Tim. "Now we just wait for Mr. Grabblemore to come and get us and I'm sure he will be really interested in hearing all about our little adventure."

"Yeah, I bet he will. Hopefully he can help me find Grandpa and Alston too," said Charlie.

"I have no doubt that he will," said Tim.

Chapter 9

Lies, Treachery and the Guildfaire

Charlie and Tim were certain that after their ordeals involving the Pit of Dulgeon, Swamp of Tomorrow and fighting with the goblins that simply waiting for Mr. Grabblemore to show up would be the easy part. They had no idea if their message actually reached their intended target but nonetheless they sat by the grate in the ceiling waiting for a response, any response to get out of this dirty, filthy situation they were now in.

Steps could be heard traveling down the hall from above and heading towards the grate. Neither of the boys made any attempt to flee. At this point in time they would just be grateful to get out of these tunnels and into some sunlight. The steps grew closer and closer until finally they stopped right before the grate and a friendly face peered in smiling from ear to ear, Mr. Grabblemore.

"Hello, my young friends. I am glad to see you here back in Wizard World safe and sound. May I ask why you did not use the orb of calling to contact me when you arrived?" asked Grabblemore.

"Mr. Grabblemore, there is a rather complicated answer for that and as soon as you get us out of here we'll gladly fill you in," said Tim.

"Children, the first thing we need to do then is get this grate open and get the both of you up here. Once that little chore is completed I highly suggest we go to a, let us say inconspicuous location. Unfortunately in a city this large and old you never know who or what is listening. I am sure you are familiar with this expression, 'the walls have ears,' and in some cases eyes for that matter," said Mr. Grabblemore.

Moments later Mr. Grabblemore waved his hand over the grate and it lifted effortlessly. He then lowered a rope that seemed to be attached to nothing but air itself and instructed both Charlie and Tim to grab on and hold on tight. The rope seemed to pull itself up and yank both Charlie and Tim right out of the tunnel, causing them to fall upon each other with a rather loud thud.

"Charlie, do you mind getting off me?"

"No, not at all, just give me a second, will ya?"

"Hurry now, we must make haste and get to a secure location known to only a select few here in the city. Once we reach our location we can talk freely and I will conjure up some food for the both of you. There is no time to explain so please follow along as swiftly as possible. At this point in our journey haste is better than stealth so no stopping for sightseeing," said Grabblemore.

Grabblemore led Tim and Charlie up a beautiful sweeping staircase from the basement and through a rather large archway and down another hallway until they reached a very impressively high spiral staircase. This staircase seemed to go up without either Charlie or Tim being able to see the final destination. After climbing stairs for what felt like hours they finally reached the top. They were now standing on a dimly lit landing that had the look of somewhere long ago forgotten. Mr. Grabblemore swatted away some cobwebs and opened an old creaky door that by the looks of it had not been opened for ages. Once entering this room a strange thing seemed to happen to the doors. Along the walls of the watchtower the doors kept randomly changing places every moment or so.

Grabblemore took a deep breath and wiped his brow. "I must say that is a bit more difficult than I remember it being the last time I ventured up here. This is the most secure and private area in the Great City. The design is rather genius if you ask me; you see, these doors rotate randomly, making it nearly impossible for someone to follow."

"Where are we?" asked Charlie.

"My dear boy, we are now in the rotating Clovodor. It was named after its creator, Mr. Theodore Clovodor, who ingeniously invented this room as a last-ditch safety blanket so to speak just in case the city was invaded or attacked and evasive action was called for," said Grabblemore.

"What's so special about these doors rotating around this room?" asked Tim.

"Tim, I am glad you asked. We will enter a door of our choosing and then obviously close the door behind us and the only way we can be followed after we close the door is if we decide to either mark the outside of the door or leave it open. Therefore, anyone trying to follow us will never be able to get to our door unless we assist him or her. So, my friends, we will be quite safe and secure for the time being. I am guessing that the information we are about to exchange called for such security so I took the liberty to lead us directly to this place," said a triumphant-looking Grabblemore.

Charlie and Tim took seats around a small table across from Mr. Grabblemore. They began to fill him in on everything down to the smallest detail that they could remember. Grabblemore kept smiling through the entire two-hour-long marathon of facts and small particulars.

First the two boys took turns explaining to Grabblemore how their key was stolen and why they had not been able to use the orb. Crystal had betrayed them and teamed up with Charlie and Tim's worst enemies, Ron, Sean, Clive, and Beth.

The account Grabblemore heard was very disconcerting and he was visibly upset when told the part of the Shifters and the overseer, Cadwalader. Talking about this was still difficult for Charlie since he was still emotionally shaken by his grandfather's unknown whereabouts. Having to relive it yet again made him feel even worse for some odd reason.

Going over the details of Crystal's betrayal was not that easy for Tim and especially Charlie. He still was noticeably upset with Crystal and did not want to see her ever again. He blamed her for his grandfather's capture and hated her for it.

"If she had not betrayed us this would never have happened and my grandfather would be safe!" said Charlie with a rather menacing face.

"Charlie, alas we cannot undo the past but only go forward into the future. There is probably a very good reason for Crystal's actions and I am sure some day they will all be explained," said Grabblemore.

"Honestly I really don't care to hear her explanations. This was supposed to be my grandfather's greatest adventure and she wrecked it," said Charlie.

"Charlie, it's okay. We will get him back, I promise," said Tim.

"Yes, my dear boy, we certainly will," said Grabblemore.

"And speaking of Ron, Sean, Beth and Clive, I was rather unceremoniously introduced to them just the other day. However, Crystal was not present when Cadwalader did the introductions. It was quite obvious that he had plans for them in the future by the way they were being treated with servants and kattergraff carts to assist in their travels. It is quite simple to figure out why she was not with them since I would have wondered where the two of you were," said Grabblemore.

"Where do you think she is?" asked Tim.

"That, Tim, I don't know but I am sure she is quite safe for the moment. I would guess that you will see them this very night but we can get into that later. So please continue on with your most harrowing story, as I am most interested in hearing it," said Grabblemore.

Grabblemore patted Charlie on the back and just smiled and said nothing. He continued to listen to the story but could not help but think this tale was strange and most disturbing. For the overseer to do something of this nature without the Council's approval was just unheard of. Gathering his thoughts, Grabblemore stated that this was a most grim situation and that he might have to call an emergency council meeting to get answers to this accusation. Then Grabblemore's mind seemed to wander elsewhere as he began staring seemingly off into space, for many silent moments he glanced at the two boys and stated he had a most ingenious idea how to handle this.

"Children, I know this is not easy for either of you but I respectfully request that you continue the rest of the story. There are most important details that are yet to be exposed. Please try to remember even the smallest amount of information; although it may seem trivial, I assure you it will be important sometime nonetheless," said Grabblemore.

Charlie and Tim reluctantly recounted the goblin attack, meeting Ambrose and later Groulder. Grabblemore became very focused. He wanted particulars of how they were assisted and what if anything either Groulder or Ambrose was told about the Shifters and the overseer. Grabblemore seemed to focus on the goblin attack and proceeded to ask many questions, sometimes repeating them as Charlie and Tim explained the attack and the eventual retreat of the attackers. Grabblemore eventually pulled out a parchment from his cloak and began to scribble down random notes. Neither Charlie nor Tim could see what he was writing and after a while gave up trying.

Grabblemore was most pleased to learn that Alston was alive at least a few days earlier and that Ambrose was aware of this. He laughed when he learned of the parchment Ambrose had given them and how they had to fend off the Cractors with the lightner.

Tim took a moment to get up and stretch and casually glanced out the window. What he saw grabbed his full attention and soon Charlie joined him. A rather large crowd could be seen scurrying throughout the entire city. There were more people than either boy recalled seeing the last time they were in the city. They also noticed large caravans all about the streets. There were many kattergraff-drawn carts and carriages filled with assorted items. They also noticed off in the distance a rather large encampment being assembled and it was growing by the minute. They could see tents being setup that were bigger than most houses.

"Mr. Grabblemore, I don't want to wander off our original discussion but what is going on out there?" asked Tim.

"Tim, that is the gathering of the guilds. We have what we call a Guildfaire once a year," said Grabblemore.

"What's the gathering for, Mr. Grabblemore?" asked Charlie.

"Each year all the guilds of the land gather here at the Great City to have a festival of sorts to celebrate another year of peace, amongst other things. This event could not have come at a better time for either of you," said Grabblemore.

"Why is that?" asked Tim.

"Each year when the festival begins the guilds select new members. We are going to use this to our advantage to get the both of you into a most advantageous situation," said Grabblemore. "We are unfortunately short of time but our plan will be simple enough so that it should not be a problem."

"Are you still going to contact the council about my grandfather?" asked Charlie.

"No, Charlie, I fear that will not help us at this point in time; however, I will personally do everything in my power to find your grandfather and Alston and get them to safety once again. For now we need to focus on other things. I know this is difficult for you, but trust in me and I will not let you down," Said Grabblemore.

"Okay, Mr. Grabblemore ,I will go along for the moment but eventually I will start looking myself if I don't hear anything soon," said Charlie.

"I know you would, my boy, and I would expect nothing less from you or Tim for that matter," said Grabblemore.

"If Charlie goes I go plain and simple; we are buds and we stick together no matter what," said Tim.

"It is about time that we end this meeting. Some of the details will need to be addressed at another time and location. Follow me down the stairs and stay close and right behind me so we can make a rather unexpected entrance. There we will begin to set our little trap," said Grabblemore.

"What trap?" asked Charlie.

"That I will explain after the scene plays out. Please have patience, my young friends. Now we must hurry so we do not miss the festivities, as they are soon to begin," said Grabblemore.

"What festivities?" asked Tim.

"You will see," said Grabblemore. "You will see."

After reaching the final landing and heading towards the entrance to the Great Hall they came face to face with a group of Shifters who were guarding the exit to what must be their final destination. Tim and Charlie started to back away but Grabblemore glanced at them both before making a waving motion of his left hand, causing the group of Shifters to promptly move to either side of the hall. Tim was gripping his staff and Charlie had his dagger out of its sheath ready for action. Grabblemore just smiled and this assurance caused both boys to relax. They were sure they were safe even standing this close to the Shifters.

"Oh yes, before I forget, here is another orb so you can call me anytime you feel the need. And please do not go off and lose this one as they are a bit trying to make. Now both of you prepare for the Guildfaire and its most extravagant beginning; it's quite the show after all," smiled Grabblemore.

Charlie and Tim stepped outside onto the largest open-roof patio either of them could imagine. Grabblemore stayed right in front of the boys and continued through the crowd towards a group of wizards and sorceresses.

"Stay close, my young friends; I am sure this will be most interesting, yes indeed. This reaction will be priceless—patience, my boys, patience. One…two…three."

"Phinneus, how wonderful to see you…. What, what are you two doing here?" asked Gershrom Cadwalader. Gershrom's face had gone completely white and he stumbled for a moment and had to gather himself so he did not fall.

"Why, Gershrom, they are here naturally as personal guests and friends of mine," said Grabblemore now grinning from ear to ear.

"What—? Why, I mean of course they are," said Gershrom.

"Why do you seem so surprised to see them again, Gershrom? You were there after all when I gave them an orb to contact me and also permission to come back as soon as they possibly could," said Grabblemore.

"Yes of course—well, I am just shocked that they have returned so quickly and—here, right here at the Guildfaire nonetheless. I must bid you all a rather hasty farewell as I have some most important business to attend to," said Gershrom.

"Must you leave right now, Gershrom, at the beginning of the Guildfaire gathering?" asked Grabblemore.

"Phinneus, you know justice never sleeps and, and…well, I have to get going. Good day," said Gershrom.

Gershrom's face had gone from white to a bright red during the few moments that had passed. The sweat was now beading up on his forehead and he was obviously flustered and Grabblemore loved every minute of it.

Hurriedly Gershrom backed away from Grabblemore and the boys. He made a strange hand gesture and seemingly out of nowhere came three

Shifters who followed right after him as he attempted a rather hasty retreat. While hurrying to get off the patio Cadwalader rather unceremoniously knocked one of the staff over, sending a food tray falling to the floor. Gershrom continued his hasty exit without bothering to even excuse himself.

Grabblemore turned and smiled at Charlie and Tim looking pleased with how the events had just played themselves out. Charlie didn't see how this was going to help them and was growing quite furious at the sight of Cadwalder leaving.

"Mr. Grabblemore, how is this going to help us? He just walked away and is about to leave," said Charlie.

"Yes, I suspect he is," said Grabblemore.

"We need to stop him or something, don't we?" asked Charlie.

"And why would we do that?" asked Grabblemore.

"Because he is getting away," said Charlie.

"Exactly," said Grabblemore.

"Charlie, use your brain for a second, will ya," said Tim.

"What?" asked a rather confused Charlie.

"He will probably go right to your grandfather and Alston and all we need to do is follow him," said Tim.

"You are bright beyond your years, Tim," said Grabblemore.

"Thanks, Mr. Grabblemore," said Tim.

"I get it," said Charlie.

"That's great, Charlie, but there is one unfortunate aspect to this plan—Cadwalader will surely vaporate and that is a very difficult form of travel to trace. I will use all my resources to track his travel and hopefully with a little luck we can find your grandfather and Alston. However, even if we do not find them this very time I am sure that this will shake things up a bit in our favor," said Grabblemore.

"How is that?" asked Charlie.

"Charlie, he will surely panic and when people panic they make mistakes. Hopefully he will make one big enough to spring the trap on his own and our work will be done for us," said Grabblemore.

"Right now things are happening that we are still not aware of. Unfortunately all we can do is wait it out. We will check even the tiniest clue or scrap of evidence but we do not have anything else to go on at this point," said Grabblemore. "Now, my young friends, we need to prepare for the official beginning of the Guildfaire gathering. Please stay close to me and enjoy the show."

Grabblemore headed through the crowd and walked to the edge of the platform. Immediately the crowd quieted and focused on Grabblemore. There were thousands of wizards and sorceresses all focused on the platform and Grabblemore. He raised his staff above his head high, the crowd seemed to ready for something, then thousands of lights and beautiful fireworks shot out the end of his staff covering the sky with beautiful flashes of blue, red, green and yellow. All sorts of shapes like dragons, wizards, sorceresses, stars, trees and many other things appeared in the clear dark sky. The flashes kept appearing, magically popping, flashing and turning into most wonderful things. Charlie and Tim were amazed with the sights and sounds and could not wait to see what the rest of the Guildfaire had to offer.

A moment later the fireworks stopped and all was perfectly quiet.

"My dear friends, welcome to the 21,971st Guildfaire gathering," said Grabblemore. The crowd roared, and it was almost deafening for the next moment or two till Grabblemore called for quiet. "My friends, please, that is much too much. Let us move on past the pleasantries and get to the most important thing." Chants of "Grabblemore" rippled through the crowd, people stamped their feet, children waved and many just clapped as loud as they could.

Moments passed and the roar of the crowd still was at a deafening level. The sound was tremendously loud; it made any attempt at communication except to the closest person nearly impossible.

Then Grabblemore raised his staff again and there was complete silence.

"My friends, we are all here today to assist in the initiation of new guild members. This is a most important time of the year for all of us since we could see some of tomorrow's leaders right here within the next few days. Now for all of you that are not familiar with the process it's quite simple—the guilds choose their new recruits and they are tested. How they choose each member is specific to each guild. These standards are not public knowledge; only the guild members past and present know how each guild chooses its recruits. The test is also specific to each guild and remains secretive to this very day. If an individual does not pass the initiation test their memory is altered and the test is stricken from it. This memory alteration is done so the individual who failed cannot assist anyone who attempts that specific guild test at a later Guildfaire gathering. This tradition has been in place since the very first Guildfaire and will remain for the rest of time."

The crowd started cheering loudly again, causing Tim and Charlie to cover their ears. Guildfaire members young and old started to raise their staffs high into the air, some actually taking flight and spinning with rather spectacular flashes and sparks. This excited the crowd again to the point of frenzy.

Grabblemore called for silence and again all was remarkably quiet.

"Now let me introduce the heads of our four guilds. First, the head of the Wilfrem Guild, Efa Vanora."

Efa Vanora was dressed in another spectacular gown that reached the floor and dragged behind her when she walked. She seemed to almost float or glide rather than actually step forward when bowing to the crowd. She gracefully turned and bowed to Grabblemore and the rest of the council who ceremoniously returned her bow. She raised her staff and the most beautiful butterflies flew about as if in formation shifting into different animals at random.

The crowd went into its usual roar of approval and started stamping feet and clapping hands again. This was hastily quieted when Efa Vanora seemed to float off to the side of the platform and the next guild head proceeded to the edge of the platform.

The next to rise was Vance Vortigern. Before he get close to the edge of the platform screams could be heard throughout the crowd and women could be seen pushing towards the front and starting small riots. Roses, small parchments of paper and some other feminine things were being thrown in the direction of the platform. The men of the group did not seem too impressed with him and just continued to clap rather quietly.

Without saying a word Vance Vortigern raised his silver- and diamond-encased staff towards the sky and large lightning bolts, booming thunder and then a great eruption of raindrops the size of softballs begin falling from the sky. However, not one drop reached the dirt as Vance waved his staff causing them to all turn into a flowing river in the sky.

The female audience broke out into song about Vance, stomping feet, screaming, crying, fainting and falling about.

Grabblemore smiled and clapped, obviously amused by the whole spectacle.

Finally Vance Vortigern was able to speak and speak he sure did!

"My dear friends, welcome to the Guildfaire. As most of you already know I represent the Calder Guild."

Again the female members of the audience erupted. It took many minutes to get them under control.

"Thank you, friends. Please try to hold your applause a bit so that I may finish speaking to the most wonderful crowd that I have ever seen."

Again eruptions of screams and screeches ripped through the crowd.

Vance held his hands up calling for quiet and finally the female portion of the crowd obliged.

"Now as I have said, my guild, the Calder Guild is of the water, we flow and bend and can break the strongest material known to man. However, we can also be soothing and comforting. We are here today to hopefully gain a few new members to each guild. I am very hopeful that the best of the best will end up in the Calder Guild."

Vortigern bowed low and waited a moment before he lifted his head.

It was apparent to Charlie and Tim that he was a bit theatrical to say the least.

A moment later he raised himself to full height and extended both arms with his staff raised high above his head.

The crowd yelled so loudly it sounded like it might burst from excitement.

Vortigern headed off to join Efa; even she had to smile at the reception he had just received.

The crowd grew silent again and whispering could be heard throughout the Guildfaire gathering.

Now heading towards the edge of the platform was someone who was not a crowd favorite.

Heading to the edge of the platform was Eblis Morfran. He was wearing his usual black robe with blood red trim. His eye patch had been changed to blood red to match the robe trims. His hat was removed to show his perfectly long black hair pulled into a tight ponytail clipped with a blood red M for Morfran.

He bowed rather shallow to the crowd, raised his staff and shadowy figures shot out the end of his staff, causing the crowd to pull away and cower into small groups, obviously fearing this man and what he was about. He smiled a rather evil-looking smile, turned and walked off to the left to join Vortigern and Vanora.

"Well, that was interesting," said Charlie.

"The crowd was so silent you could hear a feather drop a mile away," said Tim.

Now Grabblemore headed back to the edge of the platform, causing much rejoicing amongst the crowd. Grabblemore's name was being chanted, even the other members of the council, except Eblis Morfran, joined in.

"I know most all of you and am glad from the bottom of my heart to see you all here. For the few who do not know I am the head of the Golundrus Guild," said Grabblemore.

Silence led to a complete roar of "Golundrus! Golundrus! Golundrus!" The place was shaking and the mortar sounded like it would crack with the immense volume of the newest chant.

"As most of you know the Golundrus guild is of all elements: earth, wind, water and fire. We are of the spirits of the wind and the guardians of the forest. We are everywhere yet nowhere."

The chant broke out again, "Golundrus! Golundrus! Golundrus!"

Grabblemore brought his staff again high above his head; the crowd quieted, then he bellowed, "THE GUILDFAIRE GATHERING HAS OFFICIALLY BEGUN!"

Grabblemore headed towards the boys, who were smiling and enjoying the spectacle of the Guildfaire gathering. "Boys, I know you do not really understand what is going on and I will spend the next few moments explaining how this could possibly affect you and your time here in Wizard World.

"How this will affect the both of you is quite simple naturally, but first I would like to explain that the Golundrus Guild is most impressed with your accomplishments in your short time here in Wizard World. Your exploits have reached the members and they are most anxious to find out what you two have to offer.

"Now we must prepare the both of you to meet with representatives from each guild. This is done on the recommendation of a preset guild member. Without a nomination—which does not come lightly, mind you—there is no chance to even be considered for guild membership," said Grabblemore.

"So why are we meeting with the representatives then?" asked Tim.

"Tim, your journey with Charlie has been the talk of the guilds so to speak. I must confess I could not but help telling of your exploits when information became available to myself," said Grabblemore.

Tim and Charlie smiled, still not knowing where this was going to take them next. This conversation seemed to be leading them to the point of getting recognized for their rather trying journey from the Pit of Dulgeon to where they are now. What amazed most of the guild members who were aware of their trip was the fact that neither of the boys was a practicing wizard and they made the journey entirely on their wits and nothing more.

"So how did you know what was going on?" asked Charlie.

"Yeah, how did you?" asked Tim.

"My friends, let's just say a little bird told me," said a grinning Grabblemore. "However, I was not completely aware of your entire journey,

I was just getting tidbits here and there. The trickle of information was just enough for me to know you were on your way but not whom you were with or who was assisting you.

"Enough of this lengthy discussion—let us now head to the Guildfaire gathering and partake in its many different experiences of food and wonderful games of skill," said Grabblemore.

Both the boys were rather anxious to experience what seemed to closely resemble a county fair. The eagerness of both the boys was most enjoyable to Grabblemore, reminding him of when he first went to the Guildfaire himself as a young boy those many years earlier. He took a moment to remember his father and mother leading him to meet the guild members and taking his challenge, which he passed with flying colors. He also remembered how awful it was for the individuals who did not pass.

Finally they reached the Guildfaire grounds and neither of the boys was disappointed with what they were seeing.

There on both sides of the grounds were many shops, carts selling strange foods that floated about changing colors and shapes, games of skill from throwing lightning bolts through smoking rings to juggling balls of fire. There were constant sparks and small explosions, strange things flying this way and that, along with the strange animals that are native to Wizard World.

Charlie, Tim and Grabblemore stopped at the first cart they came across. Here was a man and his wife selling morphing candy.

When the cart owner noticed Charlie and Tim's interest he promptly went into action as any salesman would.

"My dear fine young gentlemen, please partake in a small sample of the most wonderful candy you will ever get to experience, 'Morphin candy.' This candy can only be purchased from Morphin's Candy and Magical Supplies."

Neither boy made a move towards the offering until Grabblemore nodded rather enthusiastically.

"Please grab one of the small samples and let me know what you think," said the overanxious salesman.

Grabblemore nodded the okay and both Tim and Charlie reached for a sample only to see each piece change into a small reflection of their heads smiling up at them. Tim jumped back at the sight of his little head, which naturally caused Charlie to laugh and reach even faster for his sample.

"It was kind of creepy," said Tim.

"Yeah, it is a little you so I guess I can see what you mean," said Charlie grinning from ear to ear.

"Funny," said Tim

The boys thanked the shop owner and moved on to the next location, a large tent that had crossed staffs above its entrance and floating swords and shields flying about.

Charlie eagerly pushed open the hanging tent door, followed by Tim and then Grabblemore. When stepping in and looking to his right Charlie was confronted by his worst enemies, Ron, Sean, Clive Beth and Crystal.

Before Charlie could take a step in their direction Cadwalader appeared as if from nowhere mere inches in front of Charlie's' face. He was sporting his usual evil grin.

"Well hello, my young friends, how are you enjoying your visit to the Guildfaire?" asked Cadwalader.

"It would be much more enjoyable if you and the group of thugs standing behind you were in prison or somewhere worse—oh, like maybe the Pit of Dulgeon," said Charlie.

"My boy, why so nasty? After all, we are all here to have a good time and see the chosen ones test to join their possible guilds. We are not here for trouble, just enjoyment. Negative attitudes like yours will surely get you into trouble someday," said Cadwalader.

"Yeah, well, just the same I still would be much happier if the lot of you were behind bars where criminals belong," said Charlie.

"Temper now, boy, you wouldn't want to have a run in with the Shifters again, now would you?" Cadwalader asked.

"Hello there, Mr. Cadwalader. How are you this most lovely evening?" asked Grabblemore.

"Grabblemore? I didn't see you there. Charlie and I were just having a friendly discussion about our first meeting and his time here in Wizard World," said Cadwalader.

"Ah yes, that's what I figured," said Grabblemore.

Ron, Sean, Clive and Beth were laughing and pointing at Charlie but Crystal wasn't saying a word and wouldn't look at either of the boys. She continued to stare at the floor, speechless and apparently wanting to be anywhere but where she was at the moment.

"We must be going—there are many things for us to prepare for. I hope the both of you enjoy the rest of your stay here in Wizard World, until we meet again," said a menacing-looking Cadwalader.

"Oh, and we will," stated Charlie.

"Yes, I am sure you will," said Cadwalader.

Ron and his gang headed out, following Cadwalader and laughing the entire way as they passed both Charlie and Tim. Crystal would not look at either of the boys but did manage a small smile as she passed by Grabblemore.

Ron stopped for a moment and asked how Charlie's grandfather was doing, giggling the entire time.

Charlie lunged for Ron but was stopped by Tim, who stepped in to stop a possible disaster from happening.

"Someday, Ron, you and your bunch of loser friends are going to get what is coming to you," said Charlie.

"Idle threats, Charlie, idle threats," said Ron.

"It's quite apparent to me that you have a bit of a maturity problem, boy," said Cadwalader.

"At least I am not a lying sneak," said Charlie.

"Careful, boy, or you will certainly get into trouble far beyond your imagination," said Cadwalader.

Grabblemore stepped closer to the group and smiled at Cadwalader, causing him to back away rather hastily.

Cadwalader followed his group out the tent door without turning back. His cheeks were again bright red, leading to the obvious that he did not appreciate being intimidated by Grabblemore.

Grabblemore turned and faced both boys with his usual smile.

"Boys, I am sure that was difficult for the both of you, but please remember that Cadwalader is under immense pressure and I am sure he will soon slip up and hopefully that will lead us to Mr. Watson," said Grabblemore.

"Yeah, but it just kills me to see him walking around here like he did nothing wrong," said Charlie.

"Yeah, Mr. Grabblemore, that just stinks," said Tim.

"I know, boys, but some things are bigger than we realize and need to be handled with very light hands and not with the rock and sword. Trust me, the haze will clear and this mystery will become all too obvious soon enough," said Grabblemore.

"Now we must head to the center of the Guildfaire. There we will find a most wonderful stage. Soon the recruits will gather hoping to get selected by one of the mentors that will be preset. Remember it does not matter if the individual wants to join a specific guild or not, their joining is dependent on who and if they are selected. So you could want to join a guild but get selected by another. If you do not pass the trial or refuse to even attempt it, your one and only chance will have passed and there will be no more. This Guildfaire meets every year, but alas, a person may only be selected once," said Grabblemore.

"So if we get selected and decide not to join that's it?" asked Charlie.

"Correct," said Grabblemore.

"That doesn't give you many options, now does it?" asked Tim.

"No, it does not," said Grabblemore. "Just remember to relax and everything will be taken care of."

"Okay, but how do we even know we want to be selected?" asked Charlie.

"That is quite simple of course—if you wish to learn magic then accept the nomination and attempt the challenge and if of course you do not then politely decline and that will be the end of it," said Grabblemore

"Magic, real magic?" asked Charlie.

"Yes, Charlie, real magic," said a smiling Grabblemore.

"Of course we want to learn magic, but we want to be together and to decide which guild we join," said Tim

"Yeah, Mr. Grabblemore, we definitely want to stay together no matter what," said Charlie.

"That, my young friends, I cannot guarantee; however, if it is meant to be then it will," said Grabblemore.

"Hopefully it's meant to be," said Charlie.

The group rounded a few more corners, passing massive tents and varying displays of magic and food. They arrived at a large stage and at its center were four pedestals with a glowing globe atop each one. There were many young boys and girls gathering about the stage sporting cloaks and hooded capes. Some were carrying staffs and others something resembling Efa Vanora's sorceress's staff that she was carrying at the opening ceremony.

Charlie and Tim followed Grabblemore to the edge of the stage. There Grabblemore bade them farewell and told them to wait here in this general area

Neither of the boys had any idea who would be chosen nor how they decided to make their choice.

"Luck seemed to play a major part in who gets selected," said Charlie.

"No, I don't think so. I bet the glowing globes have something to do with it. They might be related to the crystals that are mined in the Pit of Dulgeon," said Tim.

"I guess it's possible but I don't see how a glowing ball is going to help pick a good student or not," said Charlie.

"Things here are not what they always seem to be," said Tim. "I bet there is more to those glowing crystal globes than we are aware of."

"Take a look to your left. Don't turn around, just casually glance over there," said Charlie.

There just off to the left about ten of fifteen feet away were Ron, Clive, Sean, Beth and Crystal doing their usual bullying of a rather small boy.

Strangely enough there stood Crystal, who was not really joining in the bullying but just simply standing there and trying to ignore what was going on.

Charlie was preparing to head right on over and stop the onslaught when Cadwalader showed up and broke up the group's fun, patted the small boy on his head and sent him on his way. He then turned to face the group, smiled, laughed and put his arm around Ron.

"Ron, my boy, you remind me so much of myself when I was younger. You are going to be a very good student, I suspect," said Cadwalader. "The three of you would do well to pay attention to this fine young man and follow his lead. It is quite obvious he is going places."

"Thank you, Mr. Cadwalader. You are far too kind," said Ron.

"Now, now, my boy, it's the truth so don't be ashamed of it," said Mr. Cadwalader.

"I think I am going to be sick," said Tim.

"Yeah, me too. I guess some people get rewarded for doing nothing but the wrong thing all the time while the rest of us do-gooders muddle along picking up the pieces," said Charlie.

"Well, at least we get some pieces," said Tim.

"Good one," said Charlie.

"Look, someone is heading to the front of the stage—it's Grabblemore. I bet he is going to make an announcement," said Tim.

"Yeah, look at the crowd, it's swelled to twice the size it was only a minute ago," said Charlie.

"I guess this is it," said Tim.

"Yep," said Charlie.

"Greetings to all. Let the Choosing Ceremony begin," said Grabblemore.

The crowd roared and teenagers started to push towards the front hoping they would be one of the lucky ones.

"There are no further needs for introductions so here are the heads of the four guilds. Now please let us have quiet while the selection begins. If you are one of the selected, calmly head to the left end of the stage and proceed to stand next to the guild member that has called you. Good luck to you all," said Grabblemore.

The crowd burst into a loud cheer, chanting Grabblemore's name over and over. He gave the crowd a quick wave and there was silence once more.

"Now with no further ado let the selections begin!"

Standing behind the crystal ball to the right was Eva Vanora. She looked elegant as usual, so perfect it seemed hard to turn away from her.

She placed both hands around the glowing orb and it started to shine brighter and brighter until it was nearly impossible to look in that direction. Eva continued to stare right into the blinding light as if looking for something. She then reached out with a quill and started to write. Shooting out of the glowing orb came the name of Olindra Calandra, then another and another until finally it was over.

The selections continued until they reached the next to last glowing orb. Here came Eblis Morphran, head of the Bladgen Guild. He casually placed his hands on either side of the globe and five familiar names appeared: Ron, Clive, Sean, Beth and last but not least Crystal. They strolled up to the stage with their usual arrogance as if they owned the place, pushing and shoving others to get to the front of the line. Happily they headed over to the Bladgen Guild area joining their new friends.

The last in the line was obviously the Golundrus Guild.

Mr. Grabblemore headed to the last glowing orb and placed his hands around it just like the three earlier guild leaders had done.

The crowd was dead silent. There was not a single sound to be heard. Anxious faces filled the entire crowd. Then shot the first name high into the air and it was Tim Smittens.

Tim looked at Charlie in disbelief. He did not expect to be selected and figured they were invited here more for the show than anything else. He did not move at first and just stared blankly, not knowing how he could be selected.

Charlie nudged him and patted him on the back.

Slowly Tim headed towards the stage when another flash came from the glowing orb and there it was, Charlie Watson, flying high in the air above the crowd.

Charlie headed towards Tim smiling from ear to ear.

"I knew it, Charlie, I just knew it," said Tim.

"Yeah, I guess every now and then even the guys who just get the crumbs get lucky," said Charlie.

"I bet it had nothing to do with luck and more skill," said Tim. "However, I have no idea which skill that might be."

"Me either, but does it really matter?" asked Charlie.

"I guess not," said Tim.

The boys proceeded to stand behind Grabblemore as the crowd stomped their feet, clapped and yelled at the top of their lungs.

Grabblemore turned and smiled at the boys and they realized that this was the beginning of something very special for the both of them.

Chapter 10

Testing, Learning and Stuff

The prospective new guild members headed off towards their particular Guildfaire locations. Here they would prepare for a test which, if passed, would grant them access to knowledge and power beyond their wildest dreams.

Charlie and Tim had countless questions for Grabblemore as they headed off to their next destination. As they walked off in the distance could be seen the glow of a great fire with smoke billowing high into the sky. Slowly a clearing could be seen with many tents circling the great fire. Off to the left was a magnificent tent at least half the size of the hall at the great city. This tent was red and lined with gold just like Grabblemore's robes.

The boys kept on prodding, hoping to gather even the smallest tidbit of information from Grabblemore that might be useful on their upcoming test. Grabblemore remained firm and would not give up even the smallest hint about their upcoming test. Tim, however, kept prodding for information but Grabblemore just continued to smile and shake his head stare at the great fire.

"Let it go, Tim, it's obvious we aren't getting anything from him," said Charlie.

"You are quite right, my boy," said Grabblemore. "For if I were to help you now there would be no point in going any further. You would have failed the test and it would be over for the both of you."

"What do you mean?" asked Tim.

"Tim, even though you do not see anyone at the moment I assure you that we are no longer alone. Also there is a specific spell in place to detect any cheating or assistance that is given to any of the candidates. The rules explicitly specified that any assistance to a candidate would make their test null and void," said Grabblemore.

"Okay then, I guess we're on our own," said Charlie.

"You both have fared quite well on your own while journeying here, so I'm sure this will be a piece of cake for the both of you," said Grabblemore.

"Yeah, I'm sure it will," said Tim.

"No doubt," said Charlie.

"So let's meet with the other guild members over by the central fire. There you will meet some very interesting people—yes, indeed you will. One of the people you meet will undoubtedly become your guild mentor—that is, if either of you passes your upcoming test,"said a grinning Grabblemore.

The trio walked for a bit longer and arrived at the central fire pit. The fire's brightness seemed almost unreal. The brightness caused Charlie to squint like he was out at midday during a warm summer day. He wished he had brought a pair of sunglasses along, but who knew? Tim was squinting because of the intense light and using his hands to shade his eyes. None of this seemed to have any effect whatsoever on Grabblemore, who just continued to smile like usual.

"My boys, here we are at last. Around this fire you will meet a few of the many possible guild mentors," said Grabblemore. "Ah yes, here we have Mr. Talon Klortis, one of our best shape shifters. He is known to spend days or even months transformed into various animals. He is one of our most trusted spies and knowledgeable members. He has been in the guild for longer than any wizard or sorceress except myself of myself."

Talon Klortis was a tall, muscular man. He wore robes very similar to Grabblemore's except they were cut shorter around the knees and the sleeves were rolled up to his elbows. His hair was as white as pure snow and he sported a goatee that hung down to his navel area. Around his neck were many gold chains with some interesting amulets. He also had one large diamond ring about the size of a golf ball on his left pinky finger.

Klortis didn't bother to even cast a glance in the direction of either boy and kept poking a stick casually at the edge of the fire.

Charlie thought he caught a small grin on Klortis's face when they bowed and turned to walk towards the next guild member sitting by the fire.

"Do not be alarmed that he did not acknowledge either of you at the moment. He does not want to do anything even if it is accidentally to affect either of your tests. Klortis would make a great mentor. He is a very clever and wise and the both of you could learn much from him indeed," said Grabblemore.

Charlie could just make out the next person sitting by the fire and she was obviously female. She was sitting lazily by the fire not paying any attention to anything but the dancing flames. She was a tall blond-haired female who did not look much older than either himself or Tim. She casually glanced towards Charlie and Tim for a moment then turned back to the fire and the dancing flames that were aglow in her eyes.

Grabblemore stepped to the forefront to start the introductions.

"My young friends, let me introduce you to one of our youngest members of the Golundrus Guild, Miss Caruna Grootmore. Miss Grootmore was the youngest person ever to pass the test and join a guild. She is very wise beyond her years but luckily still playful enough to keep the rest of us ancients from getting too bored," said Grabblemore.

Caruna had hair the color of gold that was intertwined into a rather stylish ponytail. She was sporting a powder blue cape with red pants lined with gold. Her undershirt was also red and gold to complement her outfit. She carried a staff that was striped with blue, gold and red gems. Again she did not acknowledge either Charlie or Tim and kept aimlessly staring into the flames.

Charlie had a hard time turning away from her although Tim and Grabblemore were almost to the next guild member. She was quite attractive to him.

Tim yelled for Charlie and he reluctantly started to walk away when Caruna quietly said, "Good luck."

Charlie was caught off guard after the meeting with Klortis and missed his opportunity to try and get a word in. He turned to speak to her but she had turned away and was grinning and just staring at the fire.

Charlie smiled and rushed to catch up with Grabblemore and Tim. He couldn't wait to talk to Caruna as soon as he had a chance.

"Keep up, Casanova, you don't want to get lost," said Tim.

"Very funny," said Charlie.

They spent the next hour or so wandering out of this tent and that and meeting so many people it was hard to keep their names straight.

Grabblemore led them to a rather plain-looking small tent. This tent seemed to be distanced from the rest of the circular formation. All the guild members were obviously staying clear of this spot for some reason. Tentatively they followed Grabblemore into the tent and he said nothing. It was dimly lit but Tim and Charlie could tell they were not alone.

"What's going on, Mr. Grabblemore?" asked Tim.

"This is where we part ways. I will be leaving the both of you here and the rest will be explained to you very shortly," said Grabblemore.

"Where are you going?" asked Charlie.

"Yeah, Mr. Grabblemore, why are you leaving?" asked Tim looking rather nervous.

"Do not worry, my young friends, I will see you soon enough. These fine guild members will prepare you for your test. Please pay very close attention to every small detail that they may mention. None of it should be forgotten or pushed off as just idle banter," said Grabblemore. "I can say no more from this point forward. Good luck to the both of you."

Grabblemore exited the tent without another word and left Charlie and Tim in the small, dimly lit tent with two strangers.

"I guess there is nothing left but the introductions so here goes, my name is Charlie and this is Tim.

The guard on the left looked irritated by the introduction but turned to answer nonetheless. "Our names need not be mentioned at this point in time. They are trivial and will serve you with nothing but wasting precious time. We are here to make sure the both of you are prepared to take your guild test, nothing more and nothing less. We are not your friends and neither of you should be concerned with such things right now."

The guard on the right called for their total attention, and Charlie and Tim obliged, realizing what he was about to say would be invaluable on their coming test. "The first thing you must both remember is some things are not as they seem.

"The second thing to remember is to keep your wits about yourselves at all moments."

"The third thing to remember, and this is the most important of all, is that you only have one shot at this. There is no retest—you will either pass or fail, plain and simple.

"Now here is your test: You will be taken into Goldora Wood, handed an axe and expected to return with a functioning staff. There is nothing more to the test except that simple requirement. There will be no assistance from anyone allowed. If any guild member is caught assisting either of you the test is null and you have failed.

"Before we head out, please remember the three things I said to you, as they are all important to whether either of you regulars passes this test."

"There is no need to get testy now and start with the name-calling," said Tim.

Neither of the guild members paid any attention to Tim's comments and motioned for the boys to follow them out of the tent.

After exiting the tent both Charlie and Tim were handed a red cloak with gold-trimmed edges, a silver-bladed axe and a lightner.

The two guides led the boys deep into the Goldora Wood, instructed them to wait a moment and then the test would begin.

Charlie and Tim were inspecting their surroundings and turned to see what their guides were doing but they were already gone, swallowed by the dark forest, leaving the boys alone in the woods.

"I guess this is it then," said Charlie.

"Yep, I guess so," said Tim.

"We can finally have some fun with the axes, let's get to some chopping," said Charlie as he raised his axe and prepared to chop into the tree right next to him.

"Wait!!" yelled Tim. "There has to be something more to this. It can't be that easy."

Charlie stopped his swing a mere inch from the tree. "What, cutting up a tree to find a nice staff? How hard can it be? Just swing away and cut down a nice straight branch and head for dinner."

"Just hold on a minute and let me think about this."

"Okay, but I don't see the need—we each have an axe and there are plenty of trees to go around," said Charlie.

"Exactly! Remember what Alston said, he said the trees are alive. So if we cut one down I think we'll be killing one of them," said Tim.

"It's a good thing one of us has a good memory," said a smiling Charlie.

The two boys placed their axes down and leaned against a rather large tree. They were trying to work their way through the clues that the guild guides had given them earlier.

"I have to tell you I have no idea what to do. We are supposed to get staffs but not cut down any trees. We have axes and are surrounded by beautiful trees that would make awesome staffs but we cannot cut any of them or we'll probably fail this test," said Charlie.

Tim stood up and looked at the neighboring trees. "I guess we could ask one?"

Charlie looked in Tim's direction wondering if he was in a joking mood. "Are you serious? Ask a tree? Did you bump your head again?"

"Do you have a better idea?" asked Tim.

"Nope. Should I ask the tree we are leaning against right now or do you prefer another?" asked Charlie. "Why don't you go first and let me know what it says."

"Okay then, I will. Mr. Tree, can we please have a branch or two? We need at least two branches so we can make a staff or two in order to pass our guild member test," said Tim.

Moments passed and there was silence.

"I'm guessing by the response of nothing that it must be sleeping or something. Maybe we should try another tree," laughed Charlie.

"I don't hear you coming up with a better idea," said Tim.

"Maybe I will, just give me a second," said Charlie.

Charlie smiled, grabbed his axe and the lightner and headed off into the forest.

Tim leaned wearily against the large tree he had tried to speak to, not wanting to know what Charlie was up to. He could hear chopping off in the distance and was shaking his head wondering how many times they were failing this test.

Charlie could now be heard stumbling through the woods. Within moments his shadow could be made out with the assistance of his lightner. He was carrying two rather large branches and dragging them along the forest floor.

"Hey, Tim, do you mind giving me a hand."

"You didn't just do what I think you did, did you? Charlie, please tell me you didn't?"

"And what would that be?" asked Charlie

"Cut down a tree after I told you not to," said Tim while he slowly shook his head from side to side.

"No, buddy, I didn't—have a little faith already. I just found a broken tree limb and chopped off a few of its branches." That usual grin that Charlie sports was now very prevalent while he enjoyed his moment of success.

"Excellent! Now that's using your head," said a smiling Tim. "Okay, pal, here I come, just hold your branches already."

After considerable effort the boys had managed to drag the two large branches back to their makeshift headquarters. Here Tim and Charlie spent the next hour or so cleaning up the longer and straighter of the random branches until they started to finally resemble staffs that they had seen other members of the guilds carrying.

"That wasn't so hard, now was it?" asked Charlie rather sarcastically.

"I have to admit that was relatively easy. Now what do we do?" asked Tim.

"I have no idea," said Charlie.

Charlie and Tim continued to wave their newly created staffs around hoping something magical would happen. They flicked them this way and that, raised them high, smacked them together and even yelled abracadabra hoping that something, anything would happen, but nothing did. Charlie quickly grew bored with this exercise in futility and leaned casually against a tree. Soon Tim joined him sporting the same disgusted look on his face.

"Maybe we're missing something? We've tried multiple times to talk to these trees and the staffs seem to be useless at the moment. So the question is what to do next?" asked Charlie.

"At least we didn't harm any of the trees. Maybe that was the test all along," said Tim.

"Maybe," said Charlie.

Both boys froze in their tracks and were completely silent. Off in the distance branches could be heard being trampled and broken. The sound was growing louder and closer. Tim and Charlie glanced at each other and immediately thought "goblins," grabbed their newly crafted staffs and hid behind the nearest tree.

The breaking of branches had died down, making it difficult to track whoever or whatever was coming. Charlie focused in the general direction of the last sound and there in the distance he made out some movement. He pointed this out to Tim and they were both now staring and wondering if this was still part of their test. Whatever was coming had purposely slowed down and was now trying to be a bit stealthier in its approach. However, off in the not-too-distant forest the silhouettes of at least three goblins could be made out and they were definitely honed in on Charlie and Tim's hiding place. Both boys realized their makeshift headquarters would provide little or no shelter from the attack that was about to commence.

"You ready?" asked Charlie.

"I'm as ready as I'll ever be," said Tim.

"Just stay close and we'll be all right," said Charlie. "I'll take the first one as soon as he gets close and you follow right behind me."

"Okay," said Tim with a rather shaky voice.

"Here we go again, did I mention I hate goblins?" asked Charlie.

"Nope, but I kind of figured you did," said Tim.

The first goblin stepped very close to the tree that Charlie and Tim were hiding behind. Charlie jumped out from their hiding place, startling the goblin and leaving him no chance to react. Charlie cracked his staff off the right side of the goblin's head, sending it sprawling to the ground with its head twitching slightly as it hit the ground. The other two goblins, now quite aware of what had happened, began yelling what must have been a battle cry, psyching themselves up for the conflict to come, and charged at Charlie.

Charlie gestured for Tim to stay out of sight hidden behind the tree until the right time. Tim moved around to the back of the tree and waited for his moment to act.

Both goblins were bearing down on Charlie and started to flank him to the left and right. Charlie stood his ground and did not move towards either one. His staff was held at the ready as he mentally prepared for the attack to come.

The goblins rushed with reckless abandon at Charlie, totally oblivious to their surroundings. Charlie stepped to face the goblin on his left without paying any attention to his right at all.

The goblin swung high and Charlie ducked and swung low, hitting the goblin right across the knees, causing it to stumble forward and almost fall into him. The other goblin was now in position to take a swing and remove Charlie's head from his shoulders. The goblin was blinded by his range, making him relatively unaware of his surroundings and only focusing on one thing, Charlie's head, leaving it an easy target for Tim.

Tim stepped around the tree and swung his staff right into the face of the oncoming goblin. The surprise on the goblin's face was evident right up until Tim's staff hit its intended mark, dead center in the goblin's face. The swing was so vicious and powerful it sent the goblin backwards, slamming to the ground and leaving an expression of endless sleep across its face.

Charlie then turned and cracked the goblin lying right in front of him upside the head, sending him falling onto his back with his helmet cracked and his body twitching uncontrollably.

Charlie looked down with a look of disgust on his face. "I hate goblins, I really, really do."

"Yeah, me too," said Tim. "Let's get out of here before any more of the uglies show up."

Charlie and Tim gathered up their lightner and were preparing to head out when a scratchy voice that sounded like two sticks being rubbed together joined the conversation.

"Hello there," said the scratchy voice as if from nowhere. Charlie and Tim looked all around but saw no one. They both prepared for another attack but none came.

Again they heard this scratchy voice as if it came from nowhere. Tim looked about and then to his utter surprise noticed that the tree they had been leaning against seemed to have magically developed a mouth and was speaking. A tree was actually speaking!

Tim instinctively backed away, as did Charlie.

"All right there, tree, what do you want and why are you talking to us?" asked Charlie with a most disturbed look on his face.

Meanwhile Tim continued to move away with his staff at the ready. His expression was of utter disbelief. He rubbed his eyes with his left hand for a moment just to make sure he was seeing what he was seeing. But sure enough the tree was speaking, mouth moving right in the bark itself.

"What is going on?" demanded Tim. "Listen, tree, I want to know right now what or who you are and why you are talking to us?"

The scratchy voice let out what sounded like a laugh and the tree branches seemed to shake as well as the leaves.

"Trees do not talk," said Tim

"No, they most certainly do not, but I am not a tree per say; I am what you might call the spirit of the wood. I reside here watching over all the forest, from the smallest bud to the largest tree. I see and know everything that happens here. I am aware that the both of you have previously met with Alston; he is also a spirit of the wood but decides to take human form for easier communication. I, on the other hand, like to stay more traditional and take on a form of the wood, whether it is a tree, shrub or even the occasional rock or two just for variety of course."

"So what do we call you then?" Tim asked.

"Call me? Ah yes, you can call me Goldora of the Wood or just Spirit to make it simpler if you would like."

"Excellent," said Charlie, smiling broadly at the talking tree. "The guys at home will never believe this one, that's for sure."

"No kidding, talking trees, rocks—what next?" asked Tim.

"Maybe a bird or two I would suspect and when did you talk to the rock spirit if you don't mind my asking?" stated the Spirit.

"Rock spirit? Oh no, I never actually talked to it," said Tim. "Wait a second, the birds can talk too?"

"Why yes, when they feel the need to of course," said the Spirit, "and if you ask the right question naturally."

"Naturally," said Tim.

"Of course, why would they talk if you do not ask the right thing after all?" said Charlie while trying not to disrespectfully giggle too much. "So, Mr. Tree, or should I say Spirit, how can we be of service?"

The spirit looked on and its expression resembled that of a grin. "I am sure the both of you would like to know why I have appeared. That I can answer simply: I was asked to. Phinneus requested I keep an eye on the two of you in case trouble arose. Unfortunately before I could step in to assist with the goblins the both of you had the situation quite under control.

"I am sure you are going to ask me the most obvious next question and before you do I will answer; the test was simple enough and you have both passed with flying colors. The staffs that you now carry were taken from dead wood instead of a living tree, and that, my young friends, is the only way to pass after all. Naturally how could the Golundrus Guild accept someone who had killed a being here in the forest just for a piece of wood nonetheless," laughed the tree spirit, sending leaves and sticks to fall from high above pelting Charlie and Tim, who promptly backed away even farther from the tree.

"It is now time for the both of you to head back to the camp and prepare for the beginning of your next journey," said the Spirit.

"But what about the goblins?" asked Charlie.

"What goblins?" the spirit asked.

"The three that are lying just there," said Tim

"Where?" asked the Spirit.

"They're gone!! Who or what just happened?" asked Tim.

"Yeah, Spirit, what happened to the goblins?" asked Charlie.

"That is nothing for either of you to worry about. Please follow the trail of leaves that I laid out for the two of you. They will take you straight back to the camp. Good luck to the both of you. I am sure we will meet again."

"Thanks, Spirit, I am sure we will meet again and I look forward to it, I think," said Tim

"Yeah, likewise," said Charlie.

Charlie and Tim started to follow the path of leaves that were laid out by the tree spirit. They walked for a time talking happily to each other about their newest triumph and their staffs.

After reaching a heavily overgrown stretch of woods loud voices could be heard off in the distance. Charlie lowered the lightner as he and Tim cautiously moved closer to hear or see what was going on. They managed to get within thirty or so feet of the two individuals who were in quite the heated argument. They realized that one of the voices was all too familiar; it was Cadwalader, but the other unfortunately was not.

"I told you more than once there was nothing I could do," said Cadwalader. "I have already set up two attempts to capture or even kill them and both have failed. They are under the protection of Grabblemore and he has made it quite difficult and nearly impossible to complete this task."

The other person could not be identified; he was wearing a large hooded black cloak that reached the ground and entirely hid his face. He was much taller and broader then Cadwalader. It was obvious that Cadwalader feared this hooded figure immensely and kept slowly backing way. His voice sounded shaky and he was obviously nervous.

"I gave you an easy assignment that any simple-minded fool could complete and you failed miserably. Two boys with no magical skills were able to best six goblins now and you say it's not your fault!!" Yelled the unidentified man squarely into Cadwalader's face. This caused Cadwalader to go to his knees and hide his face in the dirt. He was shaking and quivering, almost squirming like a worm at this point.

"Please, I did my best and if I can only try one more time—" said Cadwalader.

"One more time?" questioned the unidentified man. "You want another chance then?"

"Oh yes, please give me one more chance and I will not fail you. I assure you I will not fail again," said Cadwalader.

"Yes, for once I agree with you—I don't think you will fail me again," said the unidentified man.

The unidentified man reached over his shoulder and pulled his staff effortlessly in front of himself, pointed it at Cadwalader, who glanced up from his quivering dirty position and started to scream, obviously terrified and fearing for his very life. The unidentified man laughed, kicked Cadwalader upside his head then yelled, "Roccism Stonum!" Red light flashed from the end of his staff, hitting Cadwalader right in the face. Cadwalader stood up for a moment, started to shake and then slowly proceeded to turn to stone, first his feet, then legs, up to his knees, then to his waist and finally his chest and head. His face was caught in a moment of sheer terror, his eyes were wide with horror and his mouth was open as if gasping for a final breath. This image was now embedded in both Charlie and Tim's minds and they would not soon forget it.

The unidentified man laughed loudly, enjoying what he had just done, and then proceeded to swing his staff right at Cadwalader's head, causing it to break into hundreds of pieces that scattered across the forest floor. He then surprisingly turned in the general direction of Charlie and Tim, staring intently for a moment, and then turned away and disappeared right before their eyes.

Charlie and Tim stayed motionless, unable to move and in total disbelief at what they had just witnessed. The events that had unfolded before them seemed to be unreal. A man was just turned to rubble before their very eyes. The boys waited for a good hour before they figured it was finally safe to speak. Tim stated that he was sick to his stomach and Charlie agreed. They could not believe what had just transpired and decided it was time to get away from this place as fast and quietly as they possibly could. They waited a few more moments, cautiously looked around and decided to run as far and as fast as they could down the trail of leaves and towards the Goludrus Guildfaire.

When they came running out of the woods, winded and tired from their nonstop sprint, they were met by members of the guild who were waiting with smiles on their faces and clapping all about. Loud cheers and fireworks were being shot into the sky as the celebration began. However, Grabblemore noticed that there was something wrong. He headed towards Charlie, who was obviously distressed and very winded from a long run. Tim fell to the ground onto his back without a word.

The guild members rushed forward with staffs at the ready and hastily formed a perimeter around the boys.

"Boys, what happened?" asked Grabblemore with a most concerned tone to his voice.

"Cadwalader dead, killed by someone in cloak, then disappeared," said Charlie.

"Dead? Cadwalader? That's nonsense. What are you talking about?" asked Talon Klortis.

"He's right," said Tim. "Dead!"

"You saw it too?" asked Klortis with a now concerned look coming across his face.

After a moment or two Charlie and Tim started to regain their wind and their wits.

"Yeah, I saw it too! There was a large man in a hooded cloak, he pointed his staff at Cadwalader, yelled something like rocks stone or something, red light came out the end of his staff and Cadwalader turned to stone. Then the cloaked guy laughed and smashed Cadwalader's head into like a million pieces and then disappeared," said Tim.

"Klortis, you and I will head into the wood to see what is going on. The rest of you please take the boys to my personal tent and set guards throughout the Guildfaire. If their story is indeed true this is a most serious turn of events," said Grabblemore.

Grabblemore and Klortis disappeared into thin air and Tim and Charlie heard that usual pop noise that always accompanied this.

Caruna and a few other unknown escorts led Charlie and Tim to Grabblemore's tent. Charlie and Tim noticed that all the members of the guild had staffs at the ready and were all on edge.

Grabblemore and Klortis arrived near the location Tim and Charlie had described. There off in the distance could be seen a headless statue, the statue of Gershrom Cadwalader.

"Phinneus, do you know what this means? Obviously this was done to make sure Gershrom could not be returned to normal using any knowledge that we currently possess," said Klortis.

"I know, Klortis. Smashing of someone's head after being turned to stone is a most heinous crime indeed. We must get to the bottom of this. I fear this is not the end but just the beginning of some most unfortunate events that will be taking place. Once this hits the public there will be utter chaos. We need to gather all the leaders of the guilds as rapidly as possible to decide what our next step should be. There is also the matter of the Shifters and who will now be placed in charge of them. This is most serious indeed," said Grabblemore.

"Klortis, please gather the heads of the guilds for me. We will meet tomorrow first light at my tent at the Golundrus Guildfaire."

"Yes, sir!" said Klortis, who then disappeared into the thin air.

Grabblemore poked around the now statue of Cadwalader wondering who or what had done this. There were no obvious clues left behind. He was most curious as to why this happened on this very day when all eyes would be here on the forest for the test that was taking place here in Goldora Wood. Why do this there and now when the perpetrator could possibly be caught? It seemed that whoever had done this wanted it to be known that no person, no matter his or her importance, was safe. This troubled Grabblemore immensely. He thought to himself there had to be something there that was eluding him, but what was it and how did the boys play into it? This was a mystery that had many twists and turns and for once left Grabblemore speechless and without answers.

Chapter 11

Learning All About Magic and Stuff

During the night many wizards and sorceresses could be heard coming and going out of Grabblemore's tent. There were numerous private conversations that Charlie and Tim found all but impossible to listen to. They were in the same tent and just separated by canvas but for some odd reason almost all but the smallest syllable was unintelligible. The events that unfolded yesterday were causing obvious waves throughout the guilds, which made it apparent to both the boys that what they had witnessed earlier in the forest was a serious incident and the repercussions from that event were just beginning.

"My friends, thank you all for coming on such short notice. These are dire times for certain. As most of you already know Mr. Gershrom Cadwalader was found dead earlier this evening. Klortis and I have verified this with a visit to the Goldora Wood. Cadwalader was killed in a most heinous way. He was turned to stone then had his head smashed by a staff. Charlie and Tim, two of our newest recruits, witnessed this while hidden in the woods nearby. They were in the forest taking their guild member tests, which they had just passed by the way, and were heading back to celebrate their glorious accomplishment when they overheard voices in the wood nearby. Luckily neither of the boys was spotted or this could have been much worse."

"So, Phinneus, the rumors are indeed true, the Overseer has been killed," said Efa Vanora. "This is a most concerning turn of events. We need to get to the bottom of this. We don't want the Shifters running around without leadership. I for one have read about the heinous crimes they committed in the past and do not want to have to experience that firsthand. We need to name a successor as quickly as possible."

Eblis listened intently to the conversation between Efa Vanora and Grabblemore and realized that now was the time for him to step to the forefront; opportunity was knocking and he had no intention of missing it. "And I suppose you know who should step in to take control of the Shifters?"

Efa Vanora didn't appreciate the tone of Eblis's voice and wanted nothing more than to quiet him once and for all but was cut off by Vance Vortigern before she could get out any form of protest.

"We do not have time to squabble amongst ourselves," said Vance Vortigern. "We need to focus on what is important and put our petty feuds and old grudges behind us at this time of great distress."

"Well said, Vance, well said." Grabblemore then motioned the group out of the tent and off into the darkness. Charlie and Tim were preparing to follow the council into the woods but were cut off by a smiling Caruna. She casually stepped in front of the boys and politely instructed them to sit back down and get comfortable.

"What is about to be discussed in the forest is of no importance to either of you at the moment," said Caruna.

"I think you're wrong, Caruna, my grandfather is still missing and Cadwalader was our only lead and now he's dead," said Charlie.

"I know your grandfather is still missing, Charlie, and I am sure that Grabblemore will come up with something; after all, he always does," said Caruna.

"I think I have every right to know what's going on. After all, it was Tim and I who witnessed Cadwalader's death. And just maybe we can help," said Charlie with a stern voice.

Caruna looked on knowing all too well how Charlie must be feeling, but she knew she had to do the right thing and follow Grabblemore's instructions. "I guess you are indeed like Grabblemore described, strong willed and very headstrong."

"Headstrong? What's that supposed to mean?" asked Charlie.

"Just that you hate to quit no matter what," said Caruna with a large grin crossing her face.

"Yeah, Charlie, you are strong in the head without a doubt, kind of like a rock," said a laughing Tim.

Grabblemore reached a clearing and the group of wizards and sorceresses began to gather and talk amongst themselves. Most of the talk was revolving around the Shifters and who was going to take control of them. They had not been without leadership for centuries since their defeat many years ago. Unfortunately there was little if any information on what or who had started that battle and how the Shifters were actually defeated in the first place. This information was lost long ago although rumors have persisted that it was still hidden and just waiting to be discovered.

"Order, please, we need order!" bellowed Grabblemore. The crowd promptly quieted and formed a semicircle with the center left empty. Grabblemore stepped to the center without hesitation.

"My good people, it is great to see all of you again and I wish it were not under such unfortunate circumstances. As all of you know Gershrom Cadwalader is dead. This is s dreadful thing and will be looked into with all our available resources. We will not stop until the culprit is brought to justice."

"Here, here," yelled the crowd.

"That is indeed an important issue but not the most pressing. With his death we were left with quite the leadership void. The Shifters are without a leader for the first time in many years and quite frankly none of us knows what to expect. So the reason for this impromptu meeting is to name a temporary leader for the Shifters and work as a group to gradually get them used to this. They are very temperamental and do not take all too well to change. Now our first order of business is to nominate at least two individuals, and we can then take a private vote to officially appoint a leader to the position."

"Now if any of you would like to—" Before Grabblemore could finish, Eblis Morfran had stepped to the forefront and announced his intention to be the next Overseer of the Shifters.

"I, Eblis Morfran of the Bladgen Guild, would like to be nominated to take on the position of Overseer and start pulling the reins, so to speak, of the Shifters. At this most trying time we need someone who can handle these dominant and sometimes almost uncontrollable powerful beings. I feel I can provide this leadership and take the Shifters and security here in Wizard World to the next level of protection and control." He then bowed slightly to Grabblemore and stepped to the right.

Efa's face reddened in utter rage at Eblis's attempt at an obvious power grab. She immediately stepped forward, and again right before Grabblemore could get another word out declared her intentions to become the next Overseer.

"It seems we have a group of mind readers present," laughed Grabblemore. "Apparently I need not finish but a word or two and everyone knows what I will say. And before I get interrupted again, is there anyone else who would like to come forward for the vacated spot of Overseer?" Grabblemore waited a moment and there were no other wizards or sorceresses stepping forward so he knew he had his two candidates.

"Please let me emphasize how important a position this is and how arduous it can be. There will be many moments where you must be forceful but not violent, where you must be wise but not overbearing and where you must be strong but not physical with these very complicated beings. They are not to be taken lightly by any means. They are after all the bringers of death and destruction and can be led astray very easily. So with that said if the two of you still wish to vie for the position of Overseer then we will take a private vote that will begin in a mere moment or so," said Grabblemore.

Both potential candidates nodded that they had understood the seriousness of the position and were prepared to take on all the responsibilities that would come with it.

"Now I will sit this cauldron atop this old stump and then we will file by one by one and cast a vote into it. I will then take a count and announce the new Overseer.

"Please take a moment to make your decision, as it is most important to all of us," said Grabblemore.

Then it began, the procession of wizards and sorceresses slowly filed one by one by the magical caldron casting his or her vote for the next Overseer. Both candidates stood together but did not speak a word or even glance in the other's direction.

Finally the last wizard past the caldron and cast his vote. Grabblemore grabbed the caldron and headed off to his tent with Klortis to examine the contents and learn of the victor.

Both wizards were shocked by the results. Neither could believe what has just transpired but nonetheless there would be a new Overseer tonight.

Grabblemore and Klortis headed back to the group of wizards and sorceresses to make the announcement.

"My friends, we have all voted and now we will announce the new Overseer—Eblis Morfran of the Bladgen Guild," said Grabblemore.

There was an immediate grumble throughout the crowd; most people shook their heads in disbelief. A chant started of recount that was promptly squashed by Grabblemore.

"I can assure everyone here without a doubt that the results are correct. This caldron cannot be tampered with in any known way by any magic that any of us possess. Therefore we must follow our guidelines and let the vote stand. So without further adieu I give you our new Overseer, Eblis Morfran."

The crowd went silent, Efa could not believe what had happened. It made no sense for anyone to vote for Eblis Morfran; after all, his brother was part of the group that tried to overthrow Wizard World those many years ago and now he will be the leader of the most dangerous beings known to this land.

"I must say I am most disappointed in this decision and I think it's an unwise choice. However, being that it is majority decision of the Council then I will support this decision any way that I can," said Efa.

"What just happened?" asked Tim.

"That is still none of your concern at the moment. I am sure when Grabblemore thinks you need to know he will let you," said Caruna.

Charlie and Tim continued to pry Caruna for any information they could get; she was not the slightest bit cooperative with either of them.

Moments later the tent flap was thrown back and Grabblemore appeared with his usual smiling face.

"My young friends, I am very sorry to have disrupted your most special night. Tomorrow we will celebrate your grand accomplishments of gaining access to the Golundrus Guild. So tonight sleep well and tomorrow morning we will have a joyous breakfast along with many introductions," said Grabblemore.

"Mr. Grabblemore, what are we going to do about my grandfather?" asked Charlie.

"My boy, do not worry; I have alerted all guilds to this matter and I am sure we will have an answer soon enough. We are not sparing a single resource to find him at this point," said Grabblemore.

"But Cadwalader was our best lead," said Tim

"Yes, he was, but nonetheless we will find him so do not worry," said Grabblemore. "There are always other ways and options to be explored, so sleep well for tomorrow will be a wondrous day for the both of you."

"Caruna, I would be most appreciative if you would remain here at the door for the rest of the evening."

"You need not ask me twice, Grabblemore, it will be my honor to assist any way that I can."

Charlie and Tim woke the next morning, tired, stressed and at the same time anxious to see what was awaiting them. The boys dressed and headed to the exit of the tent, noticing that Caruna was no longer guarding the entrance.

They stepped out into the bright sunshine and to loud cheers from the many Golundrus members who had apparently gathered the night before.

There were Grabblemore, Caruna and Klortis clapping the loudest of all. The boys, both blushing and rather embarrassed, headed towards Grabblemore while the cheering continued.

"My boys, this is your official welcome to the Golundrus Guild. After a grand feast your mentor will finally be known," said Grabblemore.

Charlie and Tim headed towards the head table and took a seat besides Grabblemore and Klortis.

The feast was spectacular as food magically appeared out of thin air. All present seemed to be having a grand time. Charlie took this moment to ask Grabblemore what had transpired last night and was told that it would all be explained later on in the day. Although not happy about having to wait, Charlie decided to enjoy the moment and worry about it later.

After hours of eating and merriment the feast was coming to its finality. Most had eaten way too much and seemed to have had enjoyable times. There was laughter and small talk going on and people standing and discussing many different subjects. Finally Grabblemore stood up called for silence and asked for the mentor to rise and let him or herself be known, and then Klortis rose to his feet with a grand smile across his face as he glanced at both boys and announced that he would take on two trainees instead of the usual one. This was not unheard of but something that is not done all too often. Grabblemore applauded this choice and thought this was well within Klortis's skill as a mentor and wizard to handle.

Klortis headed over to the boys, bowed and smiled broadly.

"My young apprentices, this is the beginning of a most important journey. Try not to think of me as a teacher but more as a guide as you head down your road of magical discovery."

The group of wizards and sorceresses slowly started towards the Guildfaire to meet with old friends and possibly some new ones. Charlie and Tim walked with Klortis, who kept randomly changing into different animals along their journey. Both boys enjoyed this but it was just a mild distraction from what Charlie was really thinking. He was more worried now than ever about the whereabouts of his grandfather. He felt like he was not getting enough information and was becoming more and more frustrated with every passing moment.

"Charlie, why so quiet?" asked Tim.

"I can't get my grandfather out of my head. I feel like I am being kept in the dark here. I am getting more and more frustrated with every passing minute. I feel like I should be doing something but all I'm doing is heading to another party while Grandpa could be stuck somewhere in a dark damp place."

"Do not worry, my young apprentice; I will personally assist in the search for your grandfather and I give you my word we will not stop until he is found," said Klortis.

"Thanks, Klortis, but I still feel like I should be doing something, anything to try and find him," said Charlie with an irritated look upon his face.

"You know you can count on me, Charlie," said Tim.

"Thanks," said Charlie.

"That, my young apprentices, is why I chose the both of you; this strength and bond that you share should not be broken under any circumstances," said Klortis.

No other words were said and there was no need. Charlie felt more confident than ever that he would find his grandfather and could not wait to begin the search.

After hours of pleasantries they were now off to their new home, the Golundrus Guildfaire. Charlie and Tim would be set up in a tent right next to Klortis and only a few tents away from Grabblemore. Their tent was the smallest in the Guildfaire and definitely the oldest and most worn. It was apparently handed down through generations of new recruits.

Once entering the tent there were very old and worn names carved into the supporting poles and the occasional hole or two was visible when the sun shined just right. Charlie and Tim each chose a room off the central chamber of the tent and started to unpack their meager belongings. Klortis had alerted them that tomorrow bright and early their training would begin. He instructed them to be in their new cloaks and to bring along the staffs they had crafted a few days earlier.

First light came and their tent was literally ripped from its tie-downs and thrown into the air by Klortis. He smiled and instructed both the boys to get a cloak on and grab their staffs. Charlie and Tim gathered the requested items and followed Klortis off into the woods where their training would begin.

They walked for thirty or so minutes and stopped in a beautiful clearing. Off to one side was a small stream and all around were small stones and broken timbers lying about.

"Let me take a moment to inspect both your staffs." Grinning, Klortis grabbed each of the staffs and threw them into water and walked away without a second glance. Tim and Charlie were about to burst with rage after all their work getting the staffs just right and now they were floating down the stream and out of sight.

"What did you do that for?" asked Tim.

"Yeah, we worked hard on those staffs," said Charlie.

"First, my boys, let me tell you that the staff is not important whatsoever. Also do not forget that you need to have faith in what I teach you and there is always a reason for what I do," said Klortis.

"But now we need new staffs," said Tim with a questioning look on his face.

"Yes, you do, but that is not important at the moment; more important is why you perceive that you needed the staff in the first place," said Klortis.

"What do you mean?" asked Tim.

"Well, it's quite simple naturally; the staff is just a vessel to channel your magical power, nothing more. You yourself produce the magic, and the staff, crystals and gems that are put into it only amplify what you can do," said Klortis.

"Well then, why did we have to make the staffs in the first place?" asked Charlie.

"That, my boy, was simply a test; the both of you could have used the axes to take the easy route and cut down a magnificent tree, ending a life, but instead you spent the time to analyze the situation and get the job done without harming anyone or anything. So that was the actual test, the staff was just to give the both of you something to focus on like a medal or trophy, nothing more," said Klortis.

"Now we will spend some time attempting a most simple exercise, trying to focus our energies on a small rock and moving it, then maybe after lunch a rock hidden in the stream itself. Do not get frustrated if you are unable to manipulate either the water or stone because it is a most difficult thing to learn," said Klortis. "Now please turn your attention to either of the stones lying over there by that tree and try to make it roll or move."

"And how are we supposed to do that?" asked Charlie.

"That, my young apprentice, is for you to figure out," said Klortis.

Charlie and Tim glanced at one another, turned, then focused on the stones but nothing happened. Try as they might neither of the stones moved even the slightest bit.

"Klortis, what are we doing wrong?" asked Tim

"Yeah, Klortis, this seems impossible," said Charlie. "How are we supposed to move a rock anyway?"

"You have to focus all your energy at the stone, nothing more, and do not get distracted by anything or let your thoughts wander even for a moment or you will not be able to complete this task. Now please try it again and remember to focus," said Klortis.

Charlie went first and focused as hard as he could but nothing happened. Then Tim took his turn and the stone wobbled for just a moment then flew into the air.

"Excellent! Tim, that was spectacular. Now try and explain what you did to Charlie and myself," said Klortis.

"Well, I just thought of what the stone would look like if it was moving or flying and then it did," Tim said.

"Now, Charlie, try again and use what Tim has just told us to try and get the stone to move," said Klortis.

Charlie closed his eyes for a moment, pictured the stone flying into his hand then opened his eyes, focused on nothing but the stone and it happened, the stone flew right at him and hit his palm, sending pain shooting up his arm along with a grin on his face.

"I am most impressed that the both of you were able to complete this test that rapidly. I figured we would be here for a month or longer before we could get either of you to even get a wiggle out of a stone, never mind get it to actually fly through the air and with accuracy too nonetheless," said Klortis.

"This was the simplest of tests on an object that you can see right in front of you. However, do you think you could manipulate a stone that you cannot see, for instance in that stream over there?" asked Klortis. "The focus is still the same, it's just that you now need to imagine the object you are trying to move although you have not actually seen it."

The boys spent the next hour sending stones flying from the water in many directions, occasionally splashing each other with well-directed shots. Klortis was constantly clapping and laughing and at the same time amazed at what the boys were able to accomplish in their first day and decided it was as good a time as any to step up the difficulty.

"Boys, here is your final test for the day. Remember your staffs that were thrown into the stream hours ago?" asked Klortis.

Both boys nodded.

"You must use what you have learned to get them back," said a now grinning Klortis.

"Get them back? They have been gone for hours and are probably miles away by now," said Tim.

"You are probably correct but the principle is the same as it was for the stone in the stream or the stones that we first started to manipulate," said Klortis

"On that last bit of advice I say goodbye and I will see the both of you for dinner when you finally complete this last challenge." Klortis turned, walked away and headed back to camp smiling all the way. He wondered to himself if either of the boys would be able complete this most complicated challenge or how long they would wait before they give up.

Charlie and Tim sat by the river wondering if what Klortis had asked them to do was even possible. Tim was sure that with the right focus this should be no different from causing rocks to fly from the bottom of the stream. Charlie was having a harder time believing this and that was part of the problem. Tim kept explaining to Charlie that if you do not believe there is just no way to make it happen.

It was decided that Tim would try this exercise first and then Charlie would go if and when Tim finally gave up or finished.

Tm closed his eyes for a moment, opened them and then began to imagine his staff floating down the river. He focused on the smallest details of his staff, the color, the texture and the slight tilt it had to the left when he held it. He kept focusing more and more about the details of the stream he had never seen and his staff, always the staff. He then stood up and held out his left hand and here came whirling back up the stream his staff. Magically it hit him right in the hand. He stepped back for a moment, smiled and then said "Next" while looking at Charlie.

Charlie, who had trouble with the earlier challenges, was looking from direction from Tim, who was not assisting in any way, shape or form. He simply said to focus just like he did before and it will happen.

Try as Charlie might the staff did not show up. He tried relaxing, getting upset and then sitting or standing. None of these things seemed to work. He was just having trouble imagining the right thing. Frustration had certainly set in after the hours passed. Charlie just could not believe that Tim was able to do this so easily and he could not. None of this made any sense whatsoever. He was actually jealous of Tim and he was furious with himself for even letting that happen for a second.

"Tim, I need your help figuring this out. I just don't get it," said a now dejected Charlie.

"Okay, buddy, we are a team after all." Tim explained to Charlie to stop making it so complicated and think of it in the most basic sense—you want your staff and you know what it looks like, so call it to you. Don't think how or why, just do it, plain and simple.

Charlie relaxed, stood up and simply thought about his staff right there in his hand. He did not think about the stream or the woods or magic, just the staff being right there in his hand.

He relaxed, calling it to him, wanting it to be with him, there was a pop and appearing out of thin air was Charlie's staff. It was a bit waterlogged and water dripped down his hand and arm.

Charlie could not believe this had happened. He was just hoping to get it to come back and he had managed to do an even more complicated calling by getting the staff to actually vaporate back to him. He could not thank Tim enough for explaining it to him. Both he and Tim were amazed that it had just appeared out of thin air and did not fly back like Tim's staff had done earlier.

"I think it's about time we head back for some supper," said Charlie.

"Yeah, I can't wait to tell Klortis about what happened," said Tim.

"Thanks a lot, Tim; without you I would never have figured out how to call the staff," said Charlie.

"Thanks, buddy, but I just helped you out a bit; it was you who figured out how to make it pop out of thin air," said Tim.

"Yeah, I have no idea how I did that so I am not sure if I can do it again," said Charlie.

"You did it once so I'm sure you will figure out how to do it again," said Tim.

Charlie and Tim were casually walking back to camp, both in good moods at what they had accomplished, when they heard a few familiar voices.

"Look what we have here, it looks like two new little wizards from the Golundrus Guild," said Ron.

"While you two were doing your little tests we have an assignment to scout these woods and report back to our mentor. I guess pebbles and little tests are all that the two of you are good for, a simple assignment for two simple-minded clowns," said Ron laughing loudly.

"Yeah, here they are all proud of themselves for getting their staffs back and moving a few little stones while we are on an actual mission," said Beth.

"Come on, Charlie, let's just walk around them and not give them any satisfaction by acknowledging any of them. They are just trying to egg us on and get us into trouble," said Tim.

"What's the matter, little Timmy, all scared of the big bad wizards from the Bladgen Guild?" asked Clive.

Tim was getting red in the face and Ron and his friends were enjoying every minute.

"Why don't you and your group of punks just go back to the hole you crawled out of," said Charlie while gripping his staff with both hands.

"Poor little Charlie is getting all tough. Just look at him gripping his staff and acting big and bad," said Ron.

"Let's just go and continue on our mission and leave them alone," said Crystal.

"What? Why would we do that? There are five of us and only two of them. What are they going to do except the usual, get beat up and crawl back to their mommies," said Clive.

"We'll see who does the crawling," said Charlie.

"Oh, the tough guy wants a fight so maybe we should give him one," said Ron.

Beth had slowly closed in on Tim and used her staff to trip him while Sean pushed him to the ground with his staff and then placed the end of it right under Tim's chin.

Charlie stepped back, closed his eyes and thought about the river; Tim seeing this did the same. Small pebbles slowly started to rise from the forest floor and flew through the trees, first hitting Beth in the face then Sean. They each backed away from Tim for a moment and he casually got to his feet, not paying attention to either Sean or Beth and focused even harder on the river and the pebbles that were at its bottom. More and more pebbles came pelting through the trees, falling like heavy rain and striking Ron, Clive, Beth, Sean and Crystal on the tops of their heads, faces, and all over, sending them running as fast as they could in any direction to get away from the constant pelting. Ron and Sean ran right into each other, sending the both of them crashing to the forest floor.

Quite a bit of blood was flowing down Ron's face from his left nostril and Sean seemed too dazed to realize that he was missing a tooth. They were helped away by Clive and Crystal, who said nothing and just kept her face covered while stumbling into the forest. Ron could be heard off in the distance with his usual threats of revenge and the usual "just wait till next time" line.

Charlie and Tim relaxed and the pebbles fell about them to the ground. After all that focus they used doing the earlier challenges set forth by Klortis and now this both the boys were spent, more mentally than physically, but spent.

"I don't know about you but I am beat. Let's take a break for a few minutes and then head back to the guild. It must be close to supper so when we get back we can relax for the rest of the night," said Tim.

"I bet Klortis will be psyched to hear what we did to Ron and his group of losers," said Charlie with a proud smile across his face.

"Yeah, he will probably give us an assignment or something for kicking their butts so easily," said Tim.

They entered camp and prepared to find Klortis and tell him all about the staffs and how they used the pebbles in the stream to get the best of Ron, Sean,

Beth, Clive and Crystal. However, when they arrived Klortis was already waiting for them and he did not look all that happy whatsoever.

"I want to know who gave either of you permission to use magic, let alone against another guild member? What were the both of you thinking?" asked Klortis.

"We were attacked and had to defend ourselves," said Charlie.

"Attacked? Did they use magic?" asked Klortis.

"No," said Tim.

"At any time were your lives in jeopardy?" Klortis asked.

"No," said Charlie.

"Well then, who gave you the right to use magic against one of our own, who?"

"No one," said a suddenly dejected Tim.

"Exactly," said Klortis. "This is a serious offense. There will be no reward for either of you recovering your staffs; instead I have something else planned for the rest of the evening. Both of you follow me please."

"But what about supper?" asked Tim.

Laughing loudly Klortis continued to walk towards a large tent billowing sweet-smelling smoke. Tim and Charlie were relieved and happy about finally getting to eat. But when they arrived at the tent they realized food was not on the menu and something much worse was dishes.

"This is where you will spend the rest of the evening," said a grinning Klortis. "This is quite the mess and I am sure the both of you will do a good job of cleaning up so do not disappoint me again."

The next four hours passed by with pruned hands and lots of dishwater. The boys washed dish after dish and were completely exhausted when they finally finished the last one. Klortis had kindly given the cook and cleaning crew the night off, telling them that two nice boys had volunteered to take up the slack for them.

Charlie and Tim were spent; they had not eaten since long before lunchtime and spent the last four hours doing more dishes than either of them had ever seen. Their hands were all water soaked and looked all wrinkled and they were soaked to the bone from all the dishwater. The boys kicked back and took up seats on a few stools waiting for their next assignment when Caruna walked in lighting the tent like she does wherever she goes.

"Hello. boys, it looks like the two have done a fine job. I'm sure that Klortis and the cleaning crew will be very pleased with your efforts," said a giggling Caruna.

"This is not funny, you know," said a now agitated Tim.

"No, it's not," said Charlie with the same look across his face.

"Maybe not, but now that your little exercise in selflessness is done we can move on to something more enjoyable," said Caruna.

Caruna led Charlie and Tim down to a small valley loaded with kattergraff. She led the boys to one of the corrals and casually leaned against the retaining fence and stared at the beautiful beasts.

"They are the most wonderful animals in the kingdom," said Caruna. "Just look at them, they are graceful, powerful and simply amazing."

"Yeah," said Tim.

Charlie said nothing and just stared at this one particular kattergraff. This kattergraff seemed to take a keen interest in him and headed in his direction.

"Why is he looking at me like that?"

"That's simple, he is yours," said Caruna.

"Are you kidding me? There is no way!!! This is unreal. He is really mine?"

"Yes, he is," said Caruna. "There is one catch and that is you have to take care of him by cleaning his pen every day along with feeding and washing him too. Oh, by the way, his name is—"

"Gregor," said Charlie.

"Exactly," said Caruna.

Tim looked on wondering if he was going to get a kattergraff all for himself too. "Hey, what about me?"

Before Caruna could answer a beautiful kattergraff heading towards Tim. It was smaller than Gregor but beautiful nonetheless. The graceful beast moved closer to Tim and casually placed her head against Tim's and made a purring sound like a rather large cat. Tim did not ask for her name because he already knew, Alicia.

"She is just beautiful," said Tim. "This is awesome! Thanks, Caruna, thanks a lot."

"There is no need to thank me, although they are from my personal herd; after all, the kattergraff chose you and I really had nothing do to with it," said Caruna. "Riding lessons will begin after you finish Klortis's lesson tomorrow," said Caruna.

"I can't wait," said Tim.

"Me either," said Charlie.

Chapter 12

History of the Land

The magic lesson seemed to mercilessly drag on all day; hour after hour, until Klortis finally brought it to an agonizing end. Finally Charlie and Tim could do what they wanted, practice riding their newest pets and friends. They enjoyed spending many long hours training with the kattergraff. The hours spent practicing was paying off. They learned to ride their kattergraff in a short period of time and already looked like seasoned veterans. Caruna was amazed at how easily they could handle the kattergraff, considering they had no prior experience with such animals in the Regular World.

After their latest riding lesson had ended they were instructed by Caruna to meet with Klortis for the next day's training.

Tired from their riding lessons and cleaning up after their new pets, Charlie and Tim reluctantly headed to Klortis's tent to find out what their next lesson would be.

The boys prepared to announce their arrival when the tent door opened and there was Klortis sitting by the fire enjoying his pipe.

"Welcome, boys, I hope the riding lessons went well. I have heard that you two are naturals; your riding skills are excelling at an incredible rate," said Klortis.

"Thanks," said Tim.

"Yeah, thanks," said Charlie beaming with happiness.

"Tomorrow I have a different lesson planned. We will not actually be learning magic but will instead be learning about Wizard World and its history," said Klortis.

Charlie frowned and Tim smiled from ear to ear.

"Now, Charlie, sometimes we need to do more than just practice magic and learn where it all started after all. How can you get to the end if you do not know the beginning?" said a smiling Klortis.

"You will be heading back to the Great City riding your kattergraff. When you arrive please see Miss Gradulip and show her the letter. She will grant access to the Library of the Ancients along with the other selected students that will arrive from other guilds. This is a great opportunity for the both of you. You will both be staying at a local inn while you are there. The arrangements have already been made so all you need do is simply get there," said Klortis.

Hearing that they would be riding their kattergraff all the way to the Great City made Charlie happier than he had been in quite some time. This made the lesson suddenly more enjoyable than he had originally figured it would be. Tim, on the other hand, was beyond excited about getting access to an entire library here in Wizard World. He was preparing to bring his backpack and his camera and as many notebooks as he could get his hands on.

"So at first light tomorrow head to the corral, saddle up your kattergraff and go. Do not worry about getting lost, as Gregor and Alycia already know the way," said Klortis.

"Really?" asked Tim.

"Yes. They are very smart animals and over time will bond with their rider. Eventually they will be able to tell when you are happy or sad, hurt or sick. They are most wonderful animals and great friends," said Klortis.

The morning could not come early enough for either of the boys; both were looking forward to the ride and Tim especially to the books that he was sure would be amazing.

Bright and early Charlie rolled out of bed and headed over to Tim's sleeping quarters only to see that he had already gone. Charlie headed out and caught up with him at the corral where Tim had already put a harness on Alicia and the riding cables too.

"Hurry up, Charlie, the faster we get there the longer we'll have to study."

"Yeah, I can't wait," said Charlie.

The dew was still fresh on the green grass and hanging leaves when the two headed out towards the Great City. At first they were cautious with their kattergraff but rapidly they realized there was no need to hold back. Charlie took Gregor deep into the forest, dodging trees with ease while Tim followed closely behind. Gregor jumped a great tree that was thrown to the ground during a recent storm with ease and Alicia followed along most happily. Alicia was very agile and could move in and out of the low-hanging tree branches with ease while Gregor had a bit of trouble with this, causing Charlie more than once to have to duck to remain on his back. Alicia clearly was not as powerful but more than made up for this with her elegance and maneuverability. Gregor would lower his head a bit and head right into the tree branches, shattering them and sending debris all over Charlie. It seemed the kattergraff were having a grand time and enjoyed their freedom.

They broke from the forest and reached the edge of a great river. The water was rushing rather rapidly and neither Tim nor Charlie was sure they would be able to cross.

"Tim, there is no way we can cross here, that water is way too deep and flowing way too fast," said Charlie.

"Yeah, let's head down the river bank and see if we can find an easier place. I bet the water will ease up and we will have no problem," said Tim.

Neither kattergraff wanted to budge. Both Gregor and Alicia turned their heads towards the rushing water and would not respond to either rider's commands to move forward.

"What's wrong, boy?" asked Charlie. "Come on now, let's head down the river's edge and try and cross at a safer place."

Gregor did not move and continued to defiantly point towards the water's edge.

Alicia paid no attention to anything Tim was saying either and moved closer to the water's edge. Neither animal would respond to their rider's pleas to go at a safer place. Alicia took three large steps backwards and jumped right into the rushing water. Tim had to use all his strength just to remain in the saddle and on her back. The water rushed up and over Tim for a moment and then Alicia moved lazily through the water without much effort whatsoever. Tim laughed and called for Charlie to follow. However, Charlie who was not such a great swimmer and was in no great rush to head into this rushing river, although it seemed that Gregor had already made up his mind and lowered his head and headed straight into the river just like Alicia had earlier. Gregor did not go under though and used his immense strength to force his way through the rushing water with great effort. Charlie was holding on for dear life while Tim was laughing loudly and patting Alicia along her neck.

Without much ado both animals had reached the other side with riders still attached. Tim was laughing and still patting Alicia while Charlie scolded Gregor for not following his command. Gregor kept his head low, visibly upset by Charlie's stern voice, and moped for the rest of the journey.

The great animals moved along rapidly through beautiful meadows, small towns and rocky terrain with great ease. There seemed to be almost nothing that could slow them down. After a bit it was decided to take a break and allow Gregor and Alicia to graze and take a drink from a local stream. Charlie and Tim sat down on a fallen tree and ate some frickta bread that they had packed the night before. Caruna had made this special for their first journey with their kattergraff.

Break was over and it was time to get on with their journey. Charlie and Tim called to Gregor and Alicia, who returned refreshed and ready to finish their trip to the Great City. They were off again at a breakneck speed. It became obvious to both Charlie and Tim that they were nearing the end of the journey and the kattergraff were excited to reach their intended goal.

Finally the Great City was in sight in all of its wonder. Smoke was billowing from small cottages, villagers hauled supplies around and small children played all about. Random villagers acknowledged the boys with slight bows. Charlie and Tim at first did not understand why but then figured it was related to the color of their cloaks and the representation of the Golundrus Guild.

Slowly they worked their way to the gates of the city and were not met by the usual Shifter but instead by two wizard guards wearing the colored cloaks of the Wilfrem Guild. Both the guards raised staffs and papers were requested. Tim reached down and pulled out the parchments that Klortis had supplied to them the day earlier and presented them to the guards. After a quick once-over by one of the guards the papers were handed back to Tim. The Guards stepped aside and the gates magically swung open, showing the complete grandness of the courtyard.

Charlie and Tim headed towards a darker section of the city where there were corrals and small run-down shops all about. Here they met with Dronus McLister, head of McLister Corral and Boarding. The boys were instructed by Caruna to leave Gregor and Alicia here while they studied at the Library of the Ancients.

"All right, Gregor, I am leaving you here in the most capable hands of Mr. McLister. He is highly recommended by Caruna and that's good enough for me," said Charlie.

"Yeah, Alicia, we will see the both of you tomorrow morning bright and early," said Tim.

"Do not worry, the kattergraff will be well taken care of here at McLister's. We are world renowned for our care and treatment of all kinds of animals," said Mr. McLister.

Charlie and Tim headed towards the center of the city and their assignment at the Library of the Ancients. On their walk through the city they enjoyed the smaller shops and many of the street vendors. Neither boy purchased anything but they did make mental notes of some of the more interesting things that were for sale.

They reached the main entrance to the library and were met by a line of at least thirty other kids carrying notes that resembled the one in their possession. There were different color cloaks representing all four guilds. Happily Ron, Clive, Sean, Beth and Crystal were nowhere to be found at the moment. They started to converse with three members of the Wilfrem Guild; their names were Ada Adara, Tara Slaine and Hannah Gareth.

The three girls were interested in hearing all about the goblins that Charlie and Tim had fought while they were taking their guild test. One member, Ada Adara, had taken a particular interest in Tim, which made him very excited, causing him to blush more than once while telling the story. Tim did not pay much attention when roll call was made and scrolls were requested since he was staring deep into Ada's eyes and looking all dumbstruck.

"Hey, Mr. Smittens, when you can spare a moment could you please pass in our scroll so we can get in and do our assignment," said Charlie.

"Sorry, here it is, Miss Gradulip," said Tim with a rather embarrassed look on his face.

"We need to get going, so can we meet up again later?"

"We sure can," said Ada, smiling and batting her beautiful green eyes. "Oh, Tim, the rest of us are heading to the Rock & Stone Inn for milkwine and frickta bread sandwiches. I hope to see you and your friend there after our lesson."

"We will definitely be there," said Tim.

"Don't even ask, of course I will go with you," said Charlie.

"Wait a second, where is the Rock &Stone Inn anyway?" asked Tim.

"Don't worry, Romeo, I am sure we can get directions," said Charlie.

The students were led through a set of golden doors highlighted with red gems, hinges and doorknob and knocker. The knocker resembled what looked like a kattergraff with a bull's ring though its nose. The knocker was the size of a beach ball and when Miss Gradulip swung it there was an echo through the entire hall. Both doors swung open to rows and rows of books as far as the eye could see. There were beautiful paintings hung all about the library along with swords, shields and many ancient-looking staffs. Most of the children were in awe at the size of this room and the unimaginable amount of books that it contained. Tim was obviously overjoyed with the learning experience that was about to be offered to them and all Charlie could think about was getting back to Gregor to check up on him

They were seated randomly throughout a great seating area that resembled a bowl with rows upon rows of chairs and small long flowing tables that went from end to end of each row. Magically parchment, quill and pen appeared out of thin air in front of every student. Miss Gradulip signaled for quiet and started to write with her quill into the air and there it stayed line after line until she waved her hand through the text and it turned to smoke and haze. After an hour or so of note taking Miss Gradulip instructed the class to head out into the library for an hour of free reading, break and then open discussion of what they had learned.

Tim hastily took the opportunity to sneak off with Ada to the section with the biggest and oldest books and didn't bother to wait for Charlie. Realizing what was happening, Charlie smiled and just went about his own search for anything related to the Pit of Dulgeon.

After looking through book after book related to caves and ancient mines he had reached an obvious dead end. However, he did learn a bit about the ancient tunnels below the Great City. This useful information Charlie decided would be best kept quiet until he had time to talk to Tim in private.

Tim and Ada returned all smiles carrying a large and rather worn, old-looking book. This book was wrapped in leather and trimmed in gold. The edges were worn from many years of handling and the binding had been broken many times over. Nonetheless both of them seemed most pleased with this particular book and they took it back to an empty table and started to giggle, laugh and take notes almost as an afterthought.

"Hey, Tim, what are you reading?" asked Charlie.

"Oh, it's a history of Wizard World. You should take a look, Charlie, it's pretty interesting. There are references in this book to the oldest wizards and sorceresses that have ever lived. One section refers to the Golundrus Cube and who and why it was created. There is a reference to a great war over this thing and then the pages are all ripped out. I think this is kind of strange, especially since we couldn't find any other references to the cube or the war," said Tim. "Ada and I figure that this stuff is really important so we're going to bring it up when we get our chance at open discussion."

"Hey, Charlie, did you find anything?"

"Nothing really," said Charlie, giving Tim that usual look, which caused him to nod and not say another word.

"Well then, why don't you join Ada and myself and take a glance at this book here," said Tim.

"Yeah, Charlie, come on over, the more the merrier," said Ada.

"Thanks," said Charlie.

Question and answer began and students had interesting questions about wizards, animals, locations and magic spells. Tim, Ada and Charlie waited their chance and finally Miss Gradulip acknowledged them. Tim didn't hesitate and held up the book they had found and referenced the chapter about the Golundrus Cube and the missing pages. Miss Gradulip's expression said it all; she was completely speechless for a moment or two before gathering herself. She let out a large sigh, shook her head repeatedly and motioned for Tim to bring the book forward.

"Students, this is a very ancient book about the history of Wizard World. There are many interesting things in this book, for instance, spells and history about some of the original wizards and of course the Golundrus Cube. Most of you will not know of the Golundrus Cube, and for good reason. This part of history has been hidden for many years to protect the entire population here in this beautiful land. I would suspect that many of you have heard tales told to you as bedtime stories or playground rhymes that children sing but don't really understand the true meaning. The truth is most of the stories are based on some real facts. However, not all the stories are real and there are some obvious exaggerations that have been told over and over until most of the real truth is lost or distorted to the point that it is no longer obvious.

"Before all the questions start, please let me reiterate that I am not sure that I should even be talking about this in the first place. If any of you are looking for more information related to the ancient object please ask Mr. Phinneus Grabblemore, and if he thinks the time is right he will tell you, or he will decide that it is not plain and simple.

"We are coming to the end of this first day of lessons so please, no more questions. I hope you all enjoyed the Library of the Ancients. We will meet here again at the same time tomorrow morning. Please make sure you report to your designated sleeping areas not long after dark or be prepared to face strict punishments, also your guild mentor will be notified. I suspect that most of you will head to the Rock & Stone Inn for refreshments," said Miss Gradulip.

"Come on, Tim, let's head out and take a quick peek at Gregor and Alicia before heading over to the Rock & Stone Inn."

After a quick stop at the corral Charlie and Tim had a rather long walk through some of the darker and seedier areas of the city before they finally reached their destination, the Rock & Stone Inn. Once they arrived they realized this was the place to be. Recognizable students already took most of the seating, making it difficult for Charlie and Tim to find the girls. Ada came running up from nowhere and dragged Charlie and Tim to the table she was sharing with her two friends.

Ada, Tara and Hannah already had drinks in front of them and were calling the bartender over to get two more. The bartender served Tim and then Charlie and walked away without a word.

The group continued on with small talk related to the Regular World and how they were able to cross through a portal using an ancient key. Tim also broke into their capture by the Shifters and being thrown into the Pit of Dulgeon, their escape and Grandpa Watson ending up missing. Ada was hanging on every word and had wrapped her hand around Tim's arm and stared deeply into his eyes lost in the conversation.

Charlie leaned back in his chair and took a deep drink of milkwine, enjoying the story. Tara pointed to the napkin that Charlie's drink was sitting on and Charlie leaned forward in his chair and picked it up. There scribbled one the napkin were the words "meet at table seventeen in thirty minutes." There was nothing more on the napkin and the bartender that had served the drink had mysteriously been replaced with someone else without them noticing.

"What is going on here, people?" asked Ada.

"Can anyone see table seventeen?" asked Tim.

"Yeah, it's right over there," pointed Tara.

"And there is someone sitting there," said Hannah, "and whoever it is they sure look creepy."

"Tim what time is it? Quick," said Charlie. "What time is it?"

"Hold your kattergraff will ya," said Tim. "Judging by that massive clock on the wall right over there and estimating when we arrived I would say you have about three minutes, give or take, to get over to that table."

"Okay, guys, I am heading over there, someone watch my back," asked Charlie.

"Yeah, buddy, I got your back, but I am heading over there with you—no buts, buddy, I am going and that's that," said Tim.

"I agree, Charlie, Tim should go with you," said Ada. "The rest of us will watch from here and keep an eye out for anything strange."

"Thanks, girls, I really appreciate it," said Charlie.

Ada leaned over and kissed Tim right on the lips and then took her seat with her friends.

Tim walked with Charlie to table seventeen in a total daze, dumbstruck from his first kiss.

"Okay, lover boy, stay sharp and pay attention to every little detail. I have no idea what or who we are going to meet over at table seventeen but for some strange reason I think that we need to be focused and pay attention to every small detail," said Charlie.

"Don't worry, buddy, I won't let you down," said Tim.

"Sit," came a voice from under a large black cloak. Charlie and Tim cautiously followed the direction and took seats opposite the cloaked figure. The voice sounded like a whisper and Charlie was sure that if he had not been the intended person to hear this then he would not have. This cloaked person was using magic to direct his voice to a specific person.

"We are short on time so listen and do not interrupt," said the cloaked figure. "You want your grandpa back, right?"

"Yeah, I do," said Charlie.

"Then the choice is up to you," said the hooded figure.

"What choice, and where is my grandfather now? Is he safe?" asked Charlie.

"Do not interrupt me again, for if you do this conversation is over. Do you understand me?" asked the hooded figure.

"Yeah, I get it," said Charlie.

"Okay then, we have something you want and you can get us something we want, plain and simple. We are offering a trade, your grandfather for a simple trinket that we would like to obtain. You go and get this trinket and hand it over to us and we will set your grandfather free," said the hooded figure.

"Just like that?" asked Charlie.

"Just like that. So we have an arrangement?" asked the hooded figure.

"Yeah, we do," said Charlie.

"We will meet here again tomorrow at the same time and I will give you the instructions. After that we will not meet again until you have either accomplished your given task or you have failed. Good day," said the hooded figure.

"Wait—" Before Charlie could finish his sentence the cloaked figure was gone in a puff of smoke. "No use staying here any longer—let's get back to the girls."

"There has to be more to this than meets the eye," said Charlie. "It just doesn't add up. What he wants must be really important, and how come he can't just get it himself?"

"You're right, Charlie, none of this makes sense. Why would such a powerful wizard need help from you? He obviously knows his stuff, being able to vaporate like that and manipulating his voice too," said Ada.

Charlie looked on with a frown on his face feeling a big insulted.

"Sorry, Charlie, I didn't mean to insult you, but it's clear that he is quite capable of magical things that we can only dream of at the moment," said Ada.

"Well, I guess I can't really argue with that," said Charlie. "And besides, I was thinking that myself. Why would he need me? I don't have any of the magical skills or experience that he obviously has. But still I can't pass this up. If getting whatever it is he wants helps my grandpa then I will do it, plain and simple."

"But, Charlie, you don't even know this guy. He could be tricking you and not help you at all," said Ada. "How do you know he even knows where your grandfather is?"

"I agree with Ada; we need to be careful," said Tara.

"No matter what, I am meeting with that stranger again tomorrow night. I will ask him for proof, like to show me something of my grandfather's or something. If he has nothing then I will walk away and tell Miss Gradulip what has happened so far," said Charlie.

"So it's settled then, tomorrow night we will meet at the Rock & Stone Inn. We can get there early and scout the place out a bit in advance," said Tim

"All right, Hannah and I will go too but we are going to sit at a different table closer to number seventeen so we can back you up a bit better just in case," said Tara

The group said their goodbyes and headed back to their sleeping quarters. All the while Tim and Charlie were walking they were sure someone was following them but they could never quite see who or what it was. Charlie was sure he had seen the cloaked figure from earlier at the Rock & Stone Inn floating above the ground almost like a ghost but he figured it must be his overactive imagination.

Morning came and after a quick discussion they broke into groups to do some research. Tim and Ada headed off in one direction while Charlie went with Tara and Hannah. Every aisle was searched down to the smallest book but they couldn't find a thing related to the Golundrus Cube. They decided to spend what little time they had left looking for a few useful spells just in case something went wrong with their meeting later on tonight. They worked on a few easy spells like the freezing spell and the binding spell. However, only Tim and Tara were able to use the spells correctly on a consistent basis so it was decided that they would be the main support if something went wrong.

The time finally came for the group to head to the inn. They arrived in separate groups so they would not draw too much attention to themselves.

However, even with their plans for an early arrival to prepare for the meeting they were too late; there seated at seventeen was the cloaked and hooded figure waving Charlie over to take a seat.

The hooded figure pushed a rolled parchment and a smooth stone across the table towards Charlie without a word. He just sat there motionless, as if he was waiting for a response from Charlie. It was obvious that he was becoming impatient and started to tap his fingers on the table quicker and quicker until he finally spoke, and what came from him was a surprising sound, a hideous hissing voice. "Well, are you going to open it or just sit there looking stupid?" asked the hooded man.

"Sorry, yeah, give me a second," said Charlie. "Okay, I see it; this looks like a map and encrypted directions. Am I supposed to follow this when I can't even read it? And what's this stone for anyway?"

There came the hissing voice again from under the hooded cloak, " Yes, you are supposed to read it. I am quite sure your friend will have no trouble translating this in no time. It's a simple encryption just so anyone who comes across it will not be able to readily recognize it and would probably throw it away. The stone is called a tracking stone; it is used to keep an eye on someone to make sure they are going where they are supposed to go and not making any unscheduled stops along the way.

"You are to follow that map and those instructions, retrieve the specified item and meet me at the River of Sorrow in three days' time by the crooked tree. If you do not arrive by that specified time the deal is off and you are on your own in finding your grandfather," said the cloaked figure.

Before either Charlie or Tim could ask him a question he was gone just like the last time, disappearing into thin air.

"There he goes again just like the last time—bark a few directions and wham, gone into thin air again. And what's up with that hissing voice? He sounds awfully creepy," said Tim.

"I know, that was really weird. He almost sounded like a snake or something," said Charlie.

"His voice sounded more like hissing through a crack or something," said Ada.

"Anyway, I need to go with Ada and translate this so we can try and figure out what the heck it means," said Tim.

"Okay then, you two go and do your thing and I will hang here with Hannah and Tara," said Charlie.

Hours later Charlie and Tim met up again at the inn where they were currently staying to discuss the evening's discoveries and what they should do next.

"Charlie, from what I can tell this map leads to some sort of ancient artifact that was created by a member of the Golundrus Guild many centuries ago. There is not a whole lot of useful information in this text except where the trinket is and that it's protected by ancient magic and can't be recovered except by the most skilled and pure."

Charlie laughed at the thought of being skilled and pure. "All right then, I guess that means me."

"Sure it does," said Tim. "Basically we are to follow the this trail to the mountains for two hours, then look to the north for the three rings, head towards the three rings and there off to the left will be the forked tongue, after that there are the two eyes of Rangnetto and in the left one is the tunnel leading down towards the cave of Flutornyia. In this cave there are three challenges to beat and then avoid the look of the ancients."

"Perfect! We can probably have that artifact in less than an hour," said a smiling Charlie.

"Hey, Tim, do you know what this sounds like—well, do ya?"

Tim shook is head, knowing all too well what this sounded like. "Yeah, Charlie, I do—it's another so-called adventure, and if they turn out like the ones in the Regular World I am sure we are in for the usual bucket load of surprises."

"Guys, I don't want to interrupt but it sounds like you need a direction finder," said Hannah.

Tim's perked up at the sound of something technical here in Wizard World. "Direction finder? Oh, you mean a compass. Yeah, that would be handy, that's for sure."

"I can make one if you would like?" asked Hannah.

"We sure would," said Tim.

"I suggest that we head out tomorrow right after class. We are going to need supplies of course, a lightner, some rope and some food and water just in case. We can leave a copy of the translated map with Ada just in case something goes wrong," said Tim. "And I am sure with the direction finder that Hannah is going to make we will be all set."

"That's a good idea, better safe than sorry I always say," said a grinning Charlie. "So tomorrow night we go for it, no surrender, we retrieve that whatever it is and then we get my grandfather back."

Their lesson with Miss Gradulip couldn't end fast enough. The members of their newly formed group wanted no part of studying, instead preferring to jot down a few notes and make copies of the map and clues that were given to them.

Class finally ended and they all headed off to the corral to say their goodbyes. Charlie and Tim saddled up Gregor and Alicia, strapped on their supplies and bade their new friends farewell. They planned on being back by the morning at the latest; if not they left specific instructions for Ada to alert the Golundrus Guild to their whereabouts give or take so a rescue mission could be mounted.

"Tim, here we go again off on another adventure to who knows where to face who knows what," said Charlie.

"Yeah, well, I would not have it any other way—magic and mystery here we come," said Tim.

Charlie and Tim headed out of town and quickly were off into the deep wood. Ada headed off the nearest tower moments after their departure and watched both Charlie and Tim until the very last moment. She turned away from the woods with tears in her eyes fearing she would not see Tim or Charlie ever again. The boys had made her promise not to tell anyone that they had left until tomorrow morning at the earliest and she was now wondering if that was a good idea.

"Tim, it's been two hours so I guess it's time to try and find the three rings to the north."

"Now, Charlie, the fun begins."

"I guess if you call this fun then it will be a blast."

Tim slowed Alicia to a trot and started looking around. "The first thing we need to do is get our bearings straight. We need to figure out which way is north and then look for three rings. They may be large or small so we really need to pay attention. We know we need to look to the north to find them so let's give it a shot."

"I am glad we packed this compass that Hannah made for us. She made that by hand and it seems to be working perfectly," said Charlie.

"Yeah, I knew that would come in handy," said Tim.

"Now looking to the north I see—mountains and more mountains. And guess what, no rings," said Charlie.

"Nope, not a one," said Tim.

"Maybe we are going about this the wrong way. Maybe the rings are not something we can see just hanging around but instead something we need to find, like a circle of flowers or rocks or just worn-out spots on the ground," said Tim

"Okay then, let's head north and see how many rings we come across along the way," said Charlie. "Gregor, this trail is not too rough, is it?" Gregor reared up and lowered his head, which he seems to do when he gets challenged. Charlie laughed and knew this was going to be nothing for him whatsoever.

Alicia followed along gracefully moving through the rock-strewn gorges with great ease.

Soon they reached ancient ruins and both knew that this was the spot. The boys climbed down from their mounts and began a semi-organized search of the area. After an hour or so they were coming up empty and frustration was setting in.

"It has to be here somewhere," said Tim.

"I don't see a thing that resembles a ring," said Charlie. "Maybe we didn't read the compass correctly or maybe Hannah did something wrong when she made it."

"I don't believe that for a second and neither do you. We are just going about this the wrong way. We need to step back for a moment and take a—" Tim stumbled backwards, falling to his butt. He had tripped over what looked like a curb that had been covered over the years by dirt and debris.

"Are you all right?" asked Charlie.

Tim just laughed, knowing that he had figured out the mystery of the rings. "Step back and take a look." Charlie did and there right on the ground were three of the largest rings he had ever seen. They were so large that neither Charlie nor Tim had noticed them and mistook them for stray stones that were lying about.

"Riddle one solved. Now off to find the forked tongue. We should be able to see it from here," said Tim.

"Yeah, well, a fork should stick out like a sore thumb," said Charlie.

"Right, just like the rings I suppose," said Tim. "Charlie, look over that way and I will look over here. One of us is bound to see the fork or whatever eventually. For all we know its right in front of us."

"Maybe not right in front of us but right above us, like way above us," said Charlie.

Tim turned and looked and sure enough there sprouting off a hanging stone was an ancient tree that had three limbs growing that closely resembled a fork.

"The question now is we can see it but how do we get there?" asked Charlie.

"Yeah, I was thinking the same thing," said Tim.

Gregor nudged Charlie from behind. Charlie turned to face him and it was obvious that Gregor thought he could make the climb. His head was down and he was waiting for Charlie to take the reins and get into the saddle. Alicia had headed over to Tim, who was already in his saddle and heading towards the cliffside at breakneck speed. Alicia climbed with great ease while Gregor struggled a bit but was making progress nonetheless. Soon they had reached the cliff where the forked tree was growing and both boys gingerly climbed out of their saddles and sat perched on a small ledge just barely big enough for them to stand on. Gregor and Alicia headed back down the mountainside and started to lazily graze on low-hanging trees awaiting their masters' return.

"Here we are—nothing to do now but pick a tunnel and go for it," said. Tim.

"Let's go for it," said Charlie. "Left eye it is and in we go—" Immediately both boys were sliding down the slick walls of the cave, unable to slow down whatsoever heading into the darkness. The cave walls seemed to be lined with a fungus that resembled cooking oil. There seemed to be grass growing out of the walls of the cave that would occasionally give a nasty cut. Both boys were covering their faces to avoid any injuries to their eyes as they continued descending into the unknown. Tim had finally caught up with Charlie and they were now tangled together as they slid uncontrollably not knowing what was coming next. Finally they slid into a pond of the gooey stuff and were completely grossed out by this.

"This stuff is stuck to us everywhere. We are never going to get it off. What is this stuff anyway?" asked Tim as he cleared both his eyes so he could take a glance at the surroundings.

"I have no idea what this stuff is, but right now I would say that's the least of our worries," said Charlie. Tim glanced over towards Charlie and could see these small shadows moving about. He had no idea what they were but he was sure it was not good.

Charlie struggled to pull his staff from his back while Tim started to back away trying to get enough of the gooey stuff off the lightner so he could see who or what was heading in their direction.

"I think we need to get out of here right now," said Tim.

Charlie glanced over and could now make out the shapes of small creatures that seemed to be made of the gooey stuff sporting six-inch-long fangs and claws to match. "Tim, I couldn't agree more; it's time to go."

The boys struggled through the gooey pond trying to reach the edge ahead of the fanged creatures that were rapidly heading in their direction and obviously gaining ground.

"They are going to get to us long before we reach the edge. This stuff is just too sticky and is slowing us down way too much," said Charlie. "Listen,

I will hold them off while you continue towards that edge over there. Once you get there throw me a line and you can pull me over."

"No way, Charlie," protested Tim. "I am not leaving you here."

"Tim, if you don't go now I am pretty sure neither of us will be getting out of here," said Charlie. "Don't worry about me, I will be fine. I am getting pretty good with the staff and I can hold them off for a few minutes. Hurry up and get going!!!"

"Okay, I will. Just tie this line around your waist and I will pull you out in a jiffy," said Tim.

Tim headed off towards the edge as fast as he possibly could. He was pushing himself to the limit. All his muscles were aching but he would not quit. He knew that he had to get to that edge or there could be some rather unpleasant results to this so-called adventure.

The first creature finally entered the range of Charlie's staff and he didn't waste a moment in taking a rather large windup, sending the staff hurling into the creature and embedding into what must be its neck. Charlie struggled to pull his staff out while the gooey creatures closed in on him from multiple directions.

Tim continued to struggle through the goo. He turned and noticed that the situation had grown increasingly dangerous for Charlie and began moving with all his might, ignoring the pain that was building in his entire body. Seeing his friend in mortal danger caused his determination to reach new heights, even surprising himself.

Charlie finally freed his staff from the creature only to realize that the swing he had taken had no effect whatsoever on the creature and it was slowly shifting back into shape again. He decided it was time to try a spell or two while he slowly backed away from creatures that were now well within reach of his staff.

"Tim, I would highly appreciate it if you would hurry. I am sure you are doing your best and all but—HURRY!" yelled Charlie.

Tim did not answer; he was far too focused on reaching the edge of the goo and did not want to be distracted by anything, fearing that wasting a moment would cost Charlie dearly.

Charlie yelled out the only spell he had learned, or thought he had learned, causing butterflies to come spouting out of the end of his staff.

"That's not going to help one bit, I suspect," said Charlie. "Tim, oh Tim, where the heck are you? I would appreciate a little he—lp."

Before he got an answer he felt a pull around his waist and was jerked backwards with such force that he almost went under for a moment. Promptly he gathered himself and started to swim through the goo with all his might. The creatures were gaining ground and were now within three feet or so of reaching him. Charlie realized that he was not going to make it so he did the only thing he could, pointed his staff in the general direction of the creatures and yelled, "Ergrono solidify!" This caused the creatures to turn solid, stopping them dead in their tracks. Charlie continued to move slowly towards the shoreline, thankful that he had paid attention to Tim when he explained that spell.

"I've got to tell you, Tim, I was getting a bit worried there for a moment or two. It was sure getting close, even close for my liking."

"Yeah, well, I had it under control the entire time," said Tim. "Now that was easy—I wonder what's next?"

"Charlie looked on with a questioning look. "Easy? Are you kidding me?"

"At any rate that's one down and two to go. How hard can the next challenges be if we figured this one out in no time?" asked Tim.

"No time? I almost became a puddle of goo in the belly of one of those things," said Charlie.

"It looks like we have to go down that tunnel over there," said Tim.

"Sure does," said Charlie. "Get out the lightner and we can take a peek and hopefully there will be some nice flowers and beautiful grass instead of ponds of goo and little green-colored Jell-O creatures with teeth as big as a my arm."

After rounding a curve in the tunnel they reached a large cavern. At the other side there was a locked door and hanging from perches high up above could be seen two of the most foul-looking creatures that Charlie or Tim had ever seen.

"I guess we reached the second challenge and judging by the look of those two things it's not going to be all that easy," said Charlie.

"I guess it won't but if we stick together we can figure it out," said Tim. "This looks really simple—get across, open that door and we are out. The only part that I have not figured out is where is the key?"

"Yeah, I was wondering that myself. Let's take our time and look around a bit before we actually head out there," said Charlie. "There has to be something we are missing. Somewhere in this place there has to be a key."

Suddenly one of the beasts swept down from the sky and landed twenty or so feet away from the boys. This thing looked like a cross between a vulture and a shark. It was absolutely hideous. It had giant scraggly-looking feathers, its head was bald and it had a large beak that resembled more the mouth of a shark than the mouth of a bird. It had large talons and feet that resembled chickens with webbing in between the talons. The eyes of this thing closely resembled a fish and seemed to have an extra eyelid that moved across it every moment or so.

The boys readied their staffs and prepared for battle.

"There is no need for weapons like that here, boys," said the creature. "They will provide you no assistance whatsoever."

"You can talk?" said Tim.

"Yes, we can. We have lived longer than any creature in this land and have seen many, many things. All come and go, yet we remain."

Then came the other creature sweeping down from the sky and landing right beside the other one. "Lived longer, have you? And what am I then, I suppose dead?"

"No, but if you don't stop with the chatter you just might be."

"Really? Are you threatening me?"

"If need be, then I will."

Charlie and Tim looked at each other shaking their heads and wondering when this challenge would ever get going.

"I don't want to interrupt, but can we get this going?" asked Tim

"Yeah, we don't have all day," said Charlie.

The first creature turned and faced the boys. "Impatience will end your challenge very fast, yes it will," said the now grinning first creature.

"Oh yes, dead, dead, dead," said the second creature.

"Okay then, let's get it going already. If your plan is to bore is to death it's working," said Charlie.

"Okay then, this is a simple test. All you need to do is outwit one of us in a mind game and the game starts right now," said the first creature.

Neither creature said another word, they just stood staring blankly at each boy as if waiting for some sort of a reaction.

"So this is it then?" asked Charlie. "Stare at us until we blink?"

"No kidding," said Tim. "I have had just about enough of this." Tim started to walk towards the creatures and was promptly pushed back with a great gust of wind from their mighty wings.

"If you attempt that again we will kill you on the spot," said the first creature.

"Yes, kill, kill, kill we will," said the second creature.

"Now the challenge is simple, yes it is. One question will be asked—answer correctly and get the key and head to the last challenge; answer wrong and be prepared to die, die, die," said the first creature.

"Pay attention, there will be no second try, answer wrong and prepare to—"
"Yeah, I know, die, die, die," said Charlie. "Let's just get on with it already—I'm not getting any younger you know."
"Okay then, prepare for here it comes: Sometimes I look red and sometimes white, I glow bright like a light, my colors change and are seen today, but they are older than this very day. Well, what am I?" asked the first creature.
"Yes, yes, yes, what is it?" said the second creature. "Die you will, die, die, die. Oh yes."
"Oh, shut it already," said Charlie. "Give us some time to figure this out."
"So impatient, that is no good, not at all," said the first creature.
"Luckily you brought me along and again so I can save your butt like usual," said Tim.
"Okay then, let them have it," said Charlie.
"What am I?" said the first creature.
"Are you kidding? Please! That's way simple. I was honestly expecting something a bit more challenging from beings supposedly as old as you two," said a now grinning Tim. "The answer is quite simple, you are the stars."
Both creatures were now speechless staring blankly at each other.
"This is entirely your fault—that was an easy question," said the second creature.
"Easy? Why, it would have taken you two millennia just to come up with a one-liner, never mind something that complicated," said the first creature.
"Excuse me, but we need a key to get out of here. We made a deal and got the answer right, so where is it?" asked Charlie
"Yes, yes, patience, my young friend," said the second creature.
"We are not your friends and we want the key. You either give it to us now or you are going to seriously regret it," said Tim.
"No need to get testy. Here is the key—go now and prepare for the third and final challenge. No one has made it past so do not bother preparing for anything but—"
"Yeah, we know—death, death, death. Come on, Tim, let's get out of here already."
As Charlie and Tim walked towards the door they could still hear the creatures bickering amongst themselves. Both boys wondered if they would ever shut up.
"One more challenge to go and then we can get my grandpa back," said Charlie.

"Yep, one more challenge," said Tim. "I bet this one will be the hardest one."

"Yep," said Charlie. "Let's get going then."

The two boys headed down a steep tunnel. The heat was rising rapidly and there was moisture building up on the walls causing the tunnel floor to become quite slippery. They slipped and slid their way dangerously close to open lava flows and steam geysers. Carefully they worked their way down the tunnel until they came to another opening and there in the middle were three statues beautifully shaped out of what must have been hot molten lava.

"Here we are," said Charlie. "Now we need to avoid the eyes of the ancients and make it over to that pedestal and get whatever that is and get the heck out of here."

"It sure sounds simple when you put it that way," said Tim.

"How bad can this look be anyway?" asked Charlie as he slowly stepped forward. Then without warning lava came bursting from the eyes of one of the ancients, almost burning him to a cinder.

"I guess we know what the look of the ancients is, so now we just need to stay alive long enough to get by it," said Charlie, now sporting a smoking and singed left sneaker.

"Talk about a hot foot," said Tim.

"Do we have any spells for this?" asked Charlie.

"We could use the water spell but I am not so sure that will be effective enough to stop that much heat," said Tim.

"Try it for a second and see what happens," said Charlie.

Tim pointed his staff in the general direction of the statue that was now facing them. He knew that this would not completely stop the lava but it might do just enough to give them a chance to get by and maneuver to another hiding place for an angle at the second statue.

Water billowed out the end of Tim's staff, meeting a steady flow of hot lava and filling the room with steam. Slowly the water was being pushed back closer and closer to the end of Tim's staff until he finally had to step back out of the chamber to avoid a burst of hot lava.

"That didn't work so well, but it did give me an idea. Obviously I can't stop the flow alone but if you kick in just enough magic at the end maybe we can cause enough steam to use it as a way of hiding us, almost like stealth," said Tim.

"That's an excellent idea," said Charlie. "We need to make a ton of steam just to make sure they don't see us since I would bet we would only get one chance at this."

"Yeah, so let's make it count. Are you ready?" asked Tim.

"Yep," said Charlie.

Tim pointed his staff at the statue facing them and yelled, "Volutis watera!!!" causing a great flow of water to burst of the end of his staff, hitting the statue right in the face. The statue reacted by shooting a large flow of lava out both its eyes heading steadily towards Tim. Charlie patiently waited until Tim's water flow started to fade and then yelled, "Volutis watera!" sending an even larger flow of water at the lava, causing so much steam that Tim and Charlie could barely see each other.

"RUN!!" yelled Tim

Charlie didn't hesitate and took off at a sprint into the steam, not knowing what would happen. He had thoughts of seeing lava come through the steam and hit either Tim or himself, causing instant death. However, this did not happen and they both reached their intended target, the pedestal.

Neither of the boys took a moment to celebrate, not knowing what would happen once they reached the pedestal, and removed the odd-shaped piece of what looked like granite.

Instantly the three statues seemed to freeze, no longer full of life or lava. The cavern seemed to lighten a bit and with that so did the moods of both Charlie and Tim.

"We did it!!" said Tim.

"No, you did it, I was just along for the ride," said a smiling Charlie.

"No way, buddy, without you I would have quit at the first challenge," said Tim.

"Can we get the heck out of here already? I am sick of talking birds, booger creatures and statues that want to burn me to death," said Charlie.

"I agree, so let's get out of here and get your grandpa back," said Tim.

Chapter 13

Capture and Freedom

"Now that we're finally out of that cave I've got to tell you I wasn't so sure we were going to make it," said Tim.

Charlie looked on grinning from ear to ear. "Really, I had total faith in you the entire time. I wasn't worried for a second."

"We really need to hurry and get back to the Great City before Ada spills the proverbial beans," said Tim

"I totally agree. Can you go any faster, Gregor?" asked Charlie.

Gregor lowered his head and picked up their speed considerably, causing Charlie to grab the reins tightly fearing he might fall off. Alicia and Gregor were moving faster than they ever had before. Trees turned into blurs along with most of the landscape. Before long the great animals slowed down a bit and Charlie and Tim were able to recognize some of the landmarks. They realized that they would easily make it back long before Ada was supposed to alert the support troops to their whereabouts.

The gates were in sight and finally the boys felt relieved although both knew this was only the beginning. They still had to meet with the mysterious hooded person who sent them on this quest in the first place and hope that all this life-risking was worth it.

They met up with Ada, Hannah and Tara to discuss their next step in getting Grandpa back.

Before Tim could get a word out of his mouth Ada was smiling, crying and hugging him all at the same time.

"I am just so happy to see the both of you. We were incredibly worried," said Ada. "I was so sure that something terrible would happen I couldn't focus on anything."

"She's not lying, that's for sure," said Hannah. "She hasn't stopped talking about either of you since you left."

"We had it under control the entire time. It was nothing really," said Tim, presenting the bravest face he could muster.

Charlie, Hannah and Tara just rolled their eyes impatiently waiting for this overly emotional moment to come to an end so they could finally get down to business.

"Okay, you two, we get the point already," said Charlie. "Right now there are more important things to worry about so can we get on with it already? Let's order another round of milkwine and frickta bread and plan for our next step, getting this piece to Mr. Creepy and getting my grandfather back."

"We have this thing that he wants and we have two more days to get it there. The ride is about half a day, give or take, so we should be able to arrive way before we are supposed to be there and easily make it back to the Golundrus Guild with time to spare," said Tim.

"We can come along too as backup because we will be heading that way too," said a smiling Ada.

"I guess that sounds about right—Hannah, Tara, are you in or what?" asked Charlie.

The girls nodded their approval.

"So today we can visit the shops about the city and then get to bed early for what I suspect will be another crazy day tomorrow," said Tim. "There are a few interesting places I wanted to stop at and check out. There's this one particular old bookstore called Kritilla's a few blocks from here that I am really anxious to get to before we leave."

"Yeah, I saw a place that looked interesting too, so I am going to head over there and we can meet up later," said Charlie.

The group split, Charlie heading one way while Tara, Tim, Hannah and Ada headed the other.

"I bet we can find something in that bookstore that will give us some useful information about the cave of Flutornia and maybe the Golundrus Cube," said Tim.

"Don't get your hopes up, Tim, I'm sure that every bookstore in this city has been picked through with a fine-tooth comb by now," said Ada. "There is probably nothing left about the cube in this city or any village within a hundred miles."

"That might be true but we have to try; the more information we can gather the better," said Tim.

Tim, Ada, Hannah and Tara reached Kritilla's bookstore and began a thorough search of the place. After spending at least two hours they determined it was a futile search. Tim decided that he would simply walk up to the front desk and ask the storekeeper if he had any reference material to the cave or the Golundrus Cube.

"Excuse me, kind sir, could you spare a minute please?" asked Tim.

A toothless, greasy-haired, balding, dirty, hunched-over man turned around, causing Tim to back away from the counter.

After gaining his wits Tim decided to just plow on forward and see what happened.

Tim put on his best look and summoned up his most polite voice and got down to work. "Sir, my friends and I are doing a research project, so to speak. We are trying to track down some information related to a cube we have heard mention of. We have tried many libraries and come up empty. We were directed to your fine establishment, being told that this was the place to find items that can't be found in, shall we say, a normal bookstore."

The creepy storekeeper looked Tim over once or twice and then leaned in real close. "Why, yes, I might have a book or two that would interest you."

"Okay then, my good man, could you kindly point me in the general direction and I will go and look for it," said Tim.

"Alas, books like that are not just lying around; they are kept safely out of the general public's view, so to speak," said the sneering the storekeeper. "Now if you would just follow me into the back I will show you what I have to offer."

Ada, Hannah and Tara started to follow but were promptly stopped.

"No, only one. The rest of you wait here and we shall return in a moment or two," said the storekeeper.

"It's okay, I'll be fine," said Tim

"Okay," said Ada, looking on with a concerned face.

The storekeeper took Tim through a large, worn, ancient door at the back of the bookstore that had a lock shaped like a lion's head. The storekeeper said "Drudis unlockis" and the lion's mouth opened and he inserted his hand and twisted it to the right. The lock clicked and the door opened.

Tim followed the storekeeper to an old glass case containing many ancient-looking books. These books were indeed very old and had been sitting in their case for many years. They were covered with dust along with a few very dead bugs. The storekeeper pulled a key off his neck and started to unlock the case. Tim greedily headed towards the now open case only to be stopped short by its keeper.

"Things of this nature do not come cheap, young sir. How will you pay?"

"I didn't think about that—can I go out front for a moment and talk to the girls? I am sure they will be able to supply me with some currency so we can reach an arrangement," said Tim.

The storekeeper looked on with a look of doubt. "You have five minutes. If you do not return by then I will lock this case and the lion's head and send you on your way never to do business again."

"Don't get all huffy now, I will be back and I'm sure we'll be doing business," said Tim

Tim headed back towards the front of the store and explained the situation to the girls. Between them they had twenty-seven knots and two red gems. Tim hoped it would be enough and hastily headed to the back of the store and into the reserved section to deal with the storekeeper.

"What have you got for me?" asked the now greedy-looking storekeeper.

"I have enough," said Tim.

"Well, how much is that?" asked the storekeeper.

"First name your price and then we can work from there," said Tim.

"I see you are a shrewd businessman," said the storekeeper.

"I dabble a little," said Tim.

"Okay then, the book on the left is called *The Literary History of the Ancient World*. It is the cheapest of the three. The second book is called *A Complete History of Wizard World* and the last one is *Ancient History, from the Dark Magical Practices to Ancient Symbols and Items*."

Tim did not say a word and tried to use his best poker face. He really wanted the last of the three, *Ancient History, from the Dark Magical Practices to Ancient Symbols and Items*, but figured he would play it coy and not let on just yet.

"All three are interesting I guess, but you and I both know that money talks," said Tim.

"It sure does, young sir. I am looking to get at least twenty knots for the first and second books, and at least fifty for the third," said the storekeeper. "All prices are final and non-negotiable. Also a book purchased in this particular case cannot be returned."

Tim tried to look unimpressed with the prices and the books themselves. "You couldn't possibly expect anyone with any knowledge whatsoever to pay a knot more than ten for either of the first two and maybe I would go as high as twenty for the last one—that depends on the authenticity of it of course."

"Thirty-five for the third book, no less," said the storekeeper.

"Okay, maybe I could do say—twenty-three," said Tim.

"No, thirty," said the storekeeper.

Tim tried to look uninterested. "Maybe I can do twenty-five."

"I will take it," said the storekeeper.

"Okay then, it's a deal, twenty-five it is. It was a pleasure doing business with you," said Tim.

"Same to you, young sir. One last thing—you didn't get this book from this store," said the storekeeper.

"What store?" asked Tim.

Tim headed out to the front of the store and happily gathered up his friends. After all, he was most pleased with his bartering skills and the way he handled the storekeeper. He was eager to start studying this book. He was sure that this book would hold some information related to the Golundrus Cube and the cave of Flutornyia.

Charlie had wandered about until he finally ended up at the Fritriggle's body enhancements and charms. He checked out many interesting items such as a mask that gave you a sort of night vision, a protective charm to stop all known freezing spells and a pair of gloves that supposedly gave the wearer the strength of at least forty men, the Gloves of Uforion. This one particular item grabbed Charlie's attention. He was daydreaming about the countless ways that he would use these gloves to help him with his quest to rescue his grandfather. He didn't notice Tim and the girls had arrived and were staring at him wondering what the fascination was with this old worn-out pair of gloves.

"Charlie? Hey, Charlie, over here," said Tim.

"Sorry, I was just thinking," said Charlie.

"About those beat-up old gloves?" asked Tim.

"Yeah, those gloves give the wearer the strength of forty men. That would be awesome," said Charlie.

"That might be true but it would make you dependent on them and give you a false sense of accomplishment," said Tim.

"Maybe, but they sure would come in handy," said Charlie.

The group headed out of the store with Charlie still thinking about the gloves. He was completely ignoring everyone, wondering if he should go back and get the gloves and keep them just in case. He figured better safe than sorry.

"Okay, let's get a table at the inn and get to work on analyzing this book," said Tim.

"You four go and I will catch up with you in a while," said Charlie. "There are a few things I still want to check up on before I call it a night."

"Do you want any company?" asked Hannah.

"Thanks, but I'm all set," said Charlie.

Tim, Ada, Hannah and Tara grabbed a corner table and started to look through the book. There were strange symbols and illegible text that would need translating but nothing about the cube or the artifact they had recovered.

"So far this book is a big waste of money," said Hannah.

"Yeah, I have to agree," said Tara.

"We need to give it time. This book has ancient texts that need to be deciphered, which hopefully will give us some insight about the cube or the artifact we found," said Tim.

"I hate to rain on your guildfaire and all, but we only have until tomorrow morning and then we have to give the artifact over to that creepy guy," said Hannah.

"Yeah, I know, Hannah, but we have to try. There must be something here that can help us out, I just know there has to be," said Tim.

"We will keep on looking all night if we have to," said Ada.

Charlie arrived without mentioning where he had been. He seemed to be in a rather happy mood considering the upcoming meeting with the hooded stranger.

"Hey, guys, how goes the research?" asked Charlie.

"Nothing yet but we are not giving up," said Ada.

"Tara used a simple spell to copy most of the pages of the book so we can split it up amongst ourselves; you know, the more the merrier," said Hannah, "so grab some pages and dig in."

"I'm on it," said Charlie.

Tim knew they had to come up with something and he was sure that the three undeciphered pages were the key. "Okay, people, from what I can see there are only three pages so far none of us have been able to figure out. So let's split into groups—Ada and myself, Hannah and Tara and unfortunately, Charlie, you are on your own. We can head to the public reading centers and check for any information related to these strange symbols. We can meet back here in two hours to discuss what if anything we have learned."

Charlie, alone and not really focused on this quest for data, was still thinking about his purchase earlier in the evening and how it would help him get his grandfather back. He wandered about the city until he met with a strange little man pushing a cart and selling useless trinkets.

"So, young fellow, are you just out for a stroll on this most wonderful night or perhaps there is something more? Yes, there is something more, isn't there?" said the old man.

"Yeah, there is, and unless you can decipher these ancient texts there is really nothing for us to talk about," said Charlie.

The comment of ancient texts seemed to perk up the old fellow. "Ancient texts you say? Yeah. Maybe I could be of some assistance, of course for the right price."

"Why would I pay you let alone trust you?" asked Charlie.

"Ah yes, that is the real question, now isn't it? Well, you have something that you need assistance with and I need assistance with my finances. Therefore we should make an arrangement that will benefit the both of us," said the old man.

"Thanks but no thanks." Charlie turned to move away from the old man after getting that creepy feeling that something wasn't right.

The stranger stepped in front of Charlie and smiled wide; before Charlie could react he was rapidly falling asleep. He could feel his eyelids getting heavier and there seemed to be nothing he could do to stop it. Charlie tried to speak but made no noise whatsoever. The stranger just stared at him smiling and not saying a word. He opened the side of his cart to reveal a large storage area and guided Charlie towards it. Charlie was close to being stuffed in the cart when he saw the strange little man fly sideways from a vicious strike of a staff to the left side of his ribs. He keeled over in pain and let out quite the cry as he crumbled to the ground.

"Charlie, are you all right?" yelled Tim. "Snap out of it, buddy. We have to get out of here. It's illegal to use a staff in the city and the Shifters will be here in no time."

Charlie was still unable to move or speak. He was just about asleep and dead weight. Tim and Ada scooped him up and headed down the nearest alley with Tara and Hannah pulling up the rear. They had just rounded the corner when that familiar popping sound could be heard; the Shifters had arrived. Unfortunately the group had chosen an alley that led to a dead end.

"Great! This is just great. It won't take the Shifters long to take a look down here, and guess what they will find—four teenagers with staffs carrying a half-sleeping guy. I don't know about the rest of you but I am pretty sure that won't turn out so well," said Ada.

"I agree," said Tim. "We need to get out of here right now. We need to try and pry one of those cellar windows open and get out of sight."

Tara and Hannah kept pulling and eventually the window gave way and opened. Hannah and Tara went in and Charlie's limp body soon followed them. Ada was next and then Tim pulled up the rear. Within a second or so of

Tim getting through the window that strange popping sound could be heard in the alley.

"Quick, over here," whispered Hannah and Tara. Tim and Ada headed over and joined them behind some old milkwine barrels. Charlie was lying next to them fast asleep. They were out of sight but definitely not safe. The Shifters could be heard poking about the alley and it wouldn't take them long to notice the open basement window.

"We have to get out of here right now. We need to head up the stairs over there and take our chances. If we stay here we are definitely going to get caught and I for one am not a big fan of the Shifters," said Tim.

"Well, neither are we, but are you sure? We have no idea where those stairs are going to take us. For all we know we might end up in a worse situation than we are in now," said Tara.

"If we stay here we are definitely going to get caught," said Ada.

"I say we go for it," said Hannah.

"Okay, Ada and I will carry Charlie and you two lead the way. Just act as casual as possible and walk right out. If anyone asks what happen to—" Tim was cut off by a surprising voice.

"What happened to whom?" asked Charlie.

"Hey, buddy, you're awake. Well, it's about time," said Tim.

"What's going on? And what happened to that old guy I met in the street a minute or so ago, and where the heck are we?" asked Charlie.

"There's no time for that now, Charlie, just play along with the rest of us," said Ada.

The group headed towards the stairs and reached the top and closed the door only seconds before that all-too-familiar popping noise could be heard in the basement. To their total amazement they had arrived in Frittleblot's food court, the largest and oldest food court in the city. In a moment they were completely engulfed by the crowd and had managed to elude the Shifters on this day knowing all too well that they might not be so lucky the next time.

They all realized that there were now even more questions than answers. They headed back to the Rock & Stone Inn to discuss the evening's events and what their plans should be for tomorrow. After the attempted kidnap of Charlie they figured remaining in a highly public place would be beneficial to their safety.

"Charlie, who was that old man and where did you meet him anyway?" asked Ada.

"I was just walking down the street and he started talking to me. He wanted me to pay him to decipher the ancient text for me. I never showed him the text or paid him and was about to leave, then all I remember is getting really tired and that's it. The next thing I knew I was in the basement waking up lying on the floor and looking up at Ada and Tim wondering what the heck was going on."

"So you didn't show that old man the papers, that's good," said Tim.

"Well no, of course I didn't," said Charlie defensively. "I was just talking randomly with him when I let it slip that I was looking to have some ancient text deciphered and that's when things got really weird."

"Just thought you should know that we did get the other pages translated and they led to nothing all that interesting and there is still one page left. Unfortunately it will have to wait until tomorrow since it is getting really late," said Hannah.

"If we wait until then it will be of little assistance since Charlie and I have to head out early tomorrow to meet with Mr. Creepy," said Tim

Charlie looked on filled with confidence. "Don't worry, Tim, I'm sure we'll be okay tomorrow. I think we can handle Mr. Creepy."

"I don't think you should underestimate him, Charlie, he is a very powerful wizard," said Tara.

"Yeah, Charlie, he can vaporate in a no-vaporate zone," said Hannah.

"Trust me, it will be okay," said Charlie. "I'm heading to the inn to get some much-needed rest and I'm reasonably sure that Tim could use some too."

"Yeah, Charlie's right, I could use some rest. All this research, hiding and carrying Charlie around really wore me out. I suggest you girls do the same since we are heading out pretty early tomorrow," said Tim.

"Okay then, we will meet at first light at the corrals to load up the kattergraff and head out," said Ada.

The groups went their separate ways, knowing they would not see each other after tomorrow for quite some time. They could send letters using the woodland animals but besides that there were no scheduled events that any of them were aware of in the coming months.

Charlie walked confidently towards the inn feeling invincible. He had purchased the Gloves of Uforion and was sure they would save the day. He would be as strong as forty men and could defeat any enemy.

Try as hard as they might most members of the group didn't sleep that well. Their dreams were filled with nightmares and disturbing thoughts and images.

When they met at first light they all looked ragged except Charlie, who slept a perfect sleep dreaming of victory and getting his grandfather back.

"Okay, team, let's head out and get to the River of Sorrow way ahead of Mr. Creepy so we can plan our defense just in case it gets ugly," said Tim.

"Guys, don't worry about it, I have it all under control," said Charlie.

"Yeah, well, better safe than sorry I always say," said Tim. "We've got backup this time so we might as well use it and use it well."

"We got your backs, guys," said Tara.

They had reached their destined location at least three hours ahead of time. They were sure this would be adequate to set up their defensive positions for the upcoming meeting with Mr. Creepy.

"Hey, guys, I just thought of something very important," said Tim

"What's that?" asked Charlie.

"The tracking stone," said Tim.

"So he already knows we are here," said Charlie.

"He most likely does," said Tim.

"So all this planning was a waste then," said. Ada

"No, not really—he knows we are here but he doesn't know any of you three are," said a grinning Tim.

"That's right! He can see where you are going but he has no idea that there are now five of us instead of the two of you," said Hannah.

"Exactly, so we can still set up just like we planned," said Tim.

"Guys, there's really nothing to worry about anyway," said Charlie. "Just relax and I will handle everything."

"What makes you think that you can handle everything? After the way that old guy was putting you into la la land so easily I wouldn't feel so confident if I were you," said Hannah.

"Yeah, he caught me off guard, that's all," said Charlie. "I'm ready this time."

"Hey, guys, I don't want to interrupt but we have about an hour or so before our creepy little friend shows up, so we really should get into position," said Tim.

Before the group had time to react that all-too-familiar popping noise could be heard throughout the woods. There had to be at least ten pops before they stopped. Tim froze in his tracks while Charlie ran for his bag and staff. He didn't say a word and reached in and pulled out these old worn-out gloves and put them on. The girls scattered into the trees, hiding high and looking somewhat camouflaged by the leaves. After all, they were part of the sorceress guild and they were highly trained in the wilderness and great at stealth. Tim had reached his backpack and pulled the artifact from it and hastily placed it behind a few rocks that were gathered by the graffla tree where Hannah and Tara were hiding.

The brush all about the clearing seemed to be stirring and loud branches were being broken by something really big heading in their direction. There came through the woods just to the left of the graffla tree four goblins leading the largest creature either Tim or Charlie had ever seen!! Immediately behind them came two more goblins wielding large rusty-looking spears and some sort of netting made of chain.

Charlie and Tim immediately backed away from this group of enemies, expecting a full frontal assault that never came.

Tim glanced up at the graffla tree only to see it engulfed in what looked like a giant spider web. The entire tree was encased in a second or two. The girls had no time to react and were instantly stuck high up in the tree. Hannah and Tara had leaves stuck to them in strange places, their eyes and all through their hair, making them look more like strange tree creatures than the girls they had resembled just moments ago.

Ada had chosen a different tree that was webbed just like the first one, causing her to suffer the same fate as her friends.

Then right behind the boys came that all-too-familiar hissing voice, "Well, hello, boys. It's nice to see you arrived nice and early and didn't keep me waiting. I noticed that you brought a few extra friends along; it's really a bother whatsoever. In a day or two the webbing will wear off and they will be free to head back to their little lives.

Charlie turned and faced the hooded individual with a rather confident look on his face.

"Listen, buddy, first you need to let my friends go and then bring my grandfather out here or this is going to get real ugly," said Charlie.

"Hey, Charlie, I don't want to sound all negative, but it sure looks like they have the upper hand at the moment," said Tim.

"Quiet, Tim, I've got it all under control," said Charlie.

Charlie stepped closer to the hooded figure, pointed his staff in his general direction and once again demanded his friends be released and his grandfather brought forward.

This brought a round of laughter from the goblins and the hooded figure, infuriating Charlie.

"I don't know what's so funny, but this is your last warning," said Charlie.

"You fool; did you actually think that those old gloves would help you?" asked the hooded figure. "I know all too well what they are and how they work. But you never learned how they actually work, did you? Judging by the look on your face I would say this is true and that's most unfortunate."

Tim looked at Charlie and Charlie looked at the gloves. The creep was right—he had no idea how they worked or if they even worked, for that matter. Charlie felt a sudden sinking feeling in his chest. He realized he made a grave mistake by not telling Tim or any of the girls about the gloves in the first place. There was ample time for one of them to help him figure out how they actually worked but his arrogance now made them useless.

"I'm sorry, Tim, this is all my fault," said Charlie. "I should have told you I bought the Gloves of Uforion and maybe they would have actually been useful."

"It's okay, Charlie, we'll figure something out," said Tim.

The hooded figure looked on, knowing that he had the upper hand and would surely get what he wanted, the ancient artifact. "Now, my friends, you have a choice to make, either surrender now or prepare to meet the Grogger; he is a most ancient creature that lives deep in the bowels of Wizard World and only answers to the goblins."

"No surrender," yelled Charlie as he prepared to swing his staff at the head of the hooded figure. Unfortunately before he could finish his windup the Grogger stepped forward and grabbed Charlie by the right arm, yanking him off the ground. His arm could be heard cracking, causing an immediate yell from Charlie. His face was distorted with pain as the group of goblins laughed along with the hooded figure.

"You can either surrender now or I will give the command for the Grogger to tear his arms off, then his legs, then his head," said the now laughing hooded figure.

"All right, just put him down right now and I will surrender," said Tim.

"That's a good boy—oh, and by the way, can you please get the artifact from the stone pile over there and bring it here now!" said the hooded figure.

"Get it yourself," said a defiant Tim.

"I will only ask one more time, boy, get it or he dies," said the hooded figure.

Tim grudgingly went to the rock pile and pulled the artifact out, causing an immediate roar from the goblins at the sight of the artifact. Charlie was then dropped hard to the ground wincing in pain from his grotesque injury he had just suffered.

Charlie rolled over and looked at the hooded figure. He wanted to get up and tear him apart but knew all too well that if he even made a move towards him that he would be instantly crushed by the Grogger.

Tim reluctantly handed the piece to the hooded figure, who then raised it high above his head and yelled, "We have it! We have it!" More popping could be heard all about. There must have been hundreds or even thousands—there were so many the sound blended into one, making it all but impossible to tell how many were actually arriving.

"You said I would get my grandfather back, so where is he?" asked Charlie.

The hooded figure looked on with delight. "Oh yes, I did, didn't I. Well, I am a man of my word so you will indeed be meeting with him in a matter of moments."

Charlie didn't like the sound of that or the feeling of getting ripped off the ground again by the Grogger. Tim stepped forward but was promptly pushed to the ground by two goblins and placed into rather heavy-looking chains. Soon Charlie joined him on the ground still wincing in pain.

"Charlie, how is your arm?" asked Tim

"It hurts but not as much as my pride. I let all of you down," said Charlie.

"No, you didn't, it's okay, we are still alive and so are the girls. We are alive and can fight another day. Look on the bright side, it sounds like they are going to take us to your grandfather so at least we know he is still alive. Once we get there we can plan our escape," said Tim.

Moments later Charlie and Tim were surrounded by goblins who then held up five red crystals simultaneously yelling "Vaporto," causing all to become blurry. It was as if they were traveling through a tunnel of sorts—the landscape was moving by far too fast to discern where they were. Soon there was a large popping noise and reality slowly started to come into focus and so did the ground, causing jolting pain to run through Charlie's right arm. He almost passed out but was able to hold it together.

They had arrived at a large goblin camp. They were in a large clearing that was entirely surrounded by steep mountain walls, making the entire area constantly shadowed.

There were many caves that could be seen off in the distance and also tunnels here and there that Tim was able to make out while trying to get a lay of the land.

The two were unceremoniously yanked off the ground and dragged towards some holding cells. There inside one of the caves an all-too-familiar face could be seen peering through the bars; it was Grandpa Watson. He looked a bit ragged and thin but good nonetheless.

The cell door was opened and the boys were thrown as easily as small children well into the back of the cell. When Charlie finally slammed into the wall he was in extreme pain. Grandpa lunged at the nearest guard and was flattened by a staff across his back. He went down but did not make a sound and waited for the last guard to exit the cell before heading over to Charlie.

Grandpa took one look at Charlie's arm and headed over to offer his assistance.

"Tim, Charlie, what happened? How did the both of you end up here?" Tim prepared to speak and was cut off by Grandpa Watson.

"Never mind that now, the important thing is that the both of you are safe. Now, Tim, can you please untie you shoe and take off your shoelace and grab the two wooden spoons over there," said Grandpa. "Charlie, this is going to hurt a bit at first, but trust me, it will be beneficial in the long run. If we don't set that bone soon the problems that will occur will be much worse than the moment or two of dare I say intense pain you are about to endure.

"Now I am going to count to three before I pull, ready—" Without warning Grandpa yanked straight down on Charlie's arm, causing him to scream in excruciating pain. It was all over in a moment, the wooden spoons were placed on opposite sides of his wrist and the shoelace was used to tie it all together to form a makeshift splint.

Charlie slouched back against the cold cave wall wishing that he had an aspirin the size of the moon to try and ease his pain. Unfortunately he not only felt the pain of his broken arm but the pain of his earlier mistake costing Tim and himself their freedom. He now felt any chance to save his grandfather was gone and there was no one else to blame but himself. His throbbing arm was a constant reminder of his careless mistake. The smallest movement of even a finger on his right hand caused sharp pain to shoot up to his shoulder. Although the pain was almost intolerable he was relieved to finally see his grandfather alive and well.

Now that they were all together the only logical thing left to do was figure a way out of this, and judging by the looks of things that was not going to be easy.

Chapter 14

Old Allies and Great Loss

Charlie and Tim spent the next few days telling Grandpa Watson about their experiences, how they battled goblins, met a giant and ended up members of the Golundrus Guild. Grandpa enjoyed every moment of every story. He had been locked up for months now and anything about the outside world was a joy to hear. He was definitely taken aback when he learned about the artifact that was now in the hands of the goblins. He did not know the particular importance of the artifact, but judging by the excitement of the goblins it was obviously a very significant find to them.

Grandpa took his turn telling the tale about how he and Alston had attempted numerous escapes, which were finally ended by their separation. Alston was now being kept two cells down on the right. The boys were glad to hear that he was alive and well. Both boys were well aware that if it were not for the sacrifice of both Alston and Grandpa Watson they might well be dead or at the very least would have spent quite a considerable amount of time as prisoners.

"Now, boys, please correct me if needed but from what the both of you have said it sounds like something big is being planned. With all the attempts at stopping the both of you from making it back to the Great City and meeting up with Mr. Grabblemore, and now this artifact, I think there is much more happening here than we are currently aware of. However, being strangers in this land and our current situation gathering information is nearly impossible at this juncture. However, there is one thing I am quite sure of—there is a large army being assembled here and I would wager it's not for peaceful purposes. When you add that with what the two of you have already told me—"

"Something really bad is about to happen," said Tim.

"Unfortunately I think you might be right," said Grandpa.

A slight tapping sound that was barely audible broke up the conversation. Grandpa called for silence and grabbed a stone and started to tap the wall himself in almost the same rhythmic pattern. Tim smiled, realizing it was a form of communication much like Morse code. "Boys, that was a message relayed from Alston. He is most pleased to see the both of you alive and well. He wants to know when the next escape attempt is. He is anxious to assist in anyway that he can.

"We have been monitoring the movement of the guards for the past week or so. Unfortunately the goblins are not very organized and their routine is hard to track. However, I'm quite sure with Tim here that he will have no trouble nailing down a pattern in no time."

Charlie and Tim realized that there wasn't much to do here but watch the guards go by and maybe enjoy the occasional stray bolt of sunlight that reached into the caves. Tim used his free time scratching detailed maps of the camp and the movements of the guards. He was ever diligent not to miss a single rotation of the guard and the routes the replacement guards took to get there and the route the exiting guards took to leave. He also kept close track of the food and water drops, figuring they might assist when they made their eventual escape.

Eventually Charlie started to work with his grandfather on basic self-defense. Grandpa Watson was well skilled in all verses of the major martial arts and was very efficient at their uses. He still moved like a man many years younger than he was.

Tim was sitting by the entrance to the cell when he noticed something quite different than he had been seeing in the prior days. There off in the distance he could see some colored cloaks, the color of the Bladgen Guild.

"Charlie, Grandpa, get over here quick, there is something the both of you have to see." Grandpa and Charlie swiftly headed over to the cell door while Tim pointed over in the general direction. There was no need for words; Ron, Sean, Clive, Beth and Crystal had arrived at the encampment.

"This was most unexpected. The plot now thickens. Maybe there is even more going on than we had ever guessed. Is it possible that the Bladgen Guild is working with the goblins? If so then this is very grave news indeed," said Grandpa.

"I can hear another message being sent. Alston has seen what we have and he is very concerned about this new turn of events. He requested we get our escape plans together and get out of here as soon as possible. He fears the longer we wait the worse the consequences for Wizard World will be. He is recommending that we make our attempt at first light tomorrow," said Grandpa.

"During the day? That will make being stealthy kind of impossible," said Charlie.

"You are quite correct, Charlie, but there is something you are not aware of that we are and this is an important part of our plan, and this fact is that goblins don't like sunlight whatsoever. Oh, they can move around in it all right and all, but they are at about half strength at best and become quite sluggish during the daylight. Haven't you noticed that the guards are always late during the day?" asked Grandpa.

"Well, of course I did," said a defiant-sounding Tim. "I wasn't quite sure what the cause was though."

"Alston and I have made most of our escape attempts during the morning hours. On more than one occasion we did reach the edge of the forest but were always caught before Alston could actually use the forest to our advantage. He is after all one of the forest spirits and once he reaches the woods will regain his full strength," said Grandpa.

"Grandpa, I just have one question."

"What's that, Charlie?"

"How do we get out of here?"

"That, Charlie, is something I have been working on for quite some time and the fruits of my labor will soon become ripe."

Grandpa led Charlie and Tim over to the very last bar of their cell and there right at the bottom covered with dirt could be seen a really worn bar. Grandpa smiled proudly and showed his secret; he had been using a piece of wire and graffla juice as an acid to slowly wear the bar away. He had learned of this from Alston and the secret was passed to every prisoner they could possibly reach. There plan was simple, a group escape at first light of the very next day. Both Alston and Grandpa were hoping with all the confusion that they could slip out of the camp relatively unnoticed and head as fast as possible to the Golundrus Guild camp.

Tim had spent every free moment tracking the movement of all the goblins that were visible to him. He noticed more than once while watching the goblins that Crystal had stopped and stared up towards their cell and embarrassingly turned away when she caught the eventual eye of Tim.

The day of the planned escape was almost upon them and all the details were being put into place. They would all break at the same moment heading in three general directions. Charlie, Tim Grandpa Watson and Alston were going to break to the east, the two cells to the right were to go west up the mountains, and the two to the left were to go east towards the deep wood. If anyone made it to safety they were to report all that they had seen and get help.

"At first light we will break the rest of that very worn bar and make for the tents down there to the left. There we will find our equipment and hopefully some supplies to assist us on our journey. Rest well tonight because I'm sure you going to need all your strength tomorrow," said Grandpa.

The morning arrived and both boys were awake well before Grandpa came over to rouse them. "Quickly now, get dressed and meet me at the cell door. Alston has alerted me that all is ready; they are just waiting for the signal, which is one of our hands waving through the bars."

Within a minute or so Grandpa had broken the bar and pulled it completely from the cage door to use as a club. He then handed Charlie and Tim two small logs he had stowed away in a small crack in the cavern wall many weeks ago to use as clubs.

"Boys, no matter what, don't stop; you must continue on and follow the plan. Even if I fall or someone else does, do not stop. We will not get another chance like this again, it's now or never."

As they headed down the trail towards the tents Alston joined them. "My boys, I am greatly relieved to see the both of you alive and well. Unfortunately I fear we are now in a worse situation than we were the first time we met. We must hurry and not waste a moment of time because it will not take the goblins long to figure out we have escaped."

No sooner had they reached the first set of tents when a large, mean-looking goblin walked out the front of one, almost knocking Tim over as he exited. Surprise was on their side and before he could react to what he was seeing Charlie smacked him in the head with his log and Grandpa Watson hit him in the back of the legs, causing him to fall over into a pot full of hot water. This ruckus immediately brought another goblin out of a large tent who took one look at what was going on and headed straight for a large ringing bell. There was no way any of the party could reach him before he would get to the bell and alert the entire camp, bringing down countless goblins all about them. However, right when he raised his right hand to ring the bell he was struck from behind by a large yellow flash and fell immediately to the ground without any noticeable movement. There standing with a staff pointed at the group was Crystal Kildroy.

"There is no time to explain, just go, and go now," said Crystal. Tim nodded to her and took off running with Grandpa and Alston but Charlie lingered for a moment.

"This doesn't make us even, you know."

"I know, but it's a start," said Crystal. "Now go, you've already wasted too much time."

Charlie turned and ran without looking back. He could hear more goblins starting to stir and knew that it would not be too long before they were discovered.

Exiting a tent with two Groggers was the hooded figure. He was not looking yet in their general direction but it was obvious that their cover would soon be blown. Alston stopped running and pulled the log from Tim's hand. He yelled for them to keep running and not turn back. Charlie immediately stopped and prepared to assist his friend in any way that he could but was stopped by his grandfather and yanked the other way.

Grandpa grabbed Charlie and pulled him along, knowing that there was not much time to get out of the camp. "There is nothing we can do to help him. If we stop now all of us will be caught again and I would suspect for the last time."

Charlie struggled but was unable to break Grandpa's steel-like grip. "Let me go, I know we can help him, just let me go."

Tim also wanted to go back but looking over the camp he came to the same realization that Grandpa had; if they stopped now to help Alston they would not be leaving.

Tim looked at Charlie then at Grandpa and then back at Alston. "Charlie, we have to go now. Alston knows what he's doing and I'm sure he'll be okay."

"But we can't just leave him to fight all of them. He will die if we do," said Charlie.

Tim grabbed Charlie to help Grandpa pull him away from the action and towards the woods and their freedom. Charlie continued to struggle the entire way, wishing he could break free for just a moment to help Alston.

The hooded figure noticed what was happening and promptly took control. He sent goblins off in all directions and sent two Groggers headed towards Alston. Mercilessly both the Groggers were bearing down on Alston, who just calmly stood his ground expressionless. He didn't move until the last possible moment to avoid having his head ripped off by a mighty swing of one of the Groggers. He then casually stepped to the right, causing the second Grogger to crash into the first, sending them both to the ground. Spinning effortlessly he then brought the log down onto the head of the first Grogger and easily the second. Before he could turn to face the hooded individual he was struck in the right shoulder blade by what looked like a red lightning bolt, causing him to fly about twenty feet through the air, spinning out of control and slamming into a nearby tent. Alston could be seen slowly pulling himself out of the mess with his good left arm while his right arm was hanging utterly useless by his side. Alston locked gazes with the hooded figure. He stood his ground defiant till the end. The hooded figure then raised his staff and pointed it directly into Alston's face and seconds seemed to drag on forever before another bolt of red lightning sent him hurtling along the ground another twenty or so feet before his limp and broken body slammed to the ground all twisted and mangled. There was obvious smoke billowing from what used to be Alston's head. The smell was nauseating.

Charlie yelled and pulled and strained with all his might to try and break free from Grandpa and Tim's grasp, but it was no good. Sadly he realized there was nothing that could be done for Alston. He was gone. Escaping was now the logical thing to do and Charlie realized this. He would, however, let this moment burn into his memory. He would not forget how Alston sacrificed himself to save a group of people he hardly knew.

Crystal witnessed the entire thing and was sick to her stomach. However, none of what had just transpired seemed to faze Ron, Clive, Sean or Beth in the slightest. They were more concerned that Charlie, Tim and Grandpa had escaped and unfortunately managed to remain unharmed throughout the entire ordeal. She now wondered even more if that day way back when if she had made the right decision.

After heading deep into the woods and remaining silent for a number of hours they were finally safe. Realizing that this information was very important, making for either the Great City or the Golundrus Guild to alert someone to what had transpired was the main goal. Alston's sacrifice would be for nothing if they were caught before they were able to alert someone to what was happening. They had seen many disturbing things, from the large gathering of the goblins to the Bladgen Guild members being in the camp. There was also the issue of the hooded man and the artifact he now had in his possession.

Charlie wanted to personally journey into the woods to tell Ambrose about his brother Alston but quickly realized that would have to wait for another time. He planned to repay Ambrose somehow no matter what the cost.

Grandpa, Charlie and Tim spent the next two days wandering about the woods tired and hungry. They had a general idea of which way they should go but no actual idea of how far they needed to travel. They spent the days covering as much ground as possible and spent the nights safely tucked away in different wooded locations. More than once they were sure that they were close to goblin patrols and once barely avoided detection by spending two hours partially submerged in a small pond.

By the end of the second day most of their supplies were nearing their end and all three were worn out from the continual movement and sneaking about. Grandpa was starting to show a bit of wear and tear and his limp was becoming much more prominent than usual. However, he never complained and easily kept pace with both the boys.

During their third day of travel the group was battered and weary to the point where their breaks became more and more frequent. Stopping every hour was now a necessity if they wanted to continue their journey. Eventually they came across a beautiful clearing and decided to rest up a bit longer than usual and spend a few hours trying to gather some nuts and berries. Grandpa quietly motioned for the boys to join him back in the clearing. He pointed out the fact that there were no animals noises whatsoever and even the insects seemed to have quieted. The forest had become eerily still, too still.

"Boys, be prepared for anything," whispered Grandpa. Wearily each grabbed their staffs and prepared for battle.

The silence continued for a long moment before that not-so-pleasant popping sound could be heard. This immediately caused some discomfort in Tim's stomach, realizing that he had just about enough of goblins and hooded figures to satisfy him for quite some time. He was in no mood for more fighting after watching Alston get killed only a few days earlier.

Charlie glanced over at Tim and this helped him with his focus. Once again he felt that determined feeling he got whenever he knew he had to help his best friend.

Still the forest remained silent; nothing moved or could be heard in any direction. Grandpa signaled for the boys to duck down a bit to get out of eyesight and pointed to the left of a large graffla tree. There off in the distance could be seen a shadow moving very stealthily about, making not a single noise and barely visible, as if almost blending into the forest.

Then a whisper could be heard as if it was riding on the wind. "Charlie, Tim, can you hear me? Hello," said the shadow. Neither of the boys answered, fearing a trick. They did not recognize this shadowy figure and after what had happened had no intention whatsoever of exposing themselves to an attack.

The voice grew closer and then off the left could be seen another shadow, slightly taller than the other and also calling for Charlie and Tim. Tim smiled at Charlie and gave the thumbs-up to Grandpa. He had figured out who it was and seemed to relax and began to stand. Charlie grabbed for his wrist but his hand was pushed aside as Tim called to Klortis and Caruna. The wizard and sorceress came running with staffs at the ready, closely followed by at least ten members of the Golundrus Guild. The group rapidly formed a loose perimeter and looked more than well prepared for any confrontation that might arise.

Klortis, who was now facing Grandpa Watson, lowered his staff and made a ceremonial bow to him. Grandpa Watson returned the bow smiling all the while. Handshakes were exchanged while Charlie and Caruna exchanged a rather emotional hug. Charlie didn't care if anyone was staring at the moment. This was the best he had felt since witnessing the murder of Alston. He could feel tears building but held it together, not wanting to completely embarrass himself. Klortis wandered over and patted him on the back and quickly moved on towards Tim.

Tim filled Klortis in on what they had witnessed. The entire time Charlie just listened, burning with rage and wanting nothing more than to kill every single goblin and the hooded man. He had no idea of his identity but would use every single spare moment of his time to find out. He would not let Alston's death go unpunished.

Caruna stayed at Charlie's side the entire time. She would not leave him alone, fearing that at any moment an attack could occur. She remembered being horrified when she heard the boys were missing. If it were not for Ada, Hannah and Tara they would have been out here for weeks or longer since there was not a single person who had any idea of their whereabouts. This small detail was not lost on Klortis, who promised once back in camp they would have a most serious conversation about what they had done and how much peril they were actually in.

Finally they prepared to leave and head to camp. The circle was formed and they were all transported using the vaporto spell in unison. Charlie and Tim had experienced this already but couldn't help but smile and laugh when seeing the excitement on Grandpa's face.

When they arrived in camp Phinneus Grabblemore himself greeted them. Only moments earlier he had been notified that the boys and Grandpa Watson had been found and were safe. He was already well aware of the death of Alston and was noticeably shaken by this news.

"Boys, this is a most pleasing moment, seeing the both of you and your missing grandfather here makes my heart feel quite a bit lighter after hearing of the most unfortunate death of Alston. He was a fine spirit and a fine friend to all and will not be forgotten," said Grabblemore. "However, right now is not the time to mourn since we have some most disturbing things to discuss. After dinner I need to see Charlie, Tim and Mr. Watson at my personal tent to go over various things. I would also like Klortis and Caruna to join us. But for now, please eat and rest and I will call for all of you later in the evening."

Grabblemore headed off to this tent without another word. He was followed by two unknown guild members and was out of sight and off into his tent.

Charlie walked off alone, not bothering to eat. He was far too frustrated and getting more and more aggravated with every passing moment. He didn't understand why Alston's death was being treated so casually.

"Just let him go, Tim, he needs time. Charlie deals with things in his own way," said Grandpa Watson.

"I know, Grandpa Watson, but he is so frustrated and angry and you know he can sometimes do some stupid things when he gets like this."

"True, but I don't think we have to worry about that right now. I am pretty sure that Charlie feels like he let Alston down and that somehow this is his fault and he should have done something to help him."

Tim looked on shaking his head. "There was nothing anyone of us could have done."

"I know, Tim, but Charlie still feels that way nonetheless. Hopefully he pushes his feelings in the right direction and not the wrong one."

"Yeah, I hope he does too."

Caruna headed off after Charlie carrying a dish of grittla meat and a small carafe of milkwine. She didn't want to leave him alone, knowing all too well how he must be feeling. "Charlie, wait up."

Charlie kept walking and didn't bother to answer her. In a moment Caruna had caught up with him and was quietly walking beside him. Neither said a word and they just walked and walked until they eventually reached a small flowing stream. Here Charlie finally stopped and sat upon a moss-covered rock. He kept his head down and said nothing.

"Charlie, you can't let it get to you like this. I know it hurts but there was nothing you could have done."

"How do you know what I am feeling? You weren't there. Alston was only thirty feet away from us and we could have helped him!"

"Charlie, if any of you had gone back to help Alston you would have certainly joined his fate. And as far as knowing what you are feeling, I know all too well—my parents were killed right in front of me in a goblin attack and there was nothing I could do. I stood there helpless holding my staff and I didn't even raise it Charlie, I just stood there frozen in fear."

"I'm sorry, Caruna, I had no idea—"

"Yeah, well, how could have known after all? You have been too busy asking for riding lessons and help with your kattergraff to bother to get to know me. And now you're wallowing in your own pity too much to think of anyone again but yourself." Caruna turned away when tears started streaming down her face.

"I—I—I'm sorry, Caruna. Now I feel even worse. I should have asked."

"Asked what?"

"Well, more about you I guess. How old were you when this happened, you know, to your parents?"

"I was four and a half and I failed. That image has been burned into my memory as an everlasting mark of my failure."

"But, Caruna, you were only four years old, what could you have done?"

"I don't know but I could have tried."

"Maybe but you probably would have—joined your parents."

"Now you see."

"I guess I do. Thanks."

"Now can we enjoy some of that milkwine and grittla meat?"

"Sure thing."

Before Charlie could enjoy the meal that Caruna had brought along, a small floating rock came upon them and began to speak. "Well, here you two are—well, it's time for the both of you to head to my tent. There is a very important meeting going on and attendance by the both of you has been requested. Your urgency also will be most appreciated," said a small rock shaped like Grabblemore's head.

"If the rock head says we must then that's what we'll do," said a laughing Caruna.

"Yeah, how can you say no to a rock head," said Charlie. "What was that anyway?"

"That's a morphin stone; we use them to communicate sometimes," said Caruna.

"Sure we do," said Charlie.

Moments later they arrived at the tent and were hastily invited in by a waiting Klortis.

"There are many things to discuss and there is little time to waste I fear," said Klortis. "Grabblemore is waiting along with Mr. Watson and Tim. I will be standing guard with Caruna until we are called upon. Caruna, please take your place opposite me and prepare for anything. We are not allowing a single person, no matter who arrives, entrance to this tent. The things that are being discussed are far too sensitive and could lead to many deaths."

"What's going on in there?" asked Caruna.

"I was asked not to discuss anything outside the walls of Grabblemore's tent. He fears there could be spies right here in this very encampment," said Klortis.

"A spy, here in the Golundrus Guild? That's just not possible, is it?" asked Caruna.

"Oh yes, my dear, it is very possible indeed. I fear that there are trying times coming and there will be many deaths," said Klortis.

"I would very much like to know what is going on, Klortis."

Charlie entered Grabblemore's tent and his attention was drawn to a smoking cauldron set off to the right with a small smoldering fire beneath it. Surprisingly the smoke was not bothering a single person in the tent and there seemed to be relatively no smell whatsoever. Charlie took the seat right beside Tim and noticed that Ambrose was sitting straight across from him. His eyes were noticeably red and he was looking very weary. Judging by the look of Ambrose it was quite obvious to Charlie that he was well aware of the death of his brother Alston. The guilt of seeing Alston die forced Charlie to turn away from Ambrose, feeling too embarrassed to look at him even for a moment.

"My friend, there is no need to turn away from me. I have heard the entire story of what my brother did and I am more than sure that he would do the same thing again, even knowing what the results would be. He valued life and did the simple math, making the ultimate sacrifice so three others could escape and live to fight another day. He knew all too well that there is something evil going on here and that the information the three of you were carrying could save thousands of lives in the near future. So do not hold a moment of guilt inside yourself and rejoice as my brother would that he was able to enjoy your friendships for as long as he did. Now please remove all sadness from your soul and someday in the future we can mourn together by the river when all of this is finally over," said Ambrose.

"Thanks, Ambrose, but I will keep the memory of his death burned into my mind all the same. I was unable to save him and that is something I never want to happen again. I will refocus myself and train twice as hard as I have been in the past. I will not forget this failure and I am forever indebted to Alston and your family for the sacrifice he made," said Charlie.

Grandpa and Tim looked on, wondering who this stranger was sitting before them. Charlie seemed to have aged many years in the past few days. He sounded mature and focused and his goals seemed clear to him.

"Now that Charlie is officially here we can begin this most important meeting. Ha, excellent, the potion has matured and is now fully effective. Charlie, would you kindly exit the tent and please ask Caruna and Klortis to join us?" asked Grabblemore.

"But who is going to guard the tent then?" asked Charlie.

"The smoking cauldron over there in the corner has taken care of that," said Grabblemore.

"How?" asked Tim.

"The smoke is actually a magical potion called Aluris Visualis. This spell makes this tent virtually invisible and impossible to detect until the counter potion is mixed," said Grabblemore.

"There is one thing that I must emphasize and please take it very seriously—not one bit of this information can be discussed outside this tent. The repercussions could be disastrous to everyone here in Wizard World. So now that the pleasantries are out of the way we can get on with this meeting.

"Now I am well aware that Charlie and Tim have spent some time researching some rather secretive things while they were at the Library of the Ancients. Boys, don't worry, as what you were doing was perfectly fine. I was told through rather dependable sources that you two were looking for information related to the Golundrus Cube."

"Sorry, Mr. Grabblemore, we had no idea that we weren't supposed to be doing that kind of research," said Tim.

"Trust me, it's quite all right. After all, you didn't really find anything that interesting, now did you?" asked Grabblemore.

"No, I guess we didn't," said Tim.

"So for now we need to let that search go until the proper time presents itself," said Grabblemore.

"When will that be?" Tim asked.

"All in good time, my boy, all in good time," said Grabblemore.

"Here is what I think you need to know at the moment and I will try to be as brief as possible. Please follow along and try not to interrupt too much as this could be a bit long winded," said Grabblemore. "We are all well aware of the artifact and the apparent interest by the hooded figure and the goblins. There is a connection between the goblins and an evil wizard who lived long ago. Now this one wizard, Bjolf Morphran—yes, one of the original guild creators—was a bit of a power-hungry wizard. He thought that the powerful magic should be used no matter what the effects it had on others. He feared that one day Regulars from the Regular World would learn all about Wizard World and gain entrance through one of the many hidden portals and destroy all that we had worked to create. He was so sure of this that he would risk anything to gain control of the most powerful object known to exist in Wizard World.

"Fortunately the creator of this object, Amore Golundrus, was alerted to his treachery and was able to stop Bjolf Morphran from gaining access to this object by sacrificing himself.

"This moment in Wizard World caused great death and destruction. The effects were felt for many centuries and some say still to this very day. Now there was one twist to this story that not even Morphran himself was aware of and now I fear his treachery is surfacing once again.

"Amore had taken to this one misfit wizard named Ludris Garlit. Now Ludris was not a very gifted wizard and was average to say the very least. However, Ludris Garlit was a very clever person and was able to finally reach Amore and convince to take him on as his scribe. Ludris was ever diligent and paid close attention to every word that Amore mentioned about anything related to this great magic. Ludris never passed this information on to either the Goblin King or Bjolf Morphran but instead made plans of his own. Ludris's plan was when the attack did occur and the inevitable defeat of Amore Golundrus and the rest of his close supporters he would then use the information he gathered to in time recover this great magic and quite possibly proclaim himself king. Ludris stored the secret information in many different places so it could not be recovered without his assistance. Unfortunately for Ludris he was killed during the attack and the rest is history, just tales and stories about hidden clues and maps to the ancient magic.

"Now I fear this hooded figure has somehow managed to get his hands on some of Ludris's papers and is using that information to his advantage, hoping to obtain some knowledge once thought lost, and that takes us to the end of this tale."

Tim listened intently and still had one more question he would like answered. "Mr. Grabblemore, I have one more question—what does the Golundrus Cube do? I know it's really important and all, but why?"

Grabblemore looked on, obviously stressed by the entire situation. "I guess there is no point in putting the rest of this conversation off any longer, so here goes, and Mr. Watson, please pay close attention as I believe you will find this most interesting.

"Many long years ago Wizard World was located in the Regular World. Wizards and sorceresses lived alongside mankind helping when and where they could. As the long years passed however, things didn't stay as friendly and our kind was looked on with disgust and jealously. We were exploited for our extraordinary powers and skills to the point where we had to move deep into the far stretches of the land to avoid persecution and exploitation. After countless moons had passed the Regular World again started to creep ever closer to our secluded locations, leaving us little or no options. So a council of the greatest wizards and sorceresses was created to come up with a plan to save us once and for all.

"Now many ideas were thrown about until the mightiest and greatest of the wizards, Amore Golundrus, stepped forward with the idea of harnessing magic into one location to be used to move all settlements to a new and secure location, creating an entirely new dimension so we could all live in peace and not worry about further persecution. His idea was to create a cube with the four most magical members each putting a great amount of magic into a separate part of the cube, and then combining it to create what is now called the Golundrus Cube. After this accomplishment most settlements were moved to the new land of Wizard World except for a scant few outposts that were left behind, which, Mr. Watson, I believe you have once visited in the past. Now besides these outposts a few wizards stayed behind just in case they were ever needed again. Also many clues were left such as keys that could be utilized to cross over to Wizard World if the need arose. Through the many centuries these keys were hidden, lost, destroyed or forgotten until you, Charlie and Tim, came across into our lands.

"Now for the final and most important thing about the cube: If it is again assembled and brought into the portal located in the Great City, Wizard World will again be thrust back into the Regular World, causing utter destruction as the two realms once again become one. Now you can see why this information was kept secret; the destruction that could be brought on by this would be utterly devastating, not only to us but your land as well.

"I don't need to get into any more of the specifics, as they are not all important at this juncture and are better left for other days and times," said Grabblemore.

Charlie, Tim and Grandpa Watson looked on in utter astonishment. Knowing now that their quests were not only important to this land but to the very survival of the Regular World put other small issues into perspective. But there were still other questions that needed to be answered.

"That's a whole lot to take in, that's for sure," said Charlie.

"I know it was, boys, but knowing this information just might help you out somewhere down the road. I discussed this with the Council and they agreed that you should be told of the gravity of this situation."

Grabblemore looked on, knowing he had done the right thing by telling them, but wondering if they would be able to handle it in the upcoming trying times that would weigh heavily upon them. "My boys, I know it all sounds overwhelming but remember you are not alone; you have every guild member's support from the lowliest wizard to the mightiest Council Member. We are all working towards a common goal and that's making sure both our lands remain safe and sound."

Charlie had a few other questions that he needed answered and didn't hesitate to ask. "Is that Bjolf Morphran related to the current head of the Bladgen guild, Eblis Morphran?"

"Yes, he is," said Grabblemore. "Bjolf is an ancient relative of Eblis Morphran."

"Why isn't he sitting in jail right now instead of leading a group of powerful wizards?" asked Charlie.

"He has never done a thing or shown any disloyalty towards any member of this land that I am aware of," said Grabblemore. "Also, he cannot be held responsible for things that happened many centuries ago. That would not be fair to him in any way. His family line was all but exterminated and the guild was removed from these lands except for a few members of the Morphran family who never demonstrated any magical powers. Eventually the family members were slowly absorbed into the community, some marrying, and eventually this allowed for the family to again regain the use of magic.

"However, not all the evil members of the Morphran guild were hunted down and some managed to avoid capture and disappeared into history, eventually lost like most of the textbooks and parchments that documented all this tragic ancient history."

"Well, seeing members of his guild at the goblin camp sure points in his direction," said Tim.

"That certainly doesn't look good for the Bladgen Guild but we must get facts before we come to conclusions," said Grabblemore.

"I must agree also with Phinneus. There is no actual proof that Eblis has done anything wrong at the moment; however, I do recommend we keep a close eye on him," said Ambrose.

"I totally agree and that's why I have called you here, Ambrose. I need you to use your great stealth and magic to infiltrate the Bladgen Guild and see if you can learn anything that might be helpful."

"You know that I will do what I can no matter what the cost," said Ambrose.

"Good, I figured you would say that. You should head out now as time is most definitely of the essence," said Grabblemore. "Good luck, my old friend."

Without another word Ambrose was gone. There were no long goodbyes, just a quick flash and that familiar popping sound.

"I think we need to increase the guild guard and send out the call to gather all our forces," said Klortis.

"Now we must not tip our hand that we are aware of what is going on since we could put events in motion far quicker than their current pace," said Grabblemore.

"But Mr. Grabblemore, what if the Bladgen Guild attacks and the goblins are with them?" asked Tim.

"Don't worry, my boy, we are quite safe in this camp from any attack that could be mustered against us. However, I do agree that increasing the guild guard and doubling the patrols is an excellent idea," said Grabblemore.

"I will get the guard in place in a matter of moments," said Klortis.

Caruna stood and prepared to leave but was stopped by Grabblemore. "I have one more thing to ask of you, Klortis, and also you, Caruna. Our young friends are in need of a crash course of magical training and I would like you to assist Klortis any way you can. I would also like to emphasize that neither boy is to be left alone for even a moment since I fear they will eventually play a rather large role in this mystery."

"Why are we so important?" asked Charlie.

"That is quite simple, my young friend, you two recovered the artifact when many others had failed. This slight detail I am quite sure was noted by the hooded figure and that was the reason for your captivity," said Grabblemore.

"So he was planning on having us go on more quests?" asked Tim.

"I am sure that was his initial plan and having the both of you slip through his fingers must be truly frustrating to him," said Grabblemore. "Now go and head back to your tent and rest. Tomorrow will bring intense training at a level neither of you are prepared for at the moment."

Chapter 15

New Spells and Secret Tunnels

Morning came and Charlie and Tim were awoken to quite the surprise; there standing in the entryway to their tent were Gregor and Alicia along with Caruna.

"I was wondering what happened to you," said Tim.

"Yeah, me too. Where the heck were the both of you?" asked Charlie

Gregor bowed his head and Charlie rubbed him behind his ears.

"They were wandering about for a bit so I used a spell I invented when I was a kid to summon them here to their home," said Caruna. "You two should head back to the food court and get some breakfast before the training starts. I have no doubt you will need all the energy you can muster."

After a hearty breakfast Tim and Charlie were led down to what looked like an obstacle course. This course more resembled an outside torture chamber than a place to train. There were many sharp objects moving about along with stray bolts of what looked like lightning and the occasional tree sprouting out of the ground at random moments. And there just next to what must be the beginning of what is this obstacle course was a smiling Klortis.

"Welcome, my boys; today begins your crash course in wizardry. Here you will learn to fight, dodge, cast spells on the move and mentally prepare for unseen challenges. This course can either make or break you, plain and simple. You will remain here until you can successfully navigate this course or cannot get up to try again."

Caruna was grinning from ear to ear and neither of the boys had any idea why.

"What's so funny?" asked Charlie.

"You'll see if and when you get to the end," said Caruna.

"Oh, I'll be at the end, don't worry about that," said Charlie.

"And so will I," said Tim.

"Charlie, please come over here and prepare for your challenge," said Klortis.

Charlie looked on, feeling a bit skittish at the sight that was before him. He could not believe that anyone could get through this without getting seriously injured or possibly killed. He wondered to himself how many students had died attempting this obstacle course. The look of panic on Charlie's face brought a smile to Klortis as he remembered the first time he attempted this course.

"Don't worry, Charlie, it's been at least two centuries since we had a recorded death, so I am sure you'll do fine."

"Yeah, I'm sure I will. Hey, Tim, make sure you take care of Gregor for me since I may not be in any condition to do so after this."

Charlie pulled his staff off his back and prepared to enter the fray of the Wizard's Obstacle Course. He slowly worked his way down the first steep wooden decline and neared the edge of a small moat. He was sure he could just jump across but decided against this, realizing it was way too easy.

"We don't have all day, Charlie," said Klortis.

"Okay then, here goes" Charlie stepped back and jumped as far and as hard as he could. Before he reached halfway across the moat he was hit with a jet of water that threw him backwards, sending him crashing rather violently to the ground. He was covered in mud from head to toe and was not looking all that happy. Klortis and Caruna were bent over in hysterics and even Tim had a hard time holding the laugher back.

"You can laugh now, buddy, but don't forget you're next," said Charlie.

Charlie revved up and prepared for his second attempt, but this time he didn't jump but walked to the edge and used his staff to check and see how deep the water was. He realized it was only a foot deep, give or take, and he could easily walk right through. He slowly placed one foot into the water and then the next and was promptly swept backwards by a rather large muddy wave. Again Klortis, Caruna and Tim broke out into uncontrollable laughter.

Charlie didn't even look in their direction; instead he took a moment to more thoroughly examine the situation. He stepped back with a smile on his face, placed one end of his staff into the water and used it as a pole vault to get across without causing a single drip to head in his general direction.

Now smiling and feeling quite proud of his accomplishment, Charlie prepared for the next challenge and what awaited him was what looked like moving padded, giant marshmallows with the occasional random lightning bolt flying about.

He stepped gingerly forward, staff at the ready prepared for almost anything, of course except for what was about to happen. Without warning the marshmallows started to close in on Charlie, who noticed this and started to swing uncontrollably with his staff, batting the marshmallows this way and that but forgetting about the lightning bolts. Of course in a matter of seconds he was struck multiple times by the bolts, causing him to lose his concentration, and the marshmallows easily overwhelmed him and all that could be seen of him was his left foot wiggling erratically from the bottom of the pile. Klortis yelled a counter spell and the marshmallows scattered and the bolts stopped.

"That's enough for now, Charlie, you did quite well," said Klortis.

"Are you kidding me? I was drenched more than once by that puddle and the marshmallows almost smothered me to death. I would hate to have seen what would have happened if I did poorly," said Charlie.

Tim took his turn and never made it by the moat, which of course had reacted to Charlie's earlier successful cross and blocked that way of crossing. After four failed attempts it was decided that they would take up tomorrow where they left off today and would now spend a few hours learning some counter spells.

After learning two attacking spells and two counter spells the group broke for lunch. Charlie and Tim spent most of this time resting as much as possible, knowing all to well that the afternoon would be no easier than the morning.

They spent hours working on staff techniques and taking quite the beating from either Klortis or Caruna. Finally Klortis called an end to the day's training and recommended both Charlie and Tim eat and spend the rest of the evening resting. There was no need to worry about tending to the kattergraff since that was being taken care of by one of Caruna's friends, Delyna Devey.

The next few days were spent training heavily with no breaks except for food and sleep. Charlie and Tim were becoming physically and mentally worn out but were encouraged by the continued support of both Caruna and Klortis.

After many days of intense training Charlie and Tim were easily traversing the obstacle course back and forth without much trouble. They had both learned the two attacking spells and defensive spells and could easily call upon them in a moment's notice. Also highly encouraging was their staff training, which had reached the point of actually causing both Caruna and Klortis to fight at very high levels to avoid getting hit.

"It looks like the both of you have finally progressed to the point that you will no longer be embarrassments to the guild," said Klortis.

"Thanks so much," said Tim.

"Now after all that continuous training there is nothing else to do but get a well-needed day off," said Klortis.

"Oh, thank you, thank you," said Tim.

"Yeah, Klortis, thanks," said Charlie.

"Now go do whatever it is the both of you would like for the next two days and then we'll start some new training regimens," said Klortis.

"Oh, I can't wait," said Tim.

"Yeah, me either," said Charlie.

"Hey, Charlie, I'd like to spend the next day checking out those old tunnels below the Great City. Remember we saw a treasure load of books and ancient artifacts when we were down there and unfortunately we had to leave all that stuff down there."

"I know and it must have broken your heart. We should ask Klortis before we go this time," said Charlie.

"You are probably right, so give me a minute and I'll drop the magic question. Hey, Klortis, wait up a minute please," said Tim.

Klortis slowed to allow Tim to catch up with him. "What is it now?"

"Charlie and I want to spend the next day checking out the old tunnels below the Great City.

Klortis looked on with a questionable look on his face. "Why would you want to do that?"

"Well, when we were down there before we came across a depository of sorts. There were books, parchments and ancient artifacts and we want to go and check them out more thoroughly."

"Do you know exactly where this depository is located?"

"Yes."

"Quickly now, we must get in touch with Grabblemore and you need to tell him about everything that you remember seeing when you were down there," said Klortis. "We must go now. Go and get Charlie and be quick about it."

Tim ran to their tent and gathered Charlie and they headed off to meet up with Klortis and now Caruna.

"Boys, Grabblemore is on his way and will arrive any moment," said Klortis.

The tent door opened and out stepped a smiling Grabblemore. "Well hello, boys. Klortis here tells me that you might have some most useful information. Now please come in and sit and talk a while."

After hearing all about their journey into the ancient tunnels below the city and the artifacts they had seen, Grabblemore realized this could be the information they had been waiting for.

"So the two of you want to spend the next day searching through the ancient tunnels?" asked Grabblemore.

"We sure do," said Tim.

"Well then, what else is there to do but go? But you must take Klortis with you since this could be a very dangerous journey," said Grabblemore.

Klortis grinned and patted Tim on the back so hard he coughed. "I knew we would make a great team eventually."

The group headed out at first light, riding their kattergraff at top speed. They soon reached the city and headed towards the secret entrance to the tunnels of Etrallia.

"Boys, these tunnels were named after a very ancient city that once stood here far before the Great City. Its inhabitants have never been identified to my knowledge," said Klortis. "I am not aware of any expeditions into these tunnels for many long years."

"Why did someone decide to build the Great City here?" asked Tim

"Tim, that's quite simple actually. The ancients thought this was a wondrous place and figured that building on it would enhance their magical abilities," said Klortis.

"Boys, keep your lightners at the ready—you never know what we will run into in the bowels of this ancient city," said Klortis.

Slowly but steadily they made progress using the reference points that Tim and Charlie had left behind. Tim did bring his GPS but it seemed to be acting strangely and he couldn't get a proper reading.

"Do you think it's broken?" Charlie asked.

"No, I suspect it's something in the air or possibly the magnetic fields down here changed since our last visit," said Tim. "At least we have the marks we left behind and they should be helpful enough in getting us pointed in the right direction."

Off they went deeper and deeper into the ancient tunnels. Soon they were running into more and more Cractors and surprisingly Tim actually thought this was a good thing. "Charlie, look at all the Cractors—this is excellent!"

"Tim, I don't exactly see what's so excellent about running into giant rats but if you say so," said Charlie.

Klortis lingered behind the boys and said nothing. It seemed he was expecting something to happen that the boys were not even aware of.

"Hey, Klortis, we're getting close, I can feel it," said Charlie.

"That's great but please remain sharp," said Klortis. "We need to remain aware of our surroundings at all times."

Charlie rounded a corner and was sure he had been here before. He recognized the scratch mark he had left during the last excursion down into the tunnels. "Hey, guys, over here! Take a look at this!" There lying against a wall half submerged were two ancient paintings. Most of the paint had worn off the bottom third of the painting from the centuries of water but the top had remained almost perfect.

"Who do you think he was?" asked Charlie.

"I am not sure but I would suspect that he must have been an important man at one point in history," said Klortis. "Centuries ago paintings like these were made to signify the royalty of the magical world. We need to alert the guild to this place so a more thorough search can be performed in the very near future. This is a treasure trove of ancient history that will be lost if it is not soon recovered."

"I felt the same way when I came down here," said Tim. "I wanted to grab every single book, picture and parchment I could carry, but unfortunately we were kind of pressed for time and surrounded by Cractors, which kind of put a damper on the entire situation."

"This is a great find and the both of you will be highly honored for it, I'm sure," said Klortis.

"I can't wait to find the center of this place and really show you something," said Tim.

The search continued and slowly confusion set it. Charlie and Tim began to get a bit testy with each other and questioned the direction they should be traveling in. However, Klortis finally stepped in and recommended using the democracy method and it seemed to get them promptly back in the right direction.

"These tunnels seem to go on forever. Who knows what is really down here," said Tim.

"We know what we saw before and I bet if we spend a bit more time down here we can find even more stuff," said Charlie.

"Stuff's good," said Tim.

"It sure is," said Charlie.

"Wait a second, did either of you just see that?" asked Charlie.

"See what/" asked Klortis.

"It looked like a shadow just over there," said Charlie.

"Are you sure? Well?" asked Klortis.

"No, maybe it's just my imagination," said Charlie.

"Stay sharp, boys, we may not be alone down here," said Klortis.

Charlie and Tim pushed on and finally their efforts would be rewarded; there just down the tunnel was the ancient statue they had seen the last time they were down here. Without waiting they took off in a sprint to get there as soon as they possibly could, disregarding the yelling of Klortis and blindly storming off down the tunnel. Klortis picked up the pace and caught up to them just as they entered the central chamber, and there in the middle of the chamber they were once again face to face with the beautiful artifact.

The ancient parchments strewn about the chamber fascinated Klortis, along with the books, but the thing that captivated him the most was the beautiful statue in the center of the chamber.

Klortis looked at the statue, transfixed by the woman's beauty. She was beyond even the fairies of the Loren Wood or the maidens of Vorlna. "Boys, you were clearly underestimating the elegance of this statue; it is unquestionably beautiful. However, I have no idea who she is, but I would suspect that if we look around here more closely we'd find something that will point us in the right direction."

"Let's get going already, this place gives me the creeps," said Charlie.

"Boys, spread out and give the area a quick once-over. We can grab all the books and parchments we find and pile them in separate piles over on that edge," said Klortis.

"What about all this art?" Charlie asked.

"We can get to that later, for now let's just focus on the books and parchments," said Klortis.

They spent hours gathering thousands or parchments and ancient books. Some of the books were water soaked and worn, making them illegible, but Tim gathered them nonetheless, hoping there would be some way to salvage them. Charlie was growing bored fishing books out of the water and started to poke around the artwork and a few of the ancient broken statues that were lying about. He noticed this one particular statue that seemed to be calling to him in some strange way. He just had to pick it up no matter what. Just as he reached for it Klortis knocked his hand away, causing him to almost fall into the water.

"What did you do that for?" asked a rather testy Charlie.

"That statue is the statue of entrancement. If you had picked it up and looked into its ruby red eyes you would have fallen into an endless trance, forever living in your mind in a fantasy world until your eventual death from starvation or dehydration," said Klortis.

"Well, thanks then," said Charlie. "Who would put that thing down here anyway?"

"Many centuries ago artifacts like these were placed in strategic locations to use as a guard of sorts without actually having to stay there and watch over whatever it is you wanted protected," said Klortis. "Be careful, I suspect there might be more ancient traps down here protecting this treasure trove of information."

"I guess it's a good idea but definitely twisted," said Charlie.

"I swore I just saw something move down there," said Tim.

"It's probably more Cractors moving about munching on something gross," said Charlie.

"We should remain alert nonetheless. As you two are all too well aware, you can never be too careful," said Klortis. "I'm going to do a bit of scouting in the general vicinity and see if anything turns up. I will return shortly. Once I return we will gather up what we have and make our way to the exit. We have been down here long enough."

Charlie and Tim kept on with their gathering of every single piece of parchment that could possibly be recovered. Slowly the pile swelled and with it the smile on Tim's face. He finally stopped working altogether and just sat down on a small broken statue and slowly started to sort through the parchments. In no time he had four piles sorted and was working on a fifth when Klortis rounded the corner and stepped into view. He was winded and holding his left side and his breathing looked labored.

"You two need to get out of here now! Just go don't look back," said Klortis.

"What's going on?" asked Charlie.

Klortis, looking weaker by the minute, seemed to be standing only thanks to the tunnel wall he was leaning against. "There's no time for that, just go—the hooded figure is here and he's right behind me."

Then rounding a corner with staff in hand came the hooded figure. Before Klortis could react he was hit in the left arm by a red lightning bolt, completely severing it just below the shoulder. He yelled in pain and fell into the murky water without another sound. The hooded figure laughed and leisurely came forward, slowing only for a moment to kick Klortis's seemingly lifeless body out of his way.

"My boys, we meet again and like usual not under the best circumstances. Ah, it looks like your friend has quite the injury there. That's a shame, but at least the Cractors will have a nice meal after we go," said the hooded figure. "Now let's get to the issue of the parchments that you so nicely organized for me."

"What did you do to Klortis?" asked Charlie.

"I merely removed some excess weight and made getting one-armed shirts a practical thing," said the laughing hooded figure.

"You are sick," said Tim.

"Boys, there is no need for insults. We should spend more time working on our growing friendship, which I am sure will eventually evolve into something, dare I say, special."

"Friends with you? I don't think so," said Charlie. "I would just as soon go spend time with a bogblagger as spend a second with you."

"Now that's not nice at all, and if you keep that up you will most certainly be joining your friend as a Cractor feast."

Charlie raised his staff and slowly pointed it in the hooded figure's general direction, preparing to use the only spell he could think of—"Chilaria!" he yelled but nothing happened to the hooded figure.

"Is that all you have learned during your intensive training over the past two weeks? Well, if that's the case then you're pathetic and so is that entire guild," said the now yelling hooded figure.

Charlie had now become enraged and something deep down was slowly brewing, stirring and preparing to be released. Charlie ran straight at the hooded figure, completely catching him off guard, and swept both his legs out from under him in a flash. The hooded figure crashed into the water, landing on his back, and dropped his staff into the murky water. Laughing he slowly sat up, looking about for his staff and not paying attention to Charlie, who was just a few feet away.

"Now that was very impressive but as you might have guessed it is now going to cost you your life." Slowly the hooded figure rose to his feet with his staff now securely in his left hand. He began to raise it in Charlie's general direction and fired a red lightning bolt that barely missed a ducking Charlie, striking the stone wall and shattering it to pieces.

Tim had slowly worked his way over to the parchment piles and had managed to gather quite a few of them, casually placing them into his backpack. He had just about finished with the entire pile when the hooded figure turned to face him.

"Now, now, there will be none of that. Please drop that parchment now or I'll blow your arms off or possibly your head."

"Okay, calm down there is no need to get all testy," said Tim, who quickly placed the final parchment down into the murky water.

"Now the both of you can step away from the books and the parchments and prepare to head back to the goblin camp with me."

"I don't think we want do to that," said Charlie.

"Unfortunately you don't really have a choice, now do you?"

"We'll see about that," said Charlie.

"You simply have no choice in the matter since your friend has picked up the parchments that I so desire to have in my possession," said the hooded figure.

"I think I'll keep them just the same and you are welcome to the rest of the books and parchments that are still here," said Tim

"You fools, do either of you have any idea what you are holding? The significance of those parchments is unequal to anything either of you could possibly understand," said the hooded figure.

"I understand enough, I think," said Charlie. "An ancient evil scribe named Ludris Garlit created these parchments many years ago to use to gain control of Wizard World."

"Very good," said the hooded figure. "Now there is one last question that must be asked: Are those ancient parchments really worth both your lives?"

"I for one am not quite sure that I'm ready to wrap it up yet, so no, they are not, but I see no reason to give them up just yet either," said Charlie.

"Maybe we can come to some sort of arrangement," said Tim.

"There will be no arrangement, boy, either hand over the parchments or die," said the hooded figure.

"That's not much of an arrangement, now is it?" asked Charlie.

"Nope," said Tim.

"There is nothing that can save either of you so just hand over the parchments and I will let you live for another day," said the hooded figure.

Charlie could see Klortis rising slowly and knew that if he could only keep the hooded figure occupied for a moment or two longer then they would at least have a chance of getting out of this.

Charlie decided it was time for some quick thinking. "Why don't you come and take them yourself if you want them so badly?"

"If death is what you wish for then I shall gladly give it to you," said the hooded figure.

"Charlie, I hope that was not your best idea, was it?" asked Tim

"Patience, Tim, just wait a moment and our chance will—There!!!"

Klortis, bloodied and badly beaten, had risen to one knee and was slowly raising his left hand—there a blue ball could be seen building. Slowly, it grew until it was the size of a soccer ball, then closing his eyes Klortis released it towards the unsuspecting hooded figure. The ball hit him in the back and instantly engulfed the hooded figure in what looked like a giant bubble of sorts. The hooded figure just laughed and yelled something illegible while Charlie and Tim ran by him. They reached Klortis and dragged him as fast as they possibly could away from the battle.

Within moments they had reached the exit and both boys were winded from carrying and half dragging Klortis's lifeless body. They gently placed him down on a soft-looking patch of grass to rest a moment.

"Charlie, he's hurt really bad. We need to do something right away. He is bleeding everywhere and looks terrible. I've never seen an injury like that."

Charlie looked down at Klortis and felt a bit squeamish at the sight before him. "I know he looks terrible. His arm is completely gone from right below the shoulder; he is bleeding from the mouth and has a nasty cut above his right eye. I'm no doctor but I think he might be blind in that eye."

"Charlie, we need to get out of here now! Who knows how long that spell will last?"

"It will last long enough," said a slightly awake Klortis.

Tim could not believe his eyes. "Klortis, we need to go. Can you get up?"

"No, but I can vaporate out of here in a moment or two. I just need to gather my strength for a moment or two and I will be able to get out of here and back to the guild. Unfortunately, my young friends—I don't think I have enough for all three of us."

"That's okay, Klortis, you go—we'll be fine. Charlie and I will just get over to our kattergraff and ride on home."

Klortis leaned forward and managed to get to one knee. "Boys, there is no time to waste—you must go now for I can feel my spell weakening and I fear it will be only a moment or two before that freak is upon us once again. Unfortunately in my current state I will be of no assistance if he does show up."

Charlie looked on amazed at the strength that Klortis possessed even with the hideous injuries he had suffered. "We're not leaving until you do."

Klortis looked stern and focused. "You will obey my orders without question. Go now and I will meet with you at the guild. Now—go—now!"

The boys rapidly headed off towards their kattergraff, knowing that this might be the last time they would see Klortis.

"Tim, this isn't right, we need to go back for him."

"He gave us a direct command, Charlie, and we need to follow it. Klortis knows what he is doing and even in his condition he can take care of himself."

"It's still not right. We can't just leave him like that to—die."

"All right, Charlie, let's go back and maybe we can still help him."

The boys reached the edge of the forest and stopped. There they could see near the tunnel entrance a most horrible sight, the hooded figure holding Klortis by the neck, feet dangling and not reaching the ground, blood oozing from his mouth, eyes and nose looking utterly lifeless.

Charlie was preparing to run and do whatever it took to save Klortis, but Tim stopped him in his tracks and pointed to Klortis's remaining hand, which was glowing blue again and getting brighter by the second. The hooded figure was laughing uncontrollably now and not paying much attention to Klortis, who had now raised enough energy to cast a mighty spell. Without warning Klortis managed to get out a laugh then disappeared into thin air right before a large rusty dagger thrust square at his face. The boys quietly cheered and hastily made their way back to their rides and headed back to the guild.

Charlie and Tim pushed their kattergraff to the limits hoping to arrive at the guild as fast as they possibly could. Tim was carrying a prize that almost cost them their lives and still might eventually cost Klortis his. They had no idea if Klortis would be living when they arrived but at least they still had hope. After all, he had managed to cast a strong and difficult spell even in his weakened condition, allowing him to narrowly escape death at the hands of the hooded figure.

"Charlie, there are guards everywhere, look."

"I know, I see them. Tim, we need to hurry and get to the guild entrance so we can find out what is going on. The parchments you are carrying must be really important so we need to get them to Grabblemore right after we check up on Klortis."

Drintonis appeared out of the thin air with his staff at the ready. "You two stop right there and prepare to be searched!"

"Hey, take it easy, will ya? It's just Tim and myself here."

"Sorry, it's just that security has been tightened since the arrival of Klortis, or what's left of him."

"So he's alive?" asked Tim. "That's excellent new, Drintonis. Where is he so we can go see him."

"Barely, but yes, he is alive and with a little luck he just might pull through. I was instructed upon your arrivals to direct the both of you to Grabblemore's tent. I was also told that you two are to remain there and not exit the tent until Grabblemore himself calls for you."

"But we need to see Klortis right now," said a now heated Tim.

"I'm sure in due time that will be possible, but Grabblemore left explicit instructions and I would suggest that the both of you follow them," said

Drintonis. "Please leave Gregor and Alicia here with me and make your way to his tent and wait for instructions."

Reluctantly Charlie and Tim headed towards Grabblemore's tent. Both boys were visibly upset and shaken by the day's earlier events and wanted to see Klortis to thank him for what he had done, but knew there really was nothing either of them could do at the moment.

Once inside the tent they both just sat quietly waiting for any information about Klortis. The tent door flew open and there was Grabblemore, looking worn and disheveled. He looked like he hadn't slept or eaten in weeks. His eyes had circles below them and he was quite pale and visibly winded.

"Well hello, boys—how are you doing?"

"How is Klortis doing? He looked awful when we last saw him. We heard from Drintonis that he made it here and is alive," said Tim.

"Unfortunately he is in what you would call a coma. I have called the Council of Elders here to assist me in creating a combination spell to try and speed up his healing."

"Is he going to—you know, make it?" asked Charlie.

"That I don't know, but as strong as he is, I would not be surprised if he indeed did pull through."

"Mr. Grabblemore, when can we see Klortis?" asked Tim.

"First he needs time to heal along with plenty of rest and quiet, and of course the thoughts and energy from all who care for him. Now there is also the matter of what has transpired the past day and the mysterious hooded figure's most unappreciated appearance and attack upon Klortis.

"Now from what I was able to learn before Klortis slipped into his deep sleep was that you two have recovered some very important parchments. These parchments may hold the key to this mystery. I know Klortis is all that the both of you are thinking about, but we need to focus our energies in a different direction at this moment, no matter how difficult it may be. There are many lives at stake and that is where our priorities need to be. Before either of you interrupt I can assure you Klortis would agree and he wouldn't want it any other way.

"We need to go over every last tidbit that was recovered from the tunnels. We cannot dispel any minute bit of information, for I fear we will need every bit of help we can get before it's all over. I have called a few others here to help us. Shortly Caruna will be joining us, along with Mr. Watson. We also have a few other members of the Wilfrem Guild who will soon be arriving to assist us in the research into all the recovered data that hopefully you have with you. Now let's take a look at what you have and see if all this was worth it."

Slowly and carefully Tim removed the worn and damp parchments from his backpack. He had managed to gather over thirty of the ancient rolled-up documents while staring down his own possible mortality.

Grabblemore looked on in amazement. "Tim, that is most excellent that you managed to gather all those scrolls while the hooded figure was standing a mere twenty or so feet from you. Well done, my boy, well done!

"Now we need some heat to take the chill out of this tent and assist with the drying of the parchments. Sparkus lothos!" yelled Grabblemore and a beautiful fire appeared in the center of his tent, instantly making the space much more comfortable and inviting.

Within moments parchments that only moments earlier were damp and barely could be handled were now dry and perfectly manageable, providing plenty of useful information. The next few days were spent reviewing data with the help of Ada, Tara and Hannah. After a few tense hours they had figured out the exact location of the second artifact. However, there was one mystery that couldn't be solved. There was one strange parchment that could not be translated no matter who looked at it. Finally Grabblemore stepped in and hastily gathered up the parchment without a word. From what Charlie and Tim were able to learn, the parchment had been sent to the Great City and was in the hands of the ancient scribes. There it would be deciphered. Grabblemore would not explain the reason for sending the parchment there except that it was urgent business and that they would all be better off not knowing the contents that it contained. Charlie and Tim decided this was a mystery best solved another day and decided to focus on the next challenge, the recovery of the second artifact.

Chapter 16

Quest for the Second Artifact

There was just one thing left to decide now that the location of the second artifact was in hand, and that was who would take on the challenge of this surely perilous journey. The heads of the guilds were in the midst of a rather heated discussion about who should be going to make the recovery attempt and if they should go at all. After all, the artifact was well guarded by ancient magic and no one could be sure if anyone else even knew its location. Grabblemore was pushing hard to send the boys again since they had managed to best the hooded figure on more than one occasion, while Morphran was leaning heavily on sending the Shifters and a few of his hand-picked high-ranking lieutenants.

Finally Morphran saw an opportunity to take the floor and voice his opinion. "I personally think we either need to send my contingent or not go at all. The two boys, or should I say Regulars, who so easily gave up the first piece are not wizards and therefore shouldn't even be considered to attempt such a recovery in the first place. They were lucky the first time, and can you count on that one aspect alone to achieve success again? I think not!"

As soon as Morphran finished Efa rapidly rose to her feet to speak her mind. "I for one cannot sit here for another second listening to this. Eblis is obviously pushing for his people to go for his own personal gain. It's no secret that his guild members were spotted at the goblin camp by very reliable sources. That alone is reason enough not to trust him or any of his guild members as far as I'm concerned."

"Although there is no evidence of wrongdoing by Morphran himself I must second that statement," said Vance. "Sorry, Eblis, but you still have not answered to those charges yet."

"Charges, that's utter rubbish. These statements were made by individuals who only months ago had never stepped foot into our world and are now a trusted source over someone who has done nothing but support this land and the Council?"

The room was getting very tense. Grabblemore decided it was time to step in and calm the situation. "Eblis, please calm down. Although Vance and Efa have made valid points there has been no conclusive evidence linking you to the event at the goblin camp. Therefore I would appreciate it if this was left out of our current conversation and saved for an official Council meeting."

There was a brief moment of silence to allow for the usual interruptions, which surprisingly did not come so Grabblemore continued on. "Now as far as the boys are concerned I for one see no reason not to send them again. They have fared very well, I must say, and I'm very impressed with the progress and loyalty they have shown since arriving here. These reasons and their uncanny ability to adapt to adverse situations under the most stressful circumstances has convinced me to send them on this most important mission. I am looking for someone to second this notion and the boys can be on their way at first light tomorrow morning."

"I for one second the notion," said Efa.

"I also back this notion," said Vance.

Morphran stood up shaking his head. "I want it duly noted that I'm against this notion and want it known that the dire consequences that could befall this great land are now out of my hands thanks to this Council. However, although I strongly disagree with the Council's decision I want it to be known that I will do everything in my power to assist them any way possible as the attempt to complete this most important mission begins."

"Your protest is duly noted, Eblis, along with your support," said Grabblemore. "So it's settled—the boys will go after the second artifact and I will also be sending Mr. Watson and Caruna along with them. They will leave at first light tomorrow. Please support them in any and all ways possible."

The boys were called to the tent and told of their nomination. They were concerned and excited to be getting another chance at recovering such an important ancient artifact. They knew all too well that there was quite a bit of luck involved in their first quest when they managed to best the set of ancient traps and were proud of this accomplishment, but they both knew all too well that the second set of challenges might not be so easy.

The morning came after a nearly sleepless night for both Charlie and Tim. They stayed up most of the night along with Grandpa Watson discussing the challenges they might have face.

When they exited their tent they were greeted by every member of the Golundrus Guild along with the Council of Elders and the members of the Wilfrem Guild.

"Let's get this show on the road," said Charlie.

"Good luck to you all. Remember, success is not only in the accomplishment but also in the choices made to get there," said Grabblemore.

Charlie and Tim just glanced at each other as they prepared to mount their kattergraff and anxiously awaited Grandpa Watson's latest attempt at this. He had fallen off at least four times yesterday and finally gave up. Frustration had set in for him and the constant laughter of Tim and Charlie didn't help the situation either. Surprisingly this time Grandpa Watson made one step and easily leaped into the saddle without much effort whatsoever. The boys shook their heads and laughed and Caruna exchanged a quick chuckle with Grandpa Watson.

The kattergraff took them south deep into the dry lands far from any established settlements. Soon they were beyond even the Groffle trees and Gratrla plants. These hearty plants thrive almost anywhere but even they don't bother trying to grow in this desolate place. While traveling Caruna took the time to point out the occasional Groppler tribe wandering about riding their Nufla mounts slowly pulling ancient carts filled with artifacts and trinkets found lying about the deserted ancient land.

Charlie and Tim had never seen such a thing as a Nufla. These creatures resembled lizards with hairy bodies like a buffalo and horns to match. The Nufla moved easily through the sand and loose gravel with their large webbed feet and well-spread clawed toes. Their eyes had the second lid of a lizard and the hair kept them cool in the heat.

Caruna decided to kill some time while on their journey and give a little history lesson. "Many, many centuries ago, even before the time of the Golundrus Cube itself, there supposedly was an ancient civilization that dominated these lands. It is said that this civilization was destroyed in some ancient cataclysm that wiped them out along with everything they had created, leaving just legends and ancient stories. Occasionally an artifact or two is recovered but unfortunately they are so few and far between that most people think it's a fairy tale. I for one have seen a few ancient ruins on my occasional treks through this barren and ancient land but have not had the time to spend exploring them until now. Hopefully if we follow an ancient path that Gregor and Alycia are very familiar with we might just get lucky and spot a ruin or two and get to spend a bit of time exploring."

"That would be awesome, but don't you think we should stick to our mission?" asked Tim.

"We will, but there's nothing wrong with a delay; after all, we are the only ones who know where we are going and the artifact's supposed location," said Caruna.

Grandpa pulled his mount up alongside Caruna to jump into the conversation. "She is quite correct, so I see no reason not to stop for a bit if we come across something, shall we say, interesting."

Grandpa could hardly control himself, happily taking the lead and using all his prior knowledge as an archaeologist and adventurer to direct the group in what he thought was the most promising direction. Grandpa Watson loved an adventure as much as the next guy but what he liked most was discovering something supposedly lost to time and drifting into legend. He kept noticing peculiar sand dunes and eventually took off at a quick gallop towards a particular set of dunes that he was sure would yield something interesting. Charlie and Tim just smiled, knowing all too well that Grandpa was on to something and there would be no stopping him now. Caruna looked on, wondering what was going on, and before she knew it they had veered significantly off the predetermined course and were heading for these strange-looking dunes.

After riding over a very high and sweeping dune Grandpa stopped and hastily raised his hand for everyone else to do the same. Everyone came to an abrupt stop and promptly realized that a mere twenty or so feet in front of Grandpa was a tribe of Gropplers casually coming and going into what looked like the remains of an ancient temple.

The columns that still stood were magnificent in size and at one time probably led to an even grander temple. The columns were intricately carved but at the current distance the details were difficult to make out. Excitedly Charlie and Caruna pulled out their looking glasses to try and make out the ancient statues and carvings. Tim pulled the looking glass away from Charlie to have a look. He spotted what was a remnant of an ancient kattergraff and Nufla wrapped together intertwined with a spear and what looked like the remnants of a staff.

Grandpa slowly worked his kattergraff down the dune and was rather close to the Gropplers. They were currently paying him little if any attention but there was no telling what they would do if they became frightened. Grandpa jumped off his mount and reached into his saddlebag and pulled out a flask of water and a piece of frickta bread.

Caruna was frantically waving in Grandpa's general direction trying desperately to get his attention. He was now getting dangerously close to the

Gropplers. She had heard stories since she was a young girl of Groppler attacks on weary travelers and the occasional assault on a village on the outskirts of the land. There were many reports that none were left alive or found again. Caruna was sure that most if not all of these stories were exaggerated to help keep the children in line and away from trouble. Nonetheless she figured it was better to be safe than sorry and decided it was time to prepare at least an escape route or two and a spell that could possibly slow down the hordes of Gropplers.

Now the Gropplers had finally taken notice of Grandpa Watson and were getting a bit edgy, swinging their Groppler staffs and loading a Groppler shot or two. Grandpa continued to edge closer and closer holding out the frickta bread and breaking off a small piece and eating it then breaking off another and offering it to who he assumed must be the leader. He then took a sip of water from the flask and gently placed it down in the sand along with the rest of the frickta bread and slowly backed away. Hesitantly the leader moved forward flanked by two Groppler guards and headed towards the small feast. He first picked up the bread, smelled it for a moment or two then pulled off a tiny piece and placed it into his mouth. He chewed it slowly, seemingly enjoying every moment of it, then picked up the flask and took a large swig with the excess running down his face and chin. He glanced at each of his guards then at Grandpa Watson, extended his left hand and smiled. Grandpa smiled back and returned the gesture with the two meeting halfway and enjoying a laugh and a strange handshake. Caruna smiled and slowly lowered her staff and Charlie and Tim dismounted and pulled a flask from each of their saddlebags and offered them to the Gropplers, who gladly accepted.

Loud cheers could be heard deep within the ruins echoing throughout the open desert plains. The flasks were being passed throughout the Gropplers without a drop being wasted. Then to their utter surprise Caruna whipped up a spell and yelled "Aquasnumerate" and magically the flasks were filled again, causing the rejoicing to reach a new level. Gropplers surrounded Caruna and she was overwhelmed with patting and shouting of unknown words. She was smiling and feeling a bit embarrassed for her earlier prejudices, now realizing that many things that she took for fact may not be after all.

They were led into the ancient ruins by the two guards and whom they figured to be the leader. With all the random chanting Gropplers one name became clear and obvious and that was Krintro. When he entered the tunnels every Groppler they passed chanted his name. It was evident this Groppler was a powerful and important leader amongst his people. They were directed into a chamber with an ancient table at the center that was cracked and worn from the many years of use. The chairs were carved out of stone, high backed and also worn from many years of use. The room was lit with torches that were submerged in what looked like mud but black like the color of oil. These crude lamps lit the entire chamber, allowing for a most beautiful view of a ceiling fresco that had been created long ago. In the center of the table was a very ancient-looking bowl that seemed to be made of clay. It had a small smoldering fire below it and occasionally billowed something that did not smell entirely well at all. Charlie, Tim, Grandpa and Caruna took seats around the table and two Gropplers placed a cup in front of each of them along with what looked like a strange-shaped mushroom. The Groppler leader used crude sign language demonstrating dipping a cup into the bowl in the center of the table and then placing the mushroom into the cup. Reluctantly all did as instructed and then the Groppler leader did the unthinkable, he gestured for all to drink and then eat the crazy-looking mushroom. Without hesitation Grandpa Watson grabbed the cup and gulped it down before he could heed the warning of Caruna. She yelled "Wait" but it was too late; Grandpa had finished the entire cup and was grinning from ear to ear. Krinto smiled at him and Grandpa returned the gesture.

"What just happened?" Tim asked.

"Just drink," said Grandpa.

Charlie looked on with a questioning look. "Are you sure?"

Grandpa just smiled. "Yes, of course I'm sure."

"Okay then, down the hatch," said Charlie, who finished the entire drink and let out a rather large burp.

Tim reluctantly followed Charlie's lead and downed his drink, although he almost lost it due to the texture of the mushroom and the nasty smell that was coming from his cup.

Caruna reluctantly followed suit, but not before she stated her concerns.

Moments later Krinto, smiling, started to talk and amazingly the group could understand every word.

"My new friends, obviously you have figured out what the potion was for. It was not meant to harm in any way," said Krinto. "We of the Groppler nation would like to officially welcome you to one of our most ancient cities, Larungra. Here we have lived since before your people even existed. We have lived here and in many other ancient locations since time itself began. Our people have seen the beginning of time and witnessed what was close to the end of time. We were there when it all began and when it was almost all destroyed.

"The ancient city that you now possess, I believe it's called the Great City, is built on our most ancient site, 'Hargrallo.' The very tunnels that your people currently use to dispose of their waste and carelessly throw anything unwanted into is the site of the very beginning of the Groppler people. Unfortunately we lost that site many, many years ago, during the ancient wars with the Giants and the Ancient Ones. The Ancient Ones were your ancestors and I'm quite sure the Giants are still around, although their numbers have been depleted through the years. After losing this great battle the surviving members of the Gropplers were forced deep into the dry lands and now here we are.

"I am sure there are many questions so please do not hesitate to ask. Although I am not the eldest of the Gropplers, I am well versed in a considerable amount of our history and a considerable amount of yours."

"You mentioned that the Great City was built on the very site where your people originated, so why haven't you tried to get it back?" asked Caruna.

"Oh, we have tried many times in the past but unfortunately failed using diplomacy so war was declared and we were soundly defeated. We were tremendously outnumbered and fought bravely even though we realized it was a lost cause. Later when the Goblin Wars broke out we did not get involved and hoped that it would turn to our advantage, but unfortunately it did not. Although we did not gain control of our ancient site of creation we did see the bright side, and that was saving of this very land itself, so in a way we are grateful," said Krinto.

"What about the war with the Ancient Ones and the Giants?" asked Tim. "Can you tell us more about that?"

"Certainly," said Krinto. "That war was waged and unfortunately the Gropplers were caught in the middle of it. We never chose a side so one was chosen for us; the Giants and the Ancient Ones teamed together and drove my people deep into the dry lands. Still to this day we do not know the reason for this attack and I suspect we never will."

"How do you know all of this past history? I mean, some must be written down and all, but you seem to know way too much," asked Charlie.

"We know much but not all," said Krinto

"What we do know is thanks to the ancient Gropplers who figured a way to save our history using crystals. These crystals we call Memory Crystals. These most valued treasures of the Groppler people have been hidden for many centuries, only made aware to the Groppler leader and his closest confidant and now all of you. I have spent many long suns and moons studying these ancient records and learned much of the past and what to expect in the coming moons," said Krinto.

"So how come there is nothing about why you were attacked?" Tim asked.

"That has been a mystery that we would love to solve but unfortunately never have been able to. It seems that a few crystals were lost, destroyed or stolen many, many moons ago," said Krinto.

"I have a question about coming moons. Am I to understand that you can actually see the coming moons before they actually happen? Are you saying you can see the future?" asked Grandpa Watson.

"Well, let me put it this way, the future is not set in stone but if paths continue on their current course then they will unfold as predicted," said Krinto.

"What's going to happen to us?" asked Charlie

"That, Charlie, is for you to determine. Your choices in the coming days and moons will decide not only the fate of you and your friends but also quite possibly the world itself," said Krinto.

"Talk about pressure," said Tim.

"No kidding," said Charlie.

"I think that's a bit much to drop on someone so young, don't you?" asked a cranky-looking Caruna.

"I only stated what I have seen, nothing more. I meant no offense so please forgive me. Sadly this is why most information, no matter the importance, is kept silent," said Krinto.

"If it's true then there's no need for apologies," said Grandpa Watson.

"When can we explore the rest of this place?" asked Charlie.

"Right after dinner, my young friend, which should be along in just a moment," said Krinto.

An hour or so passed and there was much small talk and many courses of interesting food and drink. Although the presentation was a bit lacking, the food was excellent. It reminded Charlie of Chinese food and Italian from back home.

"Now that we have finished dinner we shall take a tour of this wonderful ancient city. First we shall head to the Chamber of Crystals, then the ancient arena where Gropplers duel while mounted on their Nuflas," said Krinto.

"There's room down here for an arena? How big is this place?" asked Charlie.

"Oh, I assure you there's more here than meets the eye," said Krinto.

When they exited the chamber it was quite obvious how the Nufla could get to an arena; the tunnels were big enough to fit two Nufla side by side with plenty of room to spare. Easily eight men could walk side by side and still have room between them. This place was massive in proportion and there was much to see here, but unfortunately they were pressed for time.

They arrived at their first stop, the Chamber of Crystals. The chamber itself was too big to take in all at once. There were pedestals ranging in height and size with a crystal mounted on each one. These pedestals seemed to grow from the floor and cradle the crystal evenly on each side. The crystals were of many shapes, colors and sizes. They seemed to react to each other and to the environment. When Charlie spoke the crystals seemed to come alive, humming randomly at first, then humming together in a sort of song. Charlie smiled and laughed and again the crystals reacted singing their magical color-coded song.

Tim looked on utterly amazed. "These crystals seem like they're alive. They are actually reacting to stimuli from their environment."

"The crystals have been friends of the Gropplers for more moons than any of us can remember," said Krinto. "These crystals are singing a song with not only color but also vibrations. These vibrations can after time be understood and interpreted into a sort of language if you know what to listen for."

"So you mean to tell me you know what they are saying?" asked Grandpa Watson.

"Why, yes, of course—they are excited to meet new people, especially from the Regular World," said Krinto.

"How did they know we were from the Regular World?" Tim asked.

"The crystals can tell by your aura and the vibrations that you put out into the world. You see, every person from every place has a certain vibration that they emit depending on where they are from. Now an aura is a certain color of sorts that surrounds a person and projects strength, happiness, sadness and so forth," said Krinto

"That's excellent! So what's my aura look like?" asked Tim.

"Well, it looks strong, determined and very bright, meaning that you are smart beyond your current years," said Krinto. "I am not actually reading your aura personally; the crystals are doing it and I am listening to what they are saying. They see you more like energy than an actual person. When they vibrate I listen and that's the secret to how we read auras. Now let's move off to the next chamber and then I will show you something that I think will be most helpful on your current quest."

Caruna looked on with a suddenly angry look on her face. "We never mentioned any quest."

Krinto smiled and kept staring at Tim. "No, you didn't, but by reading Tim's aura it's quite simple to figure out what and where you are going. Now don't be alarmed, we are here to help. I can make your journey shorter than you expected by taking you through ancient passageways that will lead you very close to the location that you currently seek."

Caruna gripped her staff tightly preparing for something that never came—either guards or Nuflas or something—but nothing happened.

Krinto glanced at Caruna and noticed she was now gripping her staff in an aggressive manner. "What did you expect us to do?"

"I don't know," said Caruna.

"We would much rather the artifacts that you seek fall into the hands of people who are not looking to use it for themselves or for their own personal gain than have it fall into the hands of ones who would destroy everything if given the chance," said Krinto.

Charlie listened to the conversation more concerned than ever. "Who would destroy everything?"

"That, my friend, is the real mystery, now isn't it?" said Krinto.

"So you don't know," asked Charlie.

"Unfortunately I don't," said Krinto. "Although that answer has eluded my people and me, we can still help by getting you to your destination as rapidly as possible."

"We would definitely appreciate that," said Tim.

Krinto realized every second was precious and decided it was time to end this meeting. "Now let us not waste a second more of precious time and get you on your way. I will personally lead you along with my two most trusted guards towards the location that you seek. Once we reach the entrance to the ancient ruins our journey together will end and the most perilous part of yours will begin. Unfortunately my people cannot enter the ancient ruins by our law that has been handed down since that artifact was originally placed there those so many long moons ago. To enter for any Groppler means death; there is no discussion or question as to why it means death. We could not make any exceptions when we first created this law and it has served my people well since then. We have steadfastly stood guard over this place for all these long years with most not even knowing what they were actually doing here. But now that you have come to remove the ancient artifact I will guide my people out of these lands and head back towards civilization. Whether you are successful or not, we will still leave these ruins that have protected my people for many moons because there will be others who will come if you happen to fail and we do not want to run into any of them. Hopefully you will be successful and return from this perilous journey but don't except to find the Gropplers here to help you anymore; we will make our leave as soon as I return and will be long gone by the time you finish your mission. However, I am most certain we will meet again."

Hours passed and the group reached their destination. Krinto said his goodbyes and wished them all the luck in the world, turned and headed back down the dark and ancient tunnels, stopped for a moment and called to the group, "There is one more thing before I go, be prepared for the guards you will meet with, for they are most evil and twisted. Do not let their appearance throw you off your intended goal even for a moment or all could be lost. I can tell you no more so please, before you ask, don't."

He again turned and headed back down the ancient tunnel and back towards his people, who were finally freed from their self-imposed guardianship of this ancient artifact and site for untold centuries. They were now free of this heavy burden, along with the dangerous and inhospitable lands they called home, and can finally head back to the lush forest life they once knew many centuries ago.

"I guess this is it then," said Grandpa Watson. "Boys, kindly lead the way and Caruna will watch our backs."

They were now in a long and straight tunnel that was carved to perfection many years earlier. Ancient carved pillars and arches that matched the ruins at the entrance to the Groppler stronghold held up the tunnel with ease. Even after these many centuries most of the columns were still in perfect condition.

Slowly they could make out light at the end of the tunnel and they felt a bit more at ease and started to pick up speed to investigate this new sight. When they finally reached the end of the tunnel all were shocked at what was before them! It was as if they had wandered into a different world. Instead of reaching a cavern or ruins they came out into a lush tropical setting that did not seem at all familiar to Caruna. She had never seen or heard of a place like this in Wizard World and was completely without answer for this turn of events.

Tim immediately turned to Caruna for answers. "Caruna, anything?"

Caruna looked on, amazed at what she was seeing and concerned at the same time. "I have no idea where we are. I have never heard of this place nor remember reading about it at anytime or anywhere."

"So you mean to tell me there is no mention of this place whatsoever in your history?" asked Grandpa Watson.

Caruna shook her head. "Unfortunately no, there is nothing that I am aware of that mentions a place like this."

Tim reached into his backpack and pulled out one of his favorite gadgets. "Okay then, I guess we are flying blind with just our wits and experience to get us through this. I'll try and get a reading with my GPS and see what we come up with."

Tim spent the next ten or so minutes trying to understand what was being presented to him and it still made no sense whatsoever. "This makes no logical sense at all. From what I am reading here we are nowhere, or what I mean is anywhere that this thing can get a reading at anyway."

"So nowhere it is—who cares already, let's just get on with it," said Charlie.

"Patience, Charlie," said Grandpa. "Now I think we should spend a moment or two examining our surroundings and figure out which is the most logical direction we should head in."

Tim turned and pointed east. "I think we should go that way."

"Why?" asked Caruna.

"There's a large bridge over there that leads towards what looks like an ancient structure, see right over there."

"Okay then, towards the bridge we go," said Grandpa Watson.

The bridge was in sight and it looked easy enough to get there but something didn't seem right. This all seemed too easy to both Charlie and Tim. They were growing leery to just head off without surveying the situation. They were well aware of how invitingly easy it seemed when they attempted to recover the first artifact and then how it hastily it all changed, putting their lives on the line.

"We need to really check this out before we go any further," said Tim. "Did anyone notice the statues that are kind of hidden in the brush on either side of the bridge?"

"Now that you mention it, I do see them," said Charlie.

"I see them too, so let's be careful here," said Grandpa. "I have an idea. Let's try something simple—I'll just throw this stick onto the bridge and see what happens." No sooner did the branch touch the bridge than a giant fireball came out of the mouth of the statue on the left and almost took Grandpa's head off and left a bit of his hair smoking. If he had been even a second slower he would surely be dead.

Grandpa pulled himself up off the ground and dusted himself off grinning from ear to ear. "I suggest we take our time here and use a little patience. We should heed Tim's warning and spend a bit of time scouting the area. I bet there is a clue or two just waiting to be discovered that will help us out of this situation."

Caruna found a small worn plaque that read, "Use the sound of the ancient beast to call forth the keepers of the Flekkta beast."

"Now all we need to do is find the sound of the ancient beast," said Tim.

"It could be this," said Charlie while holding what looked like a horn from some unknown creature. "I just found it here resting on a pedestal on the opposite side of the plaque. It was hidden by the overgrown vines and brush."

"Well done," said Grandpa Watson.

"Now I guess we just blow this thing and the keepers will come forward," said Tim. "Charlie, if you please."

"This thing is kind of gross but if I have to then here goes nothing." Charlie blew the horn and out came a rather sickening sound. The sound was so awful that Tim, Grandpa and Caruna covered their ears and hoped it would end soon. Charlie stopped, grinned and noticed a cloud forming on the opposite side of the bridge. It seemed that the light itself was actually dimming, not only on the other side of the bridge but in the entire valley. The cloud grew thicker and darker and slowly enveloped the entire bank on the opposite side of the bridge.

Caruna looked across the bridge and gripped her staff tightly. "I don't like this one bit."

"Me either," said Grandpa Watson.

Tim squinted and continued looking into the cloud of smoke that had formed. "I think I see something, just over there, at the edge of the cloud."

Charlie looked and could see something moving. "Yeah, I see it too; it looks like, like a person or something."

"Be ready for anything," said Caruna.

"Whatever is coming it's getting bigger and heading across the bridge," said Grandpa.

The cloud spread rapidly and enveloped the entire party, causing them to feel like the cold itself had surrounded and wrapped them in a blanket. It was hard to see and hard to focus on what was actually happening. Tim was sure he could see Charlie for a moment then quickly realized it was who or whatever came across the bridge closing in. He was planning on moving but then realized he felt frozen, dumbfounded, and unable to react. This thing was closing in on him really fast and there was nothing he could do but stand there and wait for whatever was about to happen. Then the fog cleared, leaving what looked like an ancient, worn body, with the wrong head on its shoulders and two other heads being carried one in each hand. All Tim could think about was the stench that was coming from this thing and it was just about enough to make him throw up. His hands started trembling but he was still unable to move. This thing was mere inches from his face when it spoke, instantly releasing Tim from his trance and allowing him to fall to his knees feeling sick all over. When he finally gathered his thoughts and himself together he noticed the rest of the group was in the same position as he was, sick looking and curled up on the ground.

Charlie could barely muster enough energy to get a word out of his mouth. "What's happening to us?"

"I don't—t know," said a shivering Caruna.

Grandpa looked really ill, down on both knees and bent forward holding his head and groaning. Strangely, Charlie seemed to be gathering himself together and was now standing and pointing his staff at the strange being that stood before him. He was still not 100 percent but was up and ready nonetheless. His teeth were chattering together and he seemed to be getting heavy cramps to his stomach but stood nonetheless.

Charlie, still wincing in pain, knew he had to do something to stop this and stop it now. "I don't kn—ow what you di—d—but yyyyyyou neeeeeed to sttttttop it nowww!"

"Ahhhhh, so you are feeling it too then," said the creature. "But I am curious how you are still standing while the rest are not."

"Thattttttt's because I—I re-refuse to quit," said Charlie.

"Strong willed," said the creature.

"Indeed," said the head in the right hand.

"Any of them will do," chimed in the head on the left.

"Patience, my sisters, patience, we must first see if they are worthy before we even go any farther," said the head sitting atop the rotting corpse.

Charlie looked on in utter disbelief. "Those things can talk. What are you?"

"We are the Sisters of Treldori. We have lived longer than your little mind could ever comprehend," said the head atop the shoulders.

"And watch your tongue, boy, or we will remove it," said the right head.

"Oh sister, please—he is such a nice boy and his friends are wonderful," said the left head.

"That's enough already. M-m-make this st—uff go away now," said Charlie.

"Oh yes, my boy, just give it a minute and the effects will wear off," said the head atop the shoulders.

Charlie glanced over and noticed that indeed the effects were wearing off and Grandpa was slowly rising to his feet, along with Caruna and Tim. They all looked a bit under the weather still but were rising nonetheless.

Caruna was now standing. "Charlie, ge-t-t away from t-h-h-at thing now."

"Thing? Well, I never—how rude," said the head on the left. "Elgulous!" it yelled and Caruna was again engulfed in the black thick cloud, causing her to immediately fall to her knees and grab for her stomach. Charlie pointed his staff at the creature and yelled his own counter spell, which was deflected by the corpse's hand as if it were nothing.

"Stop it now," said Charlie. "Let her out of that stuff."

"Your friend needs a bit of a lesson in manners," said the head on the right. With a wave of the right hand and head the spell cloud was quickly dispersed and Caruna could be seen once again all curled up on the ground coughing and barely moving.

"Caruna," yelled Tim.

Caruna, still shaking, looked like she was regaining some color. "I-I-I'm okay."

Grandpa Watson, now standing, looked on with a rather disgusted look on his face. "Don't do that again."

"Now that all the pleasantries are over, let's get down to the real reason we are all here. You summoned us and now we stand before you. What is it that you want of us?" said the three heads in unison.

Grandpa promptly stepped forward and took the lead. "We need to get over that bridge and into that castle."

The heads looked at each other then towards Grandpa Watson, each head now sporting a curious look. "Really, and why would you need to do that?"

"That's none of your concern," said Grandpa.

The head on the right shook left and right. "Touchy… All right then, but why should we help you?"

Grandpa took a moment and then decided to play along. "We have no time for your bantering, either assist us or get out of our way."

"It seems we are at an impasse. Give us a moment and we will see what we can come up with." The thing turned and walked away carrying the heads that were now deep in conversation and it was getting heated.

"These fools have no idea what we are up to and by the time they figure it out it will be too late for all of them," said the head on the right.

"Keep it down, sister, or our plans will all be for naught," said the main head.

"Yes, yes, we will soon have our own bodies and we can leave this place," said the head on the left.

"Soon, sister, soon," said the main head.

Moments later the corpse wandered back and the three heads presented their offer: Recover a certain object called the MoonStone from the Flekkta and they would grant them safe passage across the bridge.

"Just point us in the right direction and we'll go get this stone of yours," said Tim.

Caruna said nothing and just kept her staff pointed at the hideous thing that was standing mere feet from the group looking and smelling disgusting and dripping strange bodily fluids from around the ankles, causing a small puddle to form.

This did not go unnoticed by any of the three heads either who seemed to become concerned. They wanted the stone retrieved as quickly as possible from the Flekkta.

"Remember you must be successful in retrieving the stone or the deal is off," said the main head.

"Yeah, we get it—success or you won't help us," said Charlie.

"Now go there off to your left and down towards that tunnel in the cliff. There you will find the Fleckta and the Moonstone," said the main head.

"Yes, that's it exactly," said the main head. Once out of earshot the strange heads started to laugh quietly at first then louder and louder until it reached an almost uncontrollable level.

The main head continued to laugh uncontrollably and had a difficult time getting out a word. "There is no way they can defeat the Flekkta and soon their screams will be heard as their heads are pulled off."

The journey down the side of the cliff was uneventful but dangerous nonetheless. The cliff's edge was barely big enough to stand on at some places and obviously had been created this way for a reason. Whatever was down there was meant to stay there.

"There is something not quite right about this," said Tim.

"I know, but what choice do we have?" asked Charlie.

"Did either of you notice the strange fluid that was coming from the corpse? It was really nasty and got the sisters quite upset," said Caruna.

"If they didn't, I did, said Grandpa Watson. "The heads were obviously anxious to get us to go after that stone and I bet it has something to do with their rotting corpse."

"And by the way, did anyone really pay attention to the plaque?" asked Tim. "It said the keeper of the Flekkta, right?"

"If they are the keepers of the Flekkta then why not just go and get the stone and bring it back themselves?" asked Charlie.

"That's what I was wondering myself. However, I'm quite sure they can turn off the flames at the bridge but there is still something more that we are missing here," said Grandpa Watson. "We need to be diligent."

"Unfortunately I also agree with Mr. Watson," said Caruna. "We must complete this side quest to get the flames at the bridge turned off, but we need to use great caution for I fear there is more here than we are aware of at the moment."

They reached the entrance to the cave and were greeted by a most grotesque sight; there lining the cave as far as the eye could see were skulls perched on spikes, piled to the ceiling and crushed into dust. Some had been hung from the cave ceiling and others were used to hold torches that lined the walls. The most disturbing thing of all was the lack of other bones. It was as if the remaining body parts had either been disposed of or removed to another location, or worse yet, eaten.

"This place is totally giving me the creeps," said Tim.

"Just be alert and ready for anything," said Caruna.

"I'll take the lead," said Grandpa Watson. "Caruna, you watch our back and, boys, please get in the middle." Slowly they worked their way through the skull-ridden cave until they came to a split in the tunnel. Neither way was lit all that well so there was no real choice but to split up and check each tunnel out. Caruna and Charlie went left and Grandpa and Tim went right.

Caruna and Charlie headed down the steep tunnel, being careful to keep their footing. They were making slow, steady progress when they became aware that the heat was rising very rapidly, causing the tunnel to become dangerously slippery.

Caruna was now more concerned than ever. "Careful, Charlie, we have no idea what's coming."

"I know. This tunnel is getting steeper with every step and the heat is killing me."

Charlie took one more step, suddenly lost his footing and was gone in an instant. He was out of sight before Caruna could react. She called to him but there was no answer. Panic started to set in and Caruna threw caution to the wind and recklessly hurried down the tunnel, hoping to catch up with Charlie. She lost her balance more than once but was able to keep her footing enough to avoid falling.

Tim and Grandpa Watson rounded a few corners and also realized the heat was rising at an alarming rate. They reached what looked like a dead end and determined the tunnel had been sealed by a recent lava flow. They turned to head back but to their surprise the tunnel was rapidly closing in on them. The lava, unbeknownst to them, had been slowly creeping down the tunnel, closing off their only escape route.

"This is quite the situation," said Tim.

"I must agree," said Grandpa Watson.

Caruna frantically called to Charlie but heard nothing as she continued headlong down the dark and slippery tunnel. She was in a panic by this point, sure that something disastrous had happened. She rounded a corner and almost joined Charlie down on a tiny edge about ten feet below her.

"Charlie, are you okay?"

"Quiet!" Charlie pointed across the chamber at a slumbering giant beast.

Caruna looked across the steamy chamber with awe; she had never seen anything like what she was seeing. There across the chamber was a beast of mammoth proportions guarding what looked like an ancient chamber door. Off to the left and right of the beast could be seen four fresh-cut trees, empty of skulls and obviously readied for the new arrivals.

This beast stood approximately twenty feet high and about twenty feet long. It possessed four arms, eight legs, and the head of a large hooded cobra with a snake's tail to match. Its limbs resembled that of the ancient giant Groddla, strong and furry along with its legs and torso. In short this creature was immense, strong and very, very dangerous.

Caruna lowered her staff hoping to pull Charlie up. "Charlie, grab my staff and I'll pull you up."

Charlie shook his head. "Shh!! Don't move. The last time I tried to reach the edge that thing started to stir. It must detect movement and we don't want to set it off."

"So what can I do?" whispered Caruna.

"Go back and get Grandpa and Tim. I don't want to leave you here alone with that thing."

"I'll be fine as long as I stay still. Hurry up, Caruna."

"Be careful, Charlie," said Caruna and she was gone as rapidly as she dared move as to not draw attention her way and wake the mighty beast.

Caruna hurried up the tunnel, moving rapidly but knowing all too well one false step and she will end up sliding back down the tunnel and possibly killing Charlie in the process. She struggled to keep her footing, wanting to go faster to get to help knowing all too well that any moment that thing could awaken. After what seemed like hours she reached the top and headed down the tunnel that Tim and Mr. Watson had taken earlier.

Tim and Grandpa Watson were stuck in quite the situation; there seemed to be no way to escape this trap.

Tim noticed something that just might be helpful. "Hey, Grandpa, look over here. We can stand on these footholds and avoid the lava till it cools and then climb down and get out of here."

Tim placed his right foot on one of the footholds and was just about to step on the other one when Grandpa reached out and grabbed the back of his cloak just before two large circular saw blades came seemingly out of nowhere nearly taking Tim's head off. The blades missed Tim's head by mere inches.

"Thanks, Grandpa."

"Don't mention it. Now we know what this trap is for; it's to put you in a situation where there is no choice but to die."

"That's no good, now is it?" asked Tim.

"No, it's not, and the unfortunate thing is that we may not have a choice, or do we?" Grandpa was silent, examining the situation without paying any attention to the lava that was now only a few feet away from them.

"Tim, quick, hand me your staff please and hang onto this rock." Grandpa then pulled his cane and pressed it into one foothold and the staff into the other. When the saw blades appeared he motioned for Tim to stuff a rock in between the blade and the wall, causing the entire system to come to a screeching halt. The lava was now just mere inches from Grandpa's feet when he stepped onto the footholds along with Tim. They were safe from the lava but it was rising fast and was now flowing steadily below both of them and climbing towards their footholds. Even though Grandpa had bought them some time it looked like it wouldn't be enough; the lava would soon engulf them.

Then came a familiar voice and hope; Caruna could be heard yelling "Chillaxia," freezing the lava right below Grandpa and Tim's feet and saving their lives.

"Caruna, thanks for the save, and where is Charlie?" asked Tim.

"He's trapped and we have to save him. Oh, and you're welcome," said Caruna.

"Let's be off then," said Grandpa Watson. "There's no time for tea and plenty of time for rescue."

Carefully they headed down the tunnel until they reached a point where they were sure they could hear Charlie yelling a spell or two. The sound was faint but audible nonetheless. Charlie was in trouble.

Tim threw caution to the wind and started far too fast down the tunnel, losing his footing and sliding uncontrollably out of sight. Grandpa yelled for him and picked up the pace, along with Caruna.

They reached the bottom miraculously without suffering any injury and found Tim lying on his back slowly crawling backwards up the tunnel. The reason was obvious; there heading towards the tunnel opening was a very strange and ominous-looking beast. This beast stood at least twenty feet tall with eight arms, four legs, snake's tail and a cobra's hooded head with one great eye.

Tim looked on speechless at the sight before him. "What the heck is that thing?"

"I suspect that's the Flekkta, Tim," said Grandpa.

"We need to move now," said Caruna. "Charlie's down there somewhere and he needs us."

There off to the left standing on what looked like a floating rock could be seen Charlie, swinging his staff and yelling any spell he could think of. He was jumping from stone to stone as they moved about the chamber like speeding projectiles. He was moving as if guided by something other than his reflexes, anticipating every move of the stones and flowing with them, becoming a part of them and their random pattern of flight.

Charlie fired spell after spell with no obvious effect on the great beast. It seemed oblivious to magic of any sorts. Finally the great beast reached a point of aggravation and swung its tail, barely missing Charlie and causing him to fall a stone or two before regaining his footing on a large floating stone. He looked worn from the heat but determined nonetheless. This motivated Caruna, who analyzed the situation along with Tim, realizing that the key had to be the stones. There had to be some way to use them to their advantage. These stones were floating in an obvious pattern to Tim. He figured that if they could coax the creature into just the right spot they could use the stones to push it into the lava.

Charlie ducked another swing of the beast's tail and nearly fell into the lava again. "I could use a little help here."

Tim was tracking the stones and could not afford any distractions. "Hold on a minute, will ya? This is not as easy as it looks, you know. There are over one thousand stones floating around here."

"Sure, take your time," said Charlie, as he dodged another swing from the creature.

"Tim, we need to do something now," said Caruna.

"I know, just give me a second to get this all figured out," said Tim.

"Charlie, keep distracting that thing while I get everyone into position," said Tim. "Just hang on a bit more."

"Sure, buddy, anything you say," said Charlie.

Charlie kept pestering the creature, keeping its total attention on him while the team moved into position. More than once Charlie just avoided not only its tail but what looked like venom shooting from its mouth at a very high rate of speed. Wherever this venom struck there wasn't much left to look at. Stones were melting and the cave walls themselves were turning to liquid wherever the stuff hit.

Charlie continued dodging left and right and running out of luck. "Hurry up, guys, or you're going to need a spoon to pick me up."

Tim smiled. "I got it—everyone listen to me. Caruna, head to the left, just after that big stone just there, and use your freezing spell to push the creature towards the middle; then Grandpa will go over to that red-looking stone there and throw this large stone twenty feet or so right there into the lava and that will cause that thing to stop momentarily, putting it into a direct path with that massive stone, the one just there. And if my calculations are correct, which they always are, it will spell instant lava bath for that thing. Wait for my signal before casting the spell and throwing the stone."

"What's the signal?" Caruna asked.

"Look for a flash from the end of my staff," said Tim. "Now go, there's no time to waste—Charlie is counting on us and we have to get this right the first time."

Everyone moved into position anxiously waiting for Tim's signal, and then it came, a flash from the end of his staff. Caruna cast her spell, Grandpa threw his stone and the waiting began. Slowly the stone closed with the back of the creature's head, closer and closer until it slammed headlong into its skull, causing a loud and cracking sound to echo through the entire chamber. The beast stumbled, barely keeping its balance, its eyes began to roll and it fell off to the side and was immediately engulfed by the lava and was not seen again. There was no struggle, just a few gasps for air before it went under.

They spent the next few minutes working their way on the floating stones towards the ancient door. They were relieved but distressed at the same time. Their goal was in reach yet there was a feeling of disappointment in the air.

There was a moment of silence then Tim reached up and pulled the key from an overhang and unlocked the door and pushed it open. There in the center of the room was the Moonstone!

Chapter 17

Treldori Sisters, Grabblemore and Two Hoods

The group exited the chamber with the Moonstone in hand. The mood was dark and the conversation was short. It was obvious the team felt used by the Treldori sisters and they were quite disturbed by this. Feeling maybe they should have handled it differently and tried to subdue the great beast or possibly cast the right spell to put it out for enough time to retrieve the Moonstone and make a quick escape instead of sending it to its doom. Although they knew this was not really an option they felt that they should have tried anyway.

While exiting the tunnels Caruna noticed what looked like tracks burnt into the floor by something very hot and large. She smiled and figured that even the lava itself was not enough to kill the Flekkta. She then started thinking of the Treldori sisters and was filled with rage. The way they had used the great beast infuriated her and she decided enough was enough and started to prepare for a spell to free the Flekkta. She instructed Charlie, Tim and Mr. Watson to head to the entrance and wait for her there. Caruna was not sure if the beast had survived or not but decided if it did then it would not be trapped here anymore. She cast spell after spell, expanding the tunnels wide enough for two Nufla to fit through, and this would easily be big enough for the Flekkta to make its escape if it did indeed survive. She worked her way back to her friends and the tunnel entrance and prepared for one more little trick; she would now create a temporary escape route by blasting away some of the cliff's edge so the great beast could work its way down into the lush valley below. She smiled at her handiwork and headed up the small rocky slope towards the Treldori sisters and the artifact. "We need to be prepared for the sisters and that spell of theirs."

Mr. Watson nodded in agreement. "We cannot afford to be put into that uncomfortable situation again. I suggest we use a divide-and-conquer tactic and try to separate the heads from that corpse if the situation calls for it."

Tim shook his head in agreement. "I concur."

"Let's do it," said Charlie.

Caruna had a plan in mind and prepared to lay the groundwork. "When we reach the bridge Tim and Charlie go off to the left and stay there until we are sure it's safe. If the sisters ask where they are we can simply state they were killed in the fight with the Flekkta. This should excite them and hopefully distract them long enough for Tim and Charlie to use the Roccism Stonum curse, turning that dead thing to stone so we can deal with the sisters on our own terms."

They split up, with Charlie and Tim quietly heading off towards their destination. Caruna and Mr. Watson headed towards the bridge and tried to look as distraught as they possibly could. They were sure this plan would work and that they would be able to trap the sisters and gain access to the ancient structure awaiting them on the other side of the bridge.

When they reached the bridge they could see the corpse slowly working its way across while holding a head in each hand and the usual one on its shoulders. The top head was yelling and trying to get the corpse to move faster, which was obviously not possible considering its current state of decay. Its flesh was starting to fall off in rather large disgusting chunks and more and more black liquid could be seen dripping from every maggot-filled hole on its body.

The main head was having a rather obvious time controlling her excitement and almost wobbled off the corpse's shoulders. "Well, well, did you get it? Did you?"

Caruna nodded. "Yeah, we got it."

"Let us see it then," said the left head.

Caruna positioned her staff, pointing it in the direction of the corpse, and grinned slightly. "Turn off the flames first, then you can see it."

"What happened to your other two companions?" asked the main head.

Grandpa hearing this promptly jumped in and played along. "They didn't make it."

At hearing this news all three heads now began grinning almost uncontrollably.

Realizing that a golden opportunity was at hand, the main head gathered her wits and calmed herself long enough to ask an important question. "So where are they now then?"

"They are still down in the caves with the Flekkta," said Caruna.

The head on the right was now bopping up and down in the corpse's hand and grinning wildly. "We must see their bodies now!"

The main head chimed in, "Shh—quiet, sister, or all could be lost."

Grandpa continued on with the ruse and played along. "Why would you want to see their bodies?" He was waiting for an answer that he knew would not come.

"It's no concern of yours," said the main head.

Caruna had now reached a point where she was barely controlling her emotions. "Really? I think it might have something to do with that body of yours that's, shall we say, looking a bit under the weather, so to speak. I have seen better bodies in the town morgue than the one you are currently using."

Before either Grandpa or Caruna could react the main head yelled that all-too-familiar spell "Elgulous," but before the spell took effect Charlie stood and Tim stood from their hiding place and simultaneously yelled "Roccism Stonum," hitting the corpse square in the back. The effects were obvious as the corpse rapidly turned to stone, leaving the heads screaming in panic and utterly trapped, unable to move and at the mercy of their captors.

Caruna and Grandpa Watson were still rolling in pain from the spell that had hit them but were smiling nonetheless. Their plan had worked perfectly. Now they held the upper hand and no longer had to fear the Treldori sisters.

Caruna slowly worked her way to her knees, then her feet; a grin was changing into a sneer and she was not looking all that friendly. "You three, I am giving you one chance to turn off the flames over there or I will turn all three of your heads to stone and smash them to pieces along with this rotting corpse of yours."

The main head, now in a total panic, realized that she had no choice but to obey. The Treldori sisters had lost the upper hand and were completely at the mercy of these strangers. "Oh yes, yes, we are so sorry."

"Do it now," yelled Caruna. "I would like nothing better than to smash the likes of you into so many small pieces they will never know who or what you were."

Without any other options the main head obeyed and yelled, "Lektus flocktus."

Charlie shook his head and came out of his hiding place happy with his spell casting. "So that's it?"

The main head was in a complete panic; her expression was that of a small child that just had its favorite toy taken. "Yes, yes, now please release our body so we may head back to the ancient city."

"No, I don't think so," said Caruna. "You will wait here until we return and then and only then will we free your corpse from the stone spell. And if we don't return you will remain here for the rest of time."

"We meant you no harm," said the head on the right.

Caruna turned with a look of disgust on her face. "NO HARM! You tried to have us all killed so you could take our bodies and you used that wonderful beast, the Flekkta, to kill innocent people for who knows how many years."

"So cruel, so cruel," said the main head.

The head on the left chimed in with a plea of her own. "PLEASE, YOU MUST RELEASE US! We did as you asked and disabled the bridge defenses so you can safely cross."

Charlie, Tim, Caruna and Grandpa Watson walked by the Treldori sisters without paying them any more attention. They felt no sadness whatsoever for the condition they left them in, figuring it was far safer for them to remain like this while they continued on with their quest.

They reached the bridge and tested to see if its defenses were actually disabled by again throwing a branch onto the bridge, and to their surprise nothing happened. It was now safe to cross and head for the second artifact.

Once crossing the bridge they soon came upon an overgrown, densely brush-covered city. There were vines growing through open windows reaching as high as the second floor, along with long-ago-broken doors, sagging roofs and fallen corrals. With a little closer inspection human bones could be seen strewn about, obviously left-over corpses that the Treldori had manipulated, used up and carelessly thrown away when something newer came along. Most of the doors were off their hinges and moving about was easy. The group methodically checked location after location and found nothing but old and worn-out furniture, empty cupboards and the occasional rodent or two.

Finally they came upon two large doors that were still in obvious working order and decided this was the way to go. The doors were pushed open revealing a wonderful sight, a well-maintained courtyard with beautifully kept plants, buildings and in the middle what looked like a group of oddly placed walls with only one entrance. This baffled the group and there seemed to be no answer.

Grandpa Watson studied the walls for a moment turning this way and that. "Well, this is a strange site for sure. I'm just not too sure what to make of it. Ideas, anyone?"

Tim rapidly stepped to the forefront with that usual look of confidence just like when he takes a test. "Now that I've had a moment or two to take it all it in it's quite obviously a maze. Take a closer look at it for a moment—the outside walls have only one break and if you stand just here on top of this cart you can make out the twists and turns leading to a central location."

Charlie jumped onto the cart along with Caruna and Grandpa Watson to get a closer look at Tim's discovery. And sure enough he was right—this was a maze and there was no doubt amongst the group that the item they were searching for would be found somewhere in it.

"There's no point in putting this off, we might as well go for it," said Tim

Charlie jumped off the cart and headed towards the entrance of the maze. "Let's not put this off any longer and go for it."

Off the group headed, into the twisting, turning maze. Within moments they were completely lost and baffled. Tim tried to climb the side of the maze and was unceremoniously struck down by what must be a very powerful magical spell making it impossible to climb the walls to get a look at the maze.

Tim fell to the dirt with a rather loud thump, rubbing his backside and cleaning off the dirt. "Well, that's no fun."

"I guess we need to do this the old-fashioned way." Charlie grabbed a rock and scratched an arrow into the wall pointing in the direction they were now heading in.

"Excellent idea, Charlie," said Grandpa Watson. "We can use these arrows to start getting our bearings."

Tim pulled a notebook from his backpack and prepared to whip up one of his usual detailed sketches. "Okay, everyone, follow my lead. Head in a different direction until you reach their first corner and put an arrow pointing back to here. Then go to the next corner and continue from there. I will stay here and coordinate this and try to get it all down on in a nice organized map."

Everyone headed off in different directions following Tim's instructions. In no time at all Tim had easily generated a crude but manageable map of the general area. "Now we need to go to the farthest point down the first alley over there and do the same thing again. We'll then head back here and do the same in each direction slowly, expanding the map until we can identify the entire place, give or take of course."

"Of course," said Charlie while shaking his head. "Give or take always makes me feel confident."

Tim turned staring down Charlie. "At least we'll have something, which will be much more productive than just wandering about hoping we get lucky."

After hours of mapping the group had become weary and bored. This, however, would not last long as an occasional bang and scraping could be heard moving just out of their mapping range.

"We need to be careful," said Tim. "There's obviously something in here with us and I bet when we finally run into it the meeting will not be fun."

"Is it ever?" asked Charlie.

"Not so far," said Tim. "We need to get going; it will be nightfall soon and I'm pretty sure this will not get any easier."

Grandpa nodded in agreement. "I recommend we do one more mapping session then settle in for the night."

Caruna seconded the motion. "We have no idea what's out there and when nightfall does arrive I want us to be prepared for anything. We can sleep in a nice tight circle with one of us standing guard for two hours then switching to another and so on. Charlie, you take the first, then Tim, and then Mr. Watson and I'll take the last one."

Nightfall was quickly upon them along with strange noises that could be heard echoing throughout the many alleys in the maze. That all-too-familiar sound of scraping and dragging could be heard echoing through the never-ending corridors growing ever closer. The sound seemed to be coming from everywhere. Charlie decided it was time to get the team up but they were already awake and prepared for battle.

Caruna cast a spell that did brighten the general area, allowing for vision up and down the few intersecting alleys.

The dragging and scraping continued to grow louder and louder; it seemed to be all around them and closing in.

"This is way creepy, like a horror movie," said Charlie.

Tim nodded in agreement.

Grandpa chimed in to get the boys focused on the task at hand. "Boys, there's no time for pleasantries at the moment. I suggest preparing yourselves in any way necessary for whatever is about to arrive. Caruna, you take the left, I'll take the right and, boys, back us up."

Grandpa had his trusty cane at the ready. He looked prepared to inflict some serious damage on whatever was coming. However, something happened that surprised Charlie and Tim; Grandpa actually backed away for a moment, so whatever was coming even gave him the creeps.

"They're corpses," yelled Grandpa as he swung his cane, sending it crashing into a face, which shattered almost like it was made from cement.

Caruna swung her staff at a feverish pace; she was almost overwhelmed by at least twenty of the stench-ridden corpses before Tim and Charlie came charging in with staffs high swinging at anything that moved. Grandpa was holding his own, swinging as fast as he could and leveling as many corpses as possible, but it seemed to be of no use. The group was slowly being pushed together into a corridor that had no escape and would eventually turn out to be deadly.

Caruna stepped forward and easily dispatched four of the corpses then yelled for Charlie and Tim to get behind her and prepare to use the stone spell.

Charlie did what he was told but looked on with a questioning look. "How will turning dead bodies to stone get us out?"

"JUST DO IT NOW!" yelled Caruna.

The boys prepared to cast their spells. Caruna ducked, rolled off to the side and yelled "NOW!" and both boys fired at the row of corpses. Then they understood. The corpses turned to stone would act like a temporary barrier, slowing the corpses down and giving the group a chance to turn their attention towards the other end of the corridor and quite possibly make their escape.

"BRAVO!" yelled Grandpa Watson as he leveled corpse after corpse until they were beginning to pile on top of each other. Caruna promptly joined in while Charlie and Tim watched their backs. Soon they had slowed the onslaught of corpses and with a little luck would be able to make their escape. After crushing what seemed like the last row of corpses the group breathed a sigh of relief and slowly rounded the next corner, only to see another nightmare heading straight for them. There standing in front of them were row after row of corpses in armor sporting spears, swords and rather nasty-looking battle axes.

Grandpa looked on shaking his head. "This is no good at all. We need to think of something and something quick."

"Our options are running out here so we need a grand idea—anyone?" said Charlie.

Tim shook his head knowing all too well that Charlie was referring to him. "All right, just give me a minute!"

Caruna looked on and smiled. "Well then, a minute it is." She then stepped forward and cast a mighty spell "Chillaxia Holdrus" and a wall of ice seemed to grow from the dirt floor, temporarily cutting off the approaching army of corpses. "There, and I suggest you don't squander even a second."

Tim for once, however, was speechless. There was a small bead of sweat on his forehead and it was becoming quite obvious that a minute would not be enough. For once he didn't have the answer.

Charlie looked on, wondering when his friend would step to the plate. "Hurry up, Tim."

Tim looked down, disgusted with himself and his lack of an idea. "I-I—got nothing. I can't think of a thing. Somebody help me."

"Okay, give me a second," said Charlie.

"Too late," said Caruna as the wall of ice began to give way. There were obvious cracks forming and spear tips and swords could be seen breaking through. Caruna began firing spell after spell but the ranks just kept refilling like there was no end to them.

"This is useless! They just keep on coming," said Caruna.

"We need an idea and we need it now, there is no time left," said Grandpa.

They were now pushed back to where they started, a wall of stone corpses at their backs and an army of heavily armed corpses to their front. There seemed to be no options left and a painful death was on its way. Grandpa looked at Charlie, ruffled his hair then did the same to Tim. He smiled, searching for the exact words to tell two fourteen-year-old boys that they were going to die and he was coming up with nothing. He guessed that words like that are sometimes just as good when not spoken, and this was obviously true when glancing in Charlie and Tim's direction; he received a warm smile then the moment was gone as the boys turned to face their destinies.

Off in the not-far distance could be heard a crashing noise that was growing ever louder. It sounded like a wrecking ball smashing wall after wall at breakneck speed. The sound grew louder and louder, causing the corpses to actually stop their forward march and start randomly glancing about trying to discern what it possibly could be. There off in the distance could be seen pieces of the maze wall flying high into the air, shards of stone raining down as if a strong storm was approaching. They had no idea what was going on but at least the corpses had stopped their forward approach.

The crashing was getting closer and closer and now pieces of the maze wall were raining down like deadly projectiles from the sky. Caruna cast a spell creating a rather thick ice wall at a perfect angle so the group could take shelter. The corpses, however, were not so lucky and were being struck down by large boulder-sized rocks, shards that embedded themselves deep into their skulls, shoulders and other random body parts, striking them down at random. The corpses were now in a panic, out of control and running into each other looking for an avenue for escape. Between the sounds, the deadly projectiles and the overall destruction, they seemed to have lost their focus and were completely out of control. Now the sound had reached a point where it was hard to communicate without shouting. The crashing had intensified along with the deadly raining debris. Soon whatever was coming would be upon them; whether this was good or bad no one knew but at least there was still a chance.

Caruna realized that their chance was coming and they would have one shot at it. "WE NEED TO GET READY TO MAKE OUR BREAK."

Grandpa nodded in agreement.

The sound was deafening and Caruna realized the only way to communicate was to yell. "WHEN WHATEVER IS COMING THROUGH THAT WALL OVER THERE FINALLY BREAKS THROUGH WE NEED TO MOVE FOR THAT HOLE AS QUICKLY AS WE POSSIBLY CAN. THERE WILL BE NO TIME FOR HESITATION BECAUSE I FEAR IT WILL COST US ALL DEARLY."

"BUT WHAT ARE WE GOING TO DO ABOUT WHATEVER IS COMING?" yelled Charlie.

"AVOID IT ANY WAY WE CAN AND LET IT BE ON WITH ITS BUSINESS OF DESTRUCTION," yelled Caruna. "NOW PREPARE YOURSELVES, FOR THE TIME IS ALMOST AT HAND."

Stones were now raining down from the sky at an incredible rate. Corpses were piled everywhere, battered, bloody and broken. The great bringer of this destruction and salvation was now within a wall or two of reaching their location. The ice wall was starting to show signs of wear with dangerously long and spiraling cracks starting to sprout in all locations.

"THIS SHIELD IS NOT GOING TO HOLD MUCH LONGER! WE HAVE TO BE READY—" Before Caruna could finish her final thought a thunderous rumble was heard and the wall next to the remaining corpses shattered into pieces along with the bodies strewn about.

There breaking through the wall, shattering it like it was nothing more than grass being crushed under a foot stood, the Flekkta. Not the Flekkta the way it looked before, but the Flekkta nonetheless. The sight of the great beast brought a smile to Caruna's face that lightened the mood of the group. Obviously creating the escape tunnel had paid dividends beyond anything any of them had expected, for there standing before them stood the freed beast, the Flekkta!!

Being in the lava had transformed the great beast into something resembling an armored giant. His skin had turned into something resembling a reddened shell. The snake scales had also changed and were bright red. His eyes were aglow with a red haze and flames seemed to dangle at the corners of his mouth. Where he had stepped moments earlier the ground had smoked and been melted to the shape of his hooves. The beast has taken on the very properties of the lava itself!

The Flekkta didn't pay them a moment's attention and continued to gore and devastate the remaining corpses. Flames bellowed from its mouth, along with strong venom that rotted the corpses through the ground before they had a chance to react. Their bodies were melted to piles of black ooze and the stench was intolerable. Soon the entire area was full of the smell and the remaining parts of the corpse army. None were left standing. Some were simply ripped to pieces, others burned to the ground, and the venom also took a large lot of them. The Flekkta seemed to be enraged by these things and was almost out of control when the last corpse finally fell.

Charlie, Tim, Caruna and Grandpa Watson were left speechless at the sight before them. Corpse upon corpse ripped, torn and melted lying about everywhere in any direction they turned to look.

Now the Flekkta had finished his work and turned to face the group! He then lowered his head as if bowing and ran off without a word, crashing though wall after wall. Soon he was gone; the only thing that could be heard was an occasional loud, distant thunderous crash as the great beast broke for freedom.

"LET'S NOT LOSE TRACK OF OUR MISSION," yelled Caruna.

Charlie laughed, knowing that they were finally safe. "Hey, Caruna, you can tone it down a bit, the crashing has stopped."

Tim looked on grinning from relief. "Yeah, Caruna, there's no need for yelling."

They headed further into the maze, killing the occasional corpse or two along the way. The farther they journeyed the more obvious the Flekkta's destruction became. Almost every alley seemed to have been touched by the great beast; there were remnants of corpses or large walls crushed to dust. This made traversing the maze much easier and soon enough they had reached the very center and were preparing to retrieve the very artifact they had come for, the second piece of the Golundrus Cube!

They made for the central part of the maze and the long-standing column at its center. There could be seen the piece of the ancient artifact they were so anxious to gain possession of. Charlie broke for the center and retrieved the piece and to everyone's surprise this was uneventful.

Charlie grinned. "Well, that was easy."

"Sure was and that's what's worrying me," said Tim.

"We must break for the bridge and head out as fast as possible," said Caruna. "There is no time to linger and enjoy our recent conquest. Our enemies are sure to be watching and waiting for any opportunity to claim this piece for themselves and their vile ideas."

The group easily worked their way through the maze and the occasional stray corpse or two. They soon arrived back at the familiar main doors where it all started and the bridge would soon be in sight.

Without much trouble they reached and crossed the bridge but what they saw when they got there took them all by surprise. They found the Treldori sisters scattered about after their lone remaining corpse had been smashed to small unidentifiable pieces. They could be heard mumbling and screaming for assistance that would never come.

"My friends, it looks like we are almost at the end of this wonderful journey. I for one found this to be a most enjoyably grand adventure," said a grinning Grandpa Watson.

"Yeah, that was great," said Charlie.

Caruna was still concerned and knew this adventure might not be over just yet. "Let's not celebrate our success just yet; we still need to reach the Kattergraff and get back to the guild before we are actually safe."

Charlie shook his head, not understanding why Caruna was still worried; they had the artifact and the Treldori sisters were out of commission. "Oh, Caruna, stop being such a party—" Then came the familiar sound; pops could be heard and this was obviously not a good thing.

"Are we expecting anyone?" asked Tim.

"NO! GET DOWN NOW!" yelled Caruna as a red bolt shot over the top of their heads shattering a tree into toothpicks.

"Break for the brid—" Before Caruna could finish her last word she was hit. She had been turned to stone right before their very eyes.

"CARUNA!" yelled Charlie at the top of his lungs, knowing all too well it was already too late for her. Charlie stood staring straight into her now cold eyes. He did not bother to duck when the next bolt flew dangerously close to his head. He was furious! How could anyone possibly know their whereabouts?

"Charlie, Charlie, we can't help her if we end up in the same state as her," said Tim. Charlie shook out of the daze he was in and drifted back into reality.

"Charlie, Tim, get down and stay put," said Grandpa Watson. "Neither of you make a sound."

The boys nodded and remained silent hiding in a small shrub. The only issue with this hiding place was that any escape would involve traversing a thousand-foot cliff to reach the valley below.

Charlie looked around realizing there was nowhere to go. "We're trapped like a cornered rat."

"I know," said Tim. "Where's Grandpa going anyway?"

Charlie looked over and could see his grandfather rising from his hiding place and heading towards the general location of the red bolt. He was surely going to sacrifice himself so the boys could make a break for it and this did not sit all too well with either of them. “I already lost Caruna and there’s no way I’m losing Grandpa. Let’s go, Tim, we have to back him up.”

Without hesitation both boys rose from their hiding places and started to run at a furious pace towards Grandpa Watson. Grandpa was now dodging spell after spell and wearing down rapidly. He was trying to get close to the area of the spells but was pushed back again and again by bolt after bolt of what must be some nasty spells.

“BOYS, I thought I told the both of you to remain in hiding,” said Grandpa while ducking a red bolt.

“I know, Grandpa, but we had to help you. After seeing Caruna we just couldn’t sit there and watch the same thing happen to you,” said Charlie.

“I understand. Okay now, the both of you stay low and we can try to outflank them and attack from multiple sides. Tim, you go left and, Charlie, you go—” Grandpa was hit! He was now turning to stone just like Caruna had moments earlier.

“GRANDPA, NOOOOOO!” yelled Charlie.

Charlie grabbed his grandfather’s hand and felt it go cold. He knew that the only way to save both Grandpa and Caruna was to defeat whoever was shooting at them and get back to the guild for help.

“Charlie, we need to get out of here now,” said Tim. “We can come back for Caruna and Grandpa.”

Charlie shook his head. “No. We just can’t leave them like this. We need to get whoever did this.”

Tim knew the odds and didn’t like them one bit. “If we don’t leave I’m pretty sure there’s a good chance we’ll end up just like them and then we’ll never be able to help them.”

Charlie conceded and agreed to reluctantly follow Tim.

The boys slowly headed left to some heavy cover. Before they could reach it they again heard that familiar popping sound. Now standing right before them were two hooded figures laughing and pointing menacing staffs down at them.

“Hello, boys, it’s strange that we keep meeting like this,” said the familiar hooded, hissing voice.

Charlie didn’t say a word but instead swung his staff right at the hooded figure’s right knee, only to have it blocked by the hooded figure just before it reached its intended target. “Now, now, there’ll be none of that going on. Just hand over the artifact you so generously recovered for us and we’ll be on our way.”

"How did you know we were here? I bet it was Morphran," said Tim.

"Morphran? And what would he have to do with this, silly boy?" asked the larger hooded figure.

"He tipped you off to where we were going," said Charlie. "He must have done it, who else would have?"

The hooded figure just laughed. "No, my boy, your friend took care of that."

Tim looked at Charlie and shrugged. "What do you mean? I would never help either of you."

"For a boy who is supposedly so bright you missed one obvious thing," said the smaller figure.

"And what's that?" asked Tim.

The small hooded figure laughed loudly, enjoying the moment. "Remember I handed you a tracking stone, you stupid boy—how careless of you to have forgotten."

Disgustedly Tim reached into his backpack and pulled out the stone and threw it as far as he could.

"Sorry, Charlie."

"It's okay, Tim, don't worry about it."

The larger hooded figure stepped to the forefront to take control. "ENOUGH! This conversation has gone on far too long for my liking. Now hand over the artifact or face death."

Charlie and Tim both defiantly raised their staffs. They were not going to give up without a fight.

"If you want the artifact so bad come and take it," said a defiant Charlie.

"Yeah, come and take it," said Tim.

"As you wish," said the larger hooded figure.

Both hooded figures laughed amongst themselves, not paying much attention to either boy or their challenge. However, before they could carry out their attack something odd happened; three pops were heard and standing before Charlie stood Phinneus Grabblemore, Vance Vortigern and Efa Vanora.

"Vance, Efa, please help Caruna and Mr. Watson and then get them all back to our guild as rapidly as possible and I will deal with our two new friends," said Grabblemore.

"NO ONE IS LEAVING UNTIL I HAVE MY ARTIFACT," screamed the large hooded figure.

"Well, hello there! We have not been properly introduced. I am Phinneus Grabblemore, head of the Golundrus Guild, and you are?"

"My name is no concern of yours, you witless old man. I was long before you and will be long after your corpse rots into the ground and that's all you need to know. SOON ALL WHO DWELL IN THIS LAND WILL CALL ME MASTER OR PERISH!"

"Interesting," said Grabblemore.

"Master, you must go, it's far too early for you to be discovered," said the smaller hooded figure.

"Never give me orders, Cadwalader." This comment was followed by a swift backhand to the side of Cadwalalder's face.

"Cadwalader," said Grabblemore. "This plot thickens with every spoken word."

Cadwalader was now on one knee, looking towards the dirt and not daring to face his master for fear of another assault.

"Master, please, I meant you no disrespect, I was only thinking of your glorious plan."

"Unfortunately you are right; it's far too early for my discovery."

"Go now, master, and I will cover your escape. I will deal with this old fool personally."

Without another word the large hooded figure turned and vaporated into nothing.

Grabblemore watched the large hooded figure disappear wondering what role he had to play in this mystery. "So, Cadwalader, you are alive after all."

"Yes, you stupid old fool, I am."

"So who is your new friend?"

"He is no concern of yours at the moment. When the time is right I am sure he will present himself and by then there will be nothing any of you can do."

"Really, and why is that?"

"Because all of you will be dead." Without warning Cadwalader raised his staff and fired spell after spell at Grabblemore, seemingly just missing time after time. After four or five spells frustration had set in and Cadwalader was firing madly in all directions hoping to get lucky.

"WHY CAN'T I KILL YOU?"

"Judging by your return from the dead and the way you keep missing me, maybe you really don't want to," said Grabblemore as he effortlessly dodged the continuing barrage of spells from Cadwalader.

By now Caruna and Mr. Watson were free of the spell that had been cast and were gingerly moving about. Cadwalader had reached a boiling point and was furious with himself for not only failing to kill Grabblemore but for letting the artifact slip through his fingers.

"Cadwalader, you can come back. There is a place for you here in Wizard World still. It's not too late for you."

"Yes, it is—you don't understand the power that he possesses. It's far too late for me to turn back now."

"Who possesses this power over you?"

"Never mind that—see, there you go again trying to trick me and distract me from my goals. I need that artifact and I need it now."

Cadwalader lunged forward and attempted to grab Charlie but was flattened by a staff from Vance to the side of his head. This sent Cadwalader stumbling for a moment, finally falling onto the ground. He then rolled over laughing with his face exposed. There under his hood could be seen his hideously distorted face, all cracked and deformed. The hissing sound of his voice was obvious with the large crack running down the center of his face where his breath was escaping. His skin had a stone color to it, almost flat as if all but lifeless.

"I see. I feel very sorry for you, Cadwalader. This fate you have brought onto yourself is beyond any magic we possess to heal," said Grabblemore.

"Heal? Why would I want that?" asked Cadwalader as he spit blood through the crack in his face. "I am more powerful than you could ever imagine."

"I am sorry you have become blinded by the treachery that you have been exposed to. You should have realized that there are more important things in life than power," said Grabblemore.

"You know nothing, you simple-minded fool." Before anyone could react Cadwalader was hit with a large red bolt straight in his face. His expression turned strangely peaceful and then he was gone, turned to dust and blowing away in the mountain breeze.

Grabblemore nodded slightly to where Cadwalader once stood. "Farewell, Cadwalader, hopefully you will find what you were looking for on the other side. It's most unfortunate that he chose the way of darkness and power instead of light and good-heartedness.

"Now let us leave this vile place and get back to the safe haven of our guild. There is much to discuss and I fear little time to do it in."

Chapter 18

Parting Ways

The group's arrival at the guild was met with large cheers from its members. Charlie and Tim were now considered heroes. No longer were they looked upon as Regulars but instead contributing members of the guild. They had battled great evil and survived. The second piece of the Golundrus Cube was safely in the possession of Phinneus Grabblemore and the Council of Elders, and the boys had managed to expose Cadwalader along the way. There was still one great mystery to be solved: Who was this hooded figure that was able to cast magic strong enough to revive Cadwalader after he was shattered into pieces? Why did he want to reassemble the Golundrus Cube and when would he strike again? There were still two more pieces of the cube to be discovered and judging by how difficult the first to were to recover, surely the last two would be no easier.

"Could I have quiet please? Thank you," said Grabblemore. "First I would like to say this has been a very strange past two years. We have suffered some terrible losses and made some wonderful gains. Our new friends from the Regular World have been a most pleasant surprise. They not only joined guilds here in Wizard World but also became wonderful friends and allies. Their contributions will not soon be forgotten. Almost single-handedly they helped discover a dangerous plot to try and reassemble the Golundrus Cube." The crowd broke out into mumbling conversation. "Quiet please. Yes, the rumors are indeed true; someone is trying to reassemble the cube and at any cost. Fortunately with the help of Charlie and Tim we were able to gain the upper hand and retrieve one piece of the cube, which is now well hidden and protected by the Council of Elders. I cannot emphasize enough how grave this threat is to everyone. Each and every guild member must treat this threat as if his or her very life depends on it, because I fear it will. If the cube is indeed assembled again and it falls into the wrong hands—I fear the results would be far more destructive than any one of us could ever image.

"We must remain ever diligent in these most perilous times. Dangerous and evil individuals would assemble the cube and use its awesome power for personal gain and utter destruction without a care for any of us. We must remain attentive and continue our quest to gather the final missing two pieces of the cube and protect them with all our power and might. This is our number one priority amongst all guild members and this now takes precedent over all other guild functions whatever they may be.

"However, not all is gray and sometimes happiness can be found even in the saddest places if you just know where to look. Now let's celebrate for the ones that were lost and the ones that were saved."

At this time Klortis rose and raised his staff high above his head, causing a roar from the crowd that was almost deafening. Charlie and Tim smiled and received a glance in their general direction from Klortis.

A great party was being put on and members from many guilds were arriving to celebrate their recovery of the second piece of the cube. All seemed good but Charlie and Tim knew it couldn't last. Soon they would have to make their way to the portal and head back to the Regular World. After long hours the festivity began winding down and there wasn't much left to do but say the many goodbyes that needed to be said.

"Boys, can I have a moment please?" said Klortis. "I would personally like to let the both of you know how impressed I am with your diligence and loyalty."

"Thanks," said Tim and Charlie.

"Please give me a moment to finish," said Klortis. "I will say this and say it only once, it if weren't for the both of you I surely would be dead. I will forever be grateful. I look forward to continuing your training when you return here once again."

Caruna arrived with tears in her eyes and both hands noticeably trembling.

"It sure won't be the same without you two around," said Caruna.

"Yeah, leaving is definitely going to be strange," said Charlie.

"I agree," said Tim. "I will miss this place and the new friends that we have to leave behind, and the library and the learning and the—"

"Okay, okay, we get it," said Charlie.

Caruna reached over and grabbed Charlie, kissing him deeply. Charlie didn't pull away. Tim just smiled and turned his face, knowing all too well that Charlie had deep feelings for her and obviously she felt the same.

Now came Phinneus Grabblemore, who presented himself with a courteous bow. "Boys, I cannot tell you how pleased I have been with your progress. I just want the both of you to know that you will always have a home here in Wizard World and especially here at the Golundrus Guild. I would be most pleased if the both of you would come back, as well as your grandfather. There is much training for the both of you and I'm sure much your grandfather would like to learn as well.

"The both of you have done great things since your arrivals here and I expect they will continue when you return. Tomorrow morning we shall lead you to the portal so you can return to the Regular World and this place will surely not be a better one while the both of you are gone. Remember to keep the stone I presented to you earlier so you can call me as soon as you do arrive, as we don't want to have any more run-ins with the Shifters again."

"Mr. Grabblemore, can I ask you a question about the cube?" asked Tim.

"Why, of course. If it's within my knowledge I will answer as best as possible," said Grabblemore.

"Who do you think is behind this and why?" asked Tim.

"That, my young friend, is an answer I cannot give you. At this very moment I have many of my most gifted and trusted friends searching for any clues to that answer. I assure you we will not leave any stone unturned to get that very answer," said Grabblemore. "Now, boys, I must be off since there are many old friends here I have not yet had a chance to chat with. I bid you both farewell and I will personally escort the both of you to the portal tomorrow."

"Thanks, Mr. Grabblemore," said Charlie as he bowed low to show as much respect as he possibly could.

"Thanks," said Tim, who also returned the earlier bow of Grabblemore.

Tim had a long goodbye with Ada and promised to return as soon as he possibly could. There was nothing left to do now but stop by the kattergraff corrals and say goodbye to Alicia and Gregor.

The next morning arrived and Charlie, Tim and Grandpa Watson, along with half the members of the Golundrus Guild headed out towards the arch and portal to give their new friends a final farewell.

They arrived at the arch knowing the next time they returned there would be many changes. It was Sunday in the Regular World and a week had passed by there, but it had been two long years here in Wizard World. However, it was time to head home to prepare for Monday's coming classes at Golvert's.

"My friends, we are at the end of this journey and the beginning of another. I am most disheartened to see the both of you go," said Grabblemore. "You two have developed so very much in the past two years and I am most impressed. You are both growing into fine young men and fine young wizards. I look forward to our next meeting, which I believe will be in approximately five years here in Wizard World, or five days where you are currently heading. Now remember to practice what you have learned even though you will not actually be doing magic while in the Regular World. Neither of you wants to fall behind on your studies during your time away, I would suspect."

"No, sir, we would not," said Tim. "Mr. Grabblemore, what do you think will come of Ron, Sean, Clive and Crystal? I mean, Crystal did help us out and if they find out—"

"If they find out, Tim, it will be most disastrous for her," said Grabblemore. "But do not despair, for I am sure she can take care of herself. I don't know what kind of reaction you should expect from her when you see here in the Regular World, but she definitely is not what she seems to be."

Charlie listened to what Mr. Grabblemore had to say but he was still furious with her and wasn't quite ready to put it behind him just yet. "She helped us and all but she's still with them and that's still bad enough in my eyes."

"Charlie, my boy, in time you will have a different attitude toward her, I am sure," said Grabblemore.

"So, my friends, at last we will part and go our separate ways. But do not fret because this is definitely not the last time we will meet. So go now and train and study and prepare for your return. I will be awaiting your call."

"Be careful, Mr. Grabblemore, and we will see you as soon as we can," said Tim.

"Thanks for everything," said Charlie.

"You are most welcome," said Grabblemore.

Grandpa bowed to Grabblemore, who smiled and returned his respectful gesture.

With that last word Grabblemore turned and then disappeared into thin air like he always does along with the other members of the guild. After seeing this so many times neither Charlie nor Tim were surprised by this.

"Charlie, this has to be the two craziest years ever."

"Without a doubt, and who would have thought that running into that gross, stinky alley full of fish guts would lead to this."

"No kidding, and we now know that Crystal isn't as bad as we originally thought and just maybe there is still hope for her."

"Yeah, Tim, but she's still hanging with Ron and his group of thugs so in my eyes nothing has changed and she is still the enemy. She joined the Bladgen Guild with Ron and the rest of them under her own free will."

"As far as we know it was under her free will, Charlie, but after she helped us escape there could be more to that story and maybe we'll figure it out in time."

"Whatever—that doesn't really matter to me at this point, Tim. I want to get through this week and go back and help Mr. Grabblemore find the last two pieces and recover the one that was stolen from us. Right now that's all that really matters to me."

After Charlie, Tim and Grandpa stepped through the portal and experienced the same flash they were strangely relieved to smell the all-too-familiar stench of rotten fish that greeted them when they arrived back in the alleyway. They walked out of the alley together not saying a word, each one thinking different thoughts and feeling different emotions. They stood silent by the corner waiting for Grandma Watson to pick them up at their prescheduled time. The stress of having no idea what was now going on in Wizard World was nearly overwhelming; the fate of both worlds was up in the air and there was nothing either boy could do at the moment but prepare for the new school week. Both boys knew that nothing would be the same when they went back to Golvert's Monday morning and when and if they finally did go back through the gate in five days to Wizard World everything would be different there too.